JOE COFFIN
SEASON TWO

JOE COFFIN SEASON TWO

KEN PRESTON

Cover Design Xavier Comas

contents

EPISODE
FIVE

spider-man is
a pussy

Garrett Stone gazed out of the cabin window, down at the wisps of white cloud below. It was a sight he had seen many times before and he was bored of it. International air travel was, for Stone, like driving on the motorway was for everyone else. Tedious, but necessary.

Stone returned to his meal. Braised beef in coconut milk, served on a bed of Basmati and Wild rice. Silver cutlery and bone china tableware. Eating was also tedious but necessary. Protein, carbs, vitamins and minerals, all vital not just for the continuation of life, but for the building of muscle and bone density. The beef and the coconut milk in this meal weren't the healthiest of options considering their high fat content. But on the long haul flights Stone liked to treat himself.

Garrett Stone wore a smartly pressed shirt and tie, expensive cufflinks, dark trousers and black shoes. He was handsome, with a square jaw and dark eyes, and his broad, muscular frame filled his seat.

The airline stewardess passed him, pushing her trolley and collecting dishes and cutlery. Stone smiled up at her and let her take his empty plate. She was pretty, with long hair tied back under her hat, and smooth, unblemished features. But Stone wasn't interested. She was an identikit copy of every other airline hostess he had encountered. Some days, Stone was convinced that none of them were real. That they were Stepford Wives robots, or they were grown in a lab, all cloned from the same tissue sample.

Not like the woman sat next to him.

Now she was an individual.

She wasn't slim, but neither was she fat. What was the best way to describe her?

Oh yes. Voluptuous.

And she was exposing plenty of that voluptuous, olive brown skin in the simple, black dress she wore. Stone checked the screen in front of him. When they had left New York the weather had been unseasonably mild, but not exactly warm. Of course the environmentalists had been in the news, proclaiming the end of the world yet again. Pissed Stone off every time they opened their stupid mouths. New York might be unseasonably mild but, according to the data on the live feed, Birmingham was a hell of a lot colder. A typical November day, in fact; cold and blustery, and threatening even more rain than usual.

Environmentalists weren't mentioning that, were they?

Stone risked another peek at the woman. Unless she had something warm to wrap up in when they landed, she was going to be bloody freezing when they left the airport.

Stone looked away and then back again, glanced at her face. He couldn't help himself. She was striking. Not beautiful, but handsome. His gaze swept down her neck, over her collarbone and down to her cleavage. The other striking aspect of her appearance were the tattoos. Curving, pointed black lines and shapes. Swirling over her skin and disappearing beneath the lines of her dress. The design was almost dizzying if he looked at it too much. And the more he did glance at it, the more convinced he became that it was all one design, and that most of it was hidden by her dress.

The black lines and tiny shapes seemed to have swarmed down her arms of their own accord. Her right arm was more covered than her left. The design swept over her shoulders and down her back and chest. When he glanced down at her legs, Stone could see the tattoo emerging from beneath the hem of her dress, creeping along her thighs.

He couldn't make sense of it. Wanted to pull her dress down and expose her breasts and her abdomen to see the full design.

It would be easy. One quick movement, and it would be off.

And he was certain she wasn't wearing a bra.

Stone looked out of the window again, steadied his breathing. Best not to get distracted. Best not to get caught looking, too. The last thing he wanted was to create a commotion, get accused of being a lech.

A stewardess passed by again, pushing another trolley with newspapers. Was she the same one as before? Stone couldn't tell. The woman sitting next to him asked for a paper.

She opened up the newspaper, the *Times*, and began leafing through the pages, quickly scanning the articles. Having found what she wanted, she folded the newspaper in on itself, and began reading.

Stone glanced at her again, trying to work out what had attracted her attention. But this time she caught him looking.

"Would you like me to buy a newspaper for you?" she said.

Stone chuckled, held up his hands. "You got me. I'm afraid it's a bad habit of mine, looking over people's shoulders, see what they're reading. Years ago, when I travelled to work by train, I managed to read a whole book by sitting next to the same woman every morning, and reading over her shoulder."

"That's the kind of thing that will get you in trouble one day."

Her voice was rich, and warm, with a slight husk to it.

"That's a lovely accent you have," Stone said. "Let me guess, Louisiana?"

"Pretty good," she said. "Although, over the years, I've lived everywhere you can imagine, and some places you can't."

"Sounds intriguing," Stone said. "A woman of mystery, but I like it." He held out his hand. "I'm Garrett."

The woman smiled and took his hand. Stone had expected her palm to be warm, hot even, although he couldn't have explained why. But her touch was cool, and she shook his hand lightly.

"Leola," she said, and smiled.

"Pleased to meet you, Leola," Stone replied. "So, what will you be doing in England? Business or pleasure?"

"You sound just like passport control. Is that your job?"

Stone laughed. "No, although I do work in the defence sector. If I could tell you the capacity in which I work, and what I actually do, I would, but a lot of it is very sensitive, classified stuff."

"Now you're the one who is sounding mysterious," Leola said.

"No, not really. I just don't want to bore you, that's all."

Stone noticed that Leola had folded her newspaper up, one hand resting on it. All the signals he was receiving from her indicated that she was interested in him, that she wanted to talk.

Here we go again, Stone thought. He'd promised himself, and Lucy, that he wouldn't. But, what the hell. You only got one life, right?

"Where in Louisiana do you live?" he said.

"New Orleans, the capital of Mardi Gras."

"Sounds like fun."

Leola smiled, and nodded slowly. "Oh yes, it's always fun."

"And what do you do?"

Leola turned and gave Stone the full force of her gaze.

"You wouldn't believe me if I told you."

"There you go with that woman of mystery thing again. Who would have thought it, that two random strangers could meet on a flight, and have professions so mysterious they couldn't tell one another what they did?"

"Maybe that is a mystery in itself. Or maybe we are both simply being careful."

Stone shifted in his seat. That dress really was too much. Such a thin layer of cotton, to do the job of covering her nakedness. Definitely not wearing a bra. And now Stone found himself wondering if she was even wearing any underwear.

"You know, I hate mysteries, and I have a violent aversion to being left in the dark."

"Is that what makes you so good at your job?" Leola said.

Stone laughed. "How do you know I'm any good at my job?"

Leola raised a perfectly manicured eyebrow. "Working in the defence sector, flying 1st class, the expensive clothes you're wearing? I'd be surprised if you weren't."

Stone resisted the urge to tug at his collar. That would be a dead giveaway to his discomfort. Not that he was unhappy with the sensations coursing through his nerve endings right now, just that it was a slightly inappropriate setting to be this aroused.

"With those deductive powers of yours, you must be a detective," he said, trying to shift his focus away from the attractions of Leola's body.

Leola chuckled, shook her head.

"You really are going to make me guess, aren't you?" Stone's hand was lying on the armrest, just inches from Leola's left thigh. With one swift movement, he could have lifted the hem of her dress, found out for sure if she was wearing any underwear or not. "Let's see, you can't tell me what you do because it's so fantastical I wouldn't believe you, and you also have to be careful who you tell. It's obvious. You're a secret agent, working for the American government, right?"

Leola flashed him a full on smile, bright white teeth a contrast to her brown skin. "You're way off base."

"But if you are a secret agent, you'd deny it," Stone said. "So how can I trust you?"

"You will just have to take my word for it."

"All right, let me think. Maybe you're an ultra-rich, billionaire playgirl, come to the UK to buy it up, and use us as your sex slaves."

Leola tilted her head back, and laughed. "And that's why I'm traveling with the common people, when really I should be flying here in my own private jet."

"Hmm, good point," Stone replied. "I know, you're a superhero, on the way to the UK to save the world from an English, eccentric, supervillain."

"If I was a superhero, wouldn't I be wearing a cape, and flying alongside the plane? I could wave at you through the window."

"Not all superheroes can fly," Stone said. "Spider-Man can't."

Leola laughed again. "Spider-Man's a pussy. I could eat him for breakfast."

"I bet you could."

"I could eat you for breakfast, too."

"Now that would be fun." Stone took a moment, thinking maybe he should change the conversation. Get back on safe ground. "But you still haven't told me what you do for a living."

Leola leaned in close, and Stone could smell her musky scent, and he gripped his arm rests tight.

"If I tell, you've got to promise to keep it a secret," she said, her voice low.

"Sure," Stone said. "Cross my heart and hope to die, as we funny English people like to say."

Leola leaned in even closer, her lips brushing his ear, her breath warm on his face.

"I organise sex parties," she whispered.

* * *

Stone grabbed Leola by her shoulders and flipped her over, on her back. He straddled her hips, and pinned her wrists to the mattress.

"I prefer being the one on top," he said.

"Making you nervous, was I?" Leola whispered.

"I was just feeling a little claustrophobic, and besides, I prefer the view from up here."

"You can drop the corny dialogue with me, mister, I've heard it a thousand times before."

"I'll bet you have," Stone murmured.

A bar of sunlight from the hotel window had fallen across Leola's breasts, and Stone let his gaze linger on the tattoo. The red and black lines curved around her breasts in a dense pattern, curling in on each other and out again. It made him a little dizzy if he looked at it for too long. The design closed in as it encircled her nipples, standing erect and still glistening with his saliva.

Stone had guessed right. The tattoo was one complete design. It covered her torso, both front and back, and crawled down her arms and over her thighs. It made him feel dizzy and faintly nauseous if he examined it for too long. Almost as though the tiny shapes and swirls came to life and started dancing and jumping across her flesh.

"Are you going to tell me about this tattoo?" Stone said.

Leola began undulating her hips against him. "Maybe. Depends."

"On what?" Stone said, as he released her wrists and stretched himself out across her body.

"On whether or not you manage to satisfy me."

Stone raised an eyebrow. "Really? You seriously think there's a chance I can't do that?"

Leola smiled. "Oh, you men, you're all the same." She ran a hand down his back, her fingers tracing a line over his buttocks, and round under his hips until she found him, hard and tight. She gave him a squeeze. "Think all you have to do is shove your little friend inside me, and wiggle him about, and I'll be screaming with pleasure in no time."

"Oh, I think I can do better than that," Stone said.

He began kissing her, and licking her brown skin, as he moved down her torso, and over her abdomen, and down between her legs. The tattoo seemed to be at its densest here. A distant part of Stone's mind wondered if it extended beneath the triangle of dark hair between her thighs.

But then Stone forgot all about the tattoo as Leola arched her back, presenting herself to him. He started licking her, his tongue playing with her. Leola gripped his shoulders, shivers of pleasure undulating through her body.

Stone ran his hands up over her stomach and down again, stroking her thighs. She was rubbing her hands over his back, caressing him as her breathing grew shallower and faster. Suddenly she dug her fingers into his back, her fingernails sinking into his flesh.

Stone yelled and pulled away.

"What the fuck?" he hissed.

"Don't stop," Leola growled.

Stone grabbed her wrist and yanked her hand around in front of him. The tips of her fingernails were red with his blood, and the sight of it excited him. Letting go of her hand he grabbed her by the hair and yanked her head back. He thrust himself inside her, clamping his mouth over hers, his tongue exploring hers. He could feel her hands running down his back again, but he was only dimly aware of the sensation, and the thought that she might scratch him again only served to build up his excitement even more.

Stone let go of Leola's hair as he came to climax, and he screwed the bed sheets up in his fists. He pulled back, his mouth leaving Leola's as he gasped.

Leola's head snapped forward. Through the roar of his blood in his head, every nerve ending in his body exploding, Stone realised she was sinking her teeth into his neck.

* * *

Leola stood at the hotel window, her naked flesh bathed in sunshine, stretching like a cat. Running her hands through her hair she watched the cars navigating traffic islands, edging into the stream of traffic on the dual carriageway. A river of tourists and frequent travellers, heading out of the airport, towards the motorways.

It had been a long time since she had been in England, and she was looking forward to seeing how much had changed.

Leola ran her hands down over her breasts and her abdomen, enjoying the sensation of her fingers on her skin. Her nerve endings were still sensitive and alive. Tiny sparks of pleasure coursed through her body at the touch of her fingers.

Leaving the window, Leola lay down on the bed, smoothing out the rumpled sheets with the flat of her hand. Her movement paused when her fingers reached the spots of red blood, and she rubbed lightly at them with her fingertips. They were dry now. Such tiny spots of blood. Did he really have to make such a big fuss about it?

The bathroom door opened and Garrett Stone stepped out, a towel wrapped around his waist. Steam curled around and over his shoulders from the shower. Leola's gaze lingered over his body, taut with muscle, his chest covered in a dark mat of curly hair.

He was holding a wad of toilet paper to his neck.

"Started bleeding again while I was showering," he said. "You sure do like to play rough."

"I was holding back," Leola said. "You should see me when I let myself go."

Stone pulled the toilet paper from his neck and examined the blobs of blood dotting the blue surface. "Looks like its stopping again. How the hell I'm going to explain this to Lucy when I get back, I have no idea."

Leola sat up. "Turn around, let me look at your back."

Stone turned around and Leola stood up, and ran her fingers down his back. Her fingertips traced the bumps of his spine, between the thick layers of muscle. Most of the scratches across his shoulder blades were light, and already the redness was fading. But there were a couple where her fingernails had gouged deeper, drawing blood. They would heal over quickly enough, though.

Her fingers found the edge of the towel, and she tugged at it.

Stone stepped away, turning back to face her, clutching the towel. "Much as I'd love to, I haven't got the time. Lucy will already be wondering where the hell I am."

Leola glanced down at the ridiculous looking protrusion in his towel. "Are you sure?"

Stone planted his hand on her chest and pushed her back down on the bed. "Yeah, I'm sure."

He let the towel fall to the floor, and walked back into the bathroom. Leola watched him, admiring his ass, the rolling bunches of muscle under his skin. When he came back out of the bathroom he had put a dressing over the wound on his neck. He bent down and began picking up his clothes, discarded across the room. Leola, reclining back on her elbows, watched him slowly covering up his beautiful nakedness with his clothes. Stone pulled on his shirt, checking that the dressing on his neck was secure, before he buttoned up the collar. When he had finished, he looked like the smartly dressed businessman she had first noticed on the flight over.

Shame.

She much preferred him naked.

Leola reclined fully on the bed. Watching Stone, she ran her hand down over her abdomen until her fingers found the thatch of hair between her thighs.

Stone picked up his hand luggage, the only bag he had travelled with, and looked down at her.

"You're not making it easy for me to leave, you know that, don't you?"

"That's the idea," she said.

"Unfortunately for you, I make it a habit of not succumbing to temptation too often." She watched his gaze sweep up and down her body. "You going to tell me what that tattoo is all about, now?"

Leola shook her head.

Stone lifted an eyebrow. "Didn't I satisfy you?"

"Nowhere near," she said.

Stone pulled a slim, silver case out of a pocket and opened it up. He produced a business card from it, and lay it on the bedside table.

"Call me before you leave England," he said. "Let's see if I can do better next time."

"Maybe," Leola said.

Stone walked over to the door and opened it. He paused in the open doorway and looked back.

"At least I found out the answer to one of my questions," he said.

"Oh?"

"As I suspected, you weren't wearing any knickers under your dress."

Leola giggled.

"What's so funny?"

"You English people, you use some funny words, that's all."

Stone looked at her some more.

"Call me," he said, and closed the door behind him.

Leola stood up and watched the traffic out of the window again. She saw Stone leave the hotel, and walk over to the taxi rank. He got in a car, and the taxi pulled out, driving around the island, and joining the flow of traffic on the main road. He never looked back once.

Leola watched as another car pulled out and eased into the flow of traffic, following Stone's cab. It took her a moment to pin down the faint tremble of unease in her stomach. She had seen the car before, when they left the airport. Had it followed them here, to the hotel?

Deciding it was none of her business, Leola stepped away from the window.

She opened up her suitcase and rummaged through the clothing until she found what she wanted. She pulled out a small, silver gadget, and took it in the bathroom. Wiping the steam from the bathroom mirror, Leola opened her mouth, and ran her tongue over her teeth.

She hadn't realised they had grown so sharp again.

She switched on the silver gadget, and it started buzzing.

Then she started filing down her teeth.

36 hours earlier...

Was that Michael Coffin?

Nick Archer strained against the cuffs, holding him up against the oven door, without taking his eyes off the boy. The kid was incredibly strong, that was obvious just from looking at him. Nick had a feeling it wouldn't be long before he had snapped the wooden table leg in half, and freed himself from the rope that currently held him. He was a wild-eyed monster, his mouth smeared with blood, and fingers like claws. For the last few minutes he had been pulling against the rope that bound him, snapping his head from side to side, and snarling. Bloody spittle had flown from his mouth, flecks of it hitting Nick in the face.

But for the moment he was quiet, his head bowed, shoulders hunched, panting from the exertion of his struggles.

And Nick was staring at him, thinking about how much he looked like Joe Coffin's dead child.

It wasn't possible. Nick had seen the crime scene photographs, even stood and looked at the kid's body in the mortuary. Michael Coffin was dead. Along with his mother, Steffanie Coffin, he'd been the first victim of the Birmingham Vampire.

So how come he was here, alive, and looking like something out of a horror movie?

Nick shoved the question out of his head. He could think about this another time, when he wasn't cuffed to an oven door in a narrowboat that looked more like a slaughterhouse. The handcuffs were rigid and strong, and there was no way on earth he could get them off without help. But the oven door handle, to which Coffin had attached him, was another matter. There was already a little bit of give in the handle where it was attached to the door. If he could keep up the pressure on it he might tear it out of its housing, and then at least he could get off this narrowboat, and get help.

But he could see he was running out of time.

The boy (*it's Michael, you know it is!*) was only small. How old? Four, maybe five? During his career in the police force, Nick Archer had seen some tough, streetwise kids. But nothing like this one. There was something in his eyes that revolted and terrified Nick, whenever the boy looked at him. Saying that he looked like a wild animal didn't cut it. The boy was beyond that. Whatever he had been through, whatever the Birmingham Vampire had done to him, had changed him into a monster.

And Nick knew that if the boy freed himself first, he would rip him apart in a bloody frenzy.

Biting down on the towel that Coffin had stuffed into his mouth, Nick pulled at the cuffs again. The rigid, hardened plastic rubbed at his wrists, peeling more skin back. His hands were slippery with blood, but he knew he had to ignore the pain and keep up the pressure. If he could pull the handle off the oven door he could get out and find help. The cuffs would be a hindrance, but they wouldn't stop him. All he had to do was run back down the towpath until he found the police searching the area for Julie Carter, and he would be safe. They could get the cuffs off him, and he could lead them back here. Then they could get that kid to safety, and find Emma again.

And arrest Joe Coffin.

Nick was going to slap the cuffs on Coffin himself.

Nick strained against the restraints, ignoring the searing pain from his wrists. When he could take no more he sank back, breathing hard through his nose. The dirty tea towel that Coffin had stuffed into his mouth was restricting his breathing, and with all this exertion, Nick felt like he was suffocating.

The kid still wasn't looking at him. For the first time he looked exhausted, his head bowed, his mop of hair sticky with blood and drooping over his face. On the table top lay Julie Carter's body, one arm hanging down off the edge beside the kid's head. Blood was dripping off her fingers, the steady *plip! plip!* of each drop hitting the sodden carpet the only sound in the cabin, over the thrumming of the rain hitting the narrowboat's roof.

The cabin was a slaughterhouse, the coppery stench of recently spilt blood thick in the air. Much longer down here and Nick knew he would throw up. He could hardly breathe, and his chest was tight with anxiety. He wondered if he'd been missed yet, if any of his colleagues had tried contacting him on his radio. They couldn't even phone him. That big fucking gorilla had thrown his mobile in the canal, too.

What the hell had Emma been thinking, leaving him here with this monster?

And what was her connection with Joe Coffin? Was it purely professional, the result of an investigative reporter's pursuit of a story, or was there more to it? Emma could have been raped and murdered by the Birmingham Vampire, but she had chosen Coffin over Nick for help. Why?

Was she having an affair with the ugly bastard?

Fear and frustration building inside his chest, Nick yanked hard at the oven door handle. Michael Coffin's head snapped up at the rattle of the cuffs, and he stared at Nick, his lips peeling back in a guttural snarl.

Nick flinched, looked away. The boy's red rimmed eyes had a fierce insanity within them. Noticing Nick once more sent him into a frenzy, and he began jerking at the rope that held him to the table leg. His trousers and shirt were stained red with blood, and his feet were bare. Even his toes were forming into claws. His toenails looked thick and sharp enough to rip through flesh with one swift slash.

The boy snarled and howled wordlessly, like a rabid dog being beaten to death with a hammer. He flung himself against his restraints, heedless of any injury he might do himself. Nick risked a glance up. Michael Coffin's face was taught with tension, straining every muscle in his body to try and reach Nick. His red, snapping teeth were less than a foot away from the detective's shoulder. Beneath all the noise the little boy was making, Nick swore he could hear the creak of the fastenings in the floorboards, slowly prising loose.

When he finally pulled himself free, the boy was going to rip Nick Archer to shreds.

He pulled at the cuffs again, ignoring the searing pain in his wrists, jerking against the restraints over and over again. His feet scrabbled on the floor as he twisted and writhed, his shoes slipping in the blood soaked carpet. The narrowboat rocked with the combined motion of Nick and the boy fighting to free themselves.

If only it wasn't raining so hard, there might have been somebody out there to hear all the commotion they were making, Michael Coffin howling and snarling and kicking his feet against the cabin floor. Where the hell were Emma and Coffin? Couldn't they hear what was going on?

Or had they left him to die here?

With a splintering of wood, Michael tore himself free from the table leg. The rope, no longer taut, began unravelling. The boy was staring at Nick the whole time, red drool hanging from his chin. Nick braced himself as, completely free of restraint, Michael threw himself at the helpless detective.

Nick kicked out, the sole of his shoe catching the boy in the throat. He spun around, and hit the floor with a sickening splat in the blood soaked carpet.

Immediately he scrambled to his feet again, and launched himself back at the policeman, like a wild dog. Nick kicked out again, catching him a glancing blow on the shoulder. It did little to stop him. Michael clamped his teeth into Nick's thigh, and bit down.

Nick howled in pain, but his screams were muffled by the tea towel that Coffin had stuffed in his mouth. It was as though someone had stabbed glowing red hot needles into his leg, and then begun twisting them, and digging them deeper. He thrashed and kicked, bucking against the cuffs holding him to the oven door. Michael held on, his teeth sinking even further into the warm flesh.

The little boy chewed and shook his head, like a dog fastened onto its prey. Bright, arterial blood sprayed from the side of his mouth and over Julie Carter's lifeless arm, hanging from the edge of the table.

With a squeal of metal and plastic, the handle ripped free of the oven door and Nick sprawled sideways. Michael lifted his head, his long teeth making a sucking noise as they slid out of the open wound. Using his uninjured leg, Nick raised his foot and kicked Michael square in the face. The little boy's head snapped backwards and hit the edge of the table. While he was still stunned, Nick kicked him in the head again, his shoe connecting solidly with the boy's temple.

Michael fell over, face down on the bloody carpet. Battling an urgent need to stand up and start stomping on the kid's head until he was sure he was dead, Nick pushed himself up onto his knees. He was bleeding profusely from the open gash in his thigh. He knew he had to get a tourniquet around his leg, or some kind of compression on the wound, before he lost too much blood.

Michael began stirring, his tiny fingers curling up into fists. The detective curled himself up into as small a shape as he could, and dragged his cuffed arms under his backside and underneath his knees. The next part was going to be awkward, as he had long legs. But he needed to get his hands in front where, even though still cuffed together, he had more opportunity to use them. He folded his right leg up as far as he could, his knee under his chin.

It wasn't enough, his foot couldn't fit through the gap between his arms.

Michael stirred again, a low, guttural moan growing in the back of his throat.

Straining every tendon in his arms and shoulders, his upper body curled up and his knee almost touching his shoulder, Nick waggled his foot. The heel of his shoe was caught on the cuffs, just an inch or two away from slipping over them. Screaming in frustration against the tea towel tied to his mouth, Nick wrenched his arms forward and his leg up, his foot suddenly springing free.

Now he had his cuffed wrists between his legs. The wound in his left thigh was still flowing with scarlet blood, and the whole leg felt like a dead weight. There was no way he could lift that leg in the same way.

Michael pushed himself up onto his hands and knees, and shook his head. His sodden hair flicked from side to side, scattering drops of blood and sweat around the stinking cabin.

With his arms cuffed between his legs, Nick was just as helpless as when they had been behind his back. He was dizzy and sick, and too weak to fight back.

But he did have a little more freedom in his arms. He was able to loop his left arm over his left knee, and bring his cuffed wrists down to his ankle. As Nick lifted his useless leg up and bent it at the knee, bringing his ankle around towards his groin, Michael slowly turned around and gazed at him.

A fierce awareness returned to his eyes.

The policeman pulled his cuffed wrists under his foot with relative ease, so that he had his hands in front.

Michael continued staring at him, as though aware that his prey had a little more power on his side now than he had before.

Pulling the dripping tea towel off his face, Nick sucked in a lungful of stagnant, stinking air.

He fumbled with the towel, ripping it from around his neck and balling it up. He pressed it against the wound in his leg with both hands. Keeping eye contact with the boy all the time, he continued taking deep breaths, trying to release the tightness in his chest.

The little boy growled, baring his red stained teeth at his victim. He seemed wary of making a move.

Nick edged backwards, towards the door. His hand slipped on the blood slicked floor as he pushed himself awkwardly along, hindered by his wrists still cuffed together. When he got to the steps, leading out onto the deck, he had to brace his good foot against a wall to help leverage himself up.

And all the time he kept his eyes locked onto the little boy, squatting in the corner, watching his every move.

Bit by bit, Nick bumped himself up the wooden steps, until his back was resting against the door. Once outside on the deck, he wasn't sure what he was going to do. The idea had been to escape, but he didn't know if he had the strength to stand up and climb off the boat. At least he would be out in the open, where he could be seen by a police search party.

If they were coming up this far.

Nick reached up, stretching his arms painfully above his head, and fumbled with the door, searching for the catch. Joe Coffin's little boy continued staring at him, his eyes narrowed down to slits.

Fucking hell, what happened to this poor kid, that turned him into a psychotic little monster like this?

His hand found the door handle, and he pulled it. The door swung out and Nick fell backwards, his head cracking against the hard, wooden deck. Cold rain hit him in the face, blurring his vision.

Lying on his back on the deck slick with water and blood, the detective realised how helpless he was. His legs were still inside the cabin, his left thigh pumping blood. By dragging himself this far, he had only opened himself up to the boy.

Confirming his worst fears, Nick heard the scuffling of claws from within the cabin. Before he had a chance to even think about moving or defending himself, Michael was on top of him. Long fingernails, more like claws, dug into Nick's stomach and chest. The little boy's contorted face appeared in his blurred vision, lips drawn back in a red snarl.

Nick raised both arms, trying to protect himself. The little boy ripped at the flesh on his arms, a blur of dark movement, like an imp from hell. Every tear in his skin registered in his head, every bite of those sharp teeth, piercing his soft flesh. He could feel his warm blood gushing from the rips in his body, running onto the narrowboat deck, and mingling with the rainwater.

Nick gave up trying to defend himself, the boy was too crazed, too wild, and just too fucking strong to be held back. The policeman rolled over, both hands on the deck, and tried pushing himself away. His hands slipped on the rain and blood slicked surface, and his right hand found the handle of the discarded Samurai sword. His fingers closed around it, and he lifted the weapon and swung it wildly at the boy.

The blade connected, and Michael's snarls turned into a gurgle. Nick kept on hacking at him, the sword making wet smacking noises as it slashed at flesh and bone. In the dark and the rain the boy was nothing more than a physical shadow, a monster. Sobbing, Nick swung the sword at the shadow, the blade slicing through skin and muscle. Finally the shadow stopped fighting, and keeled over and hit the deck with a wet slap.

Nick, panting wildly, tried crawling away from the mutilated body but there was no room on the narrowboat. He closed his eyes and stifled a sob.

"Oh, fuck," he whispered. "Fuck, fuck, *fuck!*"

Nick opened his eyes again, suddenly gripped with the fear that Michael Coffin was climbing to his feet once more, his mouth open and hands outstretched.

But the little boy lay still, blood oozing from the slashes in his body and the criss-cross pattern of wounds over his face.

Great fucking job, Archer. You just managed to kill a four year old kid.

But it had been him or Michael. Nick hadn't just been dealing with a sulky child having a tantrum, he'd been fighting for his life. The kid had bitten him and scratched him, he was like a wild animal, like a thing possessed. What was Nick supposed to do, offer him a jelly baby?

Even so, did you have to slash him to ribbons with a fucking Samurai sword?

The detective closed his eyes, and then immediately snapped them open. It was no good, every time he shut his eyes he was seized with a sudden terror of Michael climbing to his feet and leaping on him, to finish him off for good.

Maybe he's not dead. If he's still alive, and help comes soon, we can get him to a hospital. Everybody will see then, how wild he is, how totally vicious and mental and bug-eyed crazy he can be. Everybody will understand why I had to defend myself with that sword, when the boy attacks the doctors and nurses, and tries taking a bite out of a few people.

Nick hauled himself over to the boy, and shoved his fingers up under his jaw, trying to find a pulse. There was nothing.

The policeman rested his forehead against the little boy's chest. He was so tired. He just wanted to curl up into a ball, and wait for a rescue party.

No. They find you here, slumped over the body of a child and covered in his blood, they're going to arrest you. How the hell are you going to explain that the kid was a fucking crazy monster? All everyone is going to see is a defenceless little four-year-old, all cut up like sheets of coloured paper in a child's craft lesson.

And what about Coffin?

Nick sat up straighter.

If Joe Coffin found him here, with his dead son, he wasn't going to hang around and wait to hear any excuses. It didn't matter that Coffin knew exactly what his boy was like, that he'd had to defend himself from a frenzied attack, too.

No, as soon as he saw his son's bloody corpse lying on the deck he'd just go into a blind fury, and Nick would be a dead man.

Beyond the small pool of light cast by the glow of the narrowboat's windows, Nick could see nothing. There was no sign of his colleagues approaching the narrowboat along the towpath yet.

He cursed them and their stupidity, but at the same time he was grateful.

If he acted fast, he might just get away with this.

Nick clawed at the little boy's shirt with both cuffed hands, pulling him up to a sitting position. The child's head lolled forward, and there was a spurt of blood from a wound in his neck. The boy was light, but Nick was weak from loss of blood, and he couldn't stand up.

The side of the boat wasn't too high, though, and Nick was able to brace Michael's body against it and push him upwards. With a good shove, the boy teetered on the edge of the boat, his arms hanging limp from his sides.

And then fell over the edge.

Nick heard the splash of water. He wanted to drag himself up, peer over the edge of the narrowboat, check that Michael's body had disappeared from view.

But he was too weak.

He remained slumped on the blood and rain slicked deck, and closed his eyes, waiting for someone to find him.

* * *

Joe Coffin stared into the yellow and red flames, the heat from the bonfire scorching his scarred face. The sharp stink of burning flesh filled the cellar, lit by the glow of the flames chasing shadows across its damp brick walls. Black, oily smoke rolled across the ceiling, like storm clouds gathering in a time lapse movie. Coffin squatted on the floor, beside the pit where Abel Mortenson's carved up remains were being consumed by fire. Down here there was still some oxygen left, enough that Coffin could stay a while longer, and watch his family's killer burn up.

Jacob Mills had been kept prisoner here, and drained of his blood by the killer the newspapers had tagged the Birmingham Vampire. What the newspapers hadn't realised was that Birmingham's serial killer was a real vampire. Coffin had sliced him up with a chainsaw and then doused the pieces in diesel. He had set them alight, and now he was watching as the fire consumed the monster known as Abel Mortenson.

Coffin flexed his hand, rotated his shoulder. Pain spasmed through his arm. Where Abel had chewed on his shoulder, the muscles and ligaments were still painful, and lacking in strength. Coffin was going to carry the scars of their first encounter for the rest of his life. But they would serve as a reminder that Coffin had killed the vampire at the end, and so thoroughly destroyed his remains he was never coming back.

Coffin retreated from the edge of the pit as the heat grew in intensity. His skin was oily with sweat, and his lungs felt scorched. As he trudged outside, an immense weariness flooded through his system. The rain was cool on his face and shoulders.

Emma Wylde was sitting on the wet grass, under the large tree in the overgrown garden. Her clothes were soaked, her hair plastered against her head, and she was shivering.

"Hey, we need to get you somewhere warm and dry," Coffin said.

Emma didn't reply. She had her arms wrapped around her knees, and her head bowed.

Coffin squatted down beside her, wiped blood and rainwater out of his eyes. When he reached out and placed a hand on her shoulder she flinched, and pulled away.

Coffin dropped his hand by his side.

"You're in shock," he said. "We need to get you somewhere safe, and out of this rain."

"This is such a fucking mess," Emma said, her teeth chattering.

"Aren't you listening to me? We need to move, the cops will be here soon."

Emma looked up at Coffin. Strands of hair were plastered over her face, and flecks of blood dotted her cheeks and forehead. She stared at him with eyes round and wide and dark.

"And then what? Are you going to kill them too? And then the others, back at Angels, right? That's a lot of killing, Coffin, but I suppose that's what you do best, isn't it?"

"You weren't complaining earlier," Coffin said. "Fact is, you even helped me out."

Emma hugged herself tighter. "So much fucking blood."

"You're in shock, we need to get you out of here," Coffin said, and closed his hand around her forearm.

Emma twisted out of his grip. "We shouldn't have done this. I helped you murder someone, I'm a killer, just like you."

"You can't kill a monster like that, he was already dead."

Emma shook her head and turned her face away from Coffin.

"What the hell is wrong with you?" Coffin growled. "Surely you knew it would end like this. That bastard is never coming back now, he's never going to hurt anyone again. And that's because of me, because I chopped him up and burnt the pieces." Coffin grabbed Emma by the chin, his large hand swallowing up the lower half of her face, and twisted her head around to face him. "You're the one who asked me for help, Emma. You think you'd still be alive if your boyfriend got here first and tried slapping the cuffs on him?"

Coffin laughed, let go of Emma, and stood up. He towered over her, rainwater running in red streaks down his T-shirt.

"That bastard would have eaten your boyfriend alive, and then he would have raped you, before ripping you open and drinking your blood. So, yeah, you're right. Killing is what I do best."

Coffin tilted his head up to the dark sky and let the raindrops run over his face. After the heat of the fire in the enclosed cellar space, the cold had been good on his skin, but now he could feel it seeping into his bones. Much longer out here freezing cold and wet, and his teeth would be chattering too, just like Emma.

He lowered his head and looked at the woman on the ground, hugging herself tight, head bowed once more.

Turning his back on her, Coffin stepped through the gap he had made in the fence, and onto the canal towpath.

Behind him, Emma raised her head and watched Coffin as he climbed through the hole in the garden fence. Then she struggled to her feet, and followed him.

The narrowboat sat on the dark canal water, its windows glowing with light. The warm, cosy looking appearance was ruined by the streaks of blood splattered against the windows. Coffin stepped on the slick deck, the boat rocking slightly under his weight. Archer was sitting propped against the boat's side, his eyes closed, wrists cuffed in front of him. His shirt and trousers were ripped open, slashes of red covering his body, and there was a nasty wound in his leg still oozing blood.

Coffin bent down and peered into the cabin. Apart from the girl's corpse lying on the table, it was empty. The rope he had used to tie Michael up with lay in coils on the blood soaked carpet.

Coffin kicked Archer in the side.

Archer flinched, and opened his eyes. They widened when he saw Coffin standing over him, rain pouring down his face.

"Where's Michael?" Coffin said.

Archer coughed. His head lolled on his shoulders, and his eyes drooped.

"The party's over, Coffin," he said, his voice slurred. "You're going down for the rest of your fucking life, and you know what? I'm going to come and visit you every single fucking day, and look at your ugly mug, stuck in prison."

"Nice speech," Coffin said. "Where's Michael? What happened?"

"What the hell do you think happened? He fucked off down the park to play with his friends." Archer shivered, and his eyes closed momentarily.

Coffin squatted down in front of Archer, looked at the wound in his leg.

"They're on their way, Coffin," Archer whispered. "Not just looking for two missing women, but one of their own, who's not responding to calls on his handheld. You'd better get moving, you don't want to be leaving here with a police escort."

Coffin stood up, turned around, looked down the towpath. No sign of any coppers yet. He twisted around and looked in the opposite direction. Apart from a growing orange glow, flickering in the darkness as the fire began consuming No. 99, there was nothing.

Coffin noticed the Samurai sword lying on the narrowboat deck. He picked it up. Rainwater ran down its bloody edge, and over his hand.

One quick thrust through Archer's chest, and that was him out of the way. Coffin could disappear, get cleaned up, nobody would ever know he had been here.

Except Emma.

That's a lot of killing, Coffin, but I suppose that's what you do best, isn't it?

Lights, flickering between the trees, in the darkness. A search party making its way along the towpath.

In the distance, the growing wail of a siren cut its way through the night. A fire engine, summoned by reports of smoke seen billowing from the house on Forde Road, no doubt.

"Joe."

Coffin spun round. Emma was standing on the towpath, white face framed by her lank, dirty blond hair. Her arms hung by her sides, and she looked exhausted and defeated.

Coffin dropped the Samurai sword over the edge of the boat. Watched it sink from view. He followed it, lowering himself into the cold, dark canal water. He could hear voices now, approaching. A dog barking. Torch beam lights growing stronger.

Coffin swam to the opposite bank of the canal and hauled himself out.

He paused for one quick glance back at Emma, still standing on the towpath, watching him.

Turning his back on her, he forced himself through the shrubbery and disappeared into the night.

* * *

Emma climbed on the boat and knelt down beside Nick.

"Fucking kid tried shredding me into tiny pieces," Nick whispered. "What the hell's going on, Emma?"

"Shush, don't try and talk, help's almost here."

Nick swallowed, his eyelids fluttering, looked like he was going to pass out. But then he gripped Emma's wrist.

"Is he dead? The Birmingham Vampire, is he dead?"

Emma nodded. "Yes."

"Good." Nick took a deep breath, his chest hitching with the effort. "Get out of here, Emms. Get the fuck away before they arrive."

"No, I can't do that, I can't leave you," Emma said.

"You can't stay here," Nick whispered, his voice hoarse. "What are you going to say when you're down the station, and they ask you what happened here?"

"I'll tell them, I'll explain—"

Nick gripped Emma's wrist fiercely. "What? What are you going to explain? I had to kill Coffin's kid to stop him, Emma. He would have fucking ripped me apart if I hadn't done. How do you think that's going to look when everyone finds out I'm a child killer?"

"But you had to, it was self-defence."

"He was a fucking four-year-old kid!" Nick hissed. "And I hacked at him with that Samurai sword Coffin brought to the party, just kept chopping at him until he was a lump of red meat, and then I dumped his body into the canal. And you, I don't know what you're involvement in all this is, but you're in deep, right?"

Emma nodded, holding back the tears.

"Get the hell out of here, Emma, now. Go find Barry, tell him you slipped on the towpath, fell in the canal. I'll explain all this shit here."

"Nick, I—"

"Just fucking go will you?"

Emma stood up. Lights flickered through the trees. The police search party was almost around the bend in the canal. Another few seconds, and they would be able to see her.

Emma jumped off the boat, and ran.

WELCOME

Coffin kept off the towpath but followed its route, winding through the outskirts of the Birmingham suburbs. As he walked, sheets of rainwater poured down his body and washed away the blood. The houses thinned out, and his surroundings became more industrialised. When he felt he was far enough away from the police, Coffin got back on the towpath and picked up his speed.

He would have liked to double back for his Fat Boy, but it had been too risky. If the cops had found him there, covered in blood, he'd have had no chance. Archer had probably named Coffin by now, and the entire West Midlands police force would be out hunting him down.

What did it matter that Coffin had just killed one of the most vicious serial killers the country had ever known? A vampire. They would still search Coffin out, and when they found him they would toss him in the slammer, and throw away the keys. Idiots.

They didn't realise they needed Joe Coffin. The killings would start all over again very soon, and before they knew it, there would be hundreds, and then thousands, of vampires prowling the city. Steffanie, the old man, Clevon, Addison and Velvina, they had to be killed, wiped out, just like Abel. Burnt alive, or dragged out into the sunshine, until their skin bubbled and popped and sloughed off their bones.

Except Michael.

Coffin stopped walking, paused to wipe rainwater off his face, out of his eyes.

Given long enough, the vampires back at Angels would be found out at some point. Didn't matter how many people were dead by then, how many more victims had been infected and risen from the dead. They were going to be discovered, and then they would be hunted down. By the police, by the army, maybe specialist teams of vampire hunters would be set up. But someone, somewhere in power, would make the decision that the vampire threat needed to be eradicated.

And that would include Coffin's boy.

Coffin flexed his right arm, rolled his shoulder. Still hurt like a bastard, the tendons crunching together when he moved his arm. He was fairly certain the wound in his shoulder had opened up again after his fight with Abel and then his dip in the canal.

No point going back to Shaddock, that man was a quack. First priority was to get out of sight, somewhere warm and dry. Then he needed to get his arm sorted again. Get someone to look at his finger on his left hand, where Velvina had bitten the end off.

Once that was done he could start looking for Michael. Find him, get him somewhere safe, away from people. Maybe there was a cure, some way of getting his little boy back. Maybe not.

But he couldn't just abandon him.

Coffin started walking again, feet sloshing through the muddy puddles. The dark surface of the canal bubbled violently as the raindrops hit it. Over the hiss of the rain in the leaves of the trees, Coffin could hear the clank of machinery from the warehouses on the other side of a chain link fence running along the towpath.

Eventually Coffin got to a gap in the fence, and a muddy path leading between two large industrial units. The glow of a floodlight illuminating a mostly empty car park picked out his way along the path. Coffin walked out from between the warehouses and onto the industrial estate road system. He jogged along the tarmac, taking shortcuts through parking areas, until he found another footpath. This one lead into the darkness of a large area of wasteland, overgrown with stunted trees and brambles.

It would have helped if he'd had a torch, but Coffin knew his way well enough. He walked carefully through the gloom, pushing branches out of his way, the leaves dripping water on him. The footpath took him down, becoming less defined the further he penetrated the undergrowth. Finally the path disappeared altogether, but Coffin pushed on.

Five minutes later, Coffin found what he was looking for.

The manhole cover, set into the ground and thick with mud and leaves, looked rusted into place. Coffin squatted down and ran his finger around its circumference, gouging a line in the mud, defining the edge of the iron cover. Looked like it hadn't been used in years. Decades, probably.

There was no way he was opening that up. Not without the proper tools. But there had to be another entrance nearby. Coffin stood up. He needed a torch. Without a light of some kind he could spend the rest of the night stumbling around in the dark, looking for that entrance.

But he didn't have any other options. Even his mobile was dead, after his dip in the canal earlier. Coffin pushed cautiously through the undergrowth.

As a child he had spent many hours exploring down here, and he remembered there was a disused railway line that ran through this area, and alongside the industrial estate. In the age of the industrial revolution, the railways had made the canal system obsolete, but then along came cars and lorries, making the rail system redundant.

At some point the train track disappeared into a tunnel, cut into the side of Bunker's Hill. As children, Coffin and Tom Mills had tagged along once with a group of older boys, and walked through the disused rail tunnel from end to end. Somewhere in the middle of the tunnel, no daylight visible from either end, their torches had picked out an iron door set into the Victorian brickwork. The door had been locked, and so, after a brief argument about what might be on the other side, they had carried on walking.

Now Coffin wondered if that was what he was looking for.

After another ten minutes of stumbling through the darkness, he found the disused train track. The going got easier now as he walked along the rail line, until the brick archway of the tunnel appeared out of the darkness, so suddenly it almost seemed to be swallowing him up.

Coffin paused at the entrance. The interior of the tunnel was pitch black. He would have to walk carefully along one side, his hand running along the brickwork until he found the door. But if he was on the wrong side he would come out the opposite end, and then have to turn around and find his way back again on the opposite side.

At least he would be dry.

Coffin placed his palm flat against the damp, gritty surface of the tunnel wall. Behind him the rain continued to fall, the sound of it a constant hiss. Ahead there was silence, apart from the steady *plink!* of dripping water.

Coffin walked into the darkness, trailing his hand along the brickwork. For the first time in years he felt like that little kid again, stepping into the unknown.

As he walked deeper into the tunnel, the sound of the rain faded, and the silence grew. His boots crunched in the gravel with each step he took, and there was a steady drip of water into a pool somewhere ahead. But other than those two noises he could have been in a vacuum.

After walking slowly and steadily for some time, his fingers running along the wall, Coffin saw the first faint glow of light in the pitch black. He thought he was imagining it at first, it was so faint, and then as the light grew he wondered if he was approaching the opposite entrance to the tunnel. But that was wrong, because it was night, and so there was no daylight to provide that glow.

Soon there was enough light that Coffin was able to drop his hand and walk unaided. The diffuse glow resolved itself into a lightbulb set inside a metal grille, illuminating a recess in the brick wall.

In the recess was the metal door Coffin had been searching for.

The light picked out the rail lines, the sleepers set in the gravel and the puddles of oily, scummy water. At Coffin's feet, in front of the door, was a tatty, dirty hessian mat with the word WELCOME on it.

Someone was feeling house-proud, and Coffin had an idea he knew who it was.

There was a single metal handle set into the door. The last time he'd been here, thirty-some years and a whole different lifetime ago, the door had been locked, and whatever mysteries lay on the other side had remained just that. A mystery.

But last time there hadn't been a WELCOME mat at the entrance, inviting him in.

Coffin grasped the door handle and pulled.

The door opened.

He stepped through and into a concrete bunker. The grey, bare walls were illuminated by more lights in the ceiling, set inside metal grilles. Ahead lay a short corridor, finishing at the top of a set of steps. Coffin pulled the door to, the sound of it closing echoing around the empty chamber.

The concrete steps were wide and deep, lit all the way down by a series of bare bulbs. At the top of the steps, on the wall, was a tatty, old poster. Coffin smoothed it out.

In stark, black lettering it spelled out the warning signs of radiation poisoning.

Coffin started walking down the steps, his booted feet echoing around the empty stairwell.

Announcing his arrival.

At the bottom he reached another door, similar to the one at the top. But before he could reach out to grasp hold of the handle, the door opened.

"What a deliciousable consternation," Corpse said. "Desirabling to entate into our homory?"

steffanie's turn

Steffanie surveyed her kingdom. The overturned tables and chairs, the blood smeared across the floor and splashed up the walls. The silver and gold poles, glimmering softly in the club's lighting. Tom Mills lying on the floor, his head smashed in like an overripe watermelon.

His broken teeth scattered across the floor in puddle of congealed blood.

A pity about that. Tom had been useful, and so easy to manipulate. And fun, too. All that time, thinking he was in charge, that he had a way out. He had been a desperate, scared little boy, manipulated by Steffanie, and the Triads, too eager to seek revenge on Joe Coffin and Mortimer Craggs. All those years of built up resentment had withered him, sucked the life out of him like a vampire itself. He had been so intent on taking down Coffin and Craggs that he couldn't see what was going on under his nose. The Triad faction that wanted Angels back wouldn't have let him live long, if they had got what they wanted. They were using him, just like Steffanie had been, just like everyone else in his life had.

Craggs, Coffin, they had treated him like a dog, using him as their own personal slave and whipping boy. Even Laura had done the same, despite all her whining and crying about how Tom beat her. She had got her way with having a kid, when Tom hadn't wanted one, hadn't she? That snotty brat Jacob.

Tom's mistake had been the same as every other man's. All Steffanie had had to do was take him by his cock, and she could lead him anywhere. All it took was a glance, or a word, and all men lost the ability to think, and instead let their dicks lead them on. Pathetic. How on earth had the human race survived for so long, and become the dominant species? With men in charge, when all they could think of was fucking and fighting, they should have gone the way of the dinosaurs centuries ago.

But everything would change now. It might not know it, but the human species was at the twilight of its existence. The vampire race had almost been wiped out, Abel had said. But no longer.

Now they had a new beginning.

Steffanie fingered the hole in her face, where her right eye used to be. She ran her fingertips down over her cheek, and the ragged gaps in her flesh where the shotgun blast had ripped through her. Always the vampires healed up, whatever damage was done to them. Only prolonged exposure to sunlight could kill them, Abel had said. Maybe that was why she wasn't healing up properly, because she had been exposed to the sun when they left the Travelodge on the motorway. Maybe her system had been weakened.

But she felt strong now.

Steffanie had examined herself for a long time in a mirror, studying the ripped holes in her cheek, and the empty eye socket. Far from disturbing her, the sight of her ruined face excited something deep within herself. The old Steffanie was dead, so wasn't it somehow appropriate that the new Steffanie had a new face? Her grotesque appearance meant she could never appear in public again, but really, was that such a price to pay? Her face would inspire fear and disgust at the first sighting, and perhaps she could use that to her advantage.

The old man was prowling the club, picking items up and examining them as though they were artefacts from an alien planet. Which, in a way, they were, to him. For over 120 years he had been buried in the ground, in the cellar at No. 99. The world had changed a great deal in that time. He was still wearing the dirty, stiff suit that she had first seen him in back at No. 99, and fresh blood stained the front of his shirt, like a Jackson Pollock painting. But he was looking stronger, and younger, all the time. His grey hair was turning darker and thicker, his flesh was filling out, and his eyes becoming more alert.

The old man, Guttman was his name, picked up a mobile phone and turned it over and over. Inspecting it. Clearly mystified as to its purpose.

Steffanie stretched, easing out the kinks in her shoulders and spine. The need for blood coursed through her nerve endings, setting them aflame with desire. She had to control it, keep that hunger at bay. If they went out hunting too soon, there was every likelihood they would be discovered, maybe even captured, or worse. Clevon, Addison and Velvina were too young and immature to be set free amongst the human cattle just yet.

But they needed blood.

And not the sterile crap that Tom had been providing them with, either.

They needed a steady supply of fresh, warm blood.

At least whilst they hid, and built up their strength.

The club would be the ideal place to hide in. To Steffanie, after all the years spent dancing here, first for Terry Wu, and then for a short while for Craggs, Angels felt like home. But the club wasn't hers, and Craggs would want it back. Would probably send Joe back to take it off her.

Steffanie smiled. Joe had been gullible, thought that she loved him, cared for him. And, in truth, he'd had his uses. He was good in bed, for a start. And he always tried to look after her, in his big, lumbering, old fashioned way. But when she married him he had been a means to an end. A way of escaping Terry Wu and his wandering hands, and the life that she was living back then.

Was it her fault that none of it had turned out how she envisaged? She had imagined life with Joe Coffin, the Slaughterhouse Mob enforcer and Mortimer Craggs' right hand man, would be a lot more exciting than it turned out to be. The money hadn't exactly flowed like she thought it would, either. And so she'd had to keep on dancing for Terry Wu, both publicly and privately, and had settled into a life of domesticity with alarming speed.

After Michael was born, Steffanie returned to the pole dancing with a passion she'd forgotten she had. It was her outlet, her way of coping with a snotty, stinking, wailing child. Joe adored him. Steffanie just pretended to.

And then Tom approached her with his plan to film Joe Coffin murdering Terry Wu. She'd noticed him looking at her the last year or so, the growing need for her in his eyes. And she could see that he knew how much she despised Joe. Maybe he'd thought she might fuck him, when he told her the plan, but she didn't. He'd had to wait until she was dead before that happened.

Now it was all different. Everything had changed, turned on its head. The old Steffanie was dead, and the new Steffanie was going to live forever. The new Steffanie was in charge.

Craggs and the Slaughterhouse Mob might have owned Birmingham once. But not anymore.

Now it was Steffanie Coffin's turn.

"Clevon!" she shouted.

Guttman looked up at her, and dropped the mobile on the floor.

Clevon appeared in the doorway. His face was smeared with dried blood, from where he had been sucking at Tom's corpse earlier. He stared at Steffanie with eyes large and round and black.

"Find the others and bring them here," she said. "We have a lot to do."

infection

A bright hot fire blossomed behind Joe Coffin's eyelids, and he threw his arm over his face to protect himself. At first he thought he was back in his cell, the strip lights blazing overhead, the clang of prison bars being repeatedly hit somewhere in another wing. The screws would be along soon, making sure they were awake. Ferrying them to the showers and the toilets in waves of unshaven, bleary eyed prisoners.

Coffin shuffled over onto his side, still shielding his eyes from the light. He would climb out of his bed in a moment, before the screws got to him. He never gave them the satisfaction of having to drag him out of bed, like some of the others did. He was always up and ready, as soon as the lights came on. But this morning was different. He felt hot and feverish, and his shoulder hurt where Abel had ripped it apart with his teeth.

The vampire. Coffin remembered now, searching for Jacob, being attacked by Abel.

Coffin rolled onto his back again, squinting through eyelids opened only to a narrow slit. He wasn't in jail. The metal clanging noise still echoed through the concrete chamber, but other than that there was silence.

He was in the bunker. A nuclear fallout shelter, built in the late 1950s.

Coffin pulled himself upright, ran his hand over his close cropped scalp. He could see a little better now. The door came into focus, the other beds, bare mattresses lying in their metal frames. His own bed also had a bare mattress, but a scratchy blanket had fallen to the floor when he sat up.

Coffin shivered, even though he felt hot and his face was covered in a sheen of sweat. He wiped his arm across his forehead. Maybe he was coming down with something. His quick swim in the filthy, cold canal water, followed by a walk through the night wouldn't have done him any good.

Or maybe there was something in the canal, had infected the wound in his shoulder. The other scratches and bites were all starting to heal up, but the wound in his shoulder felt damp and sticky beneath his T-shirt and he could smell the stink of infection.

It hurt like a bastard, too.

Coffin stood up, reached out and planted his hand against the wall to steady himself as a wave of dizziness flushed through his system and his vision greyed out. When he could see again and his head had stopped pulsating, he let go of the wall and opened the door.

The loud, steady *Clang! Clang!* grew in volume, piercing his brain like bolts of red hot lightning during the worst hangover ever.

When he found out who was making all that noise he was going to rip their arms off.

Coffin followed the line of the corridor, the overhead strip lights buzzing in their metal cages. He found an office, a large map of the world on the wall, old fashioned dial telephones on the desks alongside heavy, black typewriters. A thick layer of dust covered everything.

Coffin moved on, heading for the source of the noise, reverberating through the corridors.

He stopped again when he reached a large dining hall. The noise, the irritant, was coming from in here. Coffin stepped inside. The dining hall had been cleared of all furniture apart from a table, with two chairs pushed neatly under it, one on either side, The table had been positioned exactly in the centre of the room, and Coffin imagined that it must be a lonely experience eating there, with the grey, featureless, concrete walls surrounding you, imprisoning you in their blankness.

At one end of the hall was a serving hatch, with a door next to it. Coffin walked past the table and chairs. Two plates had been placed on the table, the dark, scummy remains of a meal on each one.

Pushing open the kitchen door, Coffin was hit by the smell of rotting food and stagnant water. Dirty plates and cups had been piled high in a large, steel sink filled with cold, dark water, a layer of fatty scum floating on the surface. Looked like somebody had started washing up after a large dinner party, and then abandoned it abruptly.

Cupboards lined the walls, some of them open revealing shelf after shelf of tinned and dried food, and enough plates and bowls that the washing up didn't need to be restarted for some time yet.

At the opposite end of the kitchen, past the industrial sized cooker and an ancient dishwasher, there was another door, slightly ajar. The clanging noises were coming from in there and now Coffin thought he could hear muffled cries, too.

Coffin glanced around the kitchen and spotted a bread knife. He picked it up and sidled up to the open door.

Silently he pushed the door further ajar. More shelves of dried and tinned food, lining the walls and creating aisles down the centre of the stockroom. The strip lights in the ceiling threw heavy shadows across the concrete floor. Whatever was happening, whoever was making all the racket, they were down at the opposite end of the storeroom, still out of sight behind all the shelves filled with supplies.

Coffin gripped the wooden handle of the bread knife hard and walked slowly down the centre aisle. He could see movement. Crazy shadows thrown across the walls, someone swinging something, the arm raised high and then rushing down, followed by the *CLANG!* of metal upon metal.

Muffled cries, sobbing maybe, but stifled by a gag. Coffin edged forward, the knife by his side, and stepped out from between the shelving.

The first thing Coffin registered was Corpse, in his ill-fitting, dirty black suit, the sleeves riding high up his arms and the hems of his trouser legs flapping around his ankles. He looked at Coffin, holding a metal pipe in both hands above his head, like it was a sword.

When he saw Coffin he gave him a gap toothed grin, and then swung the pipe down in a wide arc.

It rebounded off a tall metal cage on wheels, once probably intended for wheeling supplies up and down the long corridors. Now it was all twisted out of shape, the metal grill bent inwards from all the abuse Corpse had heaped on it.

Inside the cage was a man. He was pinned against the opposite side of the cage by lengths of silver duct tape, criss-crossing his body and his arms and legs so that he was completely immobile. A piece of tape had been stuck across his mouth. When he saw Coffin his eyes bulged and he screamed something, his head straining forward.

Corpse hit the cage again, the metal grillwork shivering under the impact. The man screwed his eyes shut, and sobbed behind his gag. How long had Corpse been bashing at the metal cage, slowly crushing it around the man trapped inside? Even if he hadn't been strapped down, he wouldn't be able to move. The metal grillwork had collapsed inwards so much it was forming a shell around his body.

"Just stop, will you?" Coffin said, and took the pipe off Corpse. "My head's killing me."

"Well, Mr Coffin, did you have a restful sleep?"

Coffin twisted around, saw Stump sitting on a cardboard box, cradling her shiny mannequin's hand in her lap.

"How long have I been out?" Coffin said.

Stump ran her fingers up and down the mannequin hand. "Such a lack of manners, Mr Corpse. We invite him into our home, offer him safe haven from the law, and this is his response. Not a thank you passes his lips."

"You don't want thanking," Coffin replied. "You want paying back."

"True, true," Stump said.

"Handovergive me the cylindine," Corpse said, holding out a filthy hand.

Coffin ignored him. "I need a doctor. The bite in my shoulder, it's infected."

Stump stood up. For once she wasn't wearing her sunglasses. Her eyes were red and moist, and she wiped delicately at them with her plastic fingers. Coffin pulled at his T-shirt, let her take a good look at the suppurating wound, but when she reached out to touch it, he stepped back and held up his hand.

"Can you get me a doctor?"

"We can get you anything you want, Mr Coffin, you know that," Stump said, quietly.

"But it costs, yeah I know." Coffin reached out and laced his fingers through the mashed up grillwork in the cage. His head was hot, and the floor seemed to be tipping up towards him. He held onto the cage for support, and the man inside it whimpered.

"Don't you see, Mr Coffin? Have you finally realised that we need each other? You, me, Mr Corpse, we're like three bugs in a bed, peas in the pod, Mr Coffin, that's what we're like."

"Fuck that," Coffin growled. "Just tell me how much, and I'll pay it."

Stump shook her head, and greasy locks of hair escaped the black scrunchy tying her hair back, and whipped around her face.

"Oh no, a favour from you would be far more valuable than money."

"Just tell me what you want, and I'll do it."

Stump put a plastic finger in her mouth, and sucked on it for a moment. "Well, let's see, what do you think, Mr Corpse?"

"I needwish my cylindine back," Corpse said. "I'm needwishing to hitters the manbody remorely."

"Quite," Stump replied. "Well, Mr Coffin, looks like you will be owing us a debt, to be repaid at some point of our choosing in the future."

"Fine, whatever," Coffin said, and wiped sweat off his forehead. "Just get me a doctor."

He let go of the cage and handed the pipe back to Corpse.

"Ooh, splendumptious," he said, and immediately took a swing at the terrified man in the cage.

Coffin began walking slowly down between the shelves of cans and packets and then stopped, and turned around.

"Just don't bring me that fucking quack, Shaddock," he said.

they

They, whoever 'they' were, had tied him to the chair good and proper. His wrists and ankles were sore where the rope bit into his flesh and his shoulders ached from the constant tension of being pulled back. When they first grabbed him, surprising him from behind as he walked to his car, he thought he was being mugged.

But then the gag had been roughly tied over his mouth, and the hood slipped over his head before he had chance to see who had grabbed him. A worm of fear had slithered into his belly at that moment. This was too elaborate for a simple mugging. Now, after a short car ride, and having been tied to a chair in what felt like a basement, he knew he was in big trouble.

But exactly what kind of trouble, he didn't know.

Frankie Shaddock twisted and pulled at the rope that bound him, even though he knew it was useless. His wrists were on fire from straining against his bonds and, with his legs tied to the chair, he couldn't even try and break the chair by bouncing it up and down on the concrete floor.

He was losing track of time. It had still been early enough this morning that the sun hadn't risen when he was abducted on the walk to his car. Now it had to be mid-morning, or maybe even lunchtime. Hard to tell, especially when he couldn't see a damn thing with this canvas bag over his head.

Shaddock had been on his way to see Craggs. The old man was being a stubborn mule by refusing to go to hospital. Whatever had gone down at Angels, and Craggs wasn't saying, not to Shaddock anyway, he'd taken a beating all right. But he was a tough old bastard, wouldn't be ordered around by anybody.

Shaddock, though, he was beginning to think he'd had enough. He was too old for this way of life now, especially if he was going to get abducted and tied up.

Sitting here, tied to this chair, his fucking IBS was playing up. Every now and then his stomach cramped up in a wave of pain, and he needed to take a shit. His own doctor said one of the causes of IBS was stress. Another reason to leave the Slaughterhouse Mob. Shaddock wasn't sure how many years he had left, but he sure as fuck didn't want to spend them tied to a chair with a bag over his head trying not to crap himself.

The old man let out a long, noisy fart.

Thank fuck I didn't follow through, he thought.

Shaddock tried shifting his focus of attention away from his bowels. Thought about being abducted that morning. The bag over his head. Being bundled into the car.

It didn't make sense.

Who the hell would do a thing like that to him? The old days of gang warfare were practically over, in Birmingham at least. Mortimer Craggs owned this city, and the only real threat to that was the Triads.

Shaddock's stomach tightened up. Fucking hell. If a Triad gang had taken him, he was dead meat.

If he was lucky.

'Doc' Shaddock had heard all the horror stories about the Triad factions, and their predilection for torture. Not that Shaddock could imagine anyone thinking he might have information worth torturing him for.

Shaddock was pretty low down on the totem pole. He was called in when Craggs' men needed sewing up, or bullets digging out of arms and legs. Anything more serious than that, and he recommended they get themselves to hospital and forget about worrying over the coppers waiting for them when they came around from the anaesthetic. If they went under with Shaddock administering the anaesthetic, there was a good chance they wouldn't wake up again.

And fuck it, even if he did know something worth torturing him for, he wasn't going to give those chink bastards a chance to get started on him. Shaddock was loyal to Craggs, but not that loyal that he would endure having his skin peeled away, or his eyelids cut off.

No. Shaddock would spill his guts straight away, and be happy to and all.

That was it, he'd decided. If he got out of this alive and with his dick still hanging between his legs, the first thing he was going to do was tell Mortimer Craggs he was retiring as the Slaughterhouse Mob 'Doctor'.

Craggs wouldn't be happy, but fuck it, he should think about retiring himself. What the hell, did he think he was going to live forever?

Every muscle in Shaddock's body tightened as he heard a door opening. Someone was coming into the cellar, closing the door behind them. Soft footsteps on the ground, approaching him.

Frankie Shaddock decided his best line of defence was attack. Get them on the defensive, all worked up and scared shitless. Once they knew who he was and who he worked for, they'd let him go for sure. If they would only take this fucking gag off his mouth, he could give them a piece of his mind.

All that nonsense about Triads he'd been thinking about, working himself up into a frenzy, it was what they wanted. It was why they had left him down here for so long, left him to conjure up his worst fears about what was going to happen.

Fucking amateurs, obviously. Not from the old school, that was for sure. Not like Craggs. He got someone and he wanted information, he went straight in there, with a knife usually, but sometimes he was more inventive. Pepper spray once, up that bastard's arse. And then that one time with the fucking blowtorch.

Mortimer Craggs could be a fucking maniac when he wanted.

These bastards?

Shaddock could deal with them.

The footsteps drew closer. Shaddock felt the rustle of the canvas bag against his scalp as fingers closed around it, grasping it. Now was the moment of truth. Triads or not, Shaddock was about to find out.

The bag was pulled roughly off Shaddock's head and dropped on the floor. The old man blinked in the light, ducked his head down.

Fuck! The lights, it's too bright!

Shaddock could just make out a pair of black shoes in front of him as he kept his head down, and his eyes screwed down to slits. His captor stood silently in front of him, waiting. As Shaddock's eyes adjusted to the light, he slowly lifted his head.

He was right, he was in a cellar, maybe a pub cellar. He looked up, his eyes travelling over the figure's trousers and jacket, and up to the face.

Shaddock screamed, the sound muffled behind the gag. He tried to push himself away, hands and feet straining at his bonds. His stomach clenched up into a tiny knot but his bladder let go, and he pissed himself, dimly conscious of the warmth spreading around his crotch and down his legs, and the splattering noise on the floor.

Steffanie Coffin was dead, buried in the ground along with her son, and yet here she was. Half her face was missing, her teeth visible through the ragged holes in her cheek, her right eye an empty socket. She stood there, hands in her trouser pockets, her red hair cascading over her shoulders, and smiled.

"Hello, Frankie," she said.

Shaddock squirmed and strained, whipping his head from side to side, leaning as far back as he could. He tried to look away, to banish this nightmare from his sight. But he couldn't stop staring at her, at the empty eye socket, at the teeth.

Still smiling, Steffanie leaned in toward him. She took one hand out of a pocket and reached out to his face, her fingers caressing his cheek for a moment before she grasped the gag and ripped it from his mouth.

"Fucking hell!" Shaddock gasped. "Stay away from me, just stay the fuck away from me."

Steffanie stepped back, resumed her casual pose with her hands in her pockets.

"I'm sorry, it must be quite a shock for you," she said.

Shaddock sucked in a lungful of cold, damp air. His head was buzzing, like it was full of angry wasps trapped inside his skull, trying to get out.

"Well, say something, Frankie." Steffanie pouted. "Aren't you pleased to see me? You always loved to pay me so much attention, didn't you? The way you looked at me sometimes, I felt practically naked."

Shaddock looked away, tried fixating on something else, the whitewashed brick wall, anything just to avoid seeing the nightmare standing in front of him.

"Oh, Frankie, do I really look that awful now?" Steffanie cooed.

"Stay away from me," Shaddock whispered. "Don't fucking touch me."

"Really, Frankie?" Steffanie placed a hand on his chest, ran her fingers down to his abdomen where she paused. "You would have begged me to touch you once. What do you think would have happened, Frankie, if you got your wish and I fucked you? I think you would have cried, cried like a baby. What do you think, Frankie?"

Shaddock still couldn't look at Steffanie, kept his head twisted away, his eyes fixed on the floor. But he was regaining some of his composure.

"I think you should get the fuck out of here, before Mort returns and finds you here, and rips your fucking tongue out of your mouth."

"Oh, poor Frankie. Didn't Mortimer tell you? I'm in charge of Angels now, not Craggs."

Keeping his face averted from the grisly sight of Steffanie and her eyeless socket, Shaddock couldn't help but risk a glance at her. He was panting, his heart galloping in his chest, thudding against his ribcage.

"Poor Frankie," Steffanie said. "Craggs never tells you anything, does he? Sends you on his errands to patch up his boys, but never lets you in on the big, important business. Even that faggot Clevon knew more than you, I bet."

"What do you want?" Shaddock whispered.

Steffanie squatted down in front of him, and Shaddock squirmed in his seat, tried to disappear through the back of the chair.

"I am sorry they tied you up," she said. "I told them, Doctor Frankie Shaddock, he's an old man, an important man, you should treat him kindly."

Steffanie began untying his ankles from the chair legs. Shaddock flinched at the touch of her cold fingers on his flesh, even through the fabric of his trousers. Twisted his head away, his stomach cramping at the stink off death emanating from Steffanie Coffin.

"But Clevon, well, he's still angry at the way you spoke to him, at the way you treated him, the lack of respect you showed him."

Keeping his eyes averted, Shaddock mumbled, "Clevon wouldn't do this to me, he's too scared of Craggs."

Steffanie giggled, and a wave of revulsion flooded through the old man's stomach, and for a moment he thought he might throw up, decorate his lap and his shoes and the floor with the contents of his stomach.

"Not anymore," she said. "Clevon's dead, which means he doesn't have to be scared of anyone."

"That doesn't make sense," Shaddock mumbled.

"It will make sense soon, Frankie. You see, Clevon's not the only one. We're all dead here. Clevon, Addison, Velvina, me, we're all in need of urgent medical care."

Steffanie finished untying his legs and stood up. She leaned over him, and her fingers found his wrists, and she began untying the knots. Shaddock could feel her cold breath on his neck, and her hair trailed over his face and across his shoulder. She smelt of the grave, of death and sex and fear.

"You always wanted to give me a physical, didn't you, Frankie?" she whispered into his ear. "Always wanted to undress me and run your trembling hands over my body, maybe your tongue, too. Licking me and sucking at me."

Suddenly his wrists were free of the rope, but Steffanie had hold of his hands, and she guided them to her hips, running them up and down the fabric of her trousers. Shaddock stifled a sob. Seemed like he hadn't had a proper hard-on in years, all the booze and the substance abuse had killed off his libido long ago, but now he had a throbbing boner, so hard it was painful.

But the nausea was back too, and the buzzing inside his head had increased. It was so loud and painful he thought he might pop a blood vessel, and then it would be goodbye Frankie Shaddock.

Steffanie let go of his hands and stepped back. She pushed her hair off her face, revealing that empty eye socket, the broken teeth through the rips in her cheek. Running her hands through her long hair she stretched, and Shaddock imagined her on stage wearing nothing more than a silver, sparkling G-string, tiny, multi-coloured spots of light dancing across her body.

"Do you want to give me that physical now, Frankie?" she purred. "I'm all yours."

Shaddock tried to lick his lips, but the inside of his mouth was dry, his tongue thick with sticky saliva. He could imagine doing that. He could see himself reaching out and grabbing hold of Steffanie, pulling her down on top of him, ripping at the shirt she was wearing, letting her undress him.

But there was something off about that picture in his mind, something wrong with it. Never mind that she was supposed to be dead, he had seen her buried himself, and never mind that she had a fucking hole where her eye should have been, there was something else.

It was the clothes. The suit.

Shaddock closed his eyes. Tried to swallow.

Steffanie was wearing one of Mortimer Craggs' suits. She had been through his wardrobe and was wearing his clothes.

"What the fuck do you want?" he whispered.

"I want you, Frankie," Steffanie whispered, and let her hair fall over her shoulders in a mass of curls.

"No, you're dead, you're fucking dead, I must be dreaming, having a fucking nightmare," Shaddock muttered, shaking his head, eyes screwed shut.

His eyes snapped open at the crack of Steffanie's palm against his face, his head rocking back under the impact.

Steffanie leaned in close, until her mangled face was only inches from his.

"You already said that, Frankie. You're repeating yourself, didn't you realise? Is that what happens when you get old, you start saying the same thing over and over?" She tilted her head slightly, gave him a smile. "Doesn't matter how often you say it though, you still won't believe it."

Steffanie ran a finger down Shaddock's cheek, over his jawline and down his neck. When she got to his shirt she pulled at it, and the buttons popped off as she opened it up, and scattered across the concrete floor.

Shaddock was breathing heavily now, his erection so hard and stiff he thought he might come in his pants any moment, something he hadn't done since he was a teenager, snogging his first girlfriend round the back of the school toilets.

Steffanie ran a fingernail down his pale, thin chest, opening a scarlet wound in his paper thin flesh. Shaddock hissed with the pain. Blood trickled from the slit, and down his chest and abdomen.

"I could slice you open with these nails, Frankie," Steffanie said. "I could open up your belly and let you bleed out onto the floor, or I could drink your blood, lap it up like a dog. I could open up an artery in your neck, and suck the lifeblood from you, and there's nothing you can do about it. I'm stronger than you now, Frankie. Much stronger. You want to try and escape, shove me out of the way? Go on, give it a try."

Shaddock didn't move. He knew she was right, he could sense the power emanating off her, her strength, her sheer force of will. And the cold, enveloping him like a blanket of freezing fog. She would snap him in half before he even got his bony arse off the chair.

Steffanie leaned forward, opened her mouth and licked the blood off his chest and stomach. Her tongue was like a cat's, sandpapering his skin as it swept upwards.

And dear God, but he swore he heard her purr with pleasure.

Steffanie placed her lips up against Shaddock's ear.

"I've got a secret for you," she whispered, and giggled. "Do you want to know what it is?"

Shaddock nodded his head, the motion jerky.

"The secret is, I am not going to kill you. But if you don't do as I tell you, you'll wish I had."

count duckula and the little vampire

Emma sat by the window and watched the dirty light growing in the sky. The rain had finally stopped sometime in the early hours of the morning, the incessant drumming against the windows replaced by a strange, eerie silence. A gutter dripped water, the soft, steady dripping the only sound for a long time.

After soaking in a hot bath, scrubbing the mud and the blood off her body, Emma spent most of the night sitting by the window, wrapped up in a dressing gown and with a mug of coffee clasped in both hands. The right side of her face throbbed and her right eye was still swollen. But she could open it at least, and her vision in that eye was no longer blurred.

The hot bath had helped revive her a little. Not just warming her chilled body and easing her aching muscles, but giving her time to think, to process everything that had happened the last few days.

She should have slept, but she knew sleep was impossible. All the horror that she had witnessed, the blood and the killing and the vampires, most of all the vampires, had been too much. A few months ago she had been on the trail of her big, career making story. Expose the Slaughterhouse Mob, truly and fully before the police and the public gaze. Put Mortimer Craggs and Joe Coffin away for a long time.

But now it was no longer just about Coffin, or Craggs and the Mob.

"Vampires."

The word sounded strange, spoken out loud, breaking the silence of the house. Vampires should have meant Dracula, Christopher Lee, Bram Stoker, Anne Rice. Vampires should have meant movies and stories, Scooby Doo cartoons, Count Duckula and The Little Vampire.

Not anymore.

Now that word evoked images of blood smeared along the walls in the house on Forde Road, of Abel Mortenson pouncing on Julie Carter and ripping her throat out with his teeth. Michael Coffin licking the blood off Julie's corpse, and

Steffanie, her naked body dripping blood and her face ripped apart by a bullet, but alive still.

Alive.

"Vampires," she said again.

The concept was too fantastical, too otherworldly to fully grasp, to get her head around. Even after everything she had seen and been through, the rational part of her mind kept telling her to be sensible, to think about this logically. Vampires were a myth, a story and nothing more. She had to get a grip, that coldly logical reporter's voice said, and look at the facts. There was a down to earth, practical explanation for everything.

But when Emma tried doing that, when Emma examined the facts as she had seen them, she kept on coming back to that single, chilling word.

Vampires.

This was going to be a huge story, even bigger than the one she had set out to write. Birmingham gangsters, vampires, and, if Tom Mills was to be believed, Triad gangs too.

The trouble was going to be getting anyone to believe her.

Emma took a sip of her coffee, and grimaced. It was cold. She picked herself up out of her seat and padded barefoot into the kitchen. She refilled the coffee machine with water, and fresh coffee granules. Settled herself against the kitchen counter as the machine began hissing and gurgling.

No, she had a bigger problem than simply persuading Karl and everyone else, including the police, to believe that vampires existed and a bunch of them were currently setting up home in Birmingham. Emma had got herself too involved in this story. Hell, she was a part of the story. She might have a career making story on her hands, but if she published it, the fact that she had withheld vital information from the police might also be responsible for ending her career at the same time.

Which reminded her of the USB stick, and the video footage of Joe Coffin murdering Terry Wu.

Coffin was a killer, there was no other way of describing him. She had the video evidence of him committing premeditated murder, and she had seen him beating Tom Mills' head into a bloody pulp. And then there was Nick, on the narrowboat. If Emma hadn't been there, she was sure that Coffin would have killed Nick, just to get him out of the way and stop him from putting Coffin at the site of the massacre on the barge.

She should hate him for that, she should be scared of him. But that wasn't how she felt at all. Despite the cold blooded brutality in him, Emma suspected there was a gentler side. She had seen first-hand his loyalty to Craggs, and possibly the love between them, like father and son. And Coffin had rushed straight to Emma's rescue after she called him from the narrowboat.

She remembered, too, Coffin fighting Abel in the house on Forde road, the punishment he had received as Abel's teeth and claws ripped at his flesh. Coffin had been the one to find and rescue Jacob, to pull him, barely alive, from that cellar. Not the police, nor Emma Wylde, crusading reporter for the *Birmingham Herald*.

No. It had taken a hardened criminal, a killer, to rescue that child.

Emma wasn't sure anymore she could be the one to put him in jail.

And the things she had said to him last night, after seeing him burn Abel Mortenson's butchered remains? Coffin had been right, she'd been in shock. And dealing with Mortenson like that had been the only way to make sure he never came back.

The coffee machine finished gurgling and hissing, and Emma took her mug of black coffee and sat back down by the window. The day had grown a little brighter, but it was still dull and overcast. What they needed was bright, sharp sunlight. Drag Steffanie and the cadaverous old vampire with her out into the sunshine and watch them die.

How would that happen, she wondered. Would they disappear in a cloud of dust, like Christopher Lee in the old Hammer Dracula films? Or would their skin turn red raw, and bubble and pop as though they had been set on fire?

Daytime. That was when vampires were weak, and vulnerable. It had to be. Abel had seemed invincible at times, impossible to kill, but the sunlight had to be harmful to them. Why else would Tom have had to throw sheets over Steffanie and the old man when he was getting them out of No. 99? What about poor Peter Marsden, his flesh sloughing off his bones as he staggered up the road to Laura's house?

And what about the other the myths that surrounded vampires? Would garlic deter them? A crucifix worn around the neck, or held out at arm's length like a talisman to ward off evil? After all, that's what they were, evil. However cold hearted and calculating Steffanie Coffin had been before she died, she hadn't been a monster, had she?

Not until Abel Mortenson had ripped out her throat, and left her to turn into one of his kind.

A shiver passed through Emma, and she clutched the mug of hot coffee a little tighter.

His kind. Were there more like him? Where had he come from? And the old man, too. What was his involvement in all of this?

Tom Mills had explained a lot, especially about his own involvement in Steffanie's death, back at Angels. Before Coffin bashed his head into a mushy pulp. But there were still too many unanswered questions. Too many gaps in the story.

Emma's reporter mind crawled over what she knew, tugging at the dangling threads, searching for answers. As the horror of the last twenty-four hours began to recede a little, the inquisitive, investigative side of her mind grew more restless and insistent for answers.

Emma's first instinct, when she had returned home, was to clean up and then head off to Staffordshire and spend some time with her parents, away from all of this mess. But now that she had had time to think, she knew that wasn't an option. Emma needed to be here, in Birmingham, where the story was.

And more importantly than that there were still two vampires at large in the city, hiding out at Angels. Steffanie Coffin and her ancient companion. How long before they started hunting for blood? Maybe they already had. For all Emma knew, maybe they had killed the staff at the nightclub.

The blood drained from Emma's face as she realised she was wrong already. There were three vampires at large, not two.

Michael Coffin.

Nick thought he had killed the little boy, but Emma knew better. He had probably crawled from the canal hours ago, maybe even made a fresh kill. Nick had seen Abel's dead body, had seen Coffin carrying it off, so he would think that the killings were over, that the Birmingham Vampire was dead.

And he was dead.

But there were going to be many more killings to come if someone didn't do something soon.

Emma's thoughts returned to the vampire myths, the ways in which they could be killed.

Sunshine.

They were safe right now, during daylight hours. The city was safe. But the sky was heavily overcast, and the winter daylight hours were short. What time did the sun set at this time of year? Five o'clock? Four-thirty?

Emma needed to act fast.

If she could persuade enough people to go and visit Angels today, they might be in with a chance of exposing Steffanie and her companion to daylight. That would still leave Michael at large, but it would be a start.

With Steffanie and the old man out of the way, they might have a chance of eradicating the vampires before they began infecting others, and spreading their disease through Birmingham and out across the country.

Emma stood up, her mug of coffee forgotten on the side. Time to get dressed, head down to the newsroom. Karl was going to take some convincing of this particular story, but if anyone could do it, Emma could.

She hoped.

a favour
from mr coffin

For the rest of the day, Coffin drifted in and out of a disturbed, fevered sleep. He remembered being woken by a woman, tall and thin, with long dark hair, and shadows under her eyes, who said she was a doctor. She examined Coffin's shoulder, cleaning out the pus, and then bandaged it up. Finally she gave him an injection. She didn't ask what had happened, or where they were, or who he was.

When she had finished and Coffin was lying down on the stiff, metal framed bed again, she looked down at him and said, "You need to go to hospital, get that seen to by a surgeon. You're going to have problems, if you don't."

But she didn't say what kind of problems, and Coffin was too out of it to ask. He tried imagining what kind of doctor she was, that she knew people like Stump and Corpse. Or maybe they had kidnapped her and she was now trapped down here, in this underground bunker they called home, for the rest of her life.

Maybe they would put her in a metal cage, and Corpse could beat the cage until he had moulded the grill around her body.

Coffin imagined Corpse creating a collection of trapped victims, living statues wrapped in metal cages, lined up along the tunnels and vast rooms, like an art exhibit. But an art exhibit that would never have an audience.

In his feverish state, Coffin dreamt that he was wandering up and down a maze of endless, concrete corridors, lined with these twisted cages. The people inside them, men, women, children too, stared at Coffin as he passed them. Their faces were pressed against the metal grill work, eyes wide, voices pleading to be set free.

Coffin did his best to ignore them. He kept his gaze fixed straight ahead, where he was convinced he would ultimately reach the end of the underground bunker and find the steps leading up to the exit, and freedom. But when he did reach the end of the tunnel, his way was blocked with a final twisted cage. This one was the most exquisitely formed yet and moulded perfectly around the contours of the body within.

Joe Coffin was trapped inside this cage. His throat had been ripped open, the blood cascading down his chest and abdomen like a waterfall of crimson, hitting the floor with big, wet splats. The blood pooled out across the floor, the overhead lights reflected in its scarlet depths. Once the concrete floor had been covered, the blood began climbing the walls as though it was dripping towards the ceiling.

Tendrils of blood began crawling up Coffin's leg. He should have been dead by now, through the massive blood loss alone. But he wasn't, and it didn't occur to him that he was now inside the cage, when only moments ago he had been outside, looking at himself. The blood continued gushing from the gaping wound in his throat, and crawling up his body until he was completely enveloped in a pulsating mass of red.

Coffin snapped awake, his heart pounding. He was dripping wet, his T-shirt soaked through with sweat. But the fever had broken. He swung his legs off the bed and sat up, peeled his T-shirt off and dropped it on the floor. He needed fresh clothes, which was going to be a problem, as he very much doubted that Stump and Corpse owned anything that would fit him.

But he was feeling better. The light headedness and dizziness had passed, and his temperature was down. Coffin flexed his arm and his hand, rotated his shoulder. Still hurt, but not as much. A vague memory of the doctor injecting him with a local anaesthetic surfaced in his mind. When that wore off, the pain would return. But that was all right.

Coffin was used to pain.

He stood up and stretched. Noticed the fresh, clean clothes, folded up and laid on a chair by the bed. He picked them up, examined them.

They were his.

Stump and Corpse had been back to his house. Been through his possessions.

Coffin wondered what else they had taken.

And what favour he would be asked to do in return for their help.

Coffin stripped naked and dumped his filthy clothes on the floor. In his wanderings earlier he had seen a shower block and that was where he headed now. There he found a musty, scratchy towel and a bar of hard, grey soap. The shower was freezing cold, but the water came out of the shower head in a powerful jet, and he scrubbed his body clean with the soap.

When he was finished and had dried himself off with the rough towel, he stood naked in front of a cracked mirror over a sink and examined the stitches, the criss cross of wounds where Abel had slashed at his face.

That fucker wouldn't be slicing anybody else apart now.

But Coffin would be reminded of him and their first encounter every time he looked in a mirror.

Maybe he should think about plastic surgery at some point.

Or maybe not.

Coffin walked back to his room and pulled on the fresh, clean clothes, along with his leather jacket. The only other outdoor coat that he owned. Maybe he was going to have to think about doing some clothes shopping at some point.

Not yet, though.

He had two problems needed sorting right now.

First there was Steffanie and her companion, and Addison and Velvina, who needed dealing with. Killing. Carving up with a chainsaw and burnt, just like Abel, if that's what it took. But they needed sorting, and fast. Exterminating, like an infestation of rats. Left alone they would breed, create more like themselves in their own image. Hunting people down for their blood. How long would it take before Birmingham was overrun with vampires?

Not long.

But more than that, they just needed to die.

Thinking of Steffanie, Coffin's chest tightened with anger and hatred. All this time she had been cheating on him, performing sexual acts for Terry Wu in exchange for money and favours. Had they talked about him, laughed at him, while she was screwing that fat bastard?

But then she had been using Terry Wu as well, hadn't she? Knowing that Coffin was coming to kill him even while she was fucking him. And putting Coffin dead centre in the police sights, by videoing him pulling the trigger.

If he'd known all of this before Abel got to her, Coffin might well have killed the bitch himself.

But in her present blood sucking, monstrous state, she most definitely deserved to die. And Coffin was going to make sure she stayed dead this time.

That still left Michael.

And no matter what Michael had been turned into, Coffin knew he couldn't kill him. Not his own son. The boy was an innocent victim of this whole mess. He had no malice in him, no evil intent. He was still a child.

No matter what he had become, whatever monstrous urges drove him to kill and drink blood, Joe Coffin was still his father. He knew he would never be able to lay a hand against his own son.

But he had to find him, before anybody else did. Michael didn't have the cunning or the worldly knowledge that Abel had had, or Steffanie. He would be seen, make mistakes, get himself caught or killed. Coffin had to find him before that happened and get him somewhere safe.

Perhaps there might even be a cure. If Coffin could find it, he could bring Michael back, return him to the child he really was.

Coffin left his room and walked down the corridor, towards the kitchen and the storeroom. This time there was no clanging of metal against metal echoing down the corridors. No sign that Stump and Corpse were anywhere to be found.

Maybe they were outside, up to whatever it was they did together.

What kind of life did they live down here, underground? And how did they have an electricity supply, and running water? These thoughts passed only briefly through Coffin's mind. It wasn't any of his business and so it wasn't particularly of any interest to him. Even if Steffanie and Michael weren't pulling at his attention, Coffin wouldn't have thought to investigate his surroundings.

When he got to the storeroom behind the kitchen, he found Stump and Corpse there after all. Corpse was sitting on the cardboard box this time, looking weary. His arms were draped across his bony knees, his scrawny neck sticking out of his shirt collar, which was far too wide for him.

Stump was standing beside the man in the cage. The metal grillwork had been beaten into shape around his body and he had no space left to move, even if he hadn't still been pinned down with electrical tape. The malformed, squashed cage had been propped against a wall, just like one of the art exhibits in Coffin's dream.

The man's eyes were closed, and Coffin thought he was dead. But then Stump lifted a beaker of water to his face. She threaded a straw through a gap in the metal grill and between the man's lips. His eyes fluttered open, and he sucked at the drink.

"I'm leaving," Coffin said.

Corpse looked up and regarded Coffin with sad, dark eyes. He stuck a finger up his nose and rooted around inside, and then pulled it out and began sucking on the end.

"It's been a pleasure to be of assistance, Mr Coffin," Stump said, not taking her eyes off the man in the cage, who was still sucking greedily on the straw.

"Yeah, sure," Coffin said.

Stump turned her head and looked at Coffin. Her eyes were red, the capillaries inflamed and broken in the white of her eyes, the skin on her eyelids shiny and damp.

"When you see your girlfriend, Mr Coffin, please express my gratitude for her suggestion of the eye drops. My eyes are much improved now."

Emma, at his house, searching it for something when these two jokers discovered her. The USB stick with the video evidence of Coffin murdering Terry Wu. Something else Coffin needed to do. Find Emma and have a little chat with her about that. Ask her what, exactly, had her intentions been?

"I'll be sure and pass on your thanks," he said.

"We'll be in touch again," Stump said, "regarding a return favour from you, Mr Coffin."

And with that she turned her attention back to the man in the cage.

Coffin found the steps leading back up to the door, out onto the disused rail tunnel. He opened the door and stepped on to the welcome mat. The overhead light cast its pale glow against the Victorian brickwork, which disappeared into inky blackness in both directions. Coffin thought about going back down into the bunker, asking Stump and Corpse for a torch.

He decided against it. Already he was too far in their debt for his comfort. And besides, he had made it down here the previous night, wounded and shivering with the cold and the wet. He could easily walk back out again.

Thinking about a torch, his hand had automatically patted his jacket pocket, as though he might find one. It didn't, but there was something else in there.

Coffin pulled a new iPhone out of his pocket, a ragged piece of paper taped across the screen with a four digit number scrawled across it. He pulled the paper off the phone and discarded it. When he powered the phone up he tapped the number into the screen and unlocked the phone. He swiped through to the contact folder and opened it up.

It was full of names and contact numbers, including Mort's and Emma's.

Coffin looked back through the open doorway and down the stairs.

How the hell had they got hold of his contacts?

Coffin shut the door and started making his way carefully along the overgrown railway track, the light from the mobile guiding his route.

the lone ranger and tonto

The lift doors slid open to reveal the normal hustle and bustle of the *Birmingham Herald* newsroom. Emma paused before stepping out of the lift. After all the time she had spent with Joe Coffin and Mortimer Craggs recently, and in the company of vampires and killers, to see her normal working environment once more was like returning from a foreign country. Everything looked and sounded familiar, and yet slightly out of joint too.

Taking a deep breath, Emma stepped into the newsroom.

Barry looked up from his computer screen as she walked past.

"Hey, you okay?" he said.

"Sure, why wouldn't I be?" Emma replied, without breaking stride.

Barry stood up, followed her as she walked towards Karl's office.

"I don't know Emma, maybe because you look like shit, like you didn't get a wink of sleep last night and like maybe you've got this crazy look in your eyes."

Emma stopped, picked up a copy of the *Herald* lying on a desk, and looked at the headline on the front page, BIRMINGHAM VAMPIRE DEAD?

Barry almost walked into her, pulled up just in time before they collided.

"Sorry about Jessica, Barry," she said, as she glanced over the story. "I'll buy you a new umbrella, soon as I can. Who'd you like this time? Mickey Mouse? Bugs Bunny? Donald Duck? Hey! Wait a minute!"

Emma rounded on Barry and planted the newspaper in his chest.

"How come you wrote this fucking story?"

"Because I was there, maybe?" Barry said, grabbing the sheets of newsprint when Emma let go, the paper scrunching up under his hand.

"I was there too, numbnuts. I should have been the one to write this up."

"Yes, well maybe you and Barry could have worked on it together, if you had been around last night," Karl said.

Emma spun round to face her editor, stepping out of his office. His tie was off, and his shirt crumpled, his hair all mussed up. He looked exhausted.

"Bloody hell, Emma, look at the state of you."

"Charmed, I'm sure," Emma said.

"Did you mess up your eye when you fell in the canal?"

"Yeah, it looks worse than it is."

"Is that what the doctor said?"

"What doctor?"

"You got yourself checked out, right? At the hospital?"

"No, I'm fine, honestly."

"What about Nick, how's he doing?"

"I, uh, I don't know," Emma replied, her voice faltering.

"You don't know?" Karl raised an eyebrow.

"No. I went home, cleaned up, and then took some time to be by myself. I needed some headspace."

Karl gazed at Emma, his look thoughtful. Emma had to resist the urge to fidget, and blurt out everything she knew, everything that had happened last night.

"You want to come in my office?" Karl said at last. "We should talk."

"Yeah, sure."

"Grab a notebook, Barry," Karl said.

"Whoa, wait, hold on one fucking minute!" Emma said. "What's Jimmy Olsen got to do with all of this?"

"He's covering the Birmingham Vampire story now, Emma."

"Fuck that, it's my story."

"Not anymore," Karl said, rubbing a hand over his face. "You've always been a wild card, Emma, and that's partly what makes you such a good reporter. But you're off the rails at the moment, too unpredictable. I need someone steady, like Barry, who can get copy to me on time."

"Barry will kill this story, Karl. He's got the writing skills of a blind chimpanzee."

"At least he's here, Emma."

"Wait a sec," Barry said. "You just kind of agreed with her there."

"This is my story, Karl," Emma hissed. "And it's a big one, you really don't know how big."

"In which case the two of you can work on it together. Why don't you both pool information and resources right now, and write me up something good?"

"You want me to work with her, when she called me a blind chimpanzee?"

Emma turned her back on Barry, got in close to the editor. "Come on, Karl, this is my story. I can't work with Barry, he'll slow me down."

"Maybe he will, but if he does that's because he has some integrity left."

"Integrity!" Emma hissed, taking a step back, and almost treading on Barry's foot. "What the fuck is that supposed to mean?"

Karl followed her movement, keeping in close to her, his six foot frame towering over her.

"It means that he's willing to report on the story, but not be a part of the story, that's what. Have you spoken to Nick about being a witness to Coffin fighting that psychopath at the house yet? Or what about your involvement with Coffin at the service station, when Tom Mills assaulted that man and stole his car? You explained to Nick yet why you drove off with Coffin, when you should have stuck around and waited for the police? Or why you were with Coffin in the first place? Hell no, you haven't even been to see him in the hospital yet, find out how he is, or how he wound up wearing his own cuffs bleeding out from a wound in his thigh." Karl leaned in close, his face only inches from Emma's. "My guess is, you already know. You know because you were there, you were a part of it. This bullshit story you phoned in with last night, about slipping and falling in the canal, you must think I'm an idiot to believe I'd fall for that."

"I knew you wouldn't believe me if I told you the truth," Emma whispered.

"Why don't you try me? Let me be the judge of that."

"Not with him here." Emma pointed at Barry.

"That's not how it works, Emma," Karl said. "In case you forgot, I'm the editor round here. Maybe I spent too many years taking the hands off approach, believing that you were better at your job without me breathing down your neck telling you what to do. Not anymore. I've put Barry on this story with you now, and that's where he's staying."

"But—"

"No, Emma, no more arguments. I want to hear your story, but I want Barry to hear it too. Why don't we all go in my office where we can talk privately?"

Emma clenched her fists, suppressing the howl of rage building inside her chest. Karl had backed her up into a corner, and she knew there was more at stake than just this one story here. If she walked out of the newsroom now, she doubted Karl would let her back in again. She would be without a job, and without a story too.

Clenching her teeth, unwilling to open her mouth for fear of what she might say, Emma pushed past Karl and strode into his office. She sat down, and waited for Barry and Karl to join her.

* * *

Emma didn't tell them the whole story. She didn't mention her time spent on the narrowboat with Abel and Michael, and Julie, and she could see Karl knew she had left some of it out. But he didn't say anything, and Barry was too busy scribbling down notes to notice the missing details of her story.

When she finished no one said a word and the silence stretched out uncomfortably. Barry looked at Karl, as though waiting for a cue from him. Karl opened his desk drawer and took out a cigar. He spent some time peeling the wrapper off, slowly and methodically. Finally he put the cigar in his mouth and chewed thoughtfully on the end, leaning back in his chair and gazing up at the ceiling.

"Barry," he said, "just what the hell is that thing up there?"

Barry and Emma both looked up to where Karl was pointing at a plastic disk, mounted in the ceiling.

"It's a smoke detector," Barry said, his eyes flicking from Karl to Emma, and then back again, as though he couldn't decide who was crazier right now.

"Are you sure about that?" Karl replied. "I heard the other day that they might be heat detectors. I heard that smoke detectors weren't reliable enough, that they might go off because somebody burnt the toast in the kitchen, or they didn't activate the fire alarms until the fire was too well established. So these days, heat detectors are the standard safety feature in modern offices."

The *Birmingham Herald* editor leaned forward in his chair and stared at Emma, still chewing on his cigar.

"You might be wondering what the hell that has got to do with anything you just told me. It's been close on ten years since I last smoked one of these damn cigars, and more like twenty since I last smoked one at work. But if I keep chewing on them, it's almost like I'm still smoking, helps keep my stress levels down. Right now though, after hearing that crackerjack story of yours about vampires, and people returning from the dead, digging their way out of their graves like zombies, I feel just about ready to take the chance that that thing over our heads is a heat detector and not a smoke detector, and light this damn thing up and smoke it down to a stub."

"I said you wouldn't believe me," Emma said.

"Hey, Emma," Barry said, "You gotta admit, it's—"

"Did I ask for your fucking opinion?" Emma yelled, rounding on Barry.

"Maybe not, but you heard Karl, I'm writing this story now because you fucked it up, so the truth is, I don't actually need to ask your opinion on anything."

"Fuck you, Barry. You might think you're a shit hot, ace reporter, but you'd have pissed your pants and run home to Mummy if you'd seen what I have these last few days."

"Yeah, yeah, yeah," Barry said. "You're so tough, aren't you? You're always trying to outdo the boys, be tougher and harder, more fucking macho than the rest of us. Have you looked between your legs recently, Emma? I'm thinking you might have grown a pair of balls and a big fucking dick since the last time you looked."

"Enough!" Karl shouted, slamming his hand down on his desk. "I'm supposed to be running a newspaper here, not a nursery school for maladjusted kids."

Emma glanced through the window at the rest of the newsroom. Heads had turned at the sound of arguing, people craning around computer monitors to try and catch a glimpse of what was unfolding inside the editor's office. Emma fought the urge to fling open the office door and scream obscenities at them.

Instead she stared them down, until all the newsroom staff were hiding behind their computers again, pretending to work.

"First thing we need to think about doing," Karl said, "is contacting the police. We should have done that days ago, and we're going to be in a shit load of trouble for holding back until now."

"Karl, if you go to the police and tell them exactly what I just told you they'll most likely arrest me, and Coffin too."

"You're going to be in trouble for not going to them with what you know before now, but I can't see why they would arrest you. You haven't committed a crime, Emma. Have you?"

Stood by and watched while Coffin smashed Tom Mills' head into a gooey pulp. And, oh yeah, I helped Coffin dispose of a dead body.

"Besides, the police already have a manhunt on for Joe Coffin," Karl said.

"What for?"

"He killed the Birmingham Vampire. Some people might think he did the city a service, maybe he should be given a medal or something, but that's not how the cops see it."

"That makes them a bunch of idiots."

Karl sighed. Gazed at Emma.

"Vampires, Karl," she said. "I know you don't want to say the word, I know you don't want to fucking hear it, but that's what they are. The Birmingham Vampire? The headlines got it right for once."

"Emma, it's obvious you've been under a lot of stress recently, what with Steffanie Coffin's murder and her son, too. But none of that was your fault."

Emma stood up. "Shit, Karl, are you saying you think I'm seeing things? You think I'm losing my mind?"

"Sit down Emma, that's not what I'm saying."

But she couldn't sit down. She was too agitated, her limbs twitching, her heart beating hard, the walls closing in on her.

"I knew you'd find it difficult to believe what I was telling you, but I expected you to at least give it some thought, and not brush me off like I've gone off the fucking deep end."

"Emma, think about it. You say there have been some killings at Angels nightclub, right? If that's the case, we need to get the police involved. And if it turns out there are vampires there, then great, you've been vindicated, right?"

"You think they will believe me, any more than you have?"

"No, but we don't have to mention the V word, do we? We'll just say we have reason to believe there has been some violence down there, possibly a killing. They'll have to go and investigate."

"I don't know, they need to know what they're dealing with. Going in there without a clue, they're never going to come out again. Not alive, anyway."

"I can't believe you two are seriously talking about this," Barry said. "I mean, come on, vampires?"

Emma wheeled on him. "Hey, you don't believe me? I'll take you to Steffanie's grave, and Michael's too, and I'll watch while you fucking dig them up."

"That's my point, Emma. I don't need to dig them up to know that they're dead."

"Are you even listening to what I'm saying? They're not down there anymore, you knucklehead." She rapped him on the head with her knuckles.

Barry jumped to his feet, dropping his notebook on the floor. "Why do I have to take this shit off her all the time? She's fucking crazy, you know that? Absolutely dipstick, looneytunes, and you just let it go every single time."

Karl held up his hand. "Calm down, Barry, we're meant to be working together on this, remember?"

"Emma can't work with anyone, she's the fucking Lone Ranger, and you're Tonto."

"You mind explaining what the hell that is supposed to mean?" Karl said, yanking his cigar out of his mouth.

"Oh, fuck that," Barry replied, and stomped out of the office, slamming the door shut behind him.

"So much for Barry being steady and reliable, huh?" Emma said.

Karl raised an eyebrow, and sighed.

"What?" she said. "It was a joke. Can I help it if he's highly strung?"

"Looks like you've got your story back," Karl said, wearily.

Emma punched the air. "Fuck, yeah!"

"But on one condition."

"That I leave poor little Barry alone? Okay, Boss, I promise. I'll be a good girl from now on."

"Forget Barry. I'm talking about you going to the police with everything you know. And I mean everything, and I mean today, right now."

Emma held up her hands in surrender. "All right, you win."

"Really?" Karl stared at Emma. "Why do I get the feeling that was too easy?"

"No, I'm serious. I'm going straight to the police, tell them everything I know." Emma started backing out of the office. "In fact, I'm going to head down to the station right now."

"You could phone them."

"I prefer the personal touch."

"You want me to come with you?"

"Nah, that's okay." Emma opened the door, stepped out of the office. "I'll report back later Karl, okay?"

Karl Edwards watched Emma stride through the newsroom, and straight into a waiting lift.

He put the cigar back in his mouth, and chewed on it for a while.

"Shit," he said, and picked up the telephone.

brendan

Even walking down the quieter streets of Birmingham, Coffin still felt about as inconspicuous as a tarantula on a slice of wedding cake. His size and his looks gave him no chance at blending in to the background. Hell, he was sure most of the residents of the city of Birmingham must know of him by now. It seemed he had been in the news enough times over the last year.

After exiting the railway tunnel, Coffin decided to head back down to the city centre, find out how Mortimer Craggs was, and fill him in on the events of last night. The only question was, how was he going to get to him? Picking up his Harley was out of the question, he was sure the police would have impounded that by now. He could have called a taxi or found a bus stop, or a Metro station, but he didn't feel like squeezing himself into a car or a seat on public transport.

So he walked.

Coffin kept off the main roads, winding his way through the outskirts of the city in a zigzag, circuitous route that seemed to take forever. As he drew closer to the city centre he passed a newsagents, and stopped to buy a newspaper.

BIRMINGHAM VAMPIRE DEAD? the headline screamed at him.

Yeah, he's fucking dead all right, Coffin thought.

He scanned the front page story, and then opened the paper up to be confronted by a mugshot of himself.

"Shit," he growled.

Still standing outside the newsagents he glanced up, convinced he would be surrounded by a group of onlookers, all on their mobile phones and some of them taking a photograph of him whilst others called the police.

But he was on his own, and the old Asian lady who had served him inside the shop had barely looked at him. He doubted she paid much attention to the news, anyway.

But that wasn't going to be the case with everyone. The more time he spent out and about in broad daylight, the more he risked being spotted and identified.

What then? Even if he'd had a gun with him, a shootout with the police was only going to end one way.

Coffin on his back on the floor, bleeding out from a dozen gunshot wounds.

His big mistake had been letting Archer live. What the hell had he been playing at, slapping those cuffs on him and leaving him on the boat? Maybe DCI Archer hadn't seen Coffin actually kill Mortenson, but he had witnessed him picking his corpse up and taking it away to dispose of it.

He should have killed him when he had the chance. Slipped that Samurai sword between his ribs and through his heart. Would have been simpler.

Except for Emma. She was a tough character all right. She had been through a lot with him and kept her mouth shut, but watching as he shoved the pointy end of a sword through Archer's chest?

No.

That really would have been the end of a beautiful relationship.

A woman ran past, wearing black running tights and a fluorescent yellow top. White earphones were plugged into her ears, and she didn't give Coffin a second glance. A young Asian mother pushed a buggy one handed whilst pulling a toddler along behind her. Coffin was standing at a junction and traffic slowed here, drivers watching for their moment to pull out or turn right, whilst passengers gazed in boredom out of the windows.

Coffin felt completely exposed. And it would only grow worse, the closer he got to the city centre. If he wasn't spotted because of his size or distinctive appearance, he was sure that he would soon be noticed because he would start acting suspiciously. In his experience the more a person tried not to be noticed, the more they ended up announcing their presence to the world.

He had to get off the streets, find another way to get to Edwards No. 9 so he could check on Craggs. Coffin found a side street and headed down it. He pulled his mobile out and called up a contact.

"Brendan, it's Joe. Yeah, I need a favour."

Brendan Kavanagh was the landlord at O'Donoghue's, a small pub on the canal side, down a tiny lane off Broad Street. During the 1990s Birmingham city council had started its massive city regeneration project. The Victorian buildings were bought up by private companies and work began on reversing the neglect of the decades following the Second World War. Broad Street in particular was prettified, the shops and offices turned into bars and clubs where trendy young things could get hammered on alcopops and then regurgitate the contents of their stomachs on the pavement outside. Fancy restaurants moved in, along with the

Ikon art gallery, upmarket shops and, eventually, the new Library of Birmingham.

In the middle of all this upheaval O'Donoghue's stayed put and, twenty years later, it was still there, proudly unpretentious and distinctly unpretty.

It was also the busiest pub in the area.

The original O'Donoghue had been the landlord in 1880, when the pub was first opened. As was tradition amongst the Irish, it still retained the original landlord's name, despite having seen many different owners come and go.

Brendan Kavanagh was a loyal friend to Mortimer Craggs. Not a member of the Slaughterhouse Mob as such, and nor did he pay protection money to Craggs, but there was a mutual respect between the two men and a regular trade off in favours.

After finishing his call with Brendan, Coffin settled down to wait. Within fifteen minutes the Irishman had rolled up in his dirty white transit van, belching black smoke out of the exhaust. Messages had been scrawled in the dirt on the van's sides and back doors, including, 'Suck my dick', 'Brian is a wanker', and, 'Fuck off'.

The big Irishman climbed out of the cab and walked around to the back, where he yanked open the doors. He had a head of thick, red hair, and his cheeks were permanently flushed red. He looked like a heart attack waiting to happen, but Coffin had seen him in action and he wasn't a force to be messed with.

After a quick, cursory glance to check he wasn't being watched, Coffin crossed the road and jumped into the back of the van. Brendan didn't say a word. He simply slammed the doors shut, plunging Coffin into darkness. The van rocked as Brendan climbed into the cab and then the engine roared into life and they were moving.

Coffin activated the light on his iPhone. The van stank of oil, but it was empty apart from a dirty sheet covering the floor and a tyre, lying on its side. Coffin rested his back against the van's side panel and closed his eyes.

Ten minutes later the van stopped, and the growl of the engine stuttered into silence.

After a few moments the doors were flung open, the dull, grey daylight illuminating the interior and making Coffin squint.

"Let's get you inside, out of sight of the filth," Brendan said, his thick Irish accent almost transforming the words into a foreign language.

Coffin had to duck as he stepped through the doorway in the back of the pub. Brendan led him through the kitchen and out past the toilets and into the bar area. It was early and the pub was still closed. Stools had been upended and placed on the tables. The quarry tiled floor glistened with wet patches still, having recently been washed. The wall lights were on, casting their yellow glow over the seats built into the sides of the pub, the old photographs of Birmingham from a bygone era, and the bar with the beermats draped over the pumps.

One table had been cleared. Mortimer Craggs sat at it, in a darkened corner. On the table was a half-finished mug of black coffee.

Craggs looked older than Coffin ever remembered seeing him look before. His face was drawn and pale, and he sat slightly hunched over, his forearms resting on the table.

Coffin pulled a stool off a neighbouring table and sat down opposite Craggs.

"Where the hell have you been, Joe?" Craggs said.

"Taking care of business," Coffin replied.

"Is it true what the papers are saying, that the Birmingham Vampire is dead?"

Coffin nodded. "It's true, I killed him myself."

"You said that once before Joe, and you were wrong."

"Not this time. I carved him up into pieces and burnt them. He's dead."

Craggs straightened up, reached out a hand and gripped Coffin's shoulder. "Good work. Now we just need to sort out that bitch Steffanie and her friend, and take the club back."

"You've got a problem with that," Coffin said. "Addison and Clevon are vampires now. Velvina, too."

Coffin held up his hand, waggled his index finger, amputated at the first joint. The doctor that Stump and Corpse had provided for him had sewn up the wound, and redressed it.

"What the hell happened, Joe?" Craggs said.

Coffin filled him on the events at the club, and how he had to take Stut to the hospital before he bled out completely from his self-inflicted gunshot wound.

"Given what I've seen this last week," he said, "I would imagine Rob's up and about again now, developing a taste for blood and growing a set of sharp new teeth. Including that ancient bastard who looks like a stiff wind would blow him over, that makes six vampires inside Angels."

Craggs closed his eyes and tapped out a beat on the scarred table top with his long fingers. "Vampires. You believe that shit, too?"

"How else do you explain it?"

Coffin leaned in close, placed a hand over Craggs' hand, stopping the tapping. Craggs opened his eyes.

"Vampires are real, Mort. That's what they are now, Steffanie and the others.

Vampires. And if they are anything like Abel Mortenson, they're practically fucking indestructible."

"Vampires or not, I want my club back," Craggs said.

"We'll get it back," Coffin said. "There's one more thing."

He paused, held Craggs' gaze in his own for a long moment.

"Michael. I've seen him, Mort. He's one of them now."

Craggs leaned back on his seat. "Sweet Jesus in heaven, Joe. I'm sorry."

"He's out there somewhere, on his own. I want him found, Mort, and caught. But I don't want him hurt."

"You sure about that, Joe? He's your son and all, I recognise that, I understand it, but have you thought this through? What the hell are we going to do with him if we can catch him?"

"Keep him safe, lock him in a cellar or somewhere, until I think of something, until I can find a cure maybe."

"You really think there's a cure for that shit?"

"I don't know, but I can't give up on him, Mort."

"No. I understand that, Joe. I'll get some people out looking for him." Craggs winced, placed a hand against his side, and exhaled slowly. "I cracked some ribs when I fell down the stairs. Fucked up my ankle, and my shoulder, too. But I'll live."

"You had a doctor look at you?"

"Yeah, Frankie came by last night, looked me over. He should've come by Edwards this morning with more painkillers, but he never showed up, and he's not answering his phone. Bastard's probably on a bender somewhere, forgotten all about me."

"You should get yourself a proper doctor, someone who's actually qualified," Coffin said, thinking of the woman that Stump and Corpse had found for him. He had no idea if she was qualified or not, but she had been quick, efficient.

"Frankie's been my doctor most of my life, Joe, and he's never let me down yet. He'll turn up sometime soon."

Brendan walked up to their table and placed two plates of breakfast in front of them. Coffin looked at the sausages, the fried eggs, bacon, fried bread and mushrooms, and his stomach growled in anticipation. He couldn't remember the last time he'd eaten.

"I asked Patsy to cook us up a breakfast," Craggs said, picking up his knife and fork. "For an Irish lass, she cooks the best full English in town."

Coffin grunted, and dug into his food.

"And once our bellies are full, we're going to start planning," Craggs said. "That bitch might not realise it yet, but we're at war now."

two policemen and
a reporter

Emma stood on the corner of Weston Road and Sandbach Way, an unfolded newspaper held out as though she was reading it, and observed the entrance to Angels. Having the newspaper had seemed like a good idea when she first thought of it, but now she felt more conspicuous with it than if she had just been loitering without it. Perhaps she had seen a character in an American movie on a stakeout, pretending to read a newspaper as cover, and that was where the idea had sprung from.

Whatever. She was sure she looked ridiculous. Impatiently she folded the newspaper up and stuffed it into a bin.

Lunchtime crowds hurried past her, like waves around a rock on the beach. Was it Emma's imagination or were there more people out on the streets now? The story that the Birmingham Vampire was dead had only broken this morning and yet already it seemed that the city was coming back to life again. People were no longer afraid to step outside once more. That would be a relief to the city's shops and businesses, especially with the Christmas shopping season approaching.

Seeing the lunchtime crowds, Emma thought it might be a good idea to go grab lunch herself. She was no longer sure why she had even come down here to stakeout Angels, like she was a hardboiled detective in a cop film. But going to the police had never really been an option, even though that was what she had promised Karl. Not yet. Not until she talked to Coffin, at least. But every time she tried ringing his mobile she just got an automated message, telling her this person wasn't available to take calls.

Her other thought had been to head back to Edwards No. 9 and talk to Craggs, maybe even find Coffin there. But then she suspected the police would already be scouting out the Slaughterhouse Mob's known clubs and businesses, searching for Coffin, asking questions. The last thing she needed right now was to bump into one of Nick's colleagues.

So she came down here to Angels and hung around on the opposite side of the road, wondering just what the hell was going on in there right now. Was Steffanie still there? And the old man?

What about Tom Mills? If the police arrived to investigate an allegation that there had been a murder on the premises, would they find Tom's corpse still lying on the floor, his head like a squashed melon?

Or had Steffanie cleaned up?

Disposed of the body.

Perhaps Emma should go to the police. This very moment, while the sun was shining. And while Steffanie and her companion were hiding in the shadows sleeping, or doing whatever vampires did during the day. Except, Angels being a nightclub, there were no windows. In the gloom and artificial light of the club, they didn't have to worry about daylight, or stray rays of sunshine.

Which meant that it didn't matter what time of day or night the police investigated, they were dead more or less as soon as they set foot inside and the door was closed behind them.

No. Sending the police in there would be the same as murdering them herself. Emma needed to find some way of getting in touch with Coffin. He knew what he was up against. And together, maybe they could come up with a plan.

If only the cops weren't after him for Abel Mortenson's murder. That had to have been Nick. He had seen Mortenson's corpse, had seen Coffin pick it up and sling it over his shoulder, and carry it away. Nick must have told his colleagues what he had seen, even if he left out Emma's part in it all. And then the fire brigade had turned up to put out the fire at No. 99, and found the burnt body parts in the pit in the cellar.

Didn't take a genius to work out what had happened, did it? Even the West Midlands police wouldn't have too much trouble thinking that one through.

A young student walked in front of Emma. She had a large, black portfolio case slung over one shoulder and she was eating a Subway sandwich.

That's a good idea, Emma thought.

Earlier this morning, Emma had skipped breakfast. After the events of the previous night, she had thought she would never have an appetite for food ever again. Seeing Julie Carter murdered, finding Marge's dismembered head stuffed under the narrowboat seat, all that blood and ripped flesh, and then sitting with Coffin in the cellar as he barbequed Mortenson's remains had made her sick to her stomach.

But now all of a sudden she was hungry.

And a Subway would just hit the spot.

With one last glance back at the closed door to Angels, Emma headed off, threading her way through the crowds.

She found a Subway on New Street and ordered a ham salad baguette, and a Coke. There were two girls standing to one side, waiting for their order. One had piercings in her ears, lips, eyebrows and nose. They both had the large, black portfolios that Emma had grown used to seeing being carried around town, and she assumed they were for the art and design students.

"They said on the news that he chopped him up into pieces and then set fire to him," one girl said, the one without the piercings other than a silver stud in each ear. "How gross is that?"

"That's because he was a vampire," her friend replied. "It was the only way he could kill him. The police should be giving Joe Coffin a medal, not hunting him down."

"You don't really believe in vampires, do you?" the other girl whispered.

"Yeah, of course I do. And I'll bet you there's more out there, too."

Further discussion about vampires was interrupted as their sandwiches arrived. They walked out of the shop together, arguing about the existence of the supernatural.

When Emma's food arrived she decided she had lost her appetite after all. The smell of meat, and the sight of the strips of ham glistening under the lights, had turned her stomach. But she took the sandwich when it arrived and she stepped outside, and took a couple of deep breaths of the cold, city air.

Whether she felt like it or not, she decided she needed to eat.

As she walked back towards the club, Emma chewed on the sandwich. The ham and the lettuce, the cucumber and tomato, it all could have been cardboard for all she enjoyed it. But she ate it anyway, thinking that she needed the sustenance.

Especially now that you're eating for two.

The thought landed like an unexploded bomb inside her head. A bomb set to detonate in approximately nine months' time. Or less, probably. Emma had no idea how far into her pregnancy she was. She'd done the test, which was apparently 99.9% accurate, but what was she supposed to do next?

Go and visit a GP?

Start stocking up on nappies and baby grows?

Tell Nick?

He would be delighted. Or at least he would have been, before the shit hit the fan and he found out that Emma was hanging around in the company of known criminals. Especially Joe Coffin, who Nick seemed to have made it his own personal mission to put behind bars.

And he would stifle her, suffocate her with concern for her and the baby's safety. As soon as he found out he would be like a mother hen fussing around her, making her eat even when she didn't feel like it, watching her every move in case she overexerted herself. Worst of all, he would demand that she quit her job. She could see him now, worrying about her every time she set foot outside the front door. There would be no chance to meet up with Coffin again, and her story would be dead on the ground.

Maybe she should get rid of the baby, have an abortion while there was still time. Emma might not have any idea how far pregnant she was, but she had to still be in the early stages. She could get an abortion, and nobody would ever know that she had even been pregnant.

But terminating the pregnancy wasn't an option. Emma might have renounced her belief in God and rebelled against her parents' strict, religious beliefs, but their particular brand of Christianity had buried itself deep into her psyche. No matter how far off the path she strayed, there were still some 'sins' she could not commit, and 'murdering' her unborn child was one of them.

By the time she arrived back at the club, Emma had forced her way through half of the baguette. She looked at the rest and it turned her stomach. She stuffed it into the same bin she had thrown the newspaper.

A police car pulled up outside Angels.

Emma took a step back, almost as though she was getting ready to run, as though the police were there for her.

Don't be stupid, of course they're not looking for you.

Two young looking policemen climbed out the car and looked at Angels.

Karl, Emma thought. *He knew I had no intention of going to the police, so he must have called them.*

They slammed the car doors shut, and walked up to the doors, the Angels logo standing out in silver against the black of the club.

They should have sent the whole of the West Midlands police force, kitted out in full riot gear, not these two. Once inside Angels, they're dead.

Emma watched as one of the policemen pounded on the club door. She felt as though she was sitting in a movie theatre, watching the events unfold on the big screen, knowing what was about to happen but unable to intervene.

The two policemen chatted while they waited, and then the one pounded on the door again.

Maybe no one will answer, Emma thought. *Maybe they are all asleep, or whatever, and they can't even hear the door. Or maybe they're dead, maybe Coffin got there already and killed them, carved them up into bloody pieces just like Abel Mortenson.*

The two cops had turned around, and were walking back to their car, when the door opened.

Emma's stomach tightened.

She couldn't see who was standing in the doorway, hidden by the gloom of the interior. The policemen had turned back and were standing on the steps, talking to whoever was just inside the doorway.

It couldn't be Steffanie, surely? The last time Emma had seen her, half her face had been ripped away, and she looked like something out of The Walking Dead. It couldn't be the old man, either. Even though he didn't have any of his face missing, he still managed to look scarier than Steffanie.

So who the hell had answered the door?

Emma's insides clenched even tighter as she watched the two young cops walk inside the club. The doors closed behind them.

Oh shit!

They were dead. There was no doubt in Emma's mind. If she ever saw them again they wouldn't be taking statements, they would be looking for a nice, juicy piece of flesh to sink their teeth into.

Emma turned her back on the club, couldn't bear to look at the doors any longer.

"Fuck! Fuck! Fuck!" she hissed.

Damn it, Karl! Why the fuck couldn't you have just listened to me for once? Why'd you have to call the cops? It's your fault those two are dead, not mine.

No. She couldn't stand here doing nothing.

Emma spun around and ran across the pedestrianised street, dodging lunchtime students and office drones. At the front door, the Angels logo right in front of her, she pulled up short and stepped to the side.

What did she think she was doing? She had barely survived her encounter with Abel Mortenson, and it had taken Joe Coffin to rescue her from his clutches. And now she was thinking of taking on two vampires? On her own?

Emma paced up and down outside the club, unable to keep still. If only Coffin were here. He might not know what to do, but he would take action of some kind. He was like a force of nature, bulldozing his way through problems, like he would have bulldozed his way through those doors by now.

Emma pulled her mobile out, considered trying him again. But she'd been calling him all morning with no response and even if he picked up now, by the time he got here it would be too late.

Suppressing a scream of frustration, Emma screwed her eyes shut. Tried burying the images of the two cops' faces as Steffanie and her vampire companion fell on them, and began ripping at their throats. She could see the arc of blood spraying up the walls and hear the screams turning into gurgles as the cops tried to fight back, or reach for their handheld radios.

The sound of the doors opening wrenched Emma back to reality, and she flinched as she saw a dark figure stepping outside. She hadn't realised she had been holding her breath until she let it go, when she saw that one of the young policemen had stepped outside followed by his companion.

"Thank you for your time," the one said. "Sorry to inconvenience you."

"That's not a problem, officer."

The speaker was still standing just inside the entrance to the club, out of Emma's line of sight. The voice belonged to a man, probably an older man, but not Craggs she was sure of that.

And it couldn't have been Steffanie's ancient companion, could it?

The policemen said goodbye and turned to leave. The one who had spoken first saw Emma and smiled at her as they walked past. They crossed the road and climbed into the police car.

Emma watched them drive away.

When the car had turned a corner and disappeared from view, Emma pulled herself off the wall and stepped around in front of the entrance. The club doors were closed once more.

It was as though the events at Angels last night had never happened.

war council

Craggs named it a 'War Council', and Brendan took the unprecedented step of closing O'Donoghue's for the night. Brendan's mousy wife served drinks and snacks to the assembled thugs, killers, and general low-lifes who had been summoned by Craggs. A pall of cigarette and cigar smoke floated like a storm cloud above the large, round table set in the bay of the snug where they had all gathered.

These men didn't work for Craggs. Many of them were beholden to Brendan for various favours and monies owed, whilst the rest were there strictly for the cash, or to put a favour in the bank. But Craggs still held the attention of every man in the room as though they owed him their undying loyalty.

For Joe Coffin the scene was like something out of King Arthur and the Knights of the Round Table. Coffin wasn't much of a reader, but he still remembered the story of Arthur from his childhood. The teacher had read out a children's version of the tale to the class. It might have been by Enid Blyton, Coffin couldn't remember.

But he did remember being captivated by the story, and by Sir Lancelot, and Guinevere.

And here they were sitting around their own version of the round table, downing beers and whiskies, roaring with laughter and telling tall tales, cigarettes and cigars burning in overflowing ashtrays or dangling from mouths. Coffin felt at home here. Men like this, they were the ones he had grown up with, hanging out at his father's gym or with the guys at the club.

They were family.

Freddie Noonan and his brother Terry sat either side of Craggs. They were often mistaken for twins, they looked so alike with their flat noses, squinty eyes and shaven heads. But Freddie was older by eleven months. When asked what they did for a living, the Noonan brothers described themselves as builders and general labourers. This had been the case once, many years ago, but recently they had become known as the heavies to send for when everyone else had let you down.

'Punchy' Billy Adams sat next to Freddie. Another big man, with cauliflower ears and a nose that looked like it had been squashed across his face. 'Punchy' had been a boxer with a promising career ahead of him as a younger man. His problem had been a lack of self-control, and an innate rage at everyone and everything. This rage often spilled over into his fights in the ring, on some occasions helping him win, but ultimately getting him barred. Even now in his late fifties, 'Punchy' would fly into a rage at the hint of a perceived insult or grievance. And he was still capable of beating a man to death with his bare hands, which were permanently swollen and malformed from using them as weapons all his life.

Gerry Gilligan was a friend of Brendan's. He was a small, red headed, quiet man. Coffin knew nothing about him, had never met him before. He was the only man at the table not attempting to outdo everyone else with outrageous stories of heists gone wrong and revenge taken. Coffin watched him sitting silently smoking cigarette after cigarette, his eyes flitting from one man to another as they talked and laughed. It would be easy to miss Gilligan in a room full of people, or dismiss him as no one to be bothered with, but Coffin felt differently. He had a sense of coiled tension and a cunning intelligence about the man.

Antonino 'Tony' Mannoia, with his sharp suits, Mediterranean looks and black, slicked back hair was the classic Italian charmer, despite the fact that he had never set foot in Italy his whole life. His father had been brought to England as a child shortly after the end of the Second World War. Somehow, Tony had managed to cultivate an Italian accent and mannerisms, which he used to devastating effect in his chat up routines whenever the opportunity presented itself. He could always be seen around town with a different young woman on his arm, despite the fact that he was a married man with two children.

Harry Frazer was your typical East End gangster. In his sixties now, it was said that he had once worked for the Kray twins during their final years in prison. He moved up to Birmingham after Ronnie died in 1995 and attempted to set up his own criminal empire. Craggs soon put a stop to that and Frazer decided to 'retire', but the two men stayed on good terms. Frazer respected Craggs and the power he held in Birmingham with the Slaughterhouse Mob, and Craggs respected Frazer's East End connections and his history with the Krays.

Sitting next to Frazer was Danny 'The Butcher' Hanrahan. His father had owned a butchers in Lozells for many years and Hanrahan had grown up playing amongst the butchered carcasses of dead animals. But that wasn't where he got his nickname from. Hanrahan had used the skills taught to him by his father, and a few more as he grew up, to sinister effect in the criminal underworld. Not only was he an expert at the physical act of murder, but he knew more ways of disposing of a corpse than seemed possible.

Coffin let his gaze wander around the table at all these men, called together to discuss taking back Angels for Craggs. They were no doubt, along with Brendan Kavanagh, tough bastards each and every one of them. They knew how to take care of themselves and they knew how to lay on the pressure and, with the exception of 'Punchy' Billy Adams, knew when to back off.

But Coffin was the only person there who truly knew what they were up against. Sure, Craggs had been there when Steffanie and the old man invaded the club with Tom. He'd had to fight for his life, and he had seen Steffanie rise from the dead a second time, walking and talking even with half her head blown away by a shotgun blast.

But Craggs had never met Abel Mortenson, hadn't seen just how damned difficult it had been to take him down and keep him down. And Craggs hadn't seen Clevon, and Addison, hadn't watched Velvina bite Coffin's finger off, snapping it in half like it was a piece of candy.

If they were going to do this, completely and utterly wipe those blood sucking scum off the face of the earth and reclaim Angels, they had to go in hard and fast. Preferably in daytime when then they could drag each and every one of them outside, in the sun. Coffin remembered what happened to Peter, how he looked when he came stumbling up the road to Laura's house. The flesh sloughing off him, the blisters and boils, and how he was senseless with pain.

That's what they needed to do. Go in hard, take the vampires down, and drag them outside to finish them off.

Craggs began rapping his knuckles on the table and conversation stopped immediately. Despite his advanced years, and the fact that not one man here even worked for him, he was still held in high regard. This might be Brendan's pub, but Craggs was in charge.

"Thank you for coming, gentlemen," Craggs said.

This was greeted with a low, wry chuckle. Not even Tony Mannoia with his sharp clothes and suave appearance would describe himself as a gentleman.

"I expect Brendan has told you why you are here," Craggs continued.

"To take back your club from the stupid shites who thought they could mess with you, and still stay breathing," Hanrahan said.

"That's right," Craggs said, his voice low but perfectly clear.

"Then what the fuck are we waiting for?" 'Punchy' Adams said, red in the face, his eyes bulging like he wanted to mix it up there and then. "Let's go round there now and start cracking some skulls."

"Too fucking right," Terry Noonan said, and grinned at his brother, who grinned right back at him.

"Hold up a moment," Craggs said, raising his hand in the air, palm out. "There are a few things Joe and I need to tell you first, before we go in all guns blazing."

"We don't need telling how to punch some twat's face in, do we Terry?" Freddie said.

He had a black spider's web tattooed down the left side of his face and over his scalp. Terry had a matching one, mirrored on the right side of his face. Coffin had heard that they went everywhere together, shared everything, even their women.

"Nah," Terry said. "We'll fuck them over good and proper."

"Why don't we listen to what Mortimer and Joe have to tell us?" Gilligan said.

Apart from when he had said hello to everyone, and to say thank you to Brendan's wife when she handed him a whisky, this was the first time Coffin had heard Gilligan speak.

Coffin watched the quiet man carefully. Gilligan's dark eyes were narrowed to slits, and a half smoked cigarette hung from his mouth.

Once more Coffin had the impression of coiled tension. The image of a cat squatting down low, ears flat against its head, sprang to mind. All of its attention focused on the mouse as it calculated the precise moment when it should spring into action and pounce on its helpless victim.

The Noonan brothers stared at Gilligan. They obviously didn't know him either and weren't best pleased at being told what to do.

Gilligan took the cigarette out of his mouth and picked up his whisky, draining the amber liquid in one go. Placing the empty glass back on the table he returned the cigarette to his mouth, all the while completely ignoring the Noonan brothers.

"Oy," Brendan said, breaking the silence. "Neither one of you nancies could fuck a whore if you didn't have your brother to help you out. Now why don't you shut the fuck up and listen to what Mort has to say?"

"Yeah, sorry, Mr Craggs," Terry said, glancing shamefaced at the elderly Slaughterhouse Mob leader.

"That's all right, Terry," Craggs said. "I understand what you're saying, you two have been around a while now and you've proved you can take care of yourselves. There's not many in Birmingham who wouldn't think twice about taking on the Noonan brothers, and that's the way it should be. You've earned that position, by not backing down, not once."

Craggs paused, took a sip of his whisky. Coffin watched him in silence, wondering if Craggs would ask him to speak up at some point. Wondering how far Craggs would take it, what he would tell everyone. Sitting here in a fog of tobacco smoke with beer and whisky inside him, Coffin had found it hard to believe for himself the atrocities he had witnessed the last few days.

But then he shifted position slightly and his shoulder protested, sending bolts of pain down his arm. Or he reached out for his drink and saw his index finger, bitten off at the first finger joint, the white bandage stained red. Or like earlier in the evening when he went to the toilet for a piss and he glanced in the mirror and saw the livid scars slashed across his face.

These were the reminders he carried that there were vampires in Birmingham That they were real, physical beings, and they were very strong and powerful.

But none of the others gathered here had seen or experienced any of this. Even with the tremendous respect and deference they held Craggs in, would they be prepared to believe him when he uttered the word, 'Vampires'?

Craggs placed his whisky glass back on the table. Brendan's wife was hovering nearby, ready to clear away the empties and serve more drinks. The old man looked at Brendan, and then nodded.

"Patsy, it's time you made yourself scarce," Brendan said. "I'll clear up tonight. You go on to bed, while the men talk."

Patsy scuttled away like the dutiful wife she was. Coffin closed his eyes for a moment, a bolt of pain spearing him through the chest as he recalled how Steffanie would have reacted if he had ever spoken to her like that.

"These people who've taken my club," Craggs said, speaking slowly and carefully, "are like no one you have ever come across before. I barely got out alive and if it hadn't been for Joe, I wouldn't be here now."

A few of the men murmured, partly in anger and outrage, and partly in appreciation of what Coffin had done.

Hanrahan clapped his hand on Coffin's shoulder, and said, "You're a good man, Joe."

Coffin bit back a grunt of pain, as his shoulder flared up under Hanrahan's meaty hand, and resisted the urge to turn around and punch him in the face.

"But even Joe only just got out alive," Craggs said. "Twice."

The men all looked at Craggs.

Coffin spoke up.

"The second time I went back with two of our guys. Some of you might know them, Rob and Stut."

"Aye, I know Stut," Hanrahan said. "He's a good lad, but get him on a bad day and listening to the little shite try and get his words out is fucking torture."

"He's in hospital now, took a bullet to his leg. Must have hit an artery, he was close to bleeding out by the time I got him to the emergency department." Coffin decided not to tell them that Stut's injury was self-inflicted. Nobody here would have much sympathy for him knowing that he had shot himself in the leg, narrowly missing shooting his balls off. "And Rob's dead."

"Fucking hell, I were just talking with Rob a couple of days back," Terry said.

Coffin held up his hand, showed them the red stump. "And I lost my finger. A girl called Velvina bit it right off, in one go."

"Seriously, Joe?" Harry Frazer said. "You're telling us some fucking stupid bitch bit the end of your finger off?"

"That's right," Coffin said.

"And she's still alive?"

"Yeah."

"Not for long," Hanrahan said. "Not after I've got hold of her."

The men murmured their agreement again.

"That's what we're here to talk about," Craggs said. "If we go in like bulls in a china shop, I doubt all of us will come back out alive again. We need to discuss this, work it out."

"Have they got guns?" Tony Mannoia said. "If that's the case, I can get us guns. Bigger guns than they've got, that's for sure."

"No, they don't have guns," Craggs replied. "But if we go in heavily armed, that will help."

"It won't finish them off," Coffin said.

"You're not talking any sense, Joe," Frazer said. "You get a big enough piece, you can take anyone out. This gun I used once, ripped a man in half. Of course, if you're not wanting to damage the club that's a different matter. But you've got to expect some collateral damage if you're going to get these bastards out."

Freddie Noonan picked up a silver cigarette lighter and flipped the lid. A yellow flame shot almost a foot high, bathing his face in a warm glow. He relit the cigar hanging from his mouth.

"Fucking hell, Freddie," Adams said. "You almost took your fucking eyebrows off then."

Freddie grinned and snapped the lighter shut, extinguishing the flame.

"Who are these people took your club, Mort?" Hanrahan said. "They from out of town, think they can muscle their way in on your turf?"

Coffin watched Craggs, waiting for him to speak.

"No, they're not from out of town," the old man said. "In fact some of them used to be my guys. You remember Addison Lightfoot?"

"Fuck yeah," Terry said, and looked at his brother. "We laid him a new drive at his house once, remember?"

Brendan laughed. "And within a month it had cracked and buckled so bad it looked more like a mountain range."

"Not our fault that winter was cold enough to freeze the tits off a witch," Freddie said. "That's what done it, cracked open all the tarmac."

"That and the cack-handed job you pair of soft bastards made of it," Brendan said.

"You were telling us about your man, Addison," Gilligan said. "Why, exactly, did he turn against you?"

"He didn't have much choice in the matter," Craggs replied.

He picked up his cigar from the ashtray, but it had gone out. Freddie pulled his lighter from his pocket, but Craggs shook his head and placed the dead cigar back in the ashtray.

"You're going to find what I have to tell you next hard to believe. But I've seen it with my own eyes, and so has Joe. Except for you, Gerry, I know all of you men, known some of you since before you had hair on your balls. And so you'll know I'm serious when I say, if one of you fucking laughs at what I'm about to say, so help me Christ, I'll rip his fucking head off with my bare hands and piss down his neck."

"No one here would laugh at you, Mort," Tony said. "We got too much respect for you to do that."

"Vampires," Coffin said, and everyone turned to look at him. "What Mort and I are trying to tell you, is that the club has been taken over by vampires."

tongue

Wayne Davies walked across the park, his flashlight illuminating his way. The dogs were out there somewhere, he could hear them snuffling at the wet grass, and their barks as they ran around each other, but he couldn't see them. Black as midnight they were, not a cat in hell's chance of keeping track of them out here in the dark.

But they would come back as soon as he called them. At eleven months old they were still pups, really. Not that you could tell from the size of them. Bloody big bastards they were, but then that had been part of the point in getting them. Rottweilers made good guard dogs. Just one look at them would make a person think twice about starting anything.

As young as they were though, they were already very obedient and loyal.

Wayne liked walking in the dark after sundown. Even when all that crap about the Birmingham Vampire had been in the news and everyone else was staying indoors, he hadn't been afraid to take the dogs out in the park still. That sick bastard would have been welcome to try it on with him, his dogs would have soon seen him off. There wasn't a man alive who could survive a mauling by two angry Rottweilers. Not unless he had a gun, and even then the chances were stacked against him. Especially at night time, when the dogs had the advantage of better eyesight and a heightened sense of smell.

So Wayne had never once been concerned about going outside after sunset, even though his girlfriend begged him not to. No matter how many times he told her he would be safe, she always kicked up a fuss. Sometimes she even turned on the waterworks, accusing him of not loving her or, even more pathetically, not respecting her.

Of course he didn't respect her. Or love her. Staying with the silly bitch was a means to an end and nothing more. Wayne knew that if he left her, she wouldn't let him see his son anymore. Just to spite him.

That little boy was everything to Wayne. He hadn't been planned, and Wayne had thought about doing a runner when Stacie told him she was pregnant. But for some reason he could never quite work out, or put into words, he'd stayed. Maybe it was some stupid sense of doing the right thing, although nobody had ever done the right thing by him. But he had stayed, stuck it out even after the birth and their lives were filled with shitty nappies, and nights spent rocking a crying baby. Something had kept hold of Wayne, forced him to stick it out

And he was glad.

Little Tommy was two now, and he was bloody brilliant. Charging around at top speed on his stumpy little legs, he was like a mini whirlwind. Stacie whined and moaned about how much hard work he was, but Wayne ignored her. She always had to be bitching about something.

Every night when Wayne got home from work, exhausted with dried plaster in his hair and on his face and hands and splattered all over his work clothes, Tommy always charged straight for him as he stepped through the door. Wayne always hoisted him into the air and swung him around, whilst Tommy screamed with delight. Everyone said they were more like best mates than father and son and it was true. For the first time in his life, Wayne felt loved by someone just for who he was and not because of anything he had to offer, or because he was there and conveniently to hand.

His kid just loved him and Wayne felt like his heart might rip apart every time he looked at him. Wayne couldn't remember a time when he had ever felt so loved, so wanted and needed.

Stacie was jealous, Wayne knew that. But then all she ever did was shout at the poor little bastard. If it wasn't for Wayne, the poor kid would just bawl his head off the whole time.

Another reason to stick around.

Wayne whistled for the dogs. Time to be getting back.

He swung the torch around in a slow arc, listening for the thud of paws on the ground, the panting of the dogs. The torch was a heavy duty one. The bright beam picked out the blades of grass, and the tree trunks and their branches, in harsh highlights and shadows.

Wayne whistled for the dogs again. A short, sharp, commanding whistle.

Nothing.

They should have returned by now. Running around his feet, ready to have their leads fastened to their collars again. They always came back on that first whistle.

Always.

For the first time, out at night on his own, a cold creeping shadow of uneasiness began settling in his chest and stomach. He imagined the Birmingham Vampire hiding in the small wooded area, next to the church, and watching him. Wasn't this where the old homeless man had been killed?

Don't be stupid, Wayne told himself. The Birmingham Vampire was dead, killed by that gangster Joe Coffin. There were no serial killers, or vampires, out here. The dogs must have run a bit further than usual, that's all. Or they had found something fascinating to stick their noses in and were ignoring him.

Wayne whistled again.

He walked over to the small collection of trees, running his torch beam over the thin trunks, the moving shadows seeming to give the trees a life of their own. Over on the opposite side of the park he could hear traffic, and when he looked back he could see the lights of the shops, and the street lamps.

Everything down there was continuing as normal, but up here he seemed to have stepped into a different world. To his right the dark bulk of the church loomed over him. Wayne walked up to the wall separating the church graveyard from the park and swept his torch over the gravestones.

Where the hell were those dogs?

"Billy! Elvis!"

It was Stacie who had insisted on calling one of the dogs Elvis. Every time he called its name he felt like a bloody idiot. He'd had to give in to her even though the dogs were his, really. She had originally wanted to call the kid Elvis, but Wayne had put his foot down. There was no way he was lumbering any child of his with a stupid name like that.

The dog had never seemed to mind, though.

Wayne walked closer to the trees, the unease growing within him.

His foot stubbed a dark, bulky shape lying on the ground. Even before he turned the torch beam onto it, illuminating the black, glossy coat streaked with red, Wayne knew what it was. Billy lay on his side, teeth still bared in a snarl. His neck had been ripped open, and his head was lying in a pool of blood.

Wayne dropped to his knees and gently placed his hand on the dog's flank. The body was still warm, but there was no life beating beneath its rib cage. When he pulled his hand away his palm was dark with blood.

Wiping his sleeve across his eyes, angrily brushing away the tears, Wayne stood up. Whoever killed his dog was going to fucking pay for it. He was going to give them a fucking beating they would never forget.

"Elvis!" he hissed. "Elvis, come here boy!"

Stumbling between the trees, his vision blurred by more tears and the shadows swinging crazily in the wavering light of his torch, Wayne called and whistled for his dog. Within a few moments he was out the other side of the copse of trees, and he stopped.

Standing alone in the park was tiny, shadowed figure. A child, surely.

Wayne lifted the torch, its beam illuminating the small boy, four or five at the most. The little boy stood silent and motionless, his hands hanging by his sides. His head was lowered and he seemed to be looking his feet, or something on the ground.

"Are you lost?" Wayne said. "Where are your mum and dad, do you know?"

The boy said nothing, simply continued standing with his head bowed.

Wayne thought of Tommy, imagining him out here, on his own. How scared he would be, how vulnerable. It was far too late for a child of this age to be outside, even if his parents were here. But on his own? The poor little kid must be terrified.

Wayne glanced from side to side, scanning the darkness for any signs of movement. Thinking about Elvis and the sick bastard who'd killed Billy. As much as he wanted to find his dog and then kick the living shit out of the fucker who'd killed Billy, he knew his priority needed to be the boy.

If it had been Tommy out here and somebody else had found him, Wayne would want him to be looked after.

"It's okay," he said, slowly walking towards the boy. "We'll find your mummy and daddy, all right?"

The boy said nothing, but he slowly began raising his head. The beam of light, centred on the boy, quivered and Wayne realised he was shaking. A cold, prickling sensation had begun creeping down his scalp and his neck, down through his chest. He didn't want the boy to look at him, didn't want to be in this park anymore in the darkness.

For the first time in his life, Wayne was truly scared of the dark.

The boy lifted his head fully and stared at Wayne. His black pupils were fully dilated and filled his large, round eyes completely. His lips were smeared with scarlet blood. The blood had run down his chin and over his shirt.

Wayne lowered the torch, following the ghastly trail of red down the boy's torso and legs.

Elvis lay at his feet, his tongue lolling from his mouth and his throat ripped open.

Wayne didn't even have time to scream for help before the little boy was on top of him. He tried to fend off the child, who had turned into a biting, scratching, frenzied monster. Wayne dropped the torch, plunging them into darkness. They both fell to the ground and Wayne opened his mouth to scream.

He gagged instead, as the boy shoved his hand deep into Wayne's mouth and clawed at his tongue and throat. Grabbing the boy's arm with both hands, his throat filling with warm blood, the terrified man tried pulling the boy's hand out of his mouth. He coughed and spluttered blood, choking for air as the child continued ripping apart the lining of Wayne's throat.

Wayne let go of the boy's wrist and threw wild, blind punches at him. His chest heaved as he gagged and coughed, hot blood filling his throat, the child's hand filling his mouth, tearing at the soft flesh.

Just as conscious thought and all sensations of pain and panic began to slip away, the boy ripped his hand out of Wayne's mouth. Wayne rolled over onto his side and coughed up a torrent of blood. His mouth and throat were on fire with indescribable pain, and already he could feel the inside of his mouth filling up with more blood.

But the boy was leaving him alone, seemed preoccupied with something else for the moment.

Got to shout for help, while I have the chance.

Coughing up some more blood, he lifted his head and tried to scream.

But nothing came out, except a gargled hiss.

That's when Wayne saw the boy, holding Wayne's severed, bloody tongue. Strips of dark flesh dangled from its base. The boy inspected it for a moment or two, and then lifted it to his mouth and began sucking hungrily at it.

tender love and care

City hospital was turning into a second home for Emma Wylde. The last time she had been such a frequent visitor to a hospital was when she was a child, and her sister had been ill. After that experience she had hoped never to have to set foot inside a hospital again, but in the last six days she had been here three times.

Emma had no idea what the visiting times were, or even which ward Nick was on. She assumed they would have taken him to the Emergency Department first, but would he still be there? Emma wandered into the main concourse. The skylights in the ceiling were dark with the night sky, but the entrance was lit up by the warm glow of the hospital's lights.

The shops were open and busy, but the welcome desk was empty. A scattered collection of empty wheelchairs sat next to the desk. A couple of teenagers sat in two of them, attempting to perform wheelies.

Emma decided her best bet was to walk down to the Emergency Department and ask someone there. Eight o'clock in the evening, and the hospital corridors were busy with people heading for the exit. Had she missed visiting time? Six till eight sounded about right, in which case she was too late.

A tiny little problem like that wasn't going to stop Emma, though.

The Emergency Department was as busy as she had expected it to be. Most of the patients seemed to be old, and infirm. One man had been parked in the corridor on a trolley, and he was so immensely overweight that Emma had no idea how the nurses could have got him on there. The air was filled with the noise of telephones constantly ringing, and doctors and nurses shouting messages to each other across the department.

Emma knew she shouldn't be here, that she was in the way, an inconvenience. Didn't matter. She had to find out where they had taken Nick.

A young, pretty, Chinese nurse hurried past Emma.

"Excuse me," Emma said.

The nurse cast a glance back as she hurried off, and said, "Give me a moment, and I'll be right back."

Somehow Emma doubted that. She'd probably already forgotten about her.

Emma headed for the nurse's station, and stopped in front of a ward clerk, who was staring intently at a computer monitor.

"Excuse me," she said.

"I'll be with you in a second," the clerk said, not even looking up from his screen.

Emma waited, the tension winding her insides tighter and tighter. Any moment now and she was going to explode, and then he wouldn't be looking at his computer screen anymore because she would be right in his face.

A poster was pinned prominently to a notice board behind the ward clerk. On it was a photograph of a pair of handcuffs, and the words *Our staff will not accept abuse of any kind*, printed above the photograph.

Keep cool, she thought. *Lose your temper here and you'll get taken away in a police car.*

"Excuse me," she said again.

The man held up a hand, palm out. "I'll be with you in a moment."

Resisting the almost overpowering urge to lean across the desk, grab a handful of his hair and drag the ward clerk's head upright so that she would be in his line of vision, Emma closed her eyes and took a deep breath. When she opened her eyes she noticed the leaflets in the display.

PALS.

Patient Advice and Liaison Service.

Emma pulled one out and quickly scanned it. Advice on how to make a complaint.

Unfolding the leaflet to its maximum size, Emma leaned over the desk and held the leaflet in front of the computer monitor, so that it completely obscured it.

"I think I might phone these people," she said. "I've been waiting here hours, and I've been pushed around from pillar to post this whole time, and you don't even have the common decency to look at me when I try and get your attention."

The ward clerk raised his head and looked up, the hostility clear in his eyes.

"How can I be of help?" he said, his voice a flat monotone.

Emma whisked the leaflet away and gave him a sunny smile. "I'm looking for my partner, he was brought in last night."

"Last night?"

Shit, Emma thought. *My story about waiting for several hours might start unravelling now.*

"Yes, his name is Nick Archer, could you find out where he is, please?"

The ward clerk tapped the name into his computer and clicked his mouse on various boxes, until he found what he was looking for.

"He was moved up to the High Dependency Unit," he finally said. "But I'm afraid you won't be able to visit him now, visiting times are over."

Emma left without bothering to reply.

The High Dependency Unit was situated on the first floor, according to the signs opposite the lifts. Panic had begun blooming inside her stomach at the thought of how ill Nick must be, if he had been transferred to a ward with such a serious sounding name. Was that just a different name for Intensive Care, or was it something else completely?

As Emma waited for the lift to arrive, she wondered if Jacob was still here, or if he had been allowed home. The poor boy was going to live with the psychological trauma of being held captive in that cellar, by a woman he believed dead, for the rest of his life. The scars on his physical body would heal up and given time might even become so faint as to be near invisible.

But the wounds opened up in his mind and in his emotions would never heal properly.

The lift arrived and Emma stepped inside. An old man in pyjamas was standing in the corner, attached to an IV drip on a stand with wheels. Emma wondered why he hadn't got off the lift when it arrived on the ground floor, but then decided not to worry about it. If he wanted to spend his time going for a ride up and down in the elevator that was his business.

She had too many other things to worry about.

The lift door juddered open and stepped out.

The old man stayed where he was and Emma couldn't help but turn and look at him as the doors slid closed. He looked at her with rheumy, watering eyes until he disappeared behind the metal doors.

Emma followed the signs to HDU, where she also found ITU, situated next door.

She pushed at the door, which remained firmly closed. Emma checked the time. Quarter past eight.

Visiting hours looked to be most definitely over.

This wasn't going to be easy. Attacking this head on, her usual way of confronting obstacles, obviously wasn't going to work this time. Once she lost control and started shouting and swearing and demanding her own way, the hospital security would be here in a flash and she would find herself ejected from the hospital grounds.

Or worse, sitting in the back of a police car.

Emma pressed the buzzer on the wall and waited for a response.

After only a few seconds of waiting, Emma had to hold her hands behind her back to keep from jabbing at the buzzer again.

Stay cool. They'll answer in a moment, just stay cool.

Every few seconds the intercom on the wall beeped, but no one spoke through it.

Just as she was about to punch the buzzer again, someone spoke from behind. "Excuse me, young lady."

A hospital porter had appeared silently behind Emma. He was pushing a bed with a shrivelled old lady on it, only her head visible from under the sheets. His belly strained at the buttons on his shirt and his mullet haircut might have been fashionable for a month or two back in 1983, but must have looked ridiculous and sad ever since.

He scanned his security pass and pulled the bed through the open doorway and down the corridor towards the ITU ward. Emma waited as long as she dared, watching the double doors slowly swing shut, and then grabbed a door handle when it had only a gap of an inch wide left.

After taking a quick look around, Emma pulled open the door and slipped silently inside. She walked down the hospital corridor, keeping back from the porter with the mullet, and watched as he entered the ward. He hadn't swiped his pass across the scanner this time, just pulled open the doors.

Once he was inside, Emma approached the double doors. To her left was a roll of pink, plastic disposable aprons and a dispenser of sanitizing hand gel. She pulled an apron off the roll and over her head and tied the ties behind her back. She squirted hand gel into her palms and rubbed her hands together until the sticky gel had evaporated.

Grasping the door handle firmly and, trying simultaneously to look professional, as though she belonged in ITU, and invisible, Emma pulled open the door and stepped inside.

Unlike other wards she had visited, here the nurses was station was situated in the centre of the room with the beds placed around the perimeter. Fortunately there weren't that many beds and Emma quickly scanned the room until she saw Nick. He was asleep, attached to a drip. There was a monitor beside his bed, but it was switched off and unplugged, its cables coiled on top.

That looked hopeful at least.

Emma stood at the foot of the bed, looking at her partner of five years now, wondering if she should wake him up, let him know she was here. He looked so pale, so helpless. His jawline and chin were dark with stubble. Nick was the kind of man who could shave twice a day, and he would still have a five o'clock shadow. If he didn't get out of hospital soon, he would start looking like Grizzly Adams.

Emma moved down the side of the bed and took his hand, which was lying on top of the bed sheet. His fingers were cold, and yet the ward was warm. He didn't stir at all and Emma wondered if the doctors had given him something to help him sleep. Even at home he always had so much trouble sleeping, but here he would find it near impossible.

How unusual it was to see him so peaceful, his features so composed and calm. Looking at him now, Emma couldn't remember the last time she had seen him this way. The two of them were always so busy they hardly saw each other, and when they did it was to argue, or have sex. When was the last time they had simply sat down together and talked, or shared the silence of a quiet moment together?

"Hey, Nick," she whispered. "I've got some news for you. I'm pregnant."

Emma felt stupid, saying the words out loud like that. Stupid and scared. This was the first time she had spoken the word pregnant out loud, and the fact of doing so suddenly made it so very real.

"You're going to be a dad," she whispered. "How great is that?"

Emma thought about what she had just said. Did that mean she was keeping the child? Had she made a decision, without even realising it?

The course of her whole life was set to change, depending on what she decided. Her carefully mapped out plan for the rest of her career would be in tatters if she had this child.

And if she didn't?

"Nurse? Hey, n-n-nurse, get me a drink of w-water, will you?"

Emma turned to see who had spoken, and all thoughts of pregnancy disappeared.

But she was still scared.

Charlie 'Stutterer' Boyd lay in the bed next to Nick's. He looked up at Emma, expectantly waiting for her to run at his command.

"Fuck me, you're Charlie Boyd, aren't you?" Emma said, letting go of Nick's hand and crossing over to the other bed.

"That's s-some mouth you g-g-got on you, for a nurse."

"What is it everyone calls you? Stut, right?"

"Yeah, that's right," Stut said, and grinned. "You w-w-wanna climb in bed with m-me, show m-me a bit of tender love and c-c-care?"

"I'd rather fuck a rattlesnake," Emma said.

The smile disappeared. "You're not allowed to t-talk to me like that. I could report y-y-you."

"Sure you could." Now it was Emma's turn to grin. "But I'm not a nurse, so it doesn't matter to me."

Stut's smile faltered and he glanced over to the nurse's station and back again.

"Shit, you're a f-f-fucking copper, aren't you? I already told the other one, I don't f-f-fucking know what happened!"

Emma perched herself on the edge of Stut's bed, grinned at him. "I think you probably do know what happened, but that's all right, you don't have to worry. I'm not the police. But he is."

Stut turned his head to look at Nick in the next bed. Stut's skin was pale and he moved slowly, painfully. An IV drip was attached to his arm, the tube leading up to a plastic bag on a stand, looked like custard inside it.

Clipped to the side of the bed was another bag, half full with a yellow liquid.

Stut's piss, Emma guessed.

"What the f-fuck's going on?" Stut whispered.

"I was with Coffin yesterday, at Angels," Emma said. "Did you go back with him, later on?"

Stut closed his eyes. "F-f-fuck off."

Emma reached down by the side of the bed and curled her fingers around the plastic tube, leading from the urine bag and up under the bed sheets. She gave it a tug.

Stut's eyes snapped open. "Ouch!"

"Ooh, sorry," Emma said. "Did that hurt your precious little winky?"

Stut looked over to the nurse's station again. One nurse sat in front of a computer, tapping on the keyboard. The rest of the nurses were huddled around a bed on the opposite side of the ward with a doctor.

"Listen up, Charlie. I was with Coffin, when he first went to Angels. I saw him beat Tom Mills' head to a bloody pulp and I saw some other shit too, like Steffanie Coffin wandering around without a stitch of clothing on and a fucking hole you could put your fist through in the side of her head."

"St-Steffanie's dead," Stut said, but he didn't sound convinced.

"Yeah, right, she's dead, but she's still walking and talking. What about you, Stut? You went back to the club with Coffin, right? And the other one, Rob? Is he in here, too?"

"Rob's d-dead."

"Yeah, I thought so," Emma said. "Who killed him? Steffanie Coffin?"

Stut closed his eyes. Emma gave him a few moments, and then tugged on the catheter again.

"Stop d-doing that!" Stut hissed, his eyes snapping open. "Feels like you're p-pulling my d-d-dick off!"

"Aww, really? I didn't realise, sorry about that."

Stut sighed. "No, it wasn't Steffanie Coffin. Some old g-guy, looked half d-d-dead."

Steffanie's mysterious companion. Another vampire, the one that Tom had smuggled out of No. 99 under the sheets with Steffanie. And he'd been at the club, found Emma lurking out the back, and herded her inside. Tom had shot him point blank with his shotgun. Looked like Coffin had been right. The only way to kill these things was carve them up and torch them. And maybe they should think about sifting garlic through the ashes, and then burying them in holy ground as well.

"What did you go back for? To clear up the mess?"

"Yeah, and to sort out whoever was th-th-there. F-f-fuck them over, like they did to Coffin."

"But that old bastard fucked you over instead, didn't he? What about Steffanie, was she there, too?"

"N-no, I didn't see her." Stut closed his eyes and sighed. "B-but Addison and C-C-C-Clevon were there, and V-Velvina too. They were fucking m-monsters. That b-bitch V-Velvina chewed Coffin's fucking f-finger off."

Addison, Clevon, Velvina. Those names meant nothing to Emma, and she could only assume they were Angels staff, part of Craggs' gang. Which meant there were a minimum of five vampires at the club now.

Shit!

That still didn't explain who had opened the club doors earlier this morning, and let the police in for a chat. Couldn't have been Steffanie, not the way she looked the last time Emma had seen her. Couldn't have been any of the vampires, they all looked creepy once they had turned.

"What happened to you? Did you get bit as well?"

Stut shook his head, but didn't say anything.

Emma stood up. Time to go.

"It was nice chatting to you, Charlie. Next time I'll bring grapes."

"Fuck you," Stut said.

Emma laughed and turned to go, and came face to face with a nurse.

"I'm so glad you're here," Emma said, glancing back at Stut. "Charlie's shit himself, and he needs his arse wiping."

The nurse opened her mouth to reply, but Emma pushed past her and left the ward, pulling the apron off as she walked and stuffing it into a bin.

10,000

"I'm not being rude or anything, you know, but it's a fucking stupid name if you ask me."

"You say you're not being rude, but then you go and insult me! Bastard."

Mick rolled over on his side, reached out a scabbed, dirty hand and pawed at the wooden floor. "Fucking spiders are everywhere."

"You're seeing things."

Mick rolled onto his back again. "All right, I get you, y'know, I really do. An' I'm sorry if I upset you, it wasn't my intention, not one bit, y'understand?" He paused, squinting at the ceiling through red rimmed eyes, sure he could see more spiders up there. "But I don't even know what the fuck to call you anymore. Is it like, a stutter? Kuh-Kayla? Or is it like two names, like Kay-Kayla?" I mean, y'know, the fuck?"

Kkayla was sitting on the worn, leather sofa, all shiny and ripped, and covered in stains. "I fucking told you my name already. Why're you making such a big shitty deal about it?"

"Because it don't make no fucking sense, that's why. Your mother give you that name?"

"Fuck off."

Mick swiped a hand across his face, swatting at something only he could see.

Kkayla dropped the pipe on the floor, and rested her head against the sofa back. "Fuck me, this is intense."

Mick giggled. "Y'know, I'd love to fucking fuck you, but I haven't had a boner in over a month." He grabbed his crotch and gave himself a squeeze. "You think I might be impotent?"

"Let me at him, I'll make him stand to attention."

"Anytime, babe."

The windows had been boarded up. Outside the sun had risen over a cold, grey landscape. In the house the only light came from a bare bulb hanging from the ceiling. It cast a dim, sickly yellow glow over everything. The floor was bare except for a tatty red rug, which might have looked nice once, but its best days were long behind it. The old floorboards were cracked and splintered, the grooves filled with dirt. The girl sprawled on the sofa was wearing a pair of ripped, dirty jeans and a man's shirt. The buttons were undone, the shirt open, revealing her wasted body. Her hair was dirty and lank and twisted into knots.

A second man was lying on a lumpy beanbag next to the sofa. The beanbag was ripped and the tiny, white polystyrene balls were slowly leaking from the cover. The man's torso was bare and covered in tattoos and scabs. He had his eyes closed.

"I wish we'd met before we got hooked on bang, y'know," Mick said.

He was bald on top, but the grey hair at the sides and the back had grown down over his shoulders. A scraggly beard crawled over the lower half of his face and he was so skinny, Kkayla thought she could probably snap him in half if she wanted.

"Shagging isn't that great," she said. "I've fucked more men than I can remember, and some girls, too. The girls were better than the guys. Really were."

Mick threw an arm over his eyes and groaned. "I swear there's fucking spiders crawling all over the ceiling. You see them?"

"I told you, you're seeing crap, that's all. We got any more shit?"

"No, it's all gone."

"Shit." Kkayla sighed, and scrubbed her hands over her face. "It's that fucking Joe Coffin's fault."

"What is?" Mick said.

"All this shit! My fucking pathetic life, that's what."

"Who the fuck's Joe Coffin? Talk about stupid names, that's as shitty as yours."

"He's a gangster, a killer. He killed my boyfriend."

Mick opened his eyes. "Yeah? What the fuck for?"

"I don't know," Kkayla said. "You know, he wasn't really my boyfriend, he used to pay me for sex. But I liked him. He was cute."

"Cute."

"Yeah, cute. You got a problem with that?"

"Hey, no way. You like cute, I can do cute, too."

"Fuck off, you could never do cute," Kkayla said. "But me an' Jet, we were—"

Mick burst into a fit of manic giggles. "Jet? Are you fucking with me?"

"Hey, you wanna hear this story or not?"

"Yeah, sure, sure."

"Me an' Jet, we were shagging, when Joe Coffin busted into our flat with some other guy. Coffin's huge, looks like a monster, like Frankenstein."

"No he didn't," Mick said.

"Shut the fuck up, all right? I'm telling this story, and I'm telling you Coffin looks like fucking Frankenstein!"

Mick shook his head, still gazing up at the ceiling. "No, he fucking doesn't. What you're saying is that he looks like Frankenstein's monster. Frankenstein was the mad doctor who created him."

"Yeah, whatever. Anyway, Coffin, he took one look at me, and just told me to get out. I wasn't going to argue with him. I got out of there fast as I could, just grabbed my clothes and ran outside, still naked. And then I heard later he'd killed Jet, shot him in the fucking head."

"Jet owe him money or something?"

Kkayla wiped tears from her eyes. "No, nothing. Like, we'd all heard of Joe Coffin, everyone in Birmingham knows who Joe Coffin is. But Jet never had anything to do with him."

"Fuck, man. The rozzers ever catch him?"

"They're not even looking for him. I'm the only one who knows Coffin killed Jet. An' I'm not telling anyone. I don't want Joe Coffin coming after me. Not worth it. Not even for all that money."

Kkayla fell silent. Mick lay on his back, thinking that maybe he'd just heard something significant, but he couldn't think what. Next door someone turned on a TV, a chat show or something. The host was talking, and the audience kept bursting into laughter and applause.

"Money?" Mick said, finally. "What money?"

"Jet's dad, he posted a reward for information on Jet's murder."

"And you didn't say anything?"

"Fuck, no. I told you, I don't want Coffin looking for me. Get a bullet through the back of my head."

"How much was he offering?"

"Oh, I don't know. Like, maybe fifty thousand, or something."

"Fifty grand?"

Mick stifled a giggle. In an attempt to keep quiet, he shoved both fists against his mouth and bit down on his knuckles. He glanced over at Kkayla. Looked like she was falling asleep. Her eyes were closed, her mouth hanging open.

Fifty grand. Fuck.

That would see him right for a while.

What did she say her boyfriend's name was?

"Hey! Hey, Kuh-Kayla, who's this guy, after Coffin?"

Kkayla opened her eyes. "Huh?"

"Your boyfriend's dad, who is he?"

got bit by a vampire

"Ninety-four . . . Ninety-five . . . ninety-six!"

Garrett Stone paused at the top of the push up, making sure not to cheat by locking his elbows. Sweat was running down his face and dripping off his bare chest onto the gymnasium floor in fat, dark spots. He knew he had to finish these push ups fast, get to a hundred before his arms gave out. Already he could feel the tremble starting in his triceps.

"Come on, Daddy! Only four more!"

His eight year old boy sat cross legged on the floor, watching his father.

"Yes, come on, Garrett, what are you waiting for?" Lucy murmured in his ear. "It's only four more push ups."

"Those four push ups would be a whole lot easier," Garrett grunted, "if you weren't lying on my back."

"But they wouldn't be as much fun," his wife replied, and kissed him on the top of the head.

Stone lowered himself slowly down, head arched back so that he was staring straight ahead, until his chest brushed the floor. Then he propelled himself up, using all the energy left in his burning muscles in an explosive pushing motion.

"Ninety-seven!" he shouted, and began slowly lowering himself back down.

A classic push up, using perfect form. Any slight variation on the movement, a pause at the top, with elbows locked, or not going far enough down that his chest didn't touch the ground, and that push-up didn't count. Stone didn't need a commanding officer standing over him, yelling at him to keep perfect form, abusing him with insults. Stone had all that anger inside his head. And he used that anger as an aid to discipline.

"Ninety-eight!"

At forty-nine, he was fitter and stronger than he had ever been before in his life. The army had taught him discipline, and the value of exercise and physical training. But it was the SAS that had brought him to the realisation that he was fighting a losing battle with his body, that one day it would give up on him, desert him, just when he needed it the most.

"Ninety-nine!"

And the only means he had of slowing down the gradual decay of his body was by punishing it through physical exercise.

"One hundred!"

Stone held the push up at the top, his arms trembling, waiting for Lucy to climb off his back.

"Hold it, soldier," she whispered into his ear, her auburn hair hanging over his face. "Just stay right where you are."

Stone ground his teeth together, arms trembling even more. She knew he wouldn't want to give in to her, that he would wait for her at the top of his push-up, to climb off him. If he lowered himself down to the ground, he wouldn't have the strength to push himself back up again, and that would be a defeat.

He flexed his arms slightly, as though he was going to do another repetition, and then pushed, rolling sideways at the same time. Lucy tumbled off his back and onto the floor, and Stone landed on top of her.

"Ouch! That's not fair!"

"All's fair in love and war," Stone said.

Jude leapt on top of them, and Stone grabbed him and started tickling him.

The little boy started screaming and laughing, yelling, "No! Daddy, stop! Stop!"

"Don't worry, Jude, I've got him!" Lucy shouted, grabbing Stone around his waist, her fingers finding his ticklish spot.

"Hey, two against one? No that's not fair!" he shouted.

He let go of Jude and scrambled to his feet and backed away, laughing. Stone was wearing a pair of running shorts, and nothing else. He caught sight of his reflection in the floor to ceiling mirrors and took a moment to admire his taught body, the firm stomach and chest, and the arms thick with muscle. The white dressing on his neck caught his attention. An image of Leola filled his mind, lying naked on the bed, that tattoo, those swirling dark lines, closing around her hard nipple.

He pushed the thought away. Turning his back on his reflection he watched his wife and son squirming on the polished flooring as they tickled each other, giggling and screaming.

What happened to your neck, Daddy? Jude had asked him when he arrived home earlier that morning.

Got bit by a vampire, Stone had said.

Tell me the truth, Jude had replied, in his most solemn, stern voice, his eyebrows scrunched up in an effort to appear angry.

Seriously, I'm telling the truth, Stone had replied. *He attacked me from behind, took me by surprise and bit me on the neck. But I turned around really quick, and staked him through the heart before he could suck any of my blood.*

Don't listen to your daddy, he's just teasing you, Lucy had said.

But she never asked him what had happened, about the dressing on his neck, what was under there. And the subject hadn't been raised again.

A buzzing noise cut through the sounds of laughter and screams. Stone's mobile, on the floor. Vibrating, the screen glowing, demanding attention.

Stone picked up the mobile and glanced at the screen. No caller ID, and a number he didn't recognise. Stone didn't like surprises.

"I'll take this next door," he said.

Stone walked out of his personal gym, and entered a massive kitchen, the glossy tiles cool on his bare feet, and leaned against a counter.

"Garrett Stone. State your business."

"I know who murdered your boy," said a voice.

Stone's grip tightened on the mobile. "Who is this?" he said, his voice dropping an octave.

"A concerned citizen, Mr Stone. I want to do the right thing."

The voice had a slight ragged edge to it, as if the caller was a heavy smoker. And he was enunciating his words very carefully and slowly. Was he drunk? High?

"Who is this?" Stone said again.

"Like I said, Mr Stone, I am a concerned citizen, who wants to see justice done."

A pause. Stone waited.

"I know who murdered your boy," the caller said again.

Stone waited some more. Wait long enough, people had to fill the silence, the gap in the conversation. That's when they started giving things away, talking themselves into a trap.

"I heard there might be a reward?"

There it was.

"Yes. There's a reward."

"Fifty thousand pounds?"

"No."

Stone could sense the bafflement and outrage emanating from the other end of the call through the silence.

"What the fuck, she said the reward was—"

"I don't care what you've been told. The reward is ten thousand pounds."

More silence.

"Have you told anyone else what you know?" Stone said.

"No way. I'm the only one knows anything about this."

He was lying. They always lied at some point. Everyone did.

"Give me your information. I'll need to check it out. If it's solid, I can arrange transfer of the money to your account."

Silence.

"I need the money now. Give me the ten thousand, and I'll give you the name."

"That's not how it works, Mister . . ?"

"Uh, Mick."

"All right, *Mick*, this is how we do it. You give me your info, I check it out. If I gave money to everyone who called me, saying they had valuable information for me, I would be a very poor man by now. Once I know the intell you have supplied is rock solid, then we can arrange transfer of funds from my account to yours. Is that clear enough?"

A pause.

"How do I know you'll give me the cash, once you have the name? I might never hear from you again."

Stone smiled. "You'll just have to trust me."

More silence. A rustling noise on the phone, as though it was being passed from one hand to another, or the mouthpiece was being covered up. Then muffled voices in the background.

The caller came back on. "All right, we'll tell you." He'd forgotten already about his lie. "It was Joe Coffin."

Stone gazed out through the patio door at his garden. The dogs were out there, chasing each other around the lawn.

Lucy liked to sit outside in the garden in the summer, her head tipped back, her eyes closed, enjoying the sunshine. And Jude enjoyed kicking a ball about on the lawn. Four years ago Stone's other son, Isaac, had been out there, teaching his little four year old brother how to play football.

There had been a twelve year gap between their births, filled with failed IVF treatments and one miscarriage.

Their two boys had been precious. Gifts from God, his mother would have said. And now they only had one. Jude.

But Stone hadn't grieved when the police called him, and told him his son had been killed. That was the news he had been expecting for some time now. It had been inevitable, considering the downward trajectory his life had taken.

Stone had lost his firstborn son to drugs, long before he was murdered.

What was the point of grieving for him now?

"The police discounted Joe Coffin as a suspect," Stone said. "He had no connection to Isaac, and there was no evidence or reason to link him to the crime."

"Isaac, who the fuck's Isaac?" the caller said. "I'm talking about your kid, Jet."

Stone closed his eyes. A junkie, he had to be a junkie. The slurred speech, the lack of coherent thought, the need for the money plain in his voice. When Stone thought of what he had done in the army and the good friends he'd lost, how he had risked his own life in the SAS on covert missions in Afghanistan fighting for freedom just so that arsewipes like this could shoot themselves full of shit and live off handouts, he wanted to round them up and exterminate the lot of them.

To think that Isaac had been one of them. Stone rolled his shoulders, gently trying to ease the tension out of them.

"Jet was his nickname," Stone said. "It was given to him by his friends. Now, how do you know that Joe Coffin murdered Isaac? Have you any proof?"

More mumblings in the background.

"We've got a witness."

"Who?"

"A friend. She was there when it happened."

Stone continued gazing out at the large garden. They had a good life here. A nice, big house, in an exclusive cul-de-sac. Every morning, Stone went for a run along the trails in the surrounding countryside. They held parties here, and barbecues in the summer. Jude was doing well at school. He was a popular, bright boy. Everyone said so.

Isaac had become the one blot in their perfect life. Stone could never understand it, doubted he ever would. His son had wanted for nothing, had been given all the love and attention and privileges he could have asked for. And yet still, by the time he was eighteen he had managed to derail his life so utterly and completely that Stone could not envisage how he could ever get him back.

And then he took a bullet to the back of the head, in a scuzzy block of flats in an area of Birmingham so rundown it had reminded Stone of some of the war zones he had been in.

Isaac had let himself, and his family, down. But he had still been Stone's son.

And for that reason, Stone needed to find his murderer. What was it Lucy would say?

Seek closure.

"Tell me where you live. I want to meet your friend."

the stomach for it

The row of houses looked onto an industrial estate across the road. Nothing but views of corrugated sidings and concrete, pools of oil staining the cracked and pitted ground and the ever present stink and noise of machinery grinding away inside the warehouses.

The houses were all semis, built in the 1950s, with small gardens out front and paths leading to the front doors. Some of the houses had boarded up windows and gardens overgrown with weeds and long grass. A few of the houses looked lived in still, with curtains in the windows, a light on here and there, one or two of the gardens even looking as though the owners were making an effort.

But really, if you lived somewhere like this, why would you bother?

Stone looked back at his car parked a little further down the road. Ordinarily he would be reluctant to leave it unattended in a neighbourhood like this, but not today.

He flexed his fingers, bringing some life back into them. Even through the thick lining of his gloves, the cold was seeping into his joints, stiffening them up. Seemed like winter was arriving early this year. Stone had a scarf wrapped around his neck, and he was wearing a long, black winter overcoat, but his head was bare.

One day, Stone kept promising himself, he was going to take his family and move somewhere warm, where winter never came to visit. The deserts of Afghanistan and Iraq, the heat, had never caused him a problem. But the cold got him every time.

Stone wasn't sure what was keeping him here in this godforsaken country. After all, he was wealthy enough now that he could afford to live anywhere he wanted.

Maybe it was a sense of unfinished business. Isaac, tethering him to a country he despised, even though he had shed blood for that country. Had seen friends torn apart by IEDs in defence of its values and 'freedom'.

Isaac. Stone and Lucy had lost him years ago. They had lost him to the drugs and the wasters that he took to hanging around with. It had been so hard at first, seeing his son drift away from the values of loyalty, strength and independence that Stone had tried instilling in him. But eventually, both Stone and Lucy had come to accept it, to live with it.

And they had stopped trying to win him back, to sort his life out for him. Isaac had chosen his own path and Stone reasoned it was now up to him to make his own way, to fend for himself. So, when they received news of his murder, a shot to the back of his head in a scuzzy flat in Birmingham, Stone had not grieved for his son. He had finished with grieving when he first lost him, years before. As far as Stone was concerned, his son was already dead.

But that didn't mean he wasn't angry.

That didn't mean he wasn't ready to hunt down the bastard who had murdered his boy and deliver payback.

Joe Coffin.

Stone had only vaguely heard of him before the police mentioned him as a possible suspect. But then they had dismissed him just as quickly, with no connection found to link Isaac and Coffin. The investigation had been dropped the very next day, as apprehending the Birmingham Vampire quickly became a priority over everything else.

Garrett Stone never got the justice he felt was owed him.

But that was something he was going to fix.

Thinking over what he knew of the murder, Stone could see no reason why Isaac had been killed.

It was as though he had been the random victim of a gangland killing. But Stone knew it didn't work that way. A hit executed so professionally, there had to be a reason. No one got their brains blown out the front of their face and splattered across the floor without somebody planning for that to happen.

Was that somebody Joe Coffin?

Stone had done his research on Coffin. His mother dead at an early age, the child left in the care of an abusive father. The intruder, breaking into the house when Joe Coffin was a teenager and battering his father's skull in with a dumbbell.

The police never found the intruder, but Stone suspected there never had been one. Suspected the young Coffin had finally taken enough abuse one day, and retaliated. All those years of pent up rage and abuse had finally exploded, and the victim had turned on the abuser.

Stone had seen it happen before, was well versed in the power plays between bully and victim. He had used that psychological knowledge many times in the interrogation room to elicit valuable information. Physical torture had its place, but fucking up a person's mind was much more powerful than simply abusing the body.

Stone strolled along the pavement, keeping his eyes open for No. 52. Stone reckoned it would be a house with boarded up windows, maybe a boarded up door, too. They had to be squatters.

Crackheads, just like Isaac.

Didn't matter who or what they were, as long as the information they had was solid.

Stone spotted No. 52. He had been right. No point knocking on the front door, nobody was opening that without a crowbar. The windows too. Had to be black as midnight inside there.

The dead vegetation was soft and squishy beneath his feet as Stone walked carefully up to the front door. He turned right and walked along the front of the house, and then down the side. Another boarded up window. Graffiti sprayed on the wall, a massive cock and balls, the words SUCK THIS! scrawled above it.

Stone stepped slowly around the corner of the house. Another garden. Overgrown, heaps of lager cans, Styrofoam takeout cartons, mulched cigarette packets, a broken down shed, the walls leaning in on themselves, no roof to speak of.

Even despite the cold day, Stone could smell the rotting meat.

Scumbags like this, they were vermin. Deserved to be eradicated, not given hand-outs.

Stone sidled down the wall to the back door. This one hadn't been boarded up, and it was open by about an inch. The windowpane was cracked and filthy, but Stone could just about see through it and into the kitchen.

The kitchen surfaces were black with dirt, and the sink was filled with dirty dishes and more lager cans. Stone spotted a can sitting on the kitchen table, with holes punched in it. A homemade crack pipe.

He pushed at the door, but it didn't budge. The wood had swollen, jamming the door in its frame. He pushed harder, the muscles in his arm bunching up under his shirt. The door came free of the frame, its bottom edge scraping along the dirty floor.

Stone stepped inside.

"Hey!" he shouted. "Anybody home?"

Silence.

A dripping tap. The sound of traffic from the road, and the heavy machinery on the industrial estate opposite. Stone walked slowly through the kitchen, the soles of his shoes making sticky squelching noises on the linoleum. There were two doors ahead. One was open, leading into a pantry, the shelves empty and lined with yellowing newspapers.

The other door was closed, had to lead into the rest of the house. A hall maybe, or straight into a living room. The stairs to the first floor would most likely be on his right hand side as he left the kitchen. His instincts warned him of a potential surprise attack from that area. If someone was waiting for him, crouching on the third or fourth step, it would be easy for them to leap on him as he stepped through the doorway.

Stone backed up against the kitchen wall and slowly curled his hand around the plastic, pearl coloured door handle. He flung the door open, stepping back and to one side as a man stumbled towards him and through the kitchen doorway.

"What the fuck, man!" he screamed, wild eyed, fists swinging at empty air.

Stone easily avoided him. The man was wearing a pair of stained boxer shorts, and nothing else. He was all skin and bone, his face covered in a straggly beard. Stone grabbed him, and slammed him face first against the wall, twisting both arms up behind his back.

"Ow! Fuck!"

Up close, Stone could smell him, the stink of his unwashed body, his breath.

"Are you the one who called me?" he said.

"Fuck, yeah, I'm the one who called you, yeah. You're Jet's dad, yeah? Fuck, let go of me, you're fucking hurting me."

Stone let go of the man, stepped back.

"His name was Isaac."

"All right, shit, whatever." He turned around, looked Stone up and down, pushing out his scrawny chest like he was trying to impress him. "You brought the money with you?"

"Don't worry about the money," Stone said. "If your intell is good, you'll get your reward."

"Intell? What the fuck are you talking about?"

"Your information, it needs to be solid, needs to be worth my while making the trip down to this shithole."

"Oh yeah, the information's good, all right. Just don't want to go fucking about with bank accounts, y'know? We need cash. We need it now."

Stone took his time looking around the kitchen, at the cracked plaster on the walls, at the damp, and the mould in the corners, the filthy layer of grease covering everything.

"What's the hurry? Planning on decorating, are you?"

"What do you fucking care?"

The man scratched his balls, and then turned and walked back through the doorway into a dark hall, the smell of neglect and age thick in the air. Stone followed him into the front room.

There was a man sitting on the sofa next to a young woman. He was wearing a T-shirt and a pair of ripped jeans. His arms were covered in tattoos and scabs, and he was smoking a joint. The girl sitting next to him was wearing jeans too, and what looked like a man's shirt. She'd rolled up the hem, exposing her pierced navel and she had tied the shirt together, like girls used to do in the sixties.

She glanced at Stone and quickly looked away, gnawing at her thumb, the nail bitten down to the quick.

"Hey, Kkayla, this is, uh," he glanced back at Stone, his gaze vacant, slightly befuddled, "this is Isaac's dad. Isaac was, uh . . ."

"Don't be an idiot, Mick, I know," the girl said, still gnawing on her thumb.

The room was stiflingly hot. Stone spotted a portable, electric radiator, plugged in at the wall. Who was paying the electricity bill?

"Who's this?" Stone said, pointing at the tattooed man sitting next to Kkayla. He was holding his breath, letting the smoke from his joint dribble slowly out of his nostrils, and he had his eyes closed. Stone had to fight the urge to kick him in the head.

That would get his attention.

It would also be counterproductive.

"That's Shem," Mick said. He had his hand down his boxers now, furiously scratching at his balls. "Just, like, pretend he's not here, y'know. Ah, fuck."

He pulled his hand out of his boxers and inspected his fingers. The nails were tipped with blood, and pubic hairs.

"Tell me what you know," Stone said, turning to Kkayla.

The girl didn't look up, just kept on gnawing at her thumb.

"Hey, blondie, tell the man what he wants to know and then he can, like, fuck off out of here, y'know." Mick glanced at Stone. "After he's given us the fucking reward money."

Kkayla muttered something.

"What'd you say?" Mick said.

Kkayla looked up at him, lank strands of hair hanging over her face. "I said you never should have called him. I told you I was scared, I never should have told you, I don't want the fucking money."

"You stupid cow," Mick said, taking a step towards her.

Stone grabbed Mick, his hand almost encircling his skinny arm, and yanked him away from Kkayla.

"Ow! Fuck!" Mick yelled, struggling to pull away.

Stone smiled at Mick, and let go of his arm.

"Let me talk to her," he said. "You're scaring her."

Stone walked a little closer to the girl on the couch and squatted down in front of her.

"Are these two pricks your friends?"

Kkayla shook her head. "No, not really. We're just sharing this place. I've got nowhere else to go."

"Did you really know Isaac?"

She kept gnawing at her thumb, her teeth working away at a piece of loose nail and skin. Now that Stone was up close, he noticed something odd about her teeth. The biting surfaces were irregular, almost serrated. Sharp.

"Yeah," she said softly. "We lived in a flat in Birmingham for a while. Jet, uh, Isaac, was cool. He treated me nice."

Stone remembered now. The police had said something about Isaac possibly being part of a heavy metal cult that liked to pretend they were vampires. And some of them filed their teeth down to points. For a day or two, before they gave up on the investigation altogether, they had tried connecting his murder with the Birmingham Vampire killings.

But that had gone nowhere.

"Did you see who killed him?" Stone said.

Kkayla kept biting her thumb, avoiding Stone's gaze. Gently, he reached up and held her wrist, pulling her hand away from her mouth.

"Did you see him?"

"Yes," Kkayla whispered.

"Who was it?" Stone said. "Who killed my son?"

"It was Joe Coffin," the girl whispered, her voice barely audible. "There were two of them, and Joe Coffin looked angry, I've never been so scared by anyone before. And he took one look at me and told me to get out, and I was scared, and I ran. But I stopped a little way down the hall. I didn't know what to do, and then . . . and then I heard a gunshot, and I just turned and ran again."

"Are you sure it was Coffin?"

Kkayla nodded.

Stone let go of her wrist, and she started gnawing at her thumb again.

"Fuck, yeah," Mick said. "We get the fucking money now, right? Like, y'know, the reward, it's ours, yeah?"

Shem finally opened his eyes, looking groggily up at Stone, and then Mick.

"Did the stupid cow tell him?" he said, his voice thick and slurred.

Stone stood up.

Mick giggled. "She told him all right. Ten thousand quid, yeah? Oh fuck. We are fucking rich!"

"Don't be an idiot," Stone said. "Do you seriously think for one moment that I would give you that money?"

Mick's mouth dropped open. "What?"

"Look at you. You're scum. You're a leech, sucking the lifeblood out of this country, out of the people who do a decent day's work, just so that you can fuck your body up with the shit you shovel into it."

"No way, you said you was gonna pay us. We told you what you wanted to know, you should give us the fucking reward!"

"You told me nothing," Stone said. "You took what she told you, and betrayed her."

"So what the fuck do you care?" Mick shouted, spittle flying from his lips. "You wanted to know who killed your son, well now you know. Give us the fucking money."

Shem climbed unsteadily to his feet. "Give the man his fucking money, yeah?"

Stone planted his hand against Shem's chest and pushed him back down onto the tatty sofa.

"Fuck this," Mick muttered, and turned around and stalked into the kitchen.

Stone had an idea what he was going to do and strode after him. In the dark, greasy kitchen, Mick had pulled open a drawer under the kitchen counter. He pulled out a carving knife. He still had his back to Stone, his spine sticking out prominently from between sharp shoulder blades.

Stone grabbed Mick's wrist and squeezed hard. He yelled and dropped the knife in the sink. Stone planted his free hand against the back of Mick's head and shoved his face into the crockery and the cold, dirty water in the sink. Stone twisted his arm behind and up his back, until Mick screamed, bubbles of air frothing up through the greasy water.

Stone increased the pressure on Mick's arm with a sharp, upward twist, and heard the snap in his shoulder joint, and felt his arm go limp. Mick screamed louder, coughing as he sucked in dirty dishwater.

Stone let go of him and stepped back. Mick slid to the floor, crying and holding his injured arm. Dirty dishwater dripped from his hair and beard as he coughed and retched.

"You broke my fucking arm!" he sobbed.

"No, I didn't," Stone replied. "I dislocated your shoulder. Get yourself to a hospital, they can pop it back into place for you. Getting dressed is going to hurt like a bastard, though."

When Stone turned around, he saw Shem standing in the kitchen doorway, wide eyed and alert at last.

"You want some of the same?" Stone said.

Shem shook his head.

"Then get the hell out of my sight."

Shem ran past him, and out of the back door.

Stone walked back into the front room. Kkayla was sitting on the sofa still, her legs folded up in front of her, arms wrapped around them. Her wide eyes never left Stone as he approached her.

"Don't worry, I'm not going to hurt you," he said.

"You going to give me the money?" she said.

"No." Stone pulled a roll of bills from his pocket, and took the elastic band off. "Not the ten thousand."

He unrolled the money, wet his thumb, and counted out a series of twenty pound notes. He placed the money on the sofa seat, next to the girl.

"You've got a choice now," he said. "You can use that money to buy yourself a hot meal and a drink, and you could buy yourself a train ticket and move on, somewhere new where you're not surrounded by idiots who like to inject poison into their veins. You could get yourself some help, get cleaned up, become a productive member of society. Or you could use that money to buy yourself some more shit to fuck yourself up with. I don't care what you do."

Kkayla's round, wide eyes flicked from Stone to the money lying next to her, and then back again.

Stone sighed, and peeled off a few more twenties and added them to the rest.

"Did Isaac treat you well?" he said.

Kkayla nodded. "Yeah. He was cool."

"Don't waste this opportunity," Stone said. "You won't get another. Blow this money on drugs, my guess is you'll be dead this time next year."

Stone left the house by the back door, walking past Mick still lying on his side on the floor, cradling his arm and whimpering. He walked back down the garden path and along the road to his car, his breath floating from his mouth and away over his shoulder in white streams.

The car bipped, and the lights flashed once, as he unlocked it. He pulled open the door, sat in the driver's seat, and slammed the door shut.

"Did she confirm it?" Lucy said, sitting in the passenger seat, her gaze fixed on Stone. "Did Joe Coffin murder our son?"

"Yeah."

"You gave her money, didn't you?" Lucy said.

"Yeah," Stone said again, staring ahead out of the windscreen.

"How much?"

"Not enough."

"How much?"

"Does it matter?"

Lucy shook her head. "Sometimes I wonder if you have the stomach for this."

"For what?"

"Finding our son's murderer."

"What does that have to do with giving some crackhead a little cash?"

"It shows you're growing soft. Can you still do this? Do you have the stomach for it?"

"Of course I do," Stone replied, turning on the engine.

"Good," Lucy said.

She put a cigarette in her mouth, and lit it. "Let's get out of this shit hole then, and find Coffin, and kill the bastard."

EPISODE
SIX

an article of faith

Couldn't somebody stop that baby crying? Listening to it squealing and wailing, its endless screaming, was torture. Leola Cruciele could hear the mother trying to calm it, singing to it in a soft, trembling voice. Desperate for it to hush, to be quiet. But on and on it cried, sometimes pausing as it took a few hitching breaths before launching into a renewed bout of screaming.

Leola was going to have to kill that baby soon, just to get it to shut up. But then she would have to kill the mother too.

And right now she simply couldn't be bothered to do either.

Leola was lying on her back, on the ballroom floor. The dark oak floorboards had been varnished and polished so that they were almost like mirrors, but the effect was ruined by the pools of blood and the bodies.

Hanging from the ceiling, hundreds of candles in crystal chandeliers still sputtered and burned. Hundreds more candles in silver candelabras lined the perimeter of the expansive ballroom.

It had looked lovely when they first arrived. All the men and the women in their finery swaying gracefully across the dance floor, and bathed in the soft, warm light of all those candles.

It had almost seemed a sin to kill everyone.

Leola lifted a hand and wiped it across her mouth, leaving a streak of red across her cheek. The dress was ruined, the fine silk and embroidery sodden with blood. A shame, because Leola had enjoyed wearing it. She had been giddy with delight as she had cavorted around the ballroom, the skirts swishing over the floor as she twirled and danced between all the corpses while Guttman watched her.

How sad that they had to murder the members of the orchestra. They had played so beautifully whilst Leola had danced and danced. They had stared at her with eyes wide open in terror, fingers automatically plucking at strings, or dancing across the ivory keys. Such skill, such talent, to be able to play so wonderfully, even when surrounded by blood and death.

But now the orchestra was dead too. Guttman had grown tired of their playing, and he and the others had fallen upon the men in their fancy suits and ripped them apart. Their blood had sprayed over the stained glass windows, and the portraits of the Lord and Lady and their ancestors hanging from the walls of the ballroom.

And what a dreadful shrieking they had made. Afterwards, once his bloodlust had been sated, Guttman remarked that the orchestra's screaming and wailing had been more musical to his ears than their atrocious playing.

Leola didn't agree. She had loved the music, would have listened and danced to it all night if she could. But she kept this opinion to herself. Over the decades she had spent with Guttman travelling across Europe, and then to the Americas, she had learnt never to disagree with him. Guttman was a wonderful, physical lover, and it was because of him that she was now going to live forever. But he would fly into a terrible rage if he ever thought anyone of his rag tag band of followers was disagreeing with him.

Phillipe had made that mistake. Of all of them, he should have known better. Phillipe and Guttman had been together longer than the rest. Like Guttman, he could not remember a time when he wasn't a vampire. For these two men it was as if they had been born undead, that there had never been a time when they were human. As such they were regarded as the natural leaders of the group, and everyone else looked to them for guidance and decision making.

And Guttman had shared his bed with Phillipe too. Once, when Leola had discovered the two men naked and locked in a sexual embrace, Leola had disrobed and attempted to join in. But Guttman had turned on her, growling and hissing, and she had fled.

Up until that day when Phillipe had suggested an alternative course of action to Guttman's, when it had seemed that he was suggesting they flee instead of fight, there had never been a disagreement between the two vampires. But once there was, neither of them would back down until finally they fought. Guttman was the stronger man, and he quickly ripped his friend apart in a frenzy of splattered blood and torn flesh.

Guttman drank his friend's blood, and smeared it through his hair and over his face and hands. Then he ripped Phillipe's chest open and plunged his hands inside and pulled out his heart. Guttman held the dripping heart out in front of him at arm's length, and snarled at his followers that he was their leader now, nobody else.

And he would be their leader forever, or until somebody defied him and ripped his heart out of his chest.

Leola stirred as the baby started up another round of screaming. She hadn't realised it had quietened down, or that she had fallen into a slumber. The fabric of the dress made sucking noises pulling away from the sticky floor as Leola pushed herself up to a sitting position. Her companions lay in scattered groups around the ballroom, sleeping off the excesses of the last few hours. Lying amongst them were the carcasses of the men and women who had been attending the party.

The baby screamed.

Why had they left the mother and her child alive? Had there been a reason? Or had they all just reached their fill of blood?

Leola stood up, her bare feet sticking to the floor. Carefully stepping over dead bodies and the slumbering forms of her companions, Leola followed the source of the baby's cries. Even Guttman was asleep on the floor, his hand resting on the naked breast of a young girl lying next to him. Her throat had been ripped open so deep and wide that she had almost been decapitated.

Leola idly wondered why the mother hadn't taken the opportunity to escape. She could have run into the night with her child, following the road into the nearest town where she could have got help. The townsfolk might even have returned to the mansion with guns and swords, and pitchforks and crosses, and cloves of garlic.

Thankfully for the townsfolk, that wasn't going to happen.

Leola found the Creole serving girl in the hall. She was young, fifteen maybe, and the baby obviously wasn't hers, its white skin a shocking contrast to her coffee coloured flesh. The girl was naked. Her breasts were criss-crossed with bloody slashes and both her ankles had been broken, her feet twisted out at ugly angles from her legs.

Tears spilled from her large, round eyes as she watched Leola approach. Her lips quivered and moved, as she recited a chant or a prayer to herself. The baby writhed in her arms as she clutched it tight, trying to stifle its cries by placing a hand over its mouth.

Leola put a finger to her mouth.

Ssshhhhh.

The baby cried even louder, its tiny fists waving frantically as it tried to free itself of the young girl's embrace.

"Shut it up," Leola said. "Make it stop."

The young Creole girl hugged the baby to her chest, pushing its face into her breasts. But the child twisted its head from side to side, smearing the young girl's blood across its face and crying even harder and louder. Each scream pierced Leola's head, driving spikes through it and surely sending her mad if she stood here and listened to much more.

In one sudden, swift move, Leola snatched the wriggling child from the young woman's grasp. It screamed, wriggling in her hands slick with blood. The baby almost slipped from her grasp, but Leola squeezed her fingers into its soft flesh. Its ribs snapped beneath the pressure, and the baby let out a howl of agony.

Leola sank her teeth into its throat. Arterial blood sprayed from the baby's neck, splashing the walls and over the young Creole girl. Then she ripped a chunk of flesh from the baby's neck and spat it across the room, where it landed with a wet splat on the tiled floor.

Now, at last, the baby was silent.

Watching the young woman on the floor crying, Leola lifted the limp child's body over her head, and then dropped it into her lap.

Leola snapped awake, trembling and hot, the coppery taste of blood in her mouth.

A band of yellow light travelled across the ceiling as a lorry rumbled past outside. Within a moment the light had disappeared, swallowed up by the ever present darkness. Leola sat up in the single bed, the mattress lumpy and sagging. The tiny room was reminiscent of the tomb she had awoken in, all those hundreds of years ago.

When she switched on the bedside lamp, its pale glow battled weakly to illuminate her surroundings. The bedside clock told her the time: 3.00 a.m. But she needn't have bothered looking. The nightmare always came to her in the darkest hours of the morning, when it seemed she hovered between her previous life and this one.

Not a nightmare, really, but a memory of a long time ago. That other life. The centuries she had spent travelling with Guttman and his loyal band of followers. Sweeping through villages and towns and cities, visiting death upon the innocents.

Once she had been a young girl, and then Guttman had visited her in the night. And he had kissed her and 'blessed' her with eternal life. That had been her first rebirth, born again into a new life. Leola and Guttman had been lovers for years after that, until he grew old, and she watched as he was buried in a coffin full of blood.

And then Leola met the Priest. And just like Guttman had birthed her into a new existence, the Priest dragged her bloody and screaming into another life.

Your new life is an article of faith, the Priest had said. *You have been reborn in Christ, you are of God the Father, and you are filled with the Holy Ghost. But watch out that the serpent does not fill you with his lies, and entice you back into a life of sin and bloodlust.*

After her second rebirth, the Priest had told her that one day all flesh would end, and that she would be transformed into a new being, and come face to face with her Lord.

But Leola knew that wasn't going to happen. The Priest might have absolved her of sin, he might have cast out the evil that had lived within her, but he hadn't cured her of her essential vampirism.

Of her immortality.

Leola climbed out of the lumpy bed and stretched, the cool night air tingling her naked skin. What she needed right now was company, another naked human form nestling in bed with her. Male or female, it didn't matter. Switching on the bedside lamp, she noticed the business card.

Garrett Stone. Consultant, Defence Sector.

She wasn't sure why she had kept the business card, carrying it with her from the airport hotel where they had fucked and then to this dismal boarding room in Birmingham. Was it simply because she hoped to meet him again? More anonymous sex in an anonymous room somewhere?

Maybe she should call him now. Ask him to come over.

But then she remembered he was married.

And unless he had a particularly open relationship with his wife, Leola couldn't see Stone agreeing to come out here in the middle of the night to fuck another woman.

Leola returned to the bed and lay down on top of the covers. Her gaze wandered over the pattern of swirls in the ceiling, caked brown from all the years of cigarette smoke that had filled this room.

Maybe in a day or two she would call Stone. There was too much to think about at the moment, to be distracted by physical pleasures, as tempting as that might be.

Leola closed her eyes, trying to shut out the sensations of the night. The scuttling of the rats and the mice, the cats prowling through the overgrown back gardens looking for victims, the presence of life and death surrounding her like an oppressive blanket.

And always the temptation to give in to the call of the night and to join in with the hunt.

Leola lay naked on the bed, her eyes closed, and waited for the daylight.

joe coffin for mayor

Joe Coffin sat on the edge of his bed and watched the news on the old, portable black and white television. Perched on the top of a faded dressing table it looked like something out of an antique shop. The Birmingham Vampire was headline news, and Joe Coffin wasn't far behind. The police were anxious to track him down and question him about the previous night's events.

I'll bet, thought Coffin.

DCI Archer had, apparently, not regained consciousness yet after his encounter with the man the newspapers were now calling Birmingham's most notorious serial killer. According to the hospital, Archer was in a stable condition, but very poorly after losing a lot of blood from multiple lacerations all over his body.

There were also unconfirmed reports that he had been found wearing his own handcuffs.

Coffin chuckled at that.

Archer had to have been conscious long enough at some point, though, to be able to give his colleagues even a garbled account of what had happened last night. Emma and her boyfriend were the only ones to have seen Coffin, and he doubted that Emma would have talked despite how upset she had been.

The fire at No. 99 Forde road had been extinguished before spreading to the neighbouring houses. The ground floor had been completely burnt out, and much of the upstairs had suffered too. Due to the horrors that had been perpetrated there in recent weeks, and the fire damage, a decision was expected to tear the remains of the house down and sell the land on for development.

Mortenson's burnt remains had been found in the pit in the cellar, but no one was sticking their neck out to confirm that it was the Birmingham Vampire. All the police were saying was that they had found the charred remains of a body which had been cut up into pieces. Other than that, until the pathology results came back, they could say nothing else.

The BBC had sent a reporter out onto the city's streets to interview people about Coffin's alleged involvement in last night's events. Assuming that Coffin had killed the Birmingham Vampire, the reporter wanted to know, was Joe Coffin a hero now?

"Of course he isn't," one old lady said. "For all we know the two of them were working together, and they had a falling out."

"Oh, man, like Coffin was already my hero, man," one black kid said, his friends milling around behind him, giggling and gurning for the camera. "They should, like, put up a statue for him, make the dude mayor or something."

"Right on, brother," Coffin said.

He was surprised that there was no mention of Emma Wylde, but that at least confirmed his thoughts that she had not been the one to mention his involvement.

She had to have got out of there quick, before the cops turned up and found Archer and the Carter girl's body. He thought she would have stayed with her boyfriend, waited with him until they were found and gone with him to hospital. Maybe she did, but it just wasn't being mentioned on the news report. Or maybe she thought about how deep she had become involved, and decided her best option was to take after Coffin's example and scarper.

Too many questions unanswered.

Like, for example, what the hell Emma had been doing in his house when Stump and Corpse turned up. Had she been looking for him? But if that was the case why the hell did she need to break in and search his house? And if she had been searching his house, what the hell was she looking for?

Coffin picked up his mobile. He scrolled through the contacts until he found Emma's number. He was about to tap the green telephone icon when he heard the news reader mention the Birmingham Vampire again, in connection with some breaking news.

Coffin dropped his mobile on the bed.

There had been another killing in the park by the cemetery, where the old homeless man had been found last week. The body, ripped apart and lying in a congealed pool of blood, had been discovered early this morning by a jogger. There were unconfirmed reports that the corpse was missing its tongue.

Wayne Davies had been reported missing by his girlfriend last night. He had been out walking their two dogs and never returned. The police were remaining silent at the moment on the possibility that the corpse was Davies, but had said they found no dogs at the scene.

The news had broken too late for the daily papers to latch onto it, but by tomorrow every front page headline would be screaming the news that the Birmingham Vampire was back.

But they would be wrong.

Michael.

It had to be. Mortenson was dead, there wasn't a chance in hell that even he could have come back from the dead after being sawn into several pieces and burnt to a crisp. Besides which, the police had the remains now, all bagged up separately and being inspected for DNA identification.

Still, Coffin had to shove the thought away that it might be Mortenson.

Maybe it had been Steffanie, or one of the others.

But Coffin didn't think so. Steffanie was too cunning, too clever to risk being caught. Especially now. She would know that Craggs wanted his club back, that Coffin would be returning again and this time with more than two jokers and some pop guns.

No. It had to be Michael, on his own, out hunting. Had he returned to the cemetery, where he had been buried? Did he see that as a safe space, a home of some kind?

Possibly. That was where he had woken up, transformed into a creature that he couldn't possibly understand. His four year old mind was too young, too immature to be able to process what was happening to him. Hell, Coffin couldn't understand it himself.

So he would be scared and confused, perhaps seeking safety and comfort of some kind. Coffin wondered if he had any memory of his previous life, of being a normal four year old boy. Could he remember his father and his mother?

Coffin stood up and switched off the television. Crossed the tiny bedroom in a couple of steps and stood by the window. The room was warm and Coffin was wearing his usual outfit of black jeans and white T shirt. Outside was different. Men and women hurried past, wrapped up in overcoats and scarves. The wind was strong enough that it disturbed the water in the canal, creating little ripples along its surface.

After the war council, Coffin had gone to bed and slept the night through. He realised now, that was a big mistake. He should have been out looking for his son, not lying in bed, sleeping.

Coffin picked up his mobile and activated it, the screen coming to life. Emma Wylde's number still on the display.

Maybe she could help find Michael.

She had seen him, she knew what he was capable of.

The police didn't have a clue. They might even think they were still hunting for the Birmingham Vampire, or they might assume they were now after a copycat killer.

Emma, though, she had seen Mortenson's remains consumed by fire, and she had seen Michael.

And she was possibly the only one who would agree to help look for him, and protect him.

Coffin tapped the telephone icon with his thumb, and placed the mobile to his ear.

* * *

Emma closed the browser window on her iMac and leaned back in her chair. Fuelled by coffee and adrenalin she had been up most of the night, reading books on vampire mythology and chasing internet leads down virtual rabbit holes.

Part of her reluctance to sleep had been down to fear. Vampires slept during the day and came alive at night. The darkness was their hunting ground, their friend and ally. Emma was beginning to think it might be a good idea if she became nocturnal too. After all, how much more helpless could a person be than when they were curled up in bed fast asleep? But if she slept in the day and used the night time hours to investigate and work, she would be ready for an attack.

The printer finished rolling out the last of her sheets of notes and fell quiet. Emma picked up the thick wad of paper in one hand, her coffee in the other, and left Nick's office. She walked into the living room where she sat down on the sofa.

The sheets of notes were a mixture of documentation on vampires and some local history. At some point in the night, her eyes bleary from staring at a computer screen for so long, it had occurred to Emma that the house on Forde Road might be of more significance than anyone had realised so far.

So she went onto numerous local history sites, clicking through page after page of Birmingham history, until finally she found an archived newspaper article from November 1888, concerning a series of disappearances of young girls in the local area.

Now Emma curled up on the sofa and searched through her notes until she found the newspaper article.

Another Missing Girl.
John Rawdon, of Bletchley Street, reported his daughter missing to the police late last night.

Mr Rawdon, who has a history of drunken behaviour and disturbing the peace, and a record of beating his wife and daughter, was held for questioning by the police overnight.

Mary Rawdon, aged fifteen, was reported to have not returned home yesterday evening, after her shift in the factory. Her mother, Elizabeth, said that her daughter was a quiet, dutiful girl, and always came home promptly after work, and never caused any trouble.

Mary Rawdon is the seventh girl to have gone missing in the Birmingham area in the last year. Speculation has been rife that Jack the Ripper has moved up to Birmingham from London because the police were closing in on him. Unable to resist his urge to kill, he has now begun a reign of murderous terror in Birmingham.

The police are trying to quell these fears, and have pointed out that, although it is true that the Ripper killings have ceased in London, Birmingham constabulary is still dealing with missing cases, rather than murders. All the girls have been aged between fifteen and twenty-one, and none of them have the reputation associated with the victims of 'Saucy Jack', but are respectable, and in some cases, church going young women.

John Rawdon was released from police custody without charge, and the hunt for the missing young women continues.

Emma put the sheet of paper down. She had been unable to find any more references to this story, but there were huge gaps in the archive of local papers she had found. Neither had there been any reference to No. 99 Forde Road, but John and Elizabeth had lived on Bletchley Street, which was only a couple of streets away.

What could the connection be? Was she grasping at straws here? Tom Mills had explained how he had met Abel Mortenson, but he had mentioned nothing about the house and why they were there. Had Tom led Abel there? No. 99 had been empty for decades, so it would be a natural choice for someone local, if he needed a place to hide out in.

But why had there been a great big hole dug in the cellar? Had Abel done that? Or Tom? What about the old man they took everywhere with them? Had he arrived with Abel, or had he been living at No. 99 all along?

And why had the house been empty all these years? Empty houses were being bought up by developers all the time, and either torn down or renovated. How had No. 99 escaped such a fate? Had it been placed in some kind of trust, perhaps? Or had it been protected, like a listed building?

Emma made a note to contact an estate agents, see how she could find out who actually owned the house, and what had happened to the owners.

She also needed to think about how she was going to write up the Birmingham

Vampire story, without implicating herself too much in it. Karl would want something given to him today, or else he was going to give the story back to Barry. Or if Barry didn't want it, Karl might even decide to write it up himself. Whatever he decided, one outcome was certain: Emma would be off the story again, and possibly off the newspaper too.

If only Joe Coffin would get in touch she could tell him about Angels, and the mysterious individual who had answered the door to the police.

Emma's mobile buzzed, the screen glowing with sudden, urgent life. It was Coffin, it had to be, he was getting in touch at last, replying to all those messages she had left him. But when she picked up her phone, she didn't recognise the number.

"Hello?" she said.

"Is this Emma Wylde?" a female voice said.

"Yes."

"My name is Leola Cruciele, and I think we need to talk. Can I meet with you this morning?"

Emma uncurled herself off the sofa and sat up straight. "That depends. I'm very busy at the moment, I can't just drop everything to meet every stranger who calls me. What did you want to talk about?"

"The Birmingham Vampire, or Abel Mortenson as he was really known."

"Where do you want to meet?" Emma said.

the good, the bad, and the ugly

That bloody phone was ringing again. Bloody theme tune to *The Good, The Bad, and The Ugly*, playing over and over again. Surely the battery should have drained by now? Every fucking mobile that Frankie Shaddock had owned never lasted longer than a day before the thing was dead.

But not this one. It had started up ringing not long after Steffanie let Shaddock loose and brought him upstairs to meet the rest of the horror show. There was that cadaverous old man, for starters, looked like he'd been dug out of the ground only moments ago. He kept stumbling around the club, picking stuff up and looking at it like he'd never seen any of this crap before.

He was the one with the mobile that kept going off. Shaddock seriously doubted it ever belonged to him, he didn't even seem to know what the hell it was let alone how to use it. He carried it around with him in his suit pocket and jumped every time the damn thing started whistling that melody. Would have been funny if it wasn't so damn horrific.

Every single time, he pulled it out of his pocket and looked at the glowing screen in amazement and turned it over and over in his hands. Shaddock swore he even saw him sniffing the damn thing a couple of times. Like he'd never seen a mobile phone before in his life.

Fucking hell, it was obvious to Shaddock now that Steffanie and her gang were dead all right, just like she said. Dead, but up and about. Walking and talking animated corpses.

But Steffanie and the old man, they were the true horror shows of this party, even though the rest of them weren't exactly a beauty parade.

Steffanie with those holes in her head, and an empty socket where her eye should have been, scared the shit out of Shaddock every time she looked at him. It didn't help none that she was wearing one of Craggs' suits, either. Yesterday in the cellar, she'd been right when she accused him of leching after her all those years. Shaddock had seen her dancing, plenty. Moved like a fucking tiger in heat, wearing nothing but a G-String and that *fuck me* look that she could turn on you in an instant.

Even now with the left side of her face ripped apart by a bullet, Shaddock sometimes got himself a boner when she looked at him. But then his stomach rolled over in that queasy way and before he knew it he was wilting again, and he was sickened to the very core of his being.

Then there was that stupid little girl, Velvina. That bitch always thought she was something special, just because Craggs used to let her into his office sometimes to suck him off. She was wandering around the club now, looking like she owned the place. Except when Steffanie was around, and then it was obvious who the boss lady was.

Velvina had a necklace he'd never noticed before. Not that he had ever been much good at noticing what women were wearing, he'd always been more interested in imagining what they looked like when they weren't wearing anything at all. But this necklace, it was unusual and nasty. Shaddock hadn't had a good look at it, but he was reasonably sure that it was a finger bone hanging from her neck. And he was just as sure that there were still tiny scraps of blackened flesh attached to it.

Addison was here too, a gaping wound still open in his throat. But he was up and about and wearing his uniform, cleaning behind the bar, stocking it up. Reminded Shaddock of the dead bartender in that movie, *The Shining*. Addison didn't seem interested in much, other than working at getting the place looking nice again, like they were planning on reopening.

But worst of all was that fucking black kid, Clevon. He was the only one without a wound to his neck. Shaddock couldn't work it out. It was obvious that Clevon was dead, that he was a vampire with the rest of them. But they'd all had their throats ripped out at some point, except the old man. Even on Steffanie, Shaddock could see the faint crisscross of scarring, where her throat had been ripped open.

But Clevon? He didn't have a mark on him. Not that Shaddock could see, anyway.

No question that he was a blood sucking monster along with the others, though. He had that dead look in his eyes and that unsettling way in which they all moved. As though their muscles weren't powered by tiny electrical impulses from their nerve endings, but something else. Something beyond Shaddock's understanding.

Clevon might have been dead, but it was clear he still remembered Shaddock.

Every time Clevon turned those lifeless eyes on him, Shaddock could see the murderous blood lust in them; that desire to pounce on him and rip him apart. If Steffanie hadn't been around and in charge, Shaddock knew he'd be a dead man by now.

Or undead.

And then there was that other kid wandering around the club, stumbling into the tables and chairs, his throat a mass of ripped tissue. Shaddock recognised him from Edwards No. 9, but he couldn't remember his name. The others laughed at him, and sometimes Clevon pushed him over just for the hell of it, to see him hit the ground with a wet slap and then struggle back to his feet. Sometimes Velvina shimmied up to him and groped him, but he never seemed to notice. He had a permanently stunned expression on his face, as though he had been suddenly awoken from a deep sleep and didn't know what the hell was going on.

Shaddock knew how he felt.

Steffanie hadn't told Shaddock why she wanted to keep him alive, but he was sure it wasn't out of the kindness of her heart. He had free reign of the club as far as he could tell. No one had prevented him from going upstairs, or anywhere else he wanted. Not even Clevon.

But he wasn't allowed outside. There was always someone keeping an eye on him. Usually Clevon or sometimes Velvina, with her finger necklace dangling in her cleavage and her thumb in her mouth. She'd layered thick mascara on her eyelashes this morning and kept batting her eyes at Shaddock. Looked like nothing more than a zombified Betty Boop.

Even alive, Steffanie had been a cold, calculating bitch. That big, stupid bastard Coffin had been too besotted with her to see it but it was obvious to most everybody else. Or maybe he hadn't been that stupid, maybe he had known, but decided to ignore it. After all, he got to jump her bones every fucking night so who wouldn't put up with her being an ice queen the rest of the time?

Now that Steffanie was dead she was colder, even more calculating, than Shaddock had thought possible.

When they brought that first body down into the cellar earlier this morning, while it was still dark, Shaddock had a sudden inkling of what they were going to ask him to do. What Steffanie's plan was in keeping him alive.

The man was obviously homeless. His large, grey beard didn't appear to have been trimmed in decades, and his long hair was roughly tied back in a ponytail. Shaddock guessed he was in his sixties, but it was hard to tell with some of these people. They lived such a hard life, some of them turned out to be a lot younger than they looked.

He stank of piss, and his threadbare trousers and ripped parka looked as if they hadn't been washed this century.

The perfect victim for a vampire desperate for blood, but equally desperate to remain hidden. Hardly anyone would miss this man, and even those few that did would simply assume he had moved on, or died.

The fact that he was still alive was the most startling aspect of his appearance in the cellar.

And that he appeared to have no wounds on him, no blood pouring from a gash in his throat.

Clevon and Addison cleared a space in the cellar and lay him down, under Steffanie's watchful gaze. She knelt down beside him and pulled open his ripped coat. Shaddock watched her, noticing the lack of disgust that would have been clear on her expression if she had been that close to the stinking old man when she was still alive. Did vampires have a sense of smell? Or maybe when you were dead no smell, or sight, or taste, was as revolting as yourself.

The old man was wearing layers of tatty clothing under his coat, and Steffanie pulled each one apart until she exposed his wasted chest. His ribs were painfully prominent under the harsh glow of the bare bulbs illuminating the cellar.

Steffanie ran her hand down his chest, falling and rising slowly with each breath he took.

She looked up at Shaddock.

"It's your job now to keep him alive."

Go fuck yourself, you cold fucking bitch, Shaddock wanted to say.

"Why?"

"Because I am telling you to."

Shaddock wrenched his gaze from Steffanie and looked at Clevon and Addison. They were both staring at him, Clevon with that murderous look in his dark eyes.

Stupid fucking question, wasn't it? Steffanie could ask him to perform a naked jig, with his thumb up his arse while grinning like a loon, and he would jump to it. He had no other options. He wanted to stay alive.

Besides, he thought he already knew the answer to his question. And if he was right, there would most likely be another living body down here by tomorrow morning, and then another and another. And Steffanie would tell him the same thing each time.

It's your job now to keep him alive.

Because she was building up a stock of farm animals for herself and her vampire companions. A steady supply of fresh, warm blood, without the need to go outside hunting every night and risking capture, or death.

Shaddock had no idea what Steffanie's plans were, but it seemed to him that she was intending on making Angels hers, that she was going to be staying here for a long time.

That suited Shaddock just fine. Mortimer Craggs would be wanting his club back. Even if he didn't care about this place he would still want it back, if only because nobody stole from Craggs and lived to tell the tale. Even now he was probably plotting an assault on the club.

Which meant Shaddock might just have a chance of escaping this fucking mess alive, after all.

Once Clevon had tied the homeless man up, they left him in the cellar and returned to the club. Shaddock shuffled up the stairs with the rest of them, feeling for all the world like one of the undead himself.

Velvina lay on her back on a table, holding her hands up above her head and twirling them around in random patterns whilst she softly sang to herself. The other vampire, the one Shaddock recognised from Edwards No. 9, sat slumped in a chair. He had ripped open a hole in his wrist and was sucking greedily at the wound, but there was only a tiny seepage of blood.

Shaddock flinched, jumped like a little child in a haunted funhouse.

The old man in his stained, filthy burial suit, was staring intently at the mobile in his hand. It was glowing, and ringing again, the haunting, Ennio Moriccone refrain playing over and over.

Shaddock's irritation at the ringtone suddenly boiled over into anger. He rushed over to the old man and snatched the mobile from his clawed grasp.

He lifted the mobile, ready to fling it across the club and dash it to pieces, silence it forever, when a thought occurred to him.

Answer it! Answer the fucking thing, scream for help.

Shaddock's thumb tapped the connect icon just as the old man grabbed him by the wrist, his blackened teeth bared in a snarl. His grip was icy cold and strong. Shaddock cried out in pain and let go of the mobile.

It dropped to the floor, and the back popped off and the screen cracked. But it was still working and Shaddock could hear a voice squawking from it. Holding onto Shaddock's wrist, the old man looked down at the broken mobile, almost as though he expected it to jump up and walk as well as talk.

"Hello? Mr Mills? Hello?"

The voice was silenced as Steffanie placed her foot over the phone, and ground it into the floor under her heel.

She prised the old man's fingers from Shaddock's wrist and separated the two men, pushing Shaddock away. He stumbled and then righted himself. He sat down at a table, his hands shaking.

Had that been Tom's phone? Was he dead? But if the vampires had killed him, why wasn't he here now, with the rest of them?

And that voice on the phone. Shaddock wasn't entirely sure, but the man asking for Tom, insistent and demanding, he had sounded Chinese.

And for Shaddock that meant only one thing.

Triads.

he's a pussycat

Emma drove along Hagley Road in her hire car, the interior still smelling of polish and cleaning materials. The garage had phoned to say her Fiesta was repaired and ready for collection, but Emma wasn't too keen to return to the fog of old pizza and spilt milk that was her constant companion in her car. This one drove smooth and quiet, and the windscreen wipers didn't judder loudly across the glass during even the heaviest of rain.

Just a couple of hours more, and then she would return it.

Leola Cruciele had suggested they meet outside No. 99, but Emma had vetoed that idea immediately. Emma wasn't ready to go back to that house of horrors just yet.

If ever.

Besides, there might still be some limited police presence around the house and Emma didn't want to be asked any awkward questions. The other problem was, Emma knew nothing about this woman. At least Leola was happy to meet in daylight, outside and not in a darkened cellar somewhere at midnight. Emma was guessing that she wasn't a vampire.

But that didn't mean she wasn't suspicious.

Emma suggested they meet at a cafe she knew. The cafe was actually a caravan parked in a layby, on the edge of the city's limits. Leola protested, asking how would she get there, she was unfamiliar with Birmingham, and what about transport.

But Emma held firm.

You'll find it, she had said. *Just find yourself a taxi, and ask them to take you to Eddie's Burgers. They'll know where to go.*

As soon as she had finished her call with Leola, her mobile had sprung to life again. This time it was Joe Coffin.

"Where the hell have you been?" she said. "I've been trying to get hold of you."

"I went for a dip in the canal, remember?" Coffin replied. "My phone died on me."

"And it took you this long to think about calling me?"

"I've been busy. I don't know if you noticed, you being a reporter and all, but I'm all over the news right now."

"You know what, it hadn't escaped my attention. It seems the police think you're a bigger threat to world civilisation than an outbreak of Ebola, while most everybody else considers you a hero."

On the other end of the phone, Coffin grunted. "It's enough to give a person an identity crisis. Hero or villain, what do you think?"

An image of Coffin standing on the deck of the narrowboat, holding the Samurai sword and looking ready to plunge it into Nick's chest sprang into her mind.

"I don't know," she said. "I haven't made up my mind yet."

"Would it help if I gave you flowers and chocolates?"

"Not really. I hate flowers and I'm off the chocolates. A girl's got to watch her weight, you know."

"Well, that's me all out of ideas for wooing you. Where are you? We need to meet, we've got a few things to talk about."

"Funny thing is, you're not the first person to say that to me this morning."

Emma quickly filled Coffin in on the call she'd had from the mysterious Leola Cruciele and Coffin agreed to meet her at Eddie's.

Eddie's rusty, ramshackle caravan had been around forever. No one could remember a time when Eddie hadn't been parked in that layby, selling his 'Award Winning Burgers', bacon and egg sandwiches, and mugs of steaming coffee and tea. The caravan, originally white but now stained all shades of brown, was wide and long. It probably dated back to sometime in the mid-seventies but no one, not even Eddie, was sure. And maybe it had been towed into its parking spot many years ago, but it was obvious to everyone that it wasn't getting towed out again. There were some days when the wind picked up and the entire structure shook and groaned so much, Emma was convinced it would collapse in a heap of rusty debris, leaving Eddie standing there in surprise, holding a frying pan and a slotted spoon and receiving a battering from the elements.

Somehow the caravan survived, and Eddie, a huge bear of a man in a white T-shirt covered in grease spots, continued serving his food to his loyal customers. No one ever considered the possibility that the sign over his serving hatch, proclaiming his Award Winning status as a caterer, had even the slightest grain of truth in it. But he did serve up some fine burgers. And those bacon and eggs slapped between two thick wedges of white bread, accompanied by a mug of thick, strong coffee? They were enough to turn a doubter into a fan for life.

After a brief discussion with Coffin, she had agreed that she would meet Leola on her own at first while Coffin hung around in the background, and took stock of the situation.

"Could you at least try and look inconspicuous?" Emma had said.

"Yeah, right,' Coffin had growled down the phone. "I'll buy myself a fedora and some sunglasses, and hide behind a copy of The Times."

"The Telegraph," Emma had replied.

"Huh?"

"The Times reduced its size years ago to tabloid proportions, which makes it a bit more difficult to hide behind, especially for a big gorilla like you. You need a broadsheet, and The Telegraph is about the only one of those left. Besides, I tried that trick yesterday, and I just wound up looking like a pillock."

"Well I wouldn't want to look like one of those now, would I?"

Emma pulled into the layby beside Eddie's and killed her engine. A man in an expensive looking suit was standing at the serving hatch, swapping his money for one of Eddie's bacon and egg sarnies. That was the thing with Eddie, his customers came from all walks of life.

There was nobody else around, but traffic was steady on the road. A chill wind had picked up, blowing dead leaves across the pavements, and shaking the branches of the trees. Even in her car, Emma could hear the caravan groaning and protesting, as it struggled to stay together.

Coffin had said he would get there early too, but there was no sign of him or his Harley Davidson. Parked on the opposite side of the road was a large, dirty white van. Emma considered the possibility that Coffin was inside, but the van had no windows except in the cab, and Emma didn't recognise the red headed man sitting in the driver's seat smoking a cigarette and reading a newspaper.

After ten minutes of waiting, Emma was considering getting out of the car and buying herself a coffee. Eddie's coffees were famously strong enough to blow a man's head off, and keep him awake for a week. There was a hand written sign taped by the side of the serving hatch, which said, I ONLY SERV REEL COFEE HERE IF YOU WANT A CUP OF INSTANT CRAP GO SOMEWERE ELSS.

That's what Emma loved about Eddie. His amazing food and great coffee, and his fuck off attitude.

Just as Emma had made her decision to go grab a coffee a taxi pulled up. A young, dark skinned woman climbed out and handed payment to the driver through his open window.

Emma caught her breath. No doubt about it, that was Leola Cruciele, and she was stunningly beautiful. She was also most definitely not a vampire. Not unless she was wearing factor 1000 sun cream, anyway. Emma watched as she walked gracefully over to Eddie's caravan, her simple and rather short dress clinging to her body in the wind.

Wasn't she freezing in that thing?

She spoke to Eddie through the hatch, who suddenly looked as though he might roll over on his back and beg to have his tummy tickled. Emma had to check, make sure her jaw wasn't hanging open in surprise. Eddie barely cracked a smile on a good day but here he was, practically laughing and generally acting like a lovesick teenager.

Emma climbed out of the car and walked over to the caravan. Leola had her back to Emma and turned at the last moment, giving Emma a warm smile.

"I thought that was you, sitting in the car," she said.

Eddie looked at Emma, and his sunny expression disappeared like he'd just been told the food hygiene inspectors were on the way. Emma was glad. Eddie looking happy made her kind of nervous.

"Hey, Eddie, I'll have one of your famous black coffees, and what the hell, I'll have a bacon and egg sarnie as well."

Yeah, you're eating for two now, remember!

"Coming right up," Eddie growled.

Emma stuck out her hand for Leola. "Well observed, you're right, I'm Emma."

Leola took Emma's hand and they shook once.

"Pleased to meet you, Emma."

A lorry rumbled past, leaving soggy leaves twirling crazily in the wind behind it.

"You want to sit in my car, and talk there?" Emma said. "It will be more private, and we'll be out of this wind."

"All right then," Leola replied.

"Here's your coffee," Eddie grunted, handing Emma a cracked, steaming mug.

"Thanks, Eddie. I'm going back to my car, get out of this wind, would you mind bringing my sandwich over when it's ready?"

Eddie glowered at her. "This isn't a bloody restaurant, and I'm no waiter, you know." He glanced at Leola. "Sorry for the language, there. I make it a habit of not swearing in front of ladies."

"What the fuck, Eddie?" Emma said. "You want to insult me, you could at least look at me while you do it."

Eddie cracked another smile. "Aww, did I hurt your feelings?"

"Just bring me my sandwich when it's ready, and I'll forgive you."

Emma and Leola walked over to the hire car. Once inside and out of the wind, Emma untied her ponytail and tied her hair back again, capturing all the loose strands that the wind had teased out. A couple of minutes out there and Emma felt like something the cat had dragged in, but Leola still looked composed and beautiful.

"You said on the phone that you wanted to talk about the Birmingham Vampire," Emma said, deciding not to waste any time.

"Yes," Leola replied. "Is it true what the papers and the television are saying, that he is dead?"

"As far as we can tell from what the police have told us, yes." Emma had talked it over with Coffin, and they were both agreed that she would give nothing away about her involvement with Mortenson until they found out more about this woman. "You said a name earlier. Abel Mortenson. Did you know him?"

Leola turned her head away from Emma, and looked out of the passenger side window. Emma watched the back of her head, and beyond it she could see the white van parked up on the other side of the road.

"For a while, yes," Leola said, after a long silence.

"How did you know him? Was he . . . a friend?"

"It is difficult for me to talk about this." Leola turned and faced Emma again. "For a time we were friends, yes. But if he is dead, then I am glad. He was an evil man."

Emma opened up the glove compartment, to begin the job of rooting through the jumble of CDs, leaflets, documents, spare bulbs for the car, and other bits and pieces that had somehow magically accumulated in there over the years. Buried inside all that mess was her Dictaphone. Karl would cry like a baby if Emma returned with an interview with someone who actually knew the Birmingham Vampire.

But the glove compartment was bare, and the realisation suddenly dawned on Emma that her Dictaphone was in the Fiesta still, and she was sitting in the hire car.

"Fuck!" she hissed.

She slammed the glove compartment door shut. What the hell was she going to do now? She didn't even have a pencil and notepad on her.

"Is anything the matter?" Leola said.

"I wanted to interview you, record what you tell me about Mortenson. We're going to have to go back to the *Herald* offices, and you can tell me everything there."

"No, I can't do that."

"All right, well, we can go somewhere else in town. I'll buy a notepad and pen, my shorthand's pretty shitty, but I'm sure—"

"You don't understand," Leola said. "I didn't ask to meet so that I could answer your questions. I need you to answer mine."

Emma thought about replying, but she was stumped for a response. This was not what she had been expecting.

Eddie was approaching them with Emma's sandwich. She wound down her window and Eddie thrust the paper plate into the car, narrowly missing Emma's head.

"Fuck, Eddie, watch what you're doing! You almost shoved that sandwich down my ear."

"I can think of somewhere else I might shove it, you ask me to bring your food to you again," he said, and then smiled at Leola. "Nice to meet you, I hope you call by again sometime."

"Thank you," Leola replied.

With one last murderous glance at Emma, Eddie returned to his caravan, the wind whipping at his T-shirt.

Emma pulled back the top slice of thick, white bread and looked at the bacon and egg.

"Aww, fuck it, he forgot the ketchup." She lifted her head and watched the big man climbing into his caravan. "What do you think? Reckon I should go tell him?"

Leola smiled. "I don't think that would be a good idea."

"No, maybe you're right." Emma took a big bite out of her sandwich. "So what do you mean, you wanted me to answer your questions? I'm the reporter here, but so far you know more about me than I do about you. You said you knew the Birmingham Vampire."

"And the other one. Did you see him? The old man?"

Leola held Emma in her cool, unwavering gaze, and the bacon sandwich turned into cardboard in Emma's mouth. She wrapped the rest of the sandwich up in the napkin and placed it on the dashboard.

"What old man?" she said.

"You know more than you're letting on," Leola said. "I can see it in your face, in your eyes. But that's okay, I understand that you are cautious, that you don't know who I am or what I want. But you saw him, didn't you?"

Emma struggled to find an answer, wavering between denial and the truth. In the end it just seemed simpler to say it.

"Yes, I saw him."

"Do you believe in vampires, Emma Wylde?"

"If you had asked me that question a week ago, I would have ejected you from my car and put you down as a nutcase. But now? Well, let's suppose for argument's sake I say yes, maybe I do."

Leola reached up and gently touched Emma's cheek. She flinched at the woman's touch, her fingertips cool, but soft.

"This bruising on your face, the swelling, you look like you've been in a fight. Did Abel do that?"

"Yeah. He gave me some lovely scratches across my stomach as well."

"You were lucky to escape with your life."

"I know. I had some help."

"Joe Coffin."

"Yeah, that's right. How did you know that?" Emma smiled. "Wait, you've been reading up on all of this, haven't you? You know Coffin's involvement, and now I guess you're just putting two and two together, right?"

"Is he here?" Leola twisted around in her seat, looking out of the windows, steamed up from the hot coffees.

Emma sighed, pulled her mobile out of her bag and dialled Coffin's number.

"Hey, Joe, wherever you're hiding you might as well come out and join us, the game's up, you've been ousted."

She hung up before he could reply. A few seconds later and the doors on the back of the transit van opened, and Coffin climbed out. He looked different, somehow, and it took Emma a moment before she realised why. The last time she had seen him he had been covered in thick splashes of bright red blood as rainwater cascaded down his face, creating streaks of pale flesh in his scarlet mask. He was all cleaned up now, no longer looked like something out of a horror movie.

Coffin walked over to the car, and Emma rolled down her window.

"Hi, Joe. You want to get in the back?"

"Are you kidding me?" Coffin said, scowling. "If I even managed to get in this tin can, you'd have to call the fire brigade to come and cut me out. Why don't we all convene in my office?"

"What, the back of that van?"

"It looks a lot nicer on the inside. There are leather sofas, a coffee percolator, and a carpet on the floor."

"Bullshit," Emma said. "But I don't suppose we've got much choice."

"That's what I like about you, Emma. Always straight to the point."

"This is Leola," Emma said as they climbed out of the car. "She says she knew Abel Mortenson."

Coffin looked Leola up and down. He didn't seem as impressed as Eddie, but then it was difficult to tell sometimes, what Coffin was thinking. That battered face of his always appeared to be on the edge of a deep scowl. Emma wondered if she had actually seen him smile yet, but then decided probably not. It wasn't like he'd had much to smile about this last week.

"And you're the man who killed him," Leola said.

Coffin grunted and turned on his heel and headed back to the van.

"Don't worry, he's a pussycat really," Emma said.

The ghost of a smile flitted across Leola's face. "Oh I'm not worried, I've dealt with bigger men than him before."

Emma followed Coffin, muttering under her breath, "Yeah, I get the feeling you have."

The inside of the van stank of oil, and there wasn't a sofa or coffee percolator in sight. Neither were there any windows, but somebody had strung a lamp up on the inside of the van's roof, which cast a harsh light over the van's white framework. To Emma the effect was an eerie one, and gave her the impression of sitting inside the bleached ribcage of some long dead, prehistoric animal.

On the van's floor were several large tyres.

"Nice place you got here, but I'm thinking it could do with a woman's touch," Emma said.

"Take a tyre, make yourself comfortable," Coffin said.

"You're the perfect host." Emma sat down, and shifted her backside around, trying to get comfortable. "Next time, let's meet in Starbucks."

Coffin ignored Emma and scowled at Leola. "Just to be clear, before we talk about anything else, yeah, you're right. I'm the man who killed the Birmingham Vampire. And if he was here right now, I'd kill him again, only this time I might've taken a little longer over it, made him suffer some more."

"He gave you those scars on your face, didn't he?" Leola said.

Coffin half lifted a hand to his face, and then let it drop again. It was as though he had forgotten all about them.

"That's right, and he half chewed my shoulder off, too."

"And your finger?"

Coffin looked at the stump of his index finger, still wrapped in a bandage. "No. That wasn't him."

Leola's gaze flicked from Coffin to Emma. "There are more of them, aren't there?"

"Five that I know of, maybe six," Coffin said.

Emma did a quick count in her head. She had a feeling that Coffin wasn't counting Michael in amongst that number.

"Their numbers will grow quickly unless you put a stop to them," Leola said. "They are like a contagion, a virus that spreads faster than any other virus known to man. If we don't act quickly, the city will soon be overrun with their kind."

"How do you know so much about them?" Emma said.

"These others, are they in one place, or are they scattered across the city?" Leola asked, ignoring Emma's question.

"In one place," Coffin replied. "My wife is one of them. She's probably in charge by now."

"Not for long," Leola said softly.

Emma looked at her. "What do you mean?"

Leola ignored her again. "Who else is with her? The other vampires, who were they?"

"The staff at the club. Steffanie and the old man slaughtered them, and now they're wandering around looking like they've just stepped out of a horror movie."

"The old man, ancient really, looks like a walking corpse, he was at the house with Mortenson," Emma said. "Do you know who he is?"

"Merek Guttman. He will be in charge soon. He's the most powerful vampire of them all."

Coffin grunted. "He looked half dead to me."

"He's still waking up from his one hundred year sleep," Leola said. "But once he is fully revived, he will be more dangerous than anyone or anything you have ever known before."

"Great," said Emma. "And here I was thinking we were getting on top of the situation."

contains
explicit material

Eddie lay out a row of burgers on the skillet, and they began sizzling. There were no customers outside his caravan yet, but there would be soon, and Eddie had learnt over the years that these city types didn't like to wait for their lunch. Half of them didn't even have the decency to get off their mobiles while they were placing their orders and giving Eddie their money. Just jammed the phone between shoulder and ear whilst they yabbered on, revelling in the act of doing two things at once.

Multitasking.

Eddie had learnt a long time ago, you wanted to do something well, you just concentrated on one task at a time. Keep it simple. Eddie was good at cooking fast food and brewing coffee, and he'd built himself a reputation around the area that meant he had a loyal customer base, and great word of mouth.

He was never going to be rich, and he had to work godawful hard to keep the business going. And one day for sure this heap of rust and plastic he called a caravan was going to collapse around his ears. But hell, he wouldn't swap it for anything. He was his own boss and he didn't have to answer to anybody else. For Eddie that was worth more than any amount of money he might earn in an ordinary, nine to five job.

In all the years Eddie had served burgers and bacon and eggs from this spot on the side of the road, he'd seen customers come and customers go, too many to count, but he never forgot a face. Like today, he knew Joe Coffin and that reporter, Emma Wylde. And he knew Brendan, sitting in the cab of the transit. But the girl, the dark, pretty one, she was a new face.

Like this man, walking up to the serving hatch, rooting around in his pocket for change, he was new, too.

"Two coffees, please," he said, looking up at Eddie.

Eddie pulled the jug of coffee off the hotplate, and filled two chipped, old mugs almost to the brim.

"Bring the mugs back when you're finished," he growled.

The man dumped a handful of change on the counter and picked up the mugs and walked away. Eddie watched him walking past the white van, and then turning a corner until he was out of sight. He had spilt some coffee on the counter when he lifted the mugs, and Eddie took a cloth and wiped up the mess, thinking to himself, *I'd better get those mugs back.*

Eddie had been told countless times over the years that he should switch to using disposable cups, but he never did. Hated throwing stuff away. Growing up, his family had been as poor as it was possible to be, without being thrown out on the streets, and his father had taught him not to be wasteful in any way.

Almost everyone brought their mugs back, and the few times he lost one, mainly due to breakages, he replaced it with one from home.

Eddie flipped the burgers over, the raw meat sizzling against the hot cooking surface. From the small fridge by his feet he pulled out an old ice cream tub, the design on the lid faded and scratched. He opened it up and tipped chopped onions onto the burgers, stirring them into the hot fat.

A police car pulled into the parking area.

Eddie glanced at the transit van. Brendan hadn't noticed, he was engrossed in his newspaper, licking his thumb and turning over the page.

Two coppers got out of the car, one of them stretching, the other one scratching his arse. They slammed the car doors shut, and the first one nodded at the transit van and said something, and his partner looked over at it and laughed.

Eddie knew the second one, the arse scratcher, although not by name. One of the familiar faces over the years, a regular customer. The other cop, he was a new face.

Eddie stole a glance at his mobile, lying on the counter top just within arm's reach. Thought about calling Brendan, telling the stupid fucker to put down his newspaper and look out of his window. Telling him they'd got company, and Eddie wasn't one for keeping up with the news and all that, but wasn't Joe Coffin a wanted man right now, and might it make sense for Brendan to start up the van and get the hell out of there?

The two cops ambled over to Eddie's burger van, like they had all the time in the world.

"Morning, Eddie," Arse Scratcher said, and then glanced at his companion. "Or is it afternoon yet?"

He took at a look at his watch. "About twenty minutes ago."

A gust of wind hit the caravan, which creaked and protested as it shifted slightly.

"Bloody hell," Arse Scratcher's companion said. "Is this piece of shit safe? Looks like it might fall down any second."

"Eddie's caravan's a mystery to everyone, Jimmy. Been here since before I joined the force, and probably still be here when I retire. Isn't that right, Eddie?"

"What can I do for you two?" Eddie said, having to work hard not to add the word 'fuckers' on the end of that sentence.

"Two burgers and two coffees, of course. Jimmy here doesn't believe me when I tell him you serve the finest food in all Birmingham, and I'm here to prove him wrong."

"Be one minute," Eddie said, and flipped the burgers again.

Arse Scratcher handed over a crumpled banknote. Eddie unfolded it and placed it in another recycled ice cream tub. He counted out some change, and handed it to the policeman.

"Customer of yours?" The cop nodded at the transit van.

"Yeah," Eddie growled.

"He should clean his van sometime. You seen all the obscenities scrawled in the muck on that thing? It's like a walking dictionary of swear words, should have an eighteen certificate slapped on it."

"Yeah, or one of those warnings they put on CDs sometimes, 'Warning, contains explicit material'," Jimmy said.

"Except it doesn't contain explicit material does it? If it contained explicit material then that would be all right, because all that swearing, and those obscene diagrams would be on the inside, out of view. The problem we've got with that van is that the explicit material is all over the fucking shop for everybody to see."

"I'll mention it to him," Eddie said.

"Maybe I should have a word," Arse Scratcher said.

"Seriously?" Jimmy said, turning to look at the van again.

"Absolutely. If I was feeling less charitable today, I could charge him with causing offence. But no, I'm in a good mood, so I'll just wander over and advise him that he needs to put his van through a car wash."

"Your burgers are ready," Eddie said, placing two burgers in buns, and wrapped in paper napkins, on the counter.

The two men turned their backs on the transit van, and picked up their food. Eddie placed two mugs of steaming hot, black coffee in front of them.

"I'll go speak to him when I've eaten this," Arse Scratcher said.

"There's ketchup if you want it," Eddie said, pointing at the bottle on the counter.

Arse Scratcher unwrapped his burger, lifted the top half of the bun, and squirted a good sized dollop of ketchup onto the meat and the fried onions. He held out the bottle to Jimmy.

"Nah, I hate ketchup, bloody awful stuff, you ask me."

Arse Scratcher widened his eyes in mock surprise and turned to face Eddie. "You hearing this, Eddie?"

Eddie shrugged, flipped some more burgers, wondered when these two jokers were going to go and sit in their car to eat their food, and then Eddie could get on his mobile and warn Brendan off before Arse Scratcher wandered over for a friendly word.

"Who in their fucking right mind doesn't like ketchup?" Arse Scratcher said, still holding the bottle out, like it was an exhibit in a court of law.

"Let me ask you something," Jimmy said, and took a bite of his burger. "I bet you don't like tomatoes, right?"

"I don't know, I can take them or leave them, to be honest."

"Right," Jimmy said, through a mouthful of food. "And I bet, if there was a dish of sliced tomatoes on this counter here, provided by Eddie, as a . . ." he clicked his fingers, ". . . you know, what do you call them?"

"Condiments," Eddie said.

"Yeah, that's right, condiments, for you to put on your burger, I bet you wouldn't take any, right?"

Arse Scratcher bit into his burger, and thought for a moment, while he chewed.

"Probably not, no."

"So why the hell are you putting ketchup on your food, when it's made out of tomatoes?"

Arse Scratcher shook his head, and said, "I don't follow your logic. You're saying, because I wouldn't eat tomatoes with my burger, I shouldn't put ketchup on it?"

"No, that's not what I'm saying at all," Jimmy replied, and took another big bite from his burger. "What I'm saying is, that if you wanted to add the taste of tomatoes to your burger, you'd put tomatoes on there, not ketchup. But you don't, because you don't give a shit about tomatoes. You put the ketchup on, because you're addicted to all that sugar and other crap they stick in there, to make it taste nice."

Arse Scratcher looked at Eddie, and then back at Jimmy again, chewing slowly.

"And your point is?" he said, finally.

Before Jimmy could answer, the sound of the transit van side door sliding open interrupted him and they turned to look.

Joe Coffin stood framed in the open doorway, squinting at the daylight, his huge frame filling the available space.

"Fuck me, it's Joe Coffin," Arse Scratcher said, and dropped his burger on the ground.

crouch

Forensic pathologist Malcolm Crouch finished washing his hands and dried them on the paper towel from the huge dispenser beside the stainless steel sink. Pulling on a pair of plastic gloves he regarded the body laid out on the metal table, exposed beneath the harsh light of the fluorescent strips in the ceiling.

The old man had obviously been living on the streets for many years. His ribcage protruded painfully beneath his grey flesh, and his bare arms and legs were like thin sticks of driftwood. His long, grey straggly hair was fanned out on the table like a pop star having a photo shoot, and his beard, matted with crusted blood, lay over his thin chest.

Malnutrition, or exposure to the cold, or the hardship of life on the streets of Birmingham, weren't what had killed him that was for sure. Cause of death was entirely obvious. The ragged, gaping wound in his neck.

The pathologist leaned on the table and let his gaze wander up and down the corpse's naked body.

He was a busy man at the moment. After hearing the news that the man the newspapers had labelled the Birmingham Vampire was dead, Crouch had thought he would get a respite from the parade of victims stacking up in the mortuary. There had been six of them before that gangster, Joe Coffin, had allegedly put a stop to the slaughter.

Crouch had seen the burnt remains of the body himself and was a little more sceptical than everybody else. Until they had the DNA results back, and then a positive match on the database, nobody was even close to being able to say that the Birmingham Vampire was dead. Or that Coffin had killed him.

But then Crouch was old fashioned like that. He preferred facts to supposition, logic to flights of fantasy.

Despite his sceptical nature, Crouch had still hoped that the newspapers were right for once, that the killer was dead and that the bodies would stop piling up, giving him a chance to start work on his backlog. But then there had been the murder of that young man Wayne Davies last night. His tongue torn out, his throat ripped open, his flesh lacerated from head to toe.

A copycat killer? Or was the Birmingham Vampire still alive?

Because of the nature of his death, Davies had been pushed to the top of the queue. Crouch had examined the man's wounds carefully. Comparing the pattern of cuts, the size and curvature of the bite marks, and the depth of the lacerations with the other victims, Crouch was certain that they were dealing with another killer. Smaller and weaker than the Birmingham Vampire, but more ferocious perhaps. Less in control.

This evidence, this *fact*, raised a new and disturbing question. Everyone, the police, the media, the public, even the arch sceptic Forensic Pathologist Malcolm Crouch himself, had made an assumption.

That the Birmingham Vampire was one man, working alone.

But what if that hadn't been the case? What if, all along, there had been more than one killer?

Crouch pondered the evidence he had gathered from the killer's victims that he had examined so far.

First of all there had been Coffin's wife and son. The bite marks and puncture wounds on their bodies had matched. They had both been killed by one person, a grown adult, most likely a man.

Then there had been that boy, Peter Marsden. Particularly disturbing that one, as he had survived for some time after being attacked. So much so that some of his wounds had healed to an extent, whilst others had become inflamed, oozing pus and turning gangrenous. Crouch had been unable to accurately map the bites and lacerations on the young boy to effectively match them to the other victims.

After that the bodies had started piling up. There was the old homeless man, currently lying on the table in front of him, and the black maid found at the motorway service station. And then that poor girl, Julie Carter.

None of whom Malcolm Crouch had had a chance to examine.

The pathologist bent over the body and pulled the old man's beard back, so he could look at the wound in his throat.

A muffled thump made him flinch, and straighten up.

What the hell had that been? Sounded like maybe somebody had dropped something heavy, on the floor above perhaps. The mortuary was downstairs in the basement and there were some days, when he was working down here on his own, that Crouch felt like he was the only man left alive. That he was going to spend the rest of his life with no one but the dead for company.

In some ways that was an attractive thought. Other people could be such a tiresome nuisance sometimes. At least the dead didn't answer back or argue. The perfect companions for Crouch, who never liked to be disagreed with.

The pathologist was about to return to the body when he heard the dull *THUMP!* again. It hadn't come from above at all, but down the corridor. From where they stored the bodies in their drawers.

Another thump, and then another, becoming more powerful and insistent each time. Crouch walked towards the source of the noise, between the metal body slabs and into the storage room, the Meat Locker as it was sometimes known. The room was cold and empty, but the powerful thumping noise continued. A regular, rhythmic pounding.

Oh dear Lord, it was coming from inside one of the body storage drawers. Crouch had heard the stories, just like every other pathologist and mortuary practitioner, of people who had been pronounced dead waking up on the autopsy table, or in the mortuary, alone at night. But he hadn't believed any of them. It was simply too ridiculous to be true.

And yet here he was in the mortuary, listening to the muffled thumps of what could only be somebody, in one of these drawers, kicking at the door. The overhead light flickered and buzzed. For the first time in his life the pathologist experienced a thrill of unease running through his torso as he imagined what it would be like if the lights went out, and he was thrown into darkness.

With that body in the drawer, bashing at the locked door, trying to get out.

Don't be ridiculous. Pull yourself together.

Crouch flinched as whoever, or whatever, was inside that locker hit the door again.

Go get help, go upstairs now and find someone to come back down with you.

The pathologist took an involuntary step back, ready to turn and flee up the stairs, and maybe not stop to get help after all but just keep on running. This place, the mortuary with its rows of dead bodies, suddenly frightened him. Crouch had lived and worked amongst the dead for most of his adult life and never once been spooked, or unsettled. From an early age he had always considered death to be as much a part of life as anything else.

But now, this moment, Crouch was suffocatingly aware of the presence of the dead. And a thought occurred to him, terrifying in its clarity, that if all of the dead returned to life there would be no room left for the living on the earth.

THUMP!

Crouch flinched again and his mind cleared, reason and logic returning and chasing away the phantoms. What had come over him? He was acting like a child scared of the dark, of monsters in the wardrobe or under the bed.

Inside that body storage locker was a live person, someone who had mistakenly been certified as dead. This was something to write a paper on for a journal. Of course there would be an investigation and an outcry amongst the press, but as Crouch was not the examining physician who pronounced death he would be clear of controversy.

THUMP!

The muffled thud rattled through Crouch's head and chest. His imagination ran into overdrive once more, summoning visions of the dead digging their way out of their graves in the dead of night, torrential rain washing the dirt off their emaciated, rotting bodies.

Don't be stupid, Crouch thought. *Pull yourself together and get that poor person out of there. They must be terrified.*

He approached the metal door of the body locker. The handle shivered as the door was kicked from the inside. Crouch reached out, ashamed to notice that his hand was trembling slightly, grasped the handle and gave it a swift turn to unlock it. He swung the door open.

The soles of a pair of brown feet confronted him. Feminine feet. Crouch immediately knew who this was. But that was impossible. She couldn't be alive.

Crouch pulled at the sliding tray that housed the body, dragging it out on its rollers. The body was revealed feet first, then the legs, the hips, the abdomen and the breasts, until the drawer was fully extended.

The maid from the service station, found in one of the rooms collapsed in a dark, sticky pool of her own blood with her throat opened up, lay inert on the tray.

Crouch was puzzled, and yet relieved at the same time. This woman was obviously dead.

Gripping the sides of the tray to stop his hands trembling, Crouch gazed at the woman's face.

She stared up at him with eyes round and wide. Crouch stepped back, on legs suddenly turned to jelly.

It wasn't possible. It couldn't be. She should be dead. She *was* dead.

The woman sat up, her movements stiff and awkward. Never once letting her gaze drift from the terrified pathologist.

Crouch backed away, until he stumbled into the opposite wall of body lockers. The woman swung her feet to the floor and stood up. There was no fluidity to her movements, no warmth in her nakedness, or sense of life.

Crouch crabbed sideways along the wall of body storage lockers, keeping his eyes fixed on the naked woman. There had been no mistake on pronouncement of death, and there had been no miraculous restoration of life. This woman was still dead, and yet she was up on her feet, now crouching like a cat ready to spring. Her lips peeled back to reveal bare teeth that looked too long, too sharp and pointed, to be human.

Stumbling back into the mortuary, where the old man lay on his back on the dissecting table, Crouch grabbed a knife from his tray of instruments. These weren't the delicate tools used by surgeons in the operating theatre, but crude blades used for carving open dead flesh.

The woman padded barefoot towards him across the cold, tiled floor, her hands curled into claws. Crouch gripped the knife hard, and he had to fight the urge to piss himself as he heard the woman start moaning and saw long strings of drool hanging from her chin.

Ice cold fingers closed around Crouch's wrist. The pathologist screamed and dropped the knife. The old man rose from the mortuary table, his jaws opening impossibly wide. His few remaining, brown and rotted teeth dropped onto the floor, as new teeth erupted from red and inflamed gums.

Crouch screamed again, but this time his scream was cut short as the woman flew at him, and buried her teeth into his throat.

marjorie and claire

"We are so fucked," Emma said.

"Your girlfriend's got a filthy mouth on her," Brendan said.

Coffin grinned. "Hear that? Apparently you're my girlfriend now."

"No fucking way," Emma said.

"But you both look such a perfect match for each other, what with all the bruises and scars on your faces," Brendan said.

Emma touched her cheek, just under her eye where it was still sore and bruised, and flinched. Brendan was right, they were a perfect couple. Not only did they share physical characteristics, but they had both faced up to the Birmingham Vampire and lived to tell the tale.

"Fuck off," she said.

"Now Joe, you wouldn't catch my Patsy talking like that," Brendan said. "She ever swore at me, I'd show her the back of my hand, I would."

"You're a true gent, Brendan," Coffin replied. "A model of the perfect husband."

"Joe, I can hear the sarcasm in your voice there, but it's true. Me and Patsy, we've been married now for near twenty-two years. Marriage is a commitment for life, am I right? And if a man has to raise his hand every now and then, well that's just the way it is."

"You'd never catch me hitting a woman," Coffin replied. "That's the coward's way."

Emma held up her hands and turned to Leola. "I must be dreaming. I swear, any minute now, Marjorie Proops and Claire Rayner here are going to get up and hug each other, and I will wake up screaming."

"Who?" Leola said.

"Never mind. Hey, you two! When you've finished discussing the sanctity of marriage, can you come back to reality? Because, in case you'd forgotten, we've got two massive fucking problems here."

They all turned to look at the policemen lying on the van's floor, hands and legs tied up and strips of rag wound tight across their mouths. The two cops were staring bug eyed at Coffin and Brendan, but they both remained perfectly motionless. Brendan had already kicked one of them in the side for struggling against his bonds, and told them there would be more like that if they didn't keep still.

They kept still.

"She's right, Joe," Brendan said. "We should kill them now, and then take them and dump them in the canal."

Coffin grunted. One of the cops, the younger one, started shaking his head, his breathing fast and loud through his nose.

"Are you fucking serious?" Emma said. "You can't murder them."

The big Irishman turned and gazed at Emma, his eyes sad and serious. "And what else do you suggest, young lady? We've assaulted them, tied them up and we're keeping them prisoner. They've seen all our faces, and we're keeping company with a wanted man. Do you think we should just let them go? We'd have the whole of the West Midlands police force on our tail before you could eat one of Eddie's bacon sandwiches, that you would."

"That doesn't mean you can just kill them. Joe, tell him, we can't kill them, right?"

Coffin rubbed a hand over the top of his head. "I don't know. Brendan's got a point, they can identify us."

"What?" Emma had been leaning forward, and now she sank back, and rested her head against the van's side and placed her hands over her face. "I can't believe you're agreeing with him. We are so fucked."

"You already said that," Coffin said.

"I say we drive back to O'Donoghue's," Brendan said. "I've got some tarp out back we can use, I don't want to make a bloody mess of my van. A knife in the chest, nice and clean like, and then we can wrap them up in the tarp, maybe weight them down with bricks and dump them in the canal."

"You're forgetting their car," Emma said, her voice muffled from behind her hands. "You've got an empty cop car parked outside Eddie's burger van. Not exactly inconspicuous, is it?"

Coffin opened the van's doors, just a little, letting in a shaft of dirty grey light. "The car's gone. I think Eddie must have moved it out of the way, parked it around the corner, that way he won't have to answer any awkward questions about why an empty police car is parked by his caravan."

"Anybody else out there?" Brendan said.

"Yeah, Eddie's got a couple of customers, office types."

Coffin shut the doors.

"We need to get a move on, get out of here before these two pigs are missed." Brendan turned his gaze on Emma and Leola. "Now I'm not being rude, ladies, but I'm more than a little concerned about your part in all of this, too."

Emma dropped her hands from her face. "You even think about touching me and I will scratch your eyes out of their sockets and shove them down your fucking throat."

"She's a feisty one," Brendan said to Coffin.

"Yeah, and she's with me," Coffin said. "You don't have to worry about Emma."

Brendan pointed at Leola. "Now what about this one?"

Leola held Brendan's gaze, calm and composed.

"She's with me," Emma said. "And I'm with Joe."

"You all right with that, Joe?" Brendan said. "I'm putting an awful lot of trust in you, I am. I don't want none of this coming back to bite me on the arse now, do I?"

"Let's just get the hell out of here," Coffin replied.

"All right then, I suppose that will have to do for the moment."

Brendan climbed out of the van, and slammed the doors shut. A few moments later and the engine was gunned into life, and they were moving.

"You're not going to let Brendan kill these two jokers, are you?" Emma said.

The younger of the two cops started trying to say something, his mouth muffled behind the oily rag. Coffin kicked him in the thigh.

"Shut up." He turned to Emma. "No, the last thing we need is a manhunt on for cop killers. The whole city would go into lockdown. We'd have to stay hidden, hell we'd have to get out of the country, if we could."

Emma sighed. "Not exactly the reason I was thinking of to spare their lives, but at least it's something."

"I should go now," Leola said. "None of this is my concern."

"That might be the case, but it sure as hell is my concern," Coffin said. "I need to know for sure that you're not going to blab to the cops as soon as you're out of my sight."

"You don't have to worry about that. Kill them, let them go, it means nothing to me either way."

"Wow, and here I was thinking you were one of the good guys," Emma said.

"Am I the only person here who thinks maybe we shouldn't murder these two because, hey, you know, killing people is wrong?"

"Cops aren't people," Coffin said, and held onto the side of the van as Brendan turned a corner.

"I'll pretend I didn't hear you just say that," Emma said.

She was starting to feel a little queasy, sitting inside this tin box, swaying from side to side, and being jostled up and down. Felt like she was down in the cabin of a boat on the ocean.

Now really wasn't the best time to be suffering from a bout of seasickness.

"Who is this Guttman you mentioned earlier?" Coffin said. "You said something about a hundred year sleep?"

"That's right," Leola replied. "Guttman is thousands of years old, the last of the ancient ones, and the ritual burial was a way of renewing him and making him young again. Abel buried him alive, after filling his coffin with the blood of virgin girls, and left him there. "

"Wait a minute!" Emma said. "Was he buried at the house on Forde road, in the cellar?"

Leola nodded. "And then Abel must have returned, with the purpose of digging him up."

"He was buried alive for a hundred years?" Coffin said.

"More than that, probably more like a hundred and thirty years. He was left too long, and that is why the regeneration process is going so slowly. If he had been pulled out of the ground at exactly one hundred years under a gibbous moon, he would be at the height of his strength and powers by now. You were lucky."

"Great," Emma said. "This must be how it feels to win the lottery."

"And he was alive all that time he spent in his grave?" Coffin said.

Leola nodded. "Now that he is out he needs fresh blood, and plenty of it to regain his strength and youth. I don't know what dealings you have had with him already, but don't let his frailness fool you. If left to feed and gather his strength, Guttman will become an unstoppable force of nature. He is not just a vampire, he is a *revnan*, a *djab*."

"I don't understand," Coffin said.

"He is a ghost, he is a devil."

"How do you know all this?" Emma asked.

"I've made it my job to know, over the years."

The van rounded a corner and they all held onto the sides as the floor tilted and the walls swayed. One of the cops swore as he rolled over, and into his colleague.

"I am here to kill him," Leola said. "Will you help me?"

Emma glanced at Coffin. She could see they were thinking along the same lines. Was this woman for real? And how did she know all of this? That answer about making it her job to know was nothing more than a way of dodging the question.

The fact that she wanted to kill a vampire was great, that put her on their side. But there was still something distinctly off about her. They knew nothing about her, but still, it was more than that.

Emma couldn't quite pin it down, but she didn't like it.

Not one bit.

"You don't believe me," Leola said.

"Uh, well, it's not that—" Emma began.

"You don't believe me," the Creole woman said again.

The van slowed to a stop, the engine rumbling steadily. Leola opened the back door of the van and jumped out. Behind them was a row of cars, their drivers at the wheels, waiting for the traffic to start moving again.

"Wait a minute!" Emma shouted.

Leola slammed the door shut.

Emma looked at Coffin.

"Aren't you going to do something?" she said.

The van started moving again.

"Yeah," Coffin replied. "I'm going to stay here and make sure you don't untie these two."

"You really can be very infuriating and annoying sometimes."

"I know, I've been told it's one of my more endearing traits."

"Whoever told you that, they were lying."

"What did you think about that woman, then?" Coffin said. "Seemed like there was something strange about her to me."

"I know what you mean," Emma replied. "Kind of difficult to say what, though."

Coffin ran his hand over his head, and looked at the men lying bound up on the floor of the van. "We can think about her another time, I suppose. Right now we've got to work out what to do with these two."

"Do you think they've been missed yet? Don't cops have to report in every ten minutes, or something?"

"I don't know, you tell me, you're the one with a cop boyfriend."

"We've always made it a point not to discuss work. Usually leads to an argument."

"I could see how that might happen," Coffin said. "Especially considering the current circumstances."

"Did you and Brendan really have to jump these two and tie them up? Couldn't we have just driven away?"

"I suppose, but then they would have chased us, and we would have wound up on *Police, Camera, Action* one day."

Emma shifted on the tyre she was sitting on. Brendan swung the van around a few corners, and they started to slow down.

"Seriously, just what the hell are we going to do with these two?"

The van stopped, and the engine died.

"We'll talk to Mort about it," Coffin said, standing up.

"Craggs? Great. I can imagine his response when he sees you've brought the police back with you."

The van's back doors swung open, and Brendan stood in the doorway. Behind him, Emma could see a cobblestoned street, and a canal off to the side. She had a feeling she knew where they were.

"Let's get them inside, quick," Brendan said.

He jumped in the van, hauled one of the men to his feet and dragged him outside. Coffin grabbed the other one.

"Shut the van door behind you, will you?" he said to Emma, as he jumped to the ground.

Emma thought about running. All that training she did, and the fact that she was so much smaller and lighter than these two, she had to be faster. She could lose them in a matter of seconds, make a 999 call, report the two missing policemen.

Neither Brendan nor Coffin had waited for her. They had both gone inside the pub, O'Donoghue's, pretty swift. Even better.

Emma jumped out of the van and slammed the doors shut. From where she was, she could see the top of the Library of Birmingham, and the International Convention Centre. O'Donoghue's was situated in a quiet street, but less than a minute away from the city centre. This was a perfect opportunity to run.

Shit!

Emma followed the two men inside the pub.

There was a tiny, bird like woman behind the bar, wiping down the surfaces. They already had a couple of customers, old men, sitting in the darkened corners, nursing a pint of beer each. None of them batted an eyelid at the sight of the two men, bound and gagged, lying on the floor where Coffin and Brendan had dropped them. Maybe it was a regular occurrence.

"We'd better take these two downstairs," Brendan said. "We get some city types in here sometimes, having what they call a working lunch. Me, I think it's just another excuse for them to get pissed, and that on the company pay roll as well. The thing is, if they see these two, and word gets around that I'm in the habit of kidnapping coppers, business might suffer, you know what I'm saying, Joe?"

Coffin picked one of the cops up again. "Lead the way."

"Where are you taking them?" Emma said.

"Down to the cellar," Coffin said.

Emma rolled her eyes. "Have you forgotten that it was just a couple of days back you were rescuing Jacob from a cellar? Now you're in the business of keeping people prisoner in one?"

"Your young lady shouldn't be talking back at you like that all the time, Joe," Brendan said. "It's not right. It's a man's job to wear the trousers, and his woman should stand by his decisions."

"Didn't I already tell you I'm not his fucking girlfriend?" Emma said, following the two men through a low doorway.

Brendan stopped walking and turned around, his face a mask of cold fury.

"You're a solid man, Joe, and I appreciate you're not Irish, and that you don't agree with the Irish way of things, but still, if she keeps talking like that I'm going to have to give her a slap myself, so help me God."

"There won't be any need for that," Coffin said. "Emma will keep quiet from now on."

He frowned at her, and the message was clear. *Keep your mouth shut.*

Emma shut her mouth and mimed zipping her lips together, locking them up and then throwing an invisible key over her shoulder.

Apparently satisfied, Brendan turned his back on her, and began descending a narrow flight of rickety steps, pushing the policeman in front of him. Coffin followed him, holding his prisoner by his hands tied behind his back.

Emma stood at the top of the cellar steps, watching the two men descend with their captives. There was no way she was going down there. She'd had enough of cellars to last her a lifetime.

From the bottom of the cellar steps, Coffin paused before disappearing from view and called up to Emma.

"Wait there, we still need to talk, okay?"

"Sure," Emma said.

We need to talk. Great. What shall we talk about, Joe? Murder? Vampires? Holding a pair of policemen prisoner? Withholding evidence?

Or are you finally getting around to wondering what, exactly, I know about you and Terry Wu?

mightier than
the sword

Steffanie Coffin sat in Mortimer Craggs' chair, at his desk, wearing his clothes, and she smiled. This was where she belonged, where she had always belonged, in a seat of power. It was here that she had let that sweaty, oily Chinaman Terry Wu fuck her, sometimes on the desk, other times on the couch. What a big man he'd thought he was, with his nightclub, and his big desk, and his big chair, in his big office.

Had it all been an attempt to make up for his tiny little cock?

And then there was the Samurai sword, autographed by David Carradine. And what a disappointment he'd turned out to be, found hanging naked by his neck in a hotel closet, with his dick in his hand.

Pathetic, just like Terry. She'd caught him more than once sitting at his desk, tossing himself off to internet porn. That man had had the sexual appetite of a female ape on heat, and about the same level of skill, too. If only there was an Oscar for best faking of an orgasm, Steffanie would have won it. Sometimes she'd had to act pretty quick, because he was always climaxing too soon. And for a man with his voracious sexual appetite, he was so boring.

No imagination.

But he paid well. Especially on the nights when she really threw herself into her role, purring with delight, and then screaming and writhing on top of him as his hips jerked and spasmed beneath her. He always paid her handsomely then. Steffanie sometimes wondered if he knew she was acting, and this was his way of showing gratitude for not embarrassing him.

But no, in reality he simply thought he was a stud, and in moments like that he became reckless with his money.

It had been the kiddie stuff that he wanked off to that had surprised and sickened her.

Not that it bothered her now.

Terry had made a big deal of it at the time, doing his best to convince her that the children were willing participants. Trying to persuade her that none of them got hurt, that they got paid well, they even enjoyed it. Steffanie never let him stick that tiny little cock of his in her again. Sex with Terry had always repulsed her a little, but when she found out the stuff he was really into she could hardly bear the thought of him near her. By that time Tom Mills had put his plan into action, and she knew she didn't have long to wait before Craggs sent Coffin to put a bullet in Terry Wu's head. So she strung him along for a few days, teasing him with the promise of something extra special, until he was almost crazy with lust.

When she slipped back into his office later that night to download the video onto the USB stick and wipe it from the hard drive, her first emotion when she saw Terry lying on the floor, his head leaking blood, was relief. Never again would she have to endure those pudgy hands stroking her, and pinching her flesh.

But Joe? Joe was different. She hated him, too, maybe even more than she'd hated Terry Wu. But at least he was good in bed.

It was in every other way that he had disappointed her.

Steffanie slid her hands across the desk, appreciating its silky smooth surface, and the view from the seated side. How many times had she been in this office since Craggs took control of Angellicit? Especially after Coffin was put away for assaulting that man in the pub. One of the other wives, maybe that snivelling bitch Laura, must have told Craggs how Steffanie had been flirting with that guy, leading him on. Craggs and the Slaughterhouse Mob, it was like they were still living in the 1950s. Women weren't allowed to have fun, and God forbid they should talk to someone of the opposite sex.

Craggs had had a quiet word with her about that, him sitting in his big chair, whilst Steffanie stood on the other side of his big desk like a naughty schoolgirl hauled in front of the headmaster. Only the thought of what she knew, of the files she had in her possession and the video of Joe murdering Terry Wu, had stopped her from leaping across that big desk and slapping him in the face.

When Craggs had finished telling Steffanie off for basically getting her husband sent to jail, he turned on the charm, laying it on thick about how she and Michael would never want for anything while Joe was inside. They were part of the family now.

Somehow that made Steffanie want to slap him even more.

But she'd kept herself under control. She'd had to, because she had needed to escape.

Marrying Joe Coffin had meant to be her way out of her life at Angellicit. Coffin might look like God had assembled his face from all the random bits left over from a knife fight in a back alley, but he had something about him that drew her in, magnetised her. And, more importantly, she had thought he would get her out of the life. He had been a means to an end and nothing more.

What she hadn't realised at the time was that when you married a member of the Slaughterhouse Mob, you actually married the *whole* of the Slaughterhouse Mob. And Mortimer Craggs was the patriarch, almost biblical in the power he had over his 'family'.

As if that hadn't been bad enough, she then fell pregnant. Steffanie's first thought had been to have an abortion. What did she want with a screaming kid hanging off her, dribbling snot on her clothes and shitting and puking all the time? But Joe had been over the moon, giddy with delight at the prospect of having a child.

That had been one of their fiercest arguments. Steffanie had come close to flying at him in a rage, and dragging her fingernails across that beaten up face of his. Joe was a big, powerful guy, and nobody argued with him, or stood up to him.

Except Craggs and Steffanie.

She told him she was getting an abortion and that was it, there was nothing he could do about it. *She* would have to carry the fucking baby for nine months, and *she* would have to give birth to it, and *she* would have to nurse it, and didn't he realise what having a child did to a woman's figure?

So Joe backed down.

Joe Coffin might be one tough bastard out in the real world, but when it came to women he was weak.

Steffanie had about a day to relish winning her argument, getting her way, before that old bastard Craggs came for a visit.

How the hell he found out she would never know. Joe wouldn't have told him, he liked to fight his own battles, wasn't the type to go crawling to 'Daddy' every time something didn't go his way. However it happened, Craggs knew. And he wasn't happy.

Not at all.

For a man who was at the heart of one of the UK's largest and most powerful crime syndicates involving extortion, drugs, and contract killing, Mortimer Craggs had an incredibly old fashioned sense of family values. Joe had already disappointed him once when he had allowed Laura to leave him, and he wasn't going to let something like that happen again.

Craggs sent Joe off on a job, something meaningless just to get him out of the way. The old bastard didn't want Joe around to hear what he had to say.

"I always knew you were bad news," he'd said to her. "I never should have let Joe marry you, but I did, and now we all have to live with it."

Steffanie said nothing, just lit up a cigarette. The expression on Craggs' face was worth the aggravation of having to sit there listening to him pontificate. He'd looked like he was about to shit a brick.

"You shouldn't be smoking those things, not in your condition."

Steffanie took a deep drag and held it, then tipped her head back and slowly released a blue plume of smoke up to the ceiling.

Faster than she had imagined possible for a man of his age, Craggs had leaned forward and snatched the cigarette from between her fingers. He squashed it in his hand, and opened up his fist to let the crushed cigarette fall to the carpet.

Craggs never threatened her with violence, or expulsion from the Slaughterhouse Mob. He didn't even threaten to end her career as a dancer in the clubs, something he knew she loved doing, even if she hated it at the time.

It was only later, much later, after Michael was born, that she came to realise the dancing was part of her, like breathing. And it seemed to her that somehow, Craggs had already known that even before she did.

No, Craggs reasonably and calmly talked about how she needed to have the baby, about how it would be good for Joe, for her too. How it was simply the right thing to do.

By the time he left, Steffanie knew she wasn't going to have an abortion. She also knew that she hated Mortimer Craggs more than any other person alive.

That was why Craggs wasn't going to get his club back. It was hers, now. She would be the one behind the big desk, in the big chair. Not Mortimer Craggs or Terry Wu.

The door to the office opened, pulling her out of her thoughts.

"You should come downstairs," Addison said. "We've got a problem."

Steffanie stood up, pushed her long cascade of red hair over her shoulders and adjusted the cuffs on her jacket. Who would have thought that Craggs' clothes would fit her so well?

So there was a problem. Steffanie Coffin was in charge now. Not Craggs, not Mortenson, not the old man they called the Father.

Steffanie would deal with the problem.

Addison led her downstairs, past the club bar and down to the cellar. They were all down there except the Father, who was upstairs in one of the rooms, sleeping. Clevon and Velvina were standing watching Rob kneeling on the floor, hunched over something out of her view. Frankie Shaddock was pressed up against a corner of the cellar next to the beer barrels, looking like he would rather be anywhere else on the planet.

Steffanie walked around Clevon and Velvina so she could get a better view. Rob was on his knees, head down and tongue out, lapping at a large pool of blood gathering on the concrete floor.

The blood was pulsing from a gash in the homeless man's neck.

Steffanie planted her foot in Rob's side and pushed him over. He fell on his back, his lips smeared with scarlet blood, his eyes dull and lifeless. Without turning around to face him, Steffanie lifted an arm and pointed at Shaddock, and crooked her finger, signalling him to come to her.

Shaddock shuffled slowly over, the fear etched into the lines in his face.

"Give me your pen," she said, pointing at his shirt pocket.

Shaddock put a hand to his chest, where a pen was clipped to his pocket. "What?"

Steffanie snatched the pen from him, and knelt down next to Rob, who was still staring vacantly at her. Pushing him down with the palm of her hand so that he was lying flat on the concrete floor, she placed the tip of the pen over his chest, about where his heart would be.

And then she shoved hard, the pen puncturing his shirt and the flesh beneath. Red blood bubbled over Steffanie's hand as Rob kicked and screamed, his arms jerking spasmodically. Shaddock stepped back, looked like he was about to faint, and then recovered himself.

When Rob had stopped kicking and wailing, Steffanie pulled the pen out of his chest with a wet sucking sound, and turned to the old man. She plunged the pen into his chest, too. The homeless man made no movement, but Steffanie held him down anyway.

She stood up, and said to Addison and Clevon, "Take the bodies away, and burn them."

Then she turned and slipped the bloody pen back into Shaddock's pocket and patted his chest. She left bloody handprints over his shirt.

"That was unfortunate. But don't worry, we'll bring you more bodies."

"And then what? I get to watch as you kill them all, one by one?"

"No. That's not the plan. The idea is that they live, at least for a while anyway. Keep these people alive and you get to stay alive. Do you understand?"

Shaddock swallowed. Nodded.

"But I can't protect them. Not from the likes of you."

"You don't have to worry about that, it won't happen again."

"And I need medical equipment. If you want me to keep them alive while you milk them for blood, I'm going to need more than a crate for them to lie on."

"What do you need?"

"A bed, maybe, for starters. And not just any bed, but a hospital quality grade bed, and I'll need IV stands, and cannulas, and drugs."

Steffanie tossed her hair back. "Ridiculous."

Shaddock swallowed again. He was obviously terrified, but he kept eye contact with Steffanie, not giving her an inch. Despite herself, she was subtly impressed.

"Then you'll have a cellar full of rotting corpses to deal with," Shaddock said. "And no blood supply. You want me to help you, you've got to give me what I need."

Steffanie looked at Addison. "Can you get him what he needs?"

"No," Addison said, and ran his tongue thoughtfully over his newly sharp teeth. "But I know a couple of people who can."

glow in the dark eyes

Coffin's boots crunched against the gravel as he walked past the gravestones, and down the path towards the church doors. The church was closed up, its stained glass windows dark, apart from the west facing windows, which were lit up by rays of sunlight breaking through the cloud cover.

Coffin grasped the iron ring on the church door and twisted it, and pushed. The door stayed firmly shut.

"I thought churches never shut their doors," he said. "Aren't they always supposed to be open, offering sanctuary and help to those in need?"

"Are you kidding?" Emma replied. "Leaving these doors open would be an invitation to every bored teenager pissed off their heads on cheap lager to come and scrawl satanic messages all over the walls and the pews."

Coffin grunted. "I suppose so. Still doesn't seem right, though."

Emma looked back down the path towards the road, and the white Transit van parked on the opposite side, one set of wheels on the pavement.

"You think Brendan can keep his head out of the paper long enough to look out for passing coppers, this time?"

"He'd better. Craggs will rip him to shreds if he doesn't."

"I didn't think your Irish friend worked for the Mob."

"He doesn't, but Brendan fucked up big time back at Eddie's, and now we've got the problem of what to do with those two cops. He's embarrassed, that's why he was so eager to kill them, get them out of the way. He won't mess up again."

Coffin pushed at the church doors again, as though this time they might magically open.

"Just what the hell are you going to do with those two?" Emma said. "You know you can't kill them, right?"

"I don't see any other option," Coffin replied. "Besides, they're cops. Like I said before, cops aren't people."

"You don't really believe that, do you?" Emma said.

Coffin grinned. "Of course not, I just wanted to see your reaction."

"What?"

"The look on your face, it was worth it."

Emma punched him on the arm. "Hey, I'm being serious here. You and that red headed gorilla kidnapped two coppers, and now you're holding them prisoner. If you're not going to kill them, and I've just got to say once more, that really is not an option here, then you've got to let them go at some point. And I don't know if you realise this, but the courts don't look too kindly on officers of the law being kidnapped and held prisoner. So, just what the fuck are you going to do?"

"Shouldn't that be 'we'?"

"What?"

"Just what the fuck are 'we' going to do? After all, you were there, too."

"No way. I wasn't involved in catching those two jokers," Emma said, raising her hands. "You can't involve me in this mess, as well."

Coffin turned his back on Emma and began walking along the front of the church building. "You're already involved. Those two cops got a damn good look at your face in the back of Brendan's van. You're part of the gang, Emma, didn't you realise?" He paused at the corner of the church, and looked back at Emma, still standing in front of the doors. "You're part of the Slaughterhouse Mob now."

Coffin walked down the side of the church before Emma could reply, and grinned as he heard her swearing. She was just too easy to wind up.

Coffin paused, partly to let Emma catch up with him, but also to take a moment, look at the shafts of sunlight breaking through the cloud cover. The sun was low over the city skyline, and in another hour it would have disappeared completely. From his vantage point on the hill, Coffin could see beyond the rows of houses, the city skyline in the distance. There was the Library of Birmingham with its distinctive, colourful facade, and the International Convention Centre. Further on out was the National Indoor Arena. After that, hidden from Coffin's view, there was the Sea Life Centre, the Ikon Gallery, the restaurants and shops along the canal side waterfront. Then there was the city centre itself with its shops and galleries and clubs and restaurants, and on the other side of the city, Millennium Point and the Think Tank.

Birmingham had been trying so hard for so many years to become Britain's Second City, to rival London with its attractions. Never going to happen though. Not with the city's leaders steeped in so much corruption. A significant section of the council was in Craggs' pocket, and at least half of the rest were on the take in one way or another. 'Britain's Second City' was in so much debt, if it was a business it would have been declared bankrupt years ago.

Not that Coffin gave a shit about any of that.

"So, what's the plan?" Emma said.

"Come with me," Coffin replied.

He led her around to the rear of the church building. A black crow landed on a gravestone, and watched them. After a few moments it extended its wings and lifted into the air, cawing as it rose higher and flew out of sight.

"Look down there," Coffin said, pointing down towards the park, nestled next to the ancient graveyard.

Between the trees, the yellow scene of crime tape fluttered in the soft breeze, marking out the spot where the old man had been found, lying half on the park bench, his throat ripped open.

It were like a fiend from hell, the old woman had said.

The bench where the homeless man had been found was gone, taken apart and removed by the police, and a large area around it had been trampled into mud. All that was left was the scene of crime tape.

"That's where they found one of Mortenson's victims, right?" Emma said.

"That's what the papers said," Coffin replied.

"Okay,' Emma said. "But you're not so sure, is that what you're thinking?"

"According to what Tom told us back at Angels, he was supplying Mortenson and Guttman with blood. They were still in hiding at the house, waiting until Guttman was stronger before they made any kind of move is what I'm guessing."

"So if the Birmingham Vampire didn't kill the homeless man . . ."

Coffin took Emma gently by the shoulders and turned her around, so that her back was to the park, and she was facing the graveyard.

"This is where Steffanie and Michael were buried."

"Oh, shit. You think Michael killed him, don't you?"

Coffin nodded.

"Makes sense," Emma said.

"I got thinking, wondered if maybe Michael might be hiding out up here, in the church maybe. Whatever's happened to him, whatever he has been transformed into, he's still a child, and he must have been scared as hell waking up in that coffin and having to dig his way out. I don't know, it's a long shot, but I was wondering if maybe he sees this place as the nearest thing he's got to home."

"You could be right," Emma said. "If he's got no memory of anything else, this area here is where he might feel safest."

Emma spun around, facing the park once more. "Wait a minute. Isn't this where that young guy with the dogs got killed?"

"That's right. Just over the hill there, behind that line of trees. Another reason I think Michael might still be hiding out here."

"Fuck. We've got to find him, before he kills anybody else."

"No. We've got to find him before the cops catch him. Find him and then take him somewhere to safety."

"And then what?" Emma said softly. "You think you can find a cure for him? As far as I know, the only cure for vampirism is a stake through the heart."

A dark shape hurtled past them in the twilight. A bat, flying low, circling over their heads and then peeling off and around behind the church building.

"I can't believe that," Coffin said. "There has to be something we can do for him, some way I can bring him back."

Emma touched him briefly on his arm. "Joe, I know this is hard for you, but Michael's dead. Whatever unholy force is keeping him animated, giving his body the appearance of life, it's not Michael. Your boy's gone."

Coffin walked away. He weaved his way between the graves. Some of them were clean and well maintained, others with fresh flowers laid on them, but most were unkempt, weeds and grass sprouting from their bases and their stones worn and cracked with age.

When he found Steffanie's and Michael's graves he paused. The two graves looked untidy and disturbed, even though Coffin had done his best to fill them back in. Michael's grave in particular looked odd, a dip in the ground where the soil had fallen into his empty coffin.

The daylight was fading fast now, the city skyline only visible by the glow of the windows in the tower blocks, and the streetlights. And the Library of Birmingham, its multi-coloured frontage bathed in light.

Strange that a graveyard, a final resting place for the dead, should be elevated above the city, teeming with life. As though the dead were laughing in their knowledge that everything comes to an end. That no matter what towers of light we might build, what storehouses of knowledge and wisdom, when it came to the final reckoning we all finish in the ground, nothing more than food for the worms.

"It's not your fault, you know," Emma said, breaking into his thoughts.

"What isn't my fault? Global warming? Cancer? Swine flu?"

"You know what I'm saying. Michael, Steffanie, it's not your fault they died."

"No, that was Tom Mills' fault, and Mortenson's, and Steffanie too. Seems like everybody whose fault it could be is already dead, except Steffanie."

"She's dead, too, Joe."

Coffin gestured to her grave. "Then why the hell isn't she in there?"

"You know why, already. I don't know how it works, I don't know if it's biology or magic, or what the fuck it is, but somehow Mortenson infected Steffanie and Michael when he killed them, infected them with something that brought their bodies back to life with the same hunger for blood that he had. But I can't believe they are the same as they were. Whatever it was, call it their soul if you like, that made them the people they were, it's no longer there, no longer a part of them. Don't you see?"

"No, I don't see that at all," Coffin replied. "About the only thing that Tom said that made any sense before I smashed his brains in was describing Steffanie as a cold hearted bitch. I couldn't see it before, but now I can. Now, when I think back over our time together, I can see how she looked at me sometimes, almost like she pitied me and hated me all at the same moment. I just couldn't recognise it then, or maybe a part of me did, but buried it somewhere out of sight where it wouldn't hurt me."

"Why did she marry you, if she despised you so much?"

"I don't know," Coffin said. "Maybe she thought I had more money than she realised, or maybe I was supposed to be a way to get to Craggs, or get out of a life in strip clubs."

"From what I saw of her she looked like she enjoyed the dancing," Emma said.

Coffin lifted his head and looked out over the city, aglow with lights. "You never told me you'd met Steffanie before."

"Oh shit," Emma said. "I wondered when we were going to have this conversation."

"Those things Tom said, were they true?"

"Yes, they were." Emma took a deep breath. "Steffanie approached me months ago, saying she had evidence of who murdered Terry Wu, along with evidence documenting the Slaughterhouse Mob's illegal activities, the protection money, the drugs, stuff like that. Enough to put Craggs away and close down his clubs. She wanted to sell it to the papers, but the money she was asking for, it was just too much. She kept holding out and holding out, and then she got killed."

"She ever give you the video footage?"

"No." Emma paused. "Mortenson killed her before we agreed on a price."

"Is that why you broke into my house the other day? Looking for the evidence?"

"I guess your two friends told you they found me snooping around, huh?"

"They're not exactly what you would call friends."

"They're not exactly what you would call normal."

"You're avoiding the question."

Emma sighed. "Yeah. Steffanie said she'd put everything on a USB stick, and I wondered if maybe she'd hidden it at the house somewhere."

"Did you find it?"

"No. Wherever it is, your wife hid it good and proper."

Emma ducked as a bat flew past, hurtling out of the twilight and then disappearing again just as quickly.

"What were you going to do if you found the video footage of me killing Terry Wu?" Coffin said.

"I don't know," Emma replied. "My original intention, when Steffanie first approached me, was to write up a big expose, obviously."

"And now?"

"Well, now I kind of feel like I owe you one, especially after you came riding to my rescue when Mortenson had me trapped on the barge."

"Don't forget I rescued you at the house as well, when Mortenson was wanting to do the hokey poky with you."

"And let me remind you again that I was the one who bashed him over the head when he had you pinned to the floor and was getting ready to give you a love bite."

Coffin pulled a torch out of his jacket pocket and switched it on. He ran the beam of light over the graves of his wife and son, back and forth, from one to the other. Despite everything, he still found it hard to believe they weren't down there, under the dirt.

"It gets dark out here pretty damn quick, doesn't it?" he said. "You sure you didn't find that USB stick?"

"Yeah, I'm sure," Emma said. "I'd tell you if I did."

Coffin continued playing the torch light over the graves, not looking at Emma. "You haven't asked me yet if I did it, if I murdered Terry Wu."

"I don't need to. Steffanie said she had the evidence, Tom said so, too. You did it, right?"

"Yeah, I put a bullet in his head."

"Why?"

"Mort wanted him dead, wanted the club. Wu wasn't playing straight with us, he was holding money back, whining all the time, and the place was dying a slow death, hadn't turned a profit in months."

"And that was a reason to kill him?"

"Mort thought so."

"You do everything Craggs tells you to?"

Coffin thought about this for a moment. "Wu was a sick bastard, Emma. Into kiddie porn and who knows what the fuck else. He didn't deserve to live."

"That's not your decision to make, that's why we've got the police and the courts, why we've got laws. You can't go around like an angel of vengeance, dispensing death wherever you see injustice."

Coffin turned to face Emma. "You didn't protest when I was sawing Abel's remains up into little pieces, and setting fire to them."

Emma looked away. "That was different."

Coffin grunted. "Right."

"What the fuck's that supposed to mean?"

"You're making the life or death decisions now. You're saying that Wu should have lived, so that he could be tried in the courts for his crimes, but Mortenson? No, he deserved to die. You might not agree with my moral code Emma, but at least I'm consistent."

"Fuck you, Coffin," Emma said.

Coffin tipped his head back and laughed. "I'm guessing you were never invited onto the debating team at school, right?"

Emma pulled her own torch out of her jacket pocket and switched it on.

"I thought we were supposed to be looking for Michael?"

Coffin swept his torch over the graveyard, the flickering shadows bringing the gravestones to life, before being lost in the gathering gloom.

"Yeah, we were," Coffin said.

"We should have got here earlier. Vampires sleep in the day, right? There must be somewhere that he's found where he feels safe, where he can rest. For all we know he might be out hunting now."

Coffin began walking between the gravestones. "I'm not so sure about that. It's not fully dark yet, and we got here when there was still a fair bit of daylight around."

"Still, wouldn't we have been better doing this in the middle of the day?" Emma said, as she followed Coffin.

"No, I don't want him getting burnt by the sunlight. You've seen what it can do to them. I don't want him hurt."

Emma pointed. "What about up there?"

Just visible in the gloom, were the remains of a ruined chapel, situated in the farthest corner of the graveyard. Coffin had never noticed it before, but he had only been here twice, and the first time was for the funeral of his family. The second he was digging their graves up, knowing that they were empty.

He hadn't exactly been in the mood on either occasion to take stock of his surroundings.

"Let's check it out," he said.

The two of them began walking up the incline towards the chapel, their torches trained on the shadows of the ruin. Emma had to duck as another bat, or maybe the same one, flew past, the dark shape twisting and turning in a seemingly random flight pattern.

"Fuck!" she hissed. "I hate bats. Aren't they supposed to like, roost in your hair, or some shit like that?"

"Probably an old wives' tale," Coffin said.

Emma stopped walking, placed a hand on Coffin's arm.

"Can you see that?" she whispered.

"Yeah."

Two eyes had appeared in the darkness of the ruin. Someone, or something, was inside. Hidden by the shadows, it was watching them. The eyes, like a cat's, were glowing and reflecting the torch light back at Coffin and Emma. They blinked once, and continued staring at them.

"You think it's a cat?" Emma whispered.

"I don't know," Coffin murmured. "Looks too big for a cat."

"A dog, maybe?"

"Possibly. Do dog's eyes glow in the dark, like cat's?"

"Not sure," Emma said, her voice low. "Never had a dog."

The eyes blinked again.

Before he knew it had happened, Coffin realised he was now looking at two pairs of eyes staring at him from the depths of the chapel. Whatever was up there had been joined by its partner.

"Two of them, great," Emma whispered. "Maybe they're big cats, like panthers or tigers, escaped from a zoo or something."

"You know of any zoos nearby?"

"There's Dudley Zoo, but that's ten miles from here, at least."

"Even with everything else that's been going on, I think we'd have heard something on the news if a pair of big cats had escaped from the zoo, wouldn't we?" Coffin murmured.

The two pairs of eyes blinked, but otherwise held Coffin and Emma in their gaze.

"You're not still seriously considering going exploring up there, are you?" Emma said.

"I don't know," Coffin replied.

"If you get savaged by those two things, I'm not throwing you over my shoulder and carrying you back down to the main road, all right? Just so we're clear on that."

"And there I was thinking I meant so much more to you."

"Shit, they've gone."

Emma was right. Where the glowing eyes had been, there was now simply darkness. For Coffin, it was as though he had imagined the yellow eyes staring at him from the depths of the ruin.

"Come on, let's go take a closer look," he said.

"Are you fucking serious?" Emma looked at Coffin as though he was crazy. "Just because you can't see those two pairs of devil eyes, doesn't mean to say they're not there anymore. Or do you think maybe they're taking a nap, and we can sneak around them while they have a snooze?"

"All right, you stay here with your friend the bat for company. I'll be back before you know it." Coffin started walking. "Unless I get savaged by the pussycats of course."

He took the approach to the chapel slowly. Despite what he said, and his flippant tone, he knew he had to be cautious. The last thing he wanted was a pair of ferocious big cats shredding him into bite sized chunks.

There was sign on a pole set into the ground, explaining the history of the chapel, and dating it around the 1600s. Coffin didn't stop to read it.

He paused a few feet away from the ragged opening in the wall that had once, presumably, been the front entrance. The uneven stonework had been weathered smooth over the passing of the centuries, and the windows were now empty sockets in the chapel's face. Several years ago work had been started on renovating the building, by installing new rafters in the collapsed roof. But then the money had run out and the work had been abandoned, leaving a partially completed roof on the old chapel.

Consequently much of the chapel's interior was shrouded in darkness. Coffin tried illuminating it with his torch, but from where he was standing the beam was too weak to make any difference. If he was going to investigate further, he needed to get closer.

Twisting around he could see Emma still standing by the church, her torchlight dazzling him for a moment before she lowered it. He returned to facing the chapel. Apart from the distant sounds of traffic, all was still and quiet up here.

Coffin held his breath, listening for any movement inside the ruin. If it hadn't been for Emma seeing the two pairs of eyes as well, he would have been tempted to think he'd imagined the whole thing by now.

Taking a cautious step forward, Coffin paused and listened again.

Nothing.

Just the whisper of the breeze on the grass.

Do you really want to go in there?

Coffin swept the torch around again, the beam of light still doing little to penetrate the gloom. Taking another step forward, his left hand clenched into a tight fist, he raised the torch, the light barely illuminating the rafters and the nooks and crannies in the ancient stonework.

He lowered the torch again.

What the hell was he doing? There were more than enough shadowy hiding places in here for a wild animal to leap from and fasten its jaws around his arm or, even worse, his neck. As tough as he was, Coffin knew he would have little chance of not being mauled if a large dog attacked him, and much less so if there were two of them.

But he had to explore further. Just like the chapel was an excellent hiding place for a pair of vicious animals, so it was for his son. Coffin could imagine Michael finding enough shade and privacy in a hidden corner of this ruin to enable him to rest during the daytime.

Maybe Emma had been right, and they should have come here in the protective light of the sun. Surely they could have found some way of protecting his sensitive skin from the harmful effects of daylight until they had bundled him into the cool darkness of Brendan's van.

Too late for that now. Although he couldn't say why, Coffin had the feeling that if he abandoned the search for Michael now and they returned tomorrow, they would find nothing.

He took another step forward, senses heightened for the scrape of claws against stone, of a low growl perhaps, as a dark shape hurtled for him. Would he see its glowing eyes piercing the darkness before it was on top of him?

Coffin stood in the gap in the chapel's wall. At this point the grass had given way to packed dirt. Deeper inside the ruin, some of the stone flagged floor had survived, although riddled with a crazy crisscross of cracks and indentations.

Towards the opposite end of the chapel stood the remains of a baptismal font. It, too, was constructed of stone and appeared in the darkness to be like some squat, stunted stalagmite in a cave.

Coffin took a couple more furtive steps inside the ruin, swinging his torch backwards and forwards, constantly alert for any sign of movement in the deep shadows. Slowly he turned around in a complete circle until his torch was centred on the baptismal font once more.

Surely if there was someone, or something, else in here with him he would know about it by now. The big cats, if that is what they were, would have leapt upon him, their jaws going for his throat. Or Michael would have dropped from his hiding place in the roof space, also fastening his teeth around Coffin's neck.

But there was a silence and a stillness in here that befitted a place of worship.

Coffin walked up to the baptismal font and placed a hand on the cold stone.

He shone the torch down into the shallow dip, where the brass bowl for the holy water would have been placed.

Lying on the stone, illuminated by the yellow beam of light, was a severed tongue, chewed up and leeched of all blood and moisture.

Coffin picked it up, turning it round and round in his fingers.

Finally he dropped it back in the font, and left the chapel.

a burial

After leaving Emma and Coffin, Leola had headed back to her room at the B&B. Talking with Coffin, finding out that Guttman was still alive and that the infection had begun to spread already, had frightened her. She had come over to England hoping to find out that the ancient one was dead. That perhaps Abel had never returned to dig him from his coffin after the one hundred year sleep. That he was still there, under the ground in the cellar. Rotting.

Leola paced her tiny room. They should have left him beneath the dirt. No one would ever have found him.

She should have left him. To Abel the Father had always been a god of sorts. He worshipped the ancient one, just like they all did, really. But with Abel it was different, because Abel had been human when he had been Guttman's lover. Leola would never understand why Guttman would not turn Abel. They made a grotesque sight together, the ancient, wizened vampire and the young man.

There had only been a tiny number of their company left by then. After hundreds of years roaming across Europe and the Americas, sowing terror and superstition as they moved, they finally came to a halt in the middle of England during the reign of Queen Victoria. Guttman had thought it would be funny to see the Queen, to insinuate himself into her company and sink his teeth into her fat neck.

"How very amusing," he had said once. "That miserable little country would be ruled by a vampire queen, and we would be royalty amongst the human cattle."

He could have done it, too, when he was younger. Lithe and powerful, his sexuality like a hypnotic force. But not anymore. Not in those final days, after they had bought the house and Guttman would send Abel and Leola out into the night to bring back girls for him.

They were only at the house a short time before Guttman decided they needed to carry out the ceremony.

The burial.

Leola had been there that night. Despite all the years that had passed she could still remember it now, as clear as though it had been just yesterday.

Guttman standing silently in the corner, leaning heavily on his walking stick. The walking stick was thick and heavy, intricate designs and symbols carved into its surface. Guttman's dark eyes, almost hidden beneath his overarching brow, watched Abel digging. The ancient vampire was too weak to help with the manual work. His stooped frame was skeletal, his black coat hanging limply from his frail body, his scrawny neck protruding from the wing tip collars of his white shirt. Beneath the light of the oil lamp hanging from the wooden beam, he cast a long, thin shadow across the cellar floor.

Leola stood at the foot of the cellar steps watching Abel dig as Guttman barked out the occasional command, his voice still strong despite his frailty.

Abel Mortenson, bare chested, muscular and powerful, was sweating heavily despite the cold air in the cellar. The ground was hard, and he'd had to attack it with a pick-axe before he could start digging with the spade. But the soil was stony, and sometimes he had to abandon the spade and return to the pick-axe, just to loosen the ground enough so that he could continue digging.

As the long night wore on, he had begun to regard the ground as his enemy. He had to overcome his foe, and win this battle, for the hole needed to be dug. The consequences of failure were not worth contemplating.

Leola had wanted to help him, but Guttman forbade her. Abel was his special one, and it was left to him alone to perform the burial from beginning to end.

Abel dug, as Leola and the old man watched him. Occasionally he wiped his arm across his forehead, leaving smears of dirt on his face. Sometimes he had to stop digging, and rest, his chest heaving with the tortuous exertion of sucking the stale cellar air into his lungs. Leola could see that Guttman was growing unhappy with the progress.

But there was nothing he could do. If Abel didn't do this for him, nobody else could.

And the Father would die.

Abel finally finished digging. Standing in the hole, he looked up at his master, stooped in the corner of the cellar, his bald head glowing softly beneath the dirty light from the oil lamp, his hooked fingers clutching his walking stick.

"Is it finished?" he said, his voice hardly more than a strangled whisper.

The younger man massaged the back of his neck. "Yes, it is finished."

"Is it deep enough?"

Abel took a deep breath, muscles aching from the hard, physical work of the last few hours. "Six feet deep, exactly as you need."

Leaning on the walking stick, the old man shuffled forward for a better look. He stood at the edge of the rectangular hole, his feet by the top of the young man's head. Rivulets of dirt trickled down the sides of the hole.

"It will do," Guttman said. He pulled a watch from his waistcoat pocket, and snapped the lid open. "We must be quick now, time is short."

Abel threw the spade and the pick out of the hole, and hauled himself up. The cellar trapdoor leading out to the garden was open and he paused for a moment, obviously relishing the feel of the cool breeze on his naked torso. Once they had finished down here, his next task would be to carry bags of the remaining soil up the steps and outside, where he would scatter the dirt in the garden.

Then he had to get rid of the bodies.

Abel dragged a long wooden box across the cellar, positioning it by the hole.

"Are you ready?" he said.

"The blood," the old man whispered. "We need the blood."

"It's all here." The young man pointed to the rows of earthenware jars, on the far side of the cellar, their lids covered in a fine layer of dust. Abel and Leola had spent months acquiring the blood, and mixing it with red wine vinegar to help preserve it.

Upstairs, in the kitchen, were the bodies of all the young women they had killed, their throats slit, hanging upside down from meat hooks. Abel had spent endless hours draining their blood into the jars, puddles of it gathering on the table, seeping into the wood.

As Leola watched, he lifted the wooden box and lowered it into the hole. Lying at the bottom, it was a perfect fit against the sides. Next he leaned a ladder against the wall of dirt, and climbed down until he was standing in the box. Then he helped the old man climb down the ladder, holding him by the sides so that he would not fall, guiding his trembling feet onto each of the ladder's wooden rungs.

The progress was so painfully slow that Leola took a step forward to help, but Guttman turned on her, baring his yellowed teeth and hissing.

Leola stepped back into the shadows again.

Finally, Guttman was standing in the wooden box.

"Help me to sit down," he whispered.

Abel held his arm and lowered him down, until the old man was sitting in the box. Then the younger man climbed the ladder, and lifted it out behind him. The vampire lay down on his back in the wooden box, and gazed up at Abel. He looked like a corpse, laid out in his burial clothes for the mourners to gaze upon him.

"Now the blood," he whispered.

Abel hauled the first of the earthenware jars across to the edge of the hole and lifted the lid. The strong, coppery smell, combined with the vinegar, filled his nose. He tipped the jar, and the blood began pouring over the lip of the hole, onto the vampire's face, splashing into his eyes and his open mouth.

He started cackling with delight, his arms and legs twitching, and then his whole body spasming with pleasure.

"More, more!" he shouted, his voice thick and wet, and disgusting.

Abel rolled another earthenware jar across the cellar floor and poured the blood into the box. The dark, noxious syrup splashed over Guttman's suit, running down the creases in the fabric, and filling up around the shape of his body in the box. He howled in ecstasy, as his coffin filled with blood.

Abel continued alone with the work, emptying the jars of blood into the grave whilst Leola watched. When he had finished with the last one, Guttman could hardly be seen beneath the dark, scarlet liquid, spilling over the edges of the wooden box.

Abel picked up the coffin lid and slid it down into the hole, and over the vampire, until it fitted perfectly into place. Carrying a large hammer and a bag of nails, he climbed down onto the lid and began hammering it closed. Blood spurted from between gaps in the coffin with each blow of the hammer upon a nail.

When he had finished, and the coffin was nailed completely shut, Abel knelt on the coffin lid and bowed his head. The cellar was silent.

Leola walked toward the hole, towards Abel.

She climbed down, dirt spattering onto the coffin lid, until she was kneeling beside him. She ran her fingers through his hair and down over his face.

"You did it," she whispered.

Abel wiped the sweat from his forehead.

"What now?" he said.

"Now you receive your reward."

Leola lay Abel down on his back on the coffin. Dark blood seeped through tiny cracks in the coffin lid. Leola pulled off her dress, her naked flesh yellow beneath the sputtering glow of the oil lamp. Her skin was unblemished, like ivory. She lay down on top of Abel, her breasts pressed against his naked chest, and her mouth met his.

The cold blood of the virgin girls seeped through the wooden coffin lid, and Leola smeared it over Abel's body. His breathing grew quick and shallow as she took him inside her, running her hands smeared with blood through his hair. And just at the moment he came, she sank her teeth into his neck and ripped a hole in his throat, swallowing the warm blood as it spurted into her mouth.

that lock

Brendan took Emma and Coffin back to the pub. Emma had insisted that she would be fine, that she could get a taxi back home, that she didn't want to return to O'Donoghue's. She had work to do, a story to write up on the Birmingham Vampire before Karl decided to take her off the story, and possibly the newspaper, once and for all.

Brendan was having none of it. "It's best if you come back with us. You can drink as much as you like at the bar, it's on the house."

"Oh great, thanks," Emma replied, standing by the transit van and looking up and down the darkened street, trying to work out if she made a break for it how far she would get. "The thing is, I've had a manic couple of days, and I'd really rather just go home and get some sleep, if it's all the same with you."

"I think it's best you come back with us," Brendan said.

"Yeah, I know, you just said that. I'm saying no, I'm not coming back with you."

Brendan stared at her impassively. Emma wondered what would happen if she just tried walking away, but the look in his eyes warned her off that idea.

"Joe?" she said, hoping for some moral support.

"I think he's probably right, you should come back with us," Coffin said.

Emma thought she might have detected a hint of apology in his voice, but she could have been wrong.

"You think he's probably right." Emma looked from Coffin to Brendan. "You two think I'm going to go to the police as soon as I'm out of your sight, don't you?"

"Emma, no, it's not—"

"Let's not insult her intelligence, big man," Brendan said. "You're right. Joe here, he seems to trust you, and I know the two of you have been through a lot together in the last couple of days, but me, I don't know you from Eve. As far as I'm concerned the moment I let you out of my sight you could be straight down the cop shop, telling them there's two of theirs being held prisoner in the cellar at O'Donoghue's. Before I know it, my pub would be surrounded by coppers in riot gear, with somebody yelling at me through a bullhorn, and half the artillery available in the West Midlands being pointed at my front door. I don't know if you have an appreciation of the pub trade, young lady, but that kind of situation tends to be bad for business. Do you see why I might be a little concerned now?"

Emma clenched her teeth together, in an attempt to bottle up the frustration tightening up her insides.

"All right, I can see where you're coming from," she said, through gritted teeth. "But I seriously need to go home and get some shut eye, as I am running on coffee fumes at the moment, and I want to get to my bed before I crash. Joe, tell him I'm not going to go to the police."

Coffin said nothing.

"Joe?"

Coffin still said nothing.

"Fuck!" Emma hissed. "You're on his side, aren't you?"

"It's not about taking sides, Emma," Coffin said, holding his hands out. "We should stick together, keep each other safe."

"Bullshit! Either you're agreeing with him, that I can't be trusted, or you haven't got the balls to stand up to him."

Coffin sighed. "Now you're just acting like a spoilt child."

"Are you fucking serious?" Emma took a step back. "I'm leaving now. I'm going to walk down the road and call myself a taxi, and neither of you had better try and stop me."

Before Emma had even fully taken another step, Brendan had wrapped one of his hands around her slim wrist, and stopped her.

Coffin planted his hand on Brendan's chest. "Let go of her."

"She'll go straight to the police, Joe," Brendan said, still keeping a grip on Emma's wrist.

"Just fucking let go of her, Brendan," Coffin replied, drawing in close to the Irishman.

The two men eyeballed each other for what seemed like an impossibly long time. Brendan's grip on her wrist grew so tight that Emma had to hold her breath to keep from crying out. She was scared that if she made a noise, broke the silence in any way, that it would be like a spark igniting a fire, and the tension between these two men would explode. Coffin was bigger and stronger than the Irishman, but she could see that Brendan knew how to look after himself. A fight between these two would be messy and brutal, and once they got going Emma wasn't sure they would even remember she was there anymore.

Which would have been a good thing except for the fact that Brendan had hold of her. If it kicked off between them she wasn't sure she could get out of the way in time before someone's fist or boot connected with a vital part her anatomy, like her head or stomach.

Finally, Brendan let go. "All right, Joe, calm it down now. We don't want no trouble between ourselves, now, do we?"

Coffin backed off, looked at Emma. "Just get in the fucking van, and then we can get out of here."

Emma got in the van.

Coffin said nothing on the way back to O'Donoghue's, just grunted in response to anything Emma said. After a while she stopped trying to talk to him. She could see that he was brooding, but over what she wasn't sure. Was he angry at her, saw the confrontation with Brendan as her fault? Or was it Michael?

Coffin's instincts about the church had been right, the little boy had obviously been hiding out there. But now he was gone. Emma had suggested that they hang around, see if he returned, but Coffin had said no. He said they could come back at break of day, check out the chapel at first light and see if Michael had returned to his hiding place. His gut feeling though, was that they had been spotted, and his son would be spending the night looking for a new hiding place.

The pub was locked up when they got back, which Emma thought was strange as it was early evening and all the other bars and clubs were heaving with life. O'Donoghue's, on the other hand, was silent and dark, the windows shuttered, the door firmly shut.

Brendan parked round the back and they hustled in through the rear entrance. Emma was surprised to hear voices from the snug, lots of them. Maybe the pub was open after all?

Emma headed for the bar. Brendan stepped in front of her.

"I think it's best if you go upstairs. You can join Patsy in the living room, maybe watch some TV together. Patsy likes to watch all the soaps, and the house programmes, you know the ones where they take somebody's house and decorate it in five minutes flat."

"No thanks," Emma said. "I was planning on going and getting that drink you offered me."

"There's plenty to drink upstairs, so there is. Patsy would appreciate the company."

Emma was aware of Coffin's presence behind her. He had already backed Brendan up in their last confrontation, and she wondered whose side he would be on this time and how far she should take it to find that out.

"Sounds like you've got a regular party going on out front, and a private one at that," she said. "Wouldn't Patsy like to come down, join the rest of the gang for a few drinks, a couple of laughs? Must get lonely for her up there, all by herself, nothing to do but watch Homes Under the Hammer, and EastEnders."

Brendan's dark eyes gazed at her like she was a being from another planet, some exotic creature the like of which he had never encountered before, and he didn't have a clue what to do with her.

"Let her go on through, Brendan," Coffin said.

Brendan gave no sign of having registered what Coffin said, just continued staring at Emma.

Finally he stirred, as though coming out of a deep sleep. "I don't like it, Joe. She's a reporter, for fuck's sake. She's most likely writing this all up, and in the next day or two we'll be all over the front pages of the news. We should stick her down the cellar with those two pigs, while we decide what to do with her, instead of ferrying her around like the Queen of fucking Sheba."

Emma was suddenly shoved out of the way as Coffin barrelled past her, and got right in Brendan's face again.

"Don't even think about it," he growled. "I let you bring her back here, but you're not keeping her prisoner. She stays with me."

Brendan eyeballed Coffin. Two big men, neither of them willing to back down, Emma knew it was likely to come to a nasty finish. The rumble of voices continued in the other room, oblivious to the argument happening out back. But if they realised, if they came out to investigate, Emma wondered whose side they would be on.

After a few moments of glaring at each other, nose to nose, Brendan finally backed down. Not much, just a tiny movement away, enough to signal that he was stepping down for the moment.

"Craggs isn't going to think much of it, Joe, when you bring the young lady into the meet with you."

"I'll handle Mort," Coffin said.

Brendan backed up a little more. "It's on your head, then, Joe."

"Yeah."

"What's going on?" Emma said.

"Mort's got a few guys together," Coffin said. "Tomorrow morning, first thing, we're taking Angels back from those bloodsucking freaks who are in there right now."

"What about Steffanie?"

"What about her?" Coffin said, and pushed past Brendan and through into the snug.

Brendan stayed behind a moment longer. Scowled at Emma.

"You got something you want to say to me?" Emma snapped.

"No," Brendan said, his voice low. "Not one thing, young lady."

When Brendan had walked into the snug, the door swinging shut behind him, Emma let out her breath and sank against the wall. Her legs suddenly felt like they couldn't support her anymore, that they were made of rubber and string instead of bone and muscle.

What the fuck am I doing, hanging out with gangsters and killers? Of all the stupid things you've done over the years, this has got to be the craziest.

Emma glanced at the back door. There was a key in the lock, a large bunch of keys hanging from it. This was her chance to escape, right now. Out of the door, and if she took it at a sprint she could be smack in the middle of Broad Street in less than a minute. She could get help for the two cops tied up in the cellar.

When she thought over the events of the last few days, the decisions she had made, she was all right with it. Sure, she had held back information from Karl, and the police, but none of it had endangered lives. This was the biggest story she had ever worked on, and she was smack bang right in the middle of it. There was already enough here for her to write a book, enough to make her career.

But those two policemen bound and gagged in the basement? They fouled up her story big time. Coffin wasn't a cop killer, she was sure of that. But Brendan, and Craggs? How was Coffin going to stop them when they decided it was time to 'permanently disappear' those two inconveniences downstairs?

And even Coffin was aware of the problem they had on their hands. He couldn't keep them locked up forever, but as soon as they were free there would be a manhunt on for Coffin, and Brendan, and maybe even Emma too.

Emma closed her eyes, rested her head against the wall.

Fuck!

The answer was a no-brainer. She had to get out, get help.

If it fucked up her career and her story that was just too bad. Because she had no other option.

If she didn't get help, those two cops downstairs were simply marking time until their execution.

Emma stood up straight, opened her eyes.

Okay. Get out. Now.

In four quick strides, Emma was at the door. She took hold of the key, tried turning it. It was the old mortise type and the lock was ancient and rusty. The key stuck before Emma had managed to twist it. She tried waggling it free, and the keys on the bunch jingled. Emma glanced behind her, but the low rumble of voices continued uninterrupted from the snug.

No one could hear her out here. But she had to escape quick, before Coffin or Brendan began to wonder where she was and came to investigate.

The thought struck her that maybe the door hadn't been locked when they walked into the pub. Emma twisted the handle and gave the heavy door a push. It refused to budge. She twisted at the key again, and managed to turn it back to its starting position.

Okay. Deep breath. Try again.

Emma gave the key a quick, forceful turn, and it stopped in the same position as before, a third of the way through its revolution.

"Fuck, fuck, fuck!"

Now it was stuck, wouldn't turn back to its starting position. She glanced over her shoulder, fearful that someone might be coming out to investigate where she was, and froze when she saw Brendan, framed by the doorway to the snug.

"That lock's always been a bugger to open," he said, softly. "Should have replaced it years ago, but you know how it is, you get so that you can work around the problem, becomes a part of your routine. Then somebody else comes along and tries to work it, but they don't know the routine, they don't realise the special little dance you go through every day, so familiar to you that you don't even think about it anymore. I bet you've got something like that at your house, haven't you?"

Emma let go of the keys, turned so that she was fully facing the Irishman.

"Worked out well for me, really, didn't it?" he said, stepping through the doorway and letting the door swing shut behind him. "If I'd replaced that lock, well, you'd be in town by now, calling the police no doubt. I knew we shouldn't've left you alone, that we couldn't trust you. Way I've heard it, Joe's always been a bit soft in the head when it comes to the ladies, and now I know the truth of it."

"Just stay the fuck away from me."

"What are you going to do, scream for help? I'm sure your boyfriend will come running at the first peep out of you."

"What's going on?" Coffin stepped through the doorway, the sound of laughter from the snug fading as the door swung shut.

"Your girlfriend was making a bid for freedom, going to get the police, she was," Brendan said.

"Is that right?" Coffin said.

"Hey, Joe, I've got a story to write up on the Birmingham Vampire, you know?" Emma said. "If I don't get some copy in for tomorrow's edition, my editor's likely to fire me."

"What a crock of shit," Brendan said.

"We can't let you go, Emma," Coffin said. "You must realise that, we can't let you go. Not yet, anyway."

"Fuck, Joe, you're going to have to tie me up if you want to keep me here."

"You heard her, Joe," Brendan said.

"No one's tying anybody up," Coffin said. "Please, Emma, come with me, you'll be all right."

This was an argument she wasn't going to win. Her continued obstinacy was going to get her locked up in the cellar with those two cops. Not a good idea.

But she could see that there was a bigger issue here. Just like the two policemen in the cellar, Emma was turning into a problem. Joe was on her side, but Brendan and Craggs? When all of this was over, and the vampires were dead, were Brendan and Craggs really going to be happy to wave her off to the *Herald* to write up her story?

Of course not.

Perhaps it would be best just to play it cool for a while.

"All right," she said. "I'll come with you."

Taking a deep breath, Emma followed Coffin into the snug.

a corpse
just lies there

The room quietened down as Coffin walked in, with Emma following close by and Brendan behind her. The men were all sat around the same big table as before, all in the same positions, with Craggs in the position of leader. He scowled when he saw Emma, and Coffin shook his head, saying, *not now, we'll talk about it later.*

If Craggs got involved, and Brendan weighed in too, Emma was likely to blow her top and then they would be in big trouble. Bringing her in here was bloody risky but Coffin knew if he didn't keep an eye on her she would make another attempt at getting out. What she would do then he wasn't entirely sure, but those two coppers down in the cellar had changed things between them. She had seen him chainsaw Abel Mortenson up into several pieces and douse those pieces in diesel and set them alight, and she had seen him come close to killing her boyfriend. But taking those two cops and shoving them down the cellar seemed to have brought her close to tipping point.

Coffin didn't want to kill them anymore than she did, but it was a hell of a situation they'd entangled themselves in. If it came right down to it killing them might be the only option.

If only that bloody Brendan had kept his eyes open like Coffin had asked him to, they wouldn't be in this mess.

Freddie Noonan was the first to notice Emma. His face split open in a wide, lascivious grin, and he punched his brother on the arm. Terry looked up, and he grinned as well.

"Who's the lady, then, Mort?" Tony Mannoia said.

"Emma Wylde," Craggs replied. "She's a reporter with the *Birmingham Herald.*"

The atmosphere in the room immediately turned sour. Everyone stared at Emma.

For the first time in his life, Coffin had the urge to walk up to Craggs and punch him in the face.

"She also saved my life the first time I came across the Birmingham Vampire, and she was with us at the club when it all kicked off." Coffin looked pointedly at Craggs. "In fact, she helped save Mort and drove him to safety."

The tension in the room eased off, maybe just a little. 'Punchy' Billy Adams stared at Emma with his bug eyes, and the Noonan brothers whispered urgently to each other. Of all of them, Gerry Gilligan seemed the least concerned. He lit up another in his endless chain of cigarettes and gazed into space.

"Well, that's all to be appreciated and what have you," Danny 'The Butcher' Hanrahan said, "but the fact remains, she's a reporter, and the last thing I want is for my name to be appearing on the front page of the *Birmingham Herald*."

"He's right," Harry Frazer said. "I'm a little mystified as to why you brought her in here, Joe."

"Maybe Joe's in lurve," Freddie said, grinning, and burst into a fit of giggles with his brother.

Coffin's chest tightened up. This wasn't how he wanted it to go. He glanced at Emma. Her face was a tight mask of barely controlled fury. He was amazed she had managed to keep her cool for so long.

"Truth of the matter is," Brendan said, "this little bitch has been leading Joe around by his cock all day long."

"The fuck?" Emma said, wheeling around to face Brendan.

Coffin didn't let her say anymore. He shoved the flat of his hand hard against Brendan's chest. The big man stumbled back and fell onto a table. Everyone stood up, almost moving as one.

Coffin towered over the Irishman, his fist raised.

"Joe!" Craggs shouted. "Pull yourself together."

Coffin ignored him, standing motionless over Brendan lying on his back on the table. Everyone waited for Coffin to make a move, not even the Noonan brothers making a sound.

"Joe," Craggs said again, quieter this time. "What the hell do you think you're doing?"

Brendan stared up at Coffin, daring him to deliver that first punch, see where it got him.

Coffin slowly lowered his arm, uncurling his fist and taking a step back.

"Emma stays with us," he said.

"All right, Joe, that's fine," Craggs said. "She can stay."

Brendan sat up, still scowling at Coffin.

"Now everyone needs to sit down and stop acting like we're all in the school playground," Craggs said. "We've got a lot of work to do tonight, because tomorrow morning, we're taking my club back."

"Fuck yeah!" Terry Noonan said, and grinned at his brother.

Coffin backed away from Brendan, the tension still tight in his chest and back. Brendan got back on his feet, rolled his shoulders, nodded at Coffin.

"I spoke out of turn there, Joe, and I apologise," he said, and held out his hand. "Will you accept my apology?"

Coffin stared at Brendan's outstretched hand, working on controlling his breathing, letting the adrenalin drain from his body. Finally he took Brendan's hand in his and shook it once.

"Good man," Brendan said. "Now, how about I serve up a drink for everyone, on the house like?"

There was a general murmur of appreciation at this suggestion.

As Brendan busied himself behind the bar, Emma turned to Coffin and murmured, "What the hell's going on, Joe?"

"It'll be all right," he said. "Let's sit down."

Once Brendan had finished serving everyone their drinks, he came and joined the group around the large, round table. Coffin took a deep swallow of his whisky, regarding each of the assembled tough guys in turn and remembering his thought about King Arthur and his knights. Now they even had their Queen Guinevere.

"What's the plan then, Mr Craggs?" Freddie Noonan said.

"The plan is, we go in hard tomorrow morning, take those bastards out before they know what's hit them," Craggs said. "But we have to do it fast, use the element of surprise to our advantage."

"Shoot the fuckers in the head, that'll do it," Hanrahan said.

"Maybe, for a short time," Coffin said, "but it won't finish them off."

"You're not talking sense, Joe," Punchy Billy Adams said, flexing his thick, swollen fingers. His voice was hoarse and dry from a lifetime of alcohol and nicotine abuse. "A bullet to the head'll do it every time."

"Not this time," Craggs said. "Daylight is lethal to them, not bullets or clubs or knives. We need to get them outside, in the sun."

'Punchy' Adams shook his head. "None of this makes any fucking sense to me."

"It doesn't have to," Craggs said. "Just get them outside, and then you can shoot them in the head, the balls, wherever the hell you want."

"How are you going to do that? Get them outside, I mean," Harry Frazer said.

"Tear gas," Tony Mannoia said. "I'm taking delivery of a crate full of grenades and gas masks later on tonight."

"Flood the club with tear gas, and herd those fuckers out the back," Craggs said. "Once outside, they'll start burning up, they won't be able to defend themselves or attack. Then the priority is to finish each and every one of them off as quickly as possible."

"You're going to be making one hell of a racket," Frazer said, grinding a cigarette stub out in an ashtray.

"That's not a problem," Craggs said. "Apparently a stretch of pavement outside Angels needs digging up, something to do with resurfacing works. There's going to be a team of workmen out front with jackhammers. You can make as much noise as you want."

Gerry Gilligan smiled, and spoke for the first time. "I'm guessing that's not a coincidence?"

"You guess right," Craggs said. "But we've got to work fast. Brendan will be parked round the back with his van. Once they are all dead, we need to pile the bodies in the back of Brendan's van and get the hell out of there. Hanrahan and Joe will take care of disposing the bodies, the rest of you can do a sweep of the club and make sure we haven't missed anybody."

"When's this shit going down?" Terry said.

Craggs lit up a cigar, took a long puff on it. "Tomorrow morning, first thing."

Coffin flexed his shoulder, a spasm of pain shooting through it. He didn't need any reminders as to why they were doing this, but they were there anyway. The scars on his face, the chewed up shoulder, the amputated finger. But soon, in a matter of hours, the thing that Steffanie had become would be dead.

"Hey, I know I'm the token girl here and all," Emma said. "But I really feel the need to say something right now."

"Have you got concerns that we may be breaking the law a tad here, young lady?" Brendan said. "Because if that's what's worrying you, I suggest you go upstairs and join Patsy in front of the TV after all."

Emma stared at Brendan and Coffin tensed up, waiting for that smart mouth of hers to leap into action.

Fuck you, you big lump of shit!

But no. Remarkably, Emma managed to keep her tongue under control, and turned back to face the rest of the table.

"You go ahead with this plan of yours, and by this time tomorrow you're all dead, and a week from now you'll all be waking up with a new set of teeth and an aversion to sunlight. Considering what you're up against, that has got to be the worst fucking plan you could have come up with."

Silence. Coffin could sense the tension rocketing. Nobody spoke to Mortimer Craggs that way. Not if they wanted to see their next birthday, anyway.

Craggs tapped ash off his cigar. The ashtray was overflowing with cigarette butts, but without Patsy around to empty it, it was probably going to stay that way and overflow sometime soon.

"Would you mind explaining why?" Craggs said at long last, his voice low and threatening.

"You said you want to attack first thing? I don't know if you noticed, but it's November, and we're not getting much sunlight at the moment. And I don't suppose anybody checked the weather for tomorrow either?"

"What the fuck has the weather got to do with any of this?" Frazer said.

"Because, if you've got a thick blanket of cloud cover, or if it's pissing it down, which it has a habit of doing in this country, the effect of the sun on Steffanie and her crew is going to be severely diminished, that's why."

"She's fucking crazy," Adams muttered,

"The other part of your plan, flushing everybody out with tear gas? That's just as fucked up, too."

Craggs looked like he was about to murder somebody right there and then. Coffin watched as the old man balanced his cigar on the rim of the ashtray and placed both hands flat on the table.

"Tell me why," he said.

"You ever tried spraying tear gas or a can of Mace at a corpse?" Emma said. "No, me neither, but I'm guessing we all know what the corpse would do, right? It'd just lie there."

"And your point is?" Craggs said.

"My fucking point is this. Steffanie, the old man, the one they call the Father, and the others used to be your staff at Angels, they're all dead. You can spray them with tear gas all day and night if you want, and it won't make one bit of difference to them. But, unlike a regular corpse, they are not going to lie still and take it."

"She's got a point," Coffin said, breaking the uncomfortable silence.

"All due respect to you and your friend, Joe," Tony Mannoia said, "but this is grade-A, military standard tear gas. Doesn't matter who or what we're up against, if it moves, this shit will bring it down."

"All this talk about corpses, and vampires, it's fucking crazy," Frazer said. "We should stick with the plan, storm the club tomorrow morning, flush these bastards out and kill them, just like you said, Mort. You and me, we've been in the business a long time, right? Since when did either of us take orders from a woman? I can't believe you even let her in here with us. It's fucking crazy, is what it is."

"Harry's right," Hanrahan said. "You know Mort, we've all got respect for you and the Mob, but things ain't what they used to be. This girl here, she's nice to look at, sure, and she's got one hell of a dirty mouth on her, but letting her sit at the table with us, letting her speak? All due respect Mort, but you never should have let it get this far."

"All right, that's enough," Craggs said, quietly. "Who I let sit at the table and who I let speak is my business. And if you don't like it, then now's your chance to stand up and walk away. But if you do, if that's the choice you make, then let me tell you this, you won't be coming back. No man who walks out on me is welcome back in my presence again. Am I clear?"

No one spoke, and the silence stretched out.

"Good," Craggs said, finally. "Now let's get back to talking about my club, and how we're going to fuck the bastards over who took it from me."

brendan and gerry

Gerry Gilligan smoked his cigarette, blowing plumes of smoke into the cold night air. The sounds of laughter and music floated from Broad Street, but down here it was quieter. Peaceful, almost. Gilligan was standing with his back to O'Donoghue's, facing the canal. He had often contemplated buying himself a narrowboat, spending a year or two exploring Britain's canal systems. Maybe even retiring completely, living the rest of his days out on a barge, or wherever the hell he wanted.

Beholden to no one, and no one beholden to him.

It was ridiculous of course.

Once in the life, there was no way out. Everyone knew that.

Still, looking at the barges on the dark water, tied to their mooring posts, it was tempting.

Two girls walked past arm in arm, giggling. Their skirts were stupidly short, riding high up their heavy thighs and exposing their white flesh goose pimpling in the cold night air. Was that meant to be attractive?

Dressed up like a pair of tarts, but if a man came onto them they would cry rape. Bloody pathetic. The way Gilligan looked at it, you dressed up like a piece of meat on display you shouldn't be surprised when someone wanted a bite.

"All right girls?" Gilligan called out.

They glanced back at him and then hurried on, up the stone steps that led onto Broad Street.

My fucking point exactly, Gilligan thought.

He took another drag on his cigarette, the end burning bright in the darkness. A group of young men paused outside O'Donoghue's, gazing in alcohol induced puzzlement at the closed door.

"It's shut," Gilligan said. "They're having work done."

They continued on their way.

A moment later and Brendan joined Gilligan outside. He lit up his own cigarette and sucked deeply on it.

"What's happening inside?" Gilligan said.

"Nothing," Brendan replied. "Freddie and Terry are drinking the bar dry, and the others are sat around belly aching about how it's not like the old days."

"What about Joe?"

"He's sat in a corner with his girlfriend, talking about something."

The two men smoked in silence. A barge chugged slowly past, powerful lamps on the roof illuminating the canal.

"What do you make of it all, then?" Gilligan said.

Brendan inspected his nicotine stained fingers. "I don't know."

"It's a wild story now, isn't it?"

"Aye, it is."

Gilligan sucked hard on the stub of his cigarette and then flicked it away.

"Vampires," he said.

The two men said nothing for a while, gazing out over the canal and the wall of blank brickwork extending up on the opposite side.

Gilligan struck a match, the yellow flame flaring bright, and lit up another cigarette. "I know Mr Craggs is your friend and all, but do you really believe all that shit?"

Brendan shook his head. "No." Took another drag on his cigarette. "It's not just Mort, though, is it?"

"And that's the nub of it. If it was, we could just put it down to the ramblings of an old man. But Joe and that woman of his, too? How do you explain that then?"

"I don't know," Brendan said.

"What about the others, do you think they believe it?"

"That pair of fuckwits the Noonans will believe anything, and as for 'Punchy' Adams he's just glad to get the opportunity to fuck somebody over." Brendan paused, smoking some more of his cigarette. "Hanrahan, he might be the same, he enjoys killing and then disposing of the bodies. Tony, I'm not so sure about."

"And then there's that girl reporter. She worries me, Brendan, she worries me a lot."

"Aye, I know."

"She's got Joe's dick in her back pocket, and he doesn't even know it. I thought he was supposed to be a tough bastard?"

"He is, but when it comes to the women he's got a soft spot in his head."

"You ever heard the phrase 'hiding in plain sight', Brendan?"

"Yeah."

"In this business we live our whole lives, each and every fucking day from sunup to sundown, worrying about being found out. Am I right? Living outside the law, it's not an easy life, now is it? Always having to think about what you say, and who you say it to. Trusting no one. Wondering if anyone you know has turned grass, or that new man, is he an undercover copper. You know the score, don't you Brendan?"

"Aye, I do."

"That slip of a girl she's made no secret who she is, what she does for a living. None at all. And I'm just wondering, is she hiding in plain sight?"

Brendan narrowed his eyes, his face shrouded in smoke. "You want to talk to her, you're going to have to get past Joe, and you've seen what he's like with her."

"Now that there's a bit of problem, isn't it?"

"There is another way though," Brendan said. "A way we might be able to get evidence of what she's up to, without involving Joe."

Gilligan looked at Brendan. "Go on."

* * *

DCI Nick Archer had been having trouble sorting out what was real, and what was the result of his fevered dreams. It seemed like he had been in this bed forever, slipping in and out of consciousness. At least the pain had stopped. The waves of agony that had spread from his leg and up his torso.

Sometimes he could still smell the blood, that coppery stink that made him want to gag. It came and went, like the visions in his head. He wasn't sure if they were nightmares or reality. In his more lucid moments he knew he was in hospital. The feel of the clean sheets, the smell of antiseptic, the cannula in the back of his hand.

Once he had surfaced from a nightmarish vision of blood and body parts, of an enclosed space stinking of death, to find himself surrounded by shadowy figures leaning over him. Two of the doctors discussing his case had to hold him down while the nurses tried to calm him. Eventually one of the doctors had prescribed him a sedative, and he had slipped back into unconsciousness.

But now he was awake. He still felt groggy, his mind like a thick soup, his limbs heavy and unresponsive. But he was properly awake for the first time in . . . how long?

Archer had no idea. He remembered the barge, Emma captured by that maniac, Joe Coffin taking the body away. He remembered that poor girl Julie Carter, and Coffin's boy, savage and feral.

And he remembered driving the sword through the little boy's chest, and shoving the body over the edge of the boat into the dark canal water.

"Bloody hell, Nicholas, I thought you were never going to wake up."

Archer flinched. Slowly twisted his head on the pillow, the effort almost too much.

Didn't need to look to find out who it was, though. There was only one person he knew called him Nicholas.

DS Amrit Choudhry was sitting in a plastic chair next to Archer's bed. As usual he was dressed impeccably in a charcoal grey suit and black shoes, his one anti-establishment gesture being his colourful, garish tie.

Archer tried to speak, but his voice failed him. He moistened his lips, and swallowed.

Tried again.

"How long?"

Choudhry leaned forward. "What was that, Nicholas? How long?"

"Have I been out?"

Choudhry leaned back in his chair again. "About forty-eight hours."

Archer closed his eyes, worked on formulating his next sentence. "What day is it?"

Choudhry chuckled. "It is Monday evening. Where were you today, Archer? We expected you in work this morning."

Archer swallowed again. His throat was so dry. "Coffin. Have we got him?"

Choudhry frowned, smoothed his trouser legs out with the flat of his palm. "No, not yet."

"Could do with a drink."

Choudhry poured water from a jug into a plastic beaker sitting on the hospital bedside table. Carefully he held the beaker to Archer's lips, who took a couple of small sips at the lukewarm water.

"Thank you."

"Don't worry about Coffin, we'll get him. We've got a huge manhunt on for him right now. How difficult can it be to find a mountain like him?"

"Emma."

"No one's heard from her. Someone called her, let her know what happened. Have you seen her?"

Archer thought about this. "I think so." He paused, swallowed. "I don't know."

Choudhry reached out and patted Archer gently on the shoulder. "I'm sure you did. You need to rest now, Nicholas, and build your strength. There will be lots of work waiting for you when you come back."

"What do you mean?" Archer swallowed again. Talking was taking so much effort. "The Birmingham Vampire is dead, isn't he?"

Choudhry nodded. "Oh yes, as far as we know, he is."

"So?"

"There was a disturbance today, down at the police mortuary." Choudhry smoothed out the material on his trouser legs again. "The pathologist was killed."

Archer closed his eyes. "How?"

All of a sudden, Choudhry's smooth, unruffled exterior seemed slightly disturbed. "We're not entirely sure yet. At this stage it seems that the death certificates for two of the bodies down there might have been issued prematurely."

"You're saying a couple of the dead bodies woke up and murdered the pathologist?"

"Yes, that is how it is looking at the moment."

"What do you mean, that's how it's looking? Don't you know?"

"They're not entirely sure, no. The mortuary is in complete lockdown at the moment. Apparently the two, erm, people down there are like wild animals. They're proving difficult to apprehend."

A wave of tiredness washed over Archer. The simple act of talking required too much brain power, too much energy.

"I'll leave you now," Choudhry was saying. "I'll come back another time, and we can talk."

But Archer was already slipping away into the cold darkness.

Back into the night.

And the blood.

* * *

Eddie's burger van was shuttered up and silent, apart from the occasional groan and creak in the stiff wind. Screwed up paper napkins lay in a scattered heap at the base of an overflowing bin, mounted on a metal pole on the grass verge. Some of the napkins were tumbling across the road, carried by the wind.

"Someone should empty that bin, and pick up the litter," Gilligan said, gazing through the car window at the mess.

"Don't you go telling that to Eddie, now," Brendan said. He was sitting in the driver's seat, and they were parked across the road from Eddie's. "He's in an argument with the council right now. They're refusing to empty the bin, saying it's his responsibility to dispose of any waste that's generated by his business."

"And what does Eddie say?"

"What do you think? Eddie says the council is shirking its duties so that they can slap a charge on him for the amount of rubbish he will need to dispose of. Right now they're at a, what would you call it, they're at loggerheads."

"And in the meantime the streets are filled with rubbish," Gilligan said. "I'm telling you, Brendan, it's a fucking disgrace when a man has no respect for his surroundings. Eddie should clear his rubbish up, charge or no charge."

"And let those thieving bastards on the council shaft him for every penny he's got?"

"Well now, that's an entirely different issue, isn't it?" Gilligan wiped at the windscreen, clearing a patch on the misted up glass. "But that out there, that's shameful. There's such a thing as a man's civic duty, and part of his responsibility is to keep his communal space tidy and clean."

Brendan gave Gilligan a long, enquiring look. "I'm seeing a different side to you, today, Gerry. You're not going soft on me, are you?"

Gilligan smiled, a cold, humourless smile. "Of course not. But just because I'm a killer by trade, doesn't mean to say I don't have any respect for my surroundings."

Brendan pointed at the empty car parked by Eddie's van. "That's the car that reporter bitch turned up in."

"What are we waiting for, then? Let's take a look."

The two men climbed out of the van and crossed the road. Gilligan lit up a cigarette as he walked, cupping his hand around the flame to shield it from the breeze. They circled the parked car a couple of times, looking through the windows.

"Are you sure this is her car?" Gilligan said. "Looks too clean and tidy to me."

"Saw her arrive in it," Brendan replied. "Let's open it up, take a look inside."

With a quick look around to check they weren't being watched, Gilligan pulled a small crowbar from inside his jacket and wedged the tip of it in the space between the passenger door and the car body. He leaned his weight against it, jamming it further in and creating a gap.

Brendan had an old wire coat hanger, straightened out, which he shoved through the gap. He jimmied it around until its end pushed the car lock button inside the door. The car's lights flashed once, and the doors unlocked.

The two men climbed inside. Gilligan searched under the seats whilst Brendan opened up the glove box.

"It's a hire car," he said, pulling out the documentation.

"Nothing under here, I'll check the boot," Gilligan said, and climbed out of the car.

Brendan returned the paperwork to the glove box and slammed it shut.

"Look what I found," Gilligan said, holding an iPad up.

He shut the boot and joined Brendan inside the car. Brendan watched as he powered the iPad up, and the slider appeared on the welcome screen. Gilligan ran his thumb across the screen, and the passcode buttons appeared.

Gilligan tapped in a four digit number, and the tablet buzzed. Gilligan tried another random number, and the screen buzzed again.

"You know what you're doing there?" Brendan said.

"Not a fucking clue," Gilligan replied. "Just trying to get lucky."

He punched in more numbers, nothing. Tried again.

After the fifth attempt the screen went blank.

"What's happened?" Brendan said.

"It's probably set up for stupid idiots like us so that it wipes its memory after a certain number of wrong attempts at the passcode," Gilligan replied.

"So it's useless now?"

"Let's make sure, shall we?"

Gilligan climbed out of the car and dropped the iPad on the ground. He lifted his foot and brought the heel of his shoe down hard onto the tablet, and the screen cracked. After he had stamped on it several times, Gilligan kicked the mangled iPad into the grass verge.

Brendan climbed out of the hire car and shut the door.

"That's a big fucking mess you've just made there. I thought you respected your surroundings?"

"Not in the mood for respecting much of anything right now," Gilligan replied.

"We're still no wiser about what that bitch is up to," Brendan said.

"No," Gilligan said, looking thoughtfully at the mess he had made on the ground. "You know, Brendan, I've been thinking—"

"Careful now, Gerry, the last time you began a sentence with those words we wound up in jail, pissed off our heads and with nary a stitch on."

Gilligan laughed quietly. "Aye, but that was a good night now, wasn't it?"

"It was."

"But no, I've been thinking about this here situation with that reporter bitch, and Coffin and Craggs and the Slaughterhouse Mob. Now the Mob's had itself a reputation for being the toughest, cruellest gang in the British Isles since before I was born, but it seems to me that Mr Craggs is a shadow of the man he once was."

"Aye, it could be that you're right," Brendan said.

"I can't think of anyone else who would put up with that bitch shouting her mouth off like that."

"It surprised me, too."

"That and the way he lets Coffin defend her, lets him keep her around like he's the one in charge."

"Mortimer Craggs has been head of the Slaughterhouse Mob for a long, long time, Gerry."

"Aye." Gilligan was silent for a while. "You ever think about muscling in on the Mob yourself, Brendan?"

"You thinking it needs some fresh blood in charge?"

"Maybe. I'm also thinking there's a lot of potential going to waste there. The clubs, the protection money, that's all fine now, but there's new opportunities opening up these days."

"And what would those be?"

"People trafficking. The Pakis, the blacks, they're all desperate to get over here now. I'm telling you, there's big money to be made smuggling those bastards into the UK."

"Don't you think there's more than enough of them around already? The bloody country's full of immigrants anyway."

"And since when did you and I give a fuck about this country?"

Brendan nodded. "True."

"What we need to do is find out what Coffin's little bitch is really up to. That'll set the cat amongst the pigeons."

"How about paying a visit to the *Herald* offices next?"

"Aye," Gilligan said, and took a deep breath. "It's a fine night for mischief making, now isn't it?"

heat detectors

Heat detectors or smoke detectors? Heat detectors or smoke detectors?

Karl Edwards was leaning back in his chair, gazing at the white plastic disk set into the ceiling. Dear God, but he wanted a smoke more than anything else in the world right at this moment. Just get out one of his cigars and light it up, instead of chewing on it.

The *Birmingham Herald* editor opened up his desk drawer and lifted a cigar from it. He turned it around and around, the cellophane wrapper crinkling under his fingertips. In the open drawer a box of matches invited him to pick it up, slide it open and take out a match. Karl had absolutely no idea why he had a box of matches in his office drawer. They were cook's matches, the extra-long ones. The design on the lid was old fashioned, the box battered, looked like they had been in that drawer for a long time. Maybe they had been there since he gave up smoking. But hell, that would mean they had survived through one office relocation and a couple of redecorations.

Karl tore the wrapper off the cigar and jammed it into his mouth. Looked at the box of matches again.

He was the only person in the *Birmingham Herald* offices right now. If that damn thing above him was a heat detector and not a smoke detector he could light up and smoke his cigar down to the stub, and by the time the first of his staff arrived in the morning the smell would have dissipated. Nobody would be the wiser.

Karl picked the box of matches out of the drawer and laid it on his desk.

Of course, if he was wrong, and the fire alarms started screaming at the first hint of smoke, he was buggered. What the hell kind of excuse was he going to come up with when a bunch of firemen came bursting into the office?

Karl peered at the white plastic disk above him. Damn it, there should be some way of finding out. He chewed thoughtfully on the end of the cigar for a few moments.

No, it wasn't worth the risk. In fact, he was being stupid. Why not just call it a night, like everyone else had done, and head outside. He could smoke as many cigars as he wanted without fear of causing a disturbance outside.

Or he could head on home.

Tomorrow was going to be a difficult day, so it was probably best if he got his head down and grabbed himself a decent night's sleep for once. He needed to be fresh and alert in the morning.

Especially for when he called Emma in, and told her he was dismissing her from the paper.

Hurt him to do it, he'd grown fond of her over the years, foul mouth and all. Underneath all that bluster and toughness, Karl detected a scared, hurt little girl. Seemed she had only one way of coping with life, and that was to meet it head on screaming and shouting.

Like she had something to prove to everyone.

The problem was, she had got herself too involved in her latest story. Hanging around with Joe Coffin? Bad idea. Karl knew of his reputation obviously, but he had only met him the once when he turned up at the *Herald* offices looking for Emma. The once had been enough. The man had exuded violence from every pore.

And all that talk about vampires, yesterday? Karl had no idea what to think about that. Emma had talked lucidly, didn't seem like she had a screw loose even though Karl suspected that she had been through a lot more than she let on. Kind of thing that might send you off the deep end.

But vampires? What the hell was going on there?

Was that Coffin's influence? Maybe he was the one seeing blood sucking creatures of the night, and he had convinced Emma. But that seemed just as unlikely. Coffin hadn't struck Karl as the kind of man who believed in the supernatural.

The whole city had gone to hell recently, all the murders and the violence that the *Herald* was documenting at the moment. And it all started when Steffanie Coffin and her boy were slaughtered. Seemed to Karl that Joe Coffin was at the centre of this whole bloody mess. Perhaps Coffin was the one the leading Emma on, with stories of vampires and his wife and son digging their way out of their graves.

But that was almost as ridiculous as believing in actual vampires. What reason would he have for leading her on like that?

Karl sighed. He put the box of matches in his pocket and stood up. Time to go home. He would stand outside and smoke his cigar down to a stub, and then maybe find himself a shop that sold mints before he went home.

But while he was smoking that cigar, he could think on this some more. Decide what to do about Emma. Maybe letting her go was the wrong thing. Karl liked Emma, and it was obvious she was deep in a story over her head. She needed help, not dismissing from her job.

Karl looked up as the lift pinged, to signal the arrival of the car. That was odd, he'd thought he was the only one left in the building.

The doors slid open and two men stepped out, glancing quickly around the open plan newsroom. Apart from the glow of the computer monitors, and the three large screen TVs mounted on the walls still playing their endless litany of news, the room was in darkness. Only Karl's office was lit up, exposing the editor like a rare artefact in a museum.

The two men spotted Karl, and immediately headed his way. One of them was tall and well built, the other smaller and wirier. Karl didn't like the look of either of them. Whatever they were doing here, it involved trouble.

Karl stood up and opened his door.

"Can I help you gentlemen?"

Neither of the two men broke stride.

"Now would you credit that, Gerry, he just called us gentlemen."

"Aye, he did," Gilligan replied. "He obviously needs to get to know us a little better, doesn't he now?"

Karl backed up as Brendan and Gilligan strode towards his office. He didn't want to, hadn't even intended to, but he couldn't help himself.

The two men entered the office, filling it with their presence.

"Well, would you look at this?" Brendan said, twisting his head as he examined Karl's office. "Isn't this nice, now? You know, I've been buying the *Birmingham Herald* ever since I moved here, back in ninety-seven, and I never realised that my money was paying for all this nice, fancy office space."

"The man needs somewhere to work," Gilligan said. "What did you think, that he was giving his money to the church?"

"Can I help you gentlemen?" Karl said again.

"There he goes again, using that word, that label to describe us, when we've haven't even got to know each other yet," Gilligan said.

"He'll know us soon enough," Brendan replied.

"I don't know how you two got past security downstairs, but I'm going to have to ask you to leave," Karl said.

Gilligan pointed at Karl's cigar, jutting from his mouth. "Is he allowed to smoke that thing in here?"

"Maybe he thinks it makes him look tough, like those newspaper editors in those old black and white movies," Brendan said.

The *Herald* editor, suddenly self-conscious, took the cigar from his mouth and laid it on his desk.

"Now look, you've gone and upset him," Brendan said.

Gilligan poked at a stack of papers on the desk, and sent them toppling to the floor. "Not so tough after all."

"I'll have to call security if you don't leave now," Karl said, trying to sound braver than he felt.

Brendan moved closer. "I'm afraid security came over all tired very suddenly, and he is taking a little nap."

Gilligan shook his head and tutted. "You just can't get the staff these days, now can you?"

"What do you want?"

Brendan picked up the cigar and sniffed it. "Smells gorgeous, are you sure you don't want to light it up?"

"Don't be an idiot, man," Gilligan said. "You've got smoke detectors in the ceiling there, if he lit it up we'd have the fire brigade on us in no time."

"Aye, I suppose you're right." Brendan put the cigar back down.

"We're looking for Emma Wylde's computer," Gilligan said, staring at Karl.

"Emma's not here," the editor said.

Gilligan turned to his partner. "Do you think he even heard what I said just then?"

"Maybe he's hard of hearing," Brendan said.

Gilligan turned back to Karl. "Or maybe he's just a fucking retard."

"Now, now, let's give him the benefit of the doubt, shall we?" Brendan stepped right up in front of Karl's face, and shouted, "Emma Wylde's computer station, could you lead us to it, please?"

"Get out," Karl said. "Leave now, and I won't report you to the police."

Brendan tipped his head back and guffawed.

When he had fallen silent, Gilligan said, "How about we put it this way, Mr *Birmingham Herald* newspaper editor? Give us access to that reporter bitch's computer, and we won't cut your balls off. How about that, now?"

Automatically, Karl reached down and picked up his cigar. He put it back in his mouth and began chewing on it.

"Outside," he said, nodding at the desks in the newsroom.

Brendan stepped back, out of the way. "Lead us to it, then."

Karl walked out of his office and took them to Emma's desk.

"Switch it on," Gilligan said.

Karl nudged the mouse and brought the screen to life, displaying a password prompt.

Brendan chuckled. "Oh, please tell me you have the password."

Karl said nothing.

"The editor of the newspaper?" Gilligan said. "Of course he's got the fucking password."

Karl sat down at the desk and typed in the password. The computer's desktop appeared, cluttered up with folders and files.

"Your star reporter's not very organised now, is she?" Gilligan said, pushing Karl out of the chair and sitting down.

Watching Gilligan as he began opening up folders on the computer, Karl thought about running, making a dash for the lift. But he could feel Brendan's eyes on him, and he knew he would have no chance. Even if the lift was on his floor, it would take too long for the doors to open and close.

"What is she working on, Mr *Birmingham Herald* editor?" Gilligan said, as he opened and closed files. "Is she working on an expose of the Slaughterhouse Mob, is that what she's doing?"

Karl said nothing, glanced up at Brendan, decided if he did make a run for it he could take the fire escape stairs, forget about the lift altogether. He thought about Emma, running up and down those steps, doing her hill training. Wished that he was a bit fitter, that maybe he should have done some exercise the last few years and maybe eaten a few less burgers.

Gilligan was opening folders within folders on the computer. Did he even know what he was looking for?

Karl glanced at Brendan again. He was a big man, too. Probably couldn't run that fast. Gilligan was smaller, leaner, looked like he could put on some speed if he needed to. But he was sitting at a desk, and it would take him a few seconds to extricate himself. By the time he was up on his feet and running, Karl could be halfway across the newsroom, maybe more.

"Ah, now what have we got here?" Gilligan said.

Karl looked at the monitor, and saw an Mpeg4 file, simply named 'JOE'.

Gilligan double clicked it, and an image of Terry Wu filled the screen, staring out of it as though he could see them. It took Karl a few moments to realise what he was seeing, that Wu was obviously sat at his computer, being videoed by a webcam.

But from the expression on his face, he didn't seem to know he was being filmed.

Gilligan looked up at Brendan, who was staring intently at the monitor.

"Is the chink bastard having a wank?"

"Don't know," Brendan said.

Gilligan turned to Karl. "What's this, have you been planting cameras in people's offices now? I would have said that was illegal, wouldn't you, Mr Editor?"

Karl ignored Gilligan. In the background, he could see Wu's office. The door opened, and Joe Coffin stepped inside.

"Aw, fuck," Brendan whispered.

They watched the rest of the video in silence, watched Coffin shooting Terry Wu in the head.

"Jesus Christ," Brendan whispered.

"Your star reporter's got a fucking unexploded bomb here," Gilligan said. "What the hell is it doing sitting on her hard drive? Why haven't you passed it onto the police, or uploaded it to YouTube, or whatever the fuck you people do these days when you break a fucking story?"

Why hadn't she told him? Why the hell had Emma been sitting on this?

"I didn't know," Karl said. "I didn't know anything about it."

Brendan grabbed Karl by his shirt front. "Bollocks. There's got to be a reason you haven't released it yet."

Karl lifted his hands, protesting his innocence. "Honestly, I knew nothing about this."

Brendan pushed him away, his lip curled back in disgust.

Gilligan closed the video, and dragged the file to the bin. "Have you got a backup anywhere?"

"I don't know," Karl said. His heart was beating triple time in his chest. Emma should have told him. She should have told him.

Gilligan stood up and planted his hands on Karl's chest, giving him a good shove. "Of course you have a backup. Big place like this, important news story involving a murder, you'll have that file backed up every which way there is. Now tell me, where is it?"

"Honestly, I don't know!"

"He's lying," Brendan said.

Gilligan shoved Karl again, and the editor fell onto another desk, scattering pens and sheets of paper. The two men towered over him, getting in close. Karl leaned away from them, his back touching a computer monitor.

"I know nothing about this file," he said. "But if she was going to back it up, she would have put it on the shared drive."

Gilligan returned to Emma's desk, sat down in front of the computer. "Which one is that, then?"

"The 'm' drive," Karl replied.

Brendan stayed close to Karl, towering over the editor, whilst Gilligan tapped at the keyboard.

"I can't find any other copies," he said, finally.

"What about her iPad?" Brendan said, not taking his eyes of Karl for a moment. "Maybe that was her backup."

"Maybe," Gilligan said.

Brendan pointed at Karl. "What are we going to do about him?"

Gilligan came and stood by Brendan, and the two men stared at the editor, still sitting on the desk.

"I don't know. Take him with us?"

"What, and throw him down the cellar with those two coppers? I don't know if you'd noticed, Gerry, but my cellar's not that big, and there's only so many people it can fit. Besides which, I'm in the pub trade, not the bed and breakfast business."

"Aye, you're right," Gilligan replied.

"What about you, Mr Editor? You'll be on the phone to the cop shop before the lift has even got to the ground floor, now, won't you?"

Karl kept his mouth shut. He could try denying it, but all three of them would know it was a lie.

"Well, there's not many options left now, is there?" Gilligan said.

"We could tie him up."

"We could, we could."

"Or we could kill him."

"We could do that, too."

Karl still had his cigar clamped between his teeth. The end was soggy, but still holding together. He could taste the tobacco, and that urge to light it up and smoke it came over him again.

He reached for the matches in his pocket, but Gilligan grabbed his wrist and stopped him.

"Hold it there, I don't like it when people make unexpected moves like that."

"My matches," Karl said. "I just want to light my cigar."

Gilligan let go of his wrist, and watched carefully as Karl produced the box of matches. He slid the box open and pulled out a single match. His hands were shaking, and he dropped it on the desk.

Brendan and Gilligan watched him.

"What's this now, has the condemned man asked for a final smoke?" Brendan said.

"Looks that way," Gilligan said.

Karl managed to steady his hands enough that he picked up the match and struck it. The flame flared bright and hot, and he held it to the cigar end, drawing on it until the end glowed red.

Gilligan pulled a snub nosed revolver from his jacket.

"Is that how it's to be, then?" Brendan said.

"It is," Gilligan said.

"Well, hold up a moment or two, and let the man enjoy his cigar a little longer, shall we?" Brendan said.

Karl tipped his head back, closed his eyes, and blew smoke towards the ceiling.

Heat detectors or smoke detectors?

Heat detectors or smoke detectors?

uglier than a monkey's arse

Garrett Stone sat in his car, the heater on and the engine running. For twenty minutes now he had been watching cars driving by on Peartree Lane, their headlights cutting through the darkness of the industrial estate. At midnight the street lights had flickered off, one by one down the road, until they were all out. It was the council's way of saving money, the lights staying off until five o'clock, when they would stutter back into life again.

Stone reckoned they could save a lot more money by sacking the thieving bastards who had their fingers in the till. But then if they did that, there'd be nobody left on the council, would there?

Earlier when he had parked up in the small car park, overgrown with weeds poking through the cracked tarmac, Stone had switched off his own headlights. The car was facing the entrance to the car park, and Stone would immediately see anyone who drove in but they wouldn't necessarily notice him straight away.

The smell of stale cigarette smoke hung in the air, filling the car's interior. Lucy knew that Stone hated her smoking in his car, hated the stink of it, the way the cigarette smoke clung to the seats and the plastic coating on the steering wheel and the fittings. She had her own car she could sit and smoke her cancer sticks in, but she never did.

So why light up in his?

It had been a deliberate action, an act of revenge, a way of letting him know that she knew all about his sordid little session with that woman from the Deep South. Lucy wouldn't know any of the details, obviously, but she was an intelligent woman. Stone had enough past history of extra-marital, one night stands for her not to have to work too hard to figure out what had happened when she saw the dressing on his neck.

Stone pressed a button in the door, and the window slid down with a faint hum. He stopped it halfway, breathing in the cold night air.

Lucy always liked to keep him check, give him a gentle reminder every now and then who was in charge.

His mobile buzzed, the screen lighting up with a call. He picked it up, hesitated before accepting the call. The number wasn't one he recognised. That was the second time this had happened in the last couple of days, an unusual occurrence to say the least. Somebody else claiming to have information about his son's murder, and looking to claim the reward money?

Stone swiped the accept button on the screen.

"Garrett Stone. State your business."

"It's Leola. Where are you?"

Stone swallowed. Stared ahead into the dark.

"Why?"

"Because I want to know how soon you can get here and undress me."

Stone swallowed again. Already his pants were growing tight. Had he ever known any other woman who could have such an immediate effect upon him?

"Tell me where you are," he said.

Leola gave him the address.

Headlights washed over him as a car pulled into the car park.

"I'll be there soon, I just have a little business to attend to first."

The car pulled up beside Stone's, facing the opposite direction so that the two driver's side doors were next to each other. The window slid down, and a heavily bearded man looked at Stone, and grinned.

"A nice spot for a bit of dogging, eh, Stone?"

"I wouldn't know," Stone replied.

"Aye, I know, you prefer to get your jollies in private, right? Just you, a DVD and a box of tissues."

Stone said nothing.

Shocker Stronach was a huge, bearded mountain of a man, and his first nickname in the unit had been 'Grizzly', after Grizzly Adams. Then there had been the incident with the live electrical cable, the bucket of water, and the Iraqi prisoner. Ever since then he had been known as Shocker. Sitting next to him in the passenger seat was Shanks Longworth who, in contrast to his companion, was tall and lean. Nobody knew the origins of his nickname as he had brought it to the unit with him, and he refused to tell.

"All right, then, Stone, you were never one for small talk," Shocker said, his Scottish accent so thick it made whatever he said almost indecipherable to most people he met.

"Not unless he's trying to chat up one of the ladies," Shanks said. "Our boy

Stone can turn on the charm then."

"True, true, which is a good job for him, as the poor bastard's face is uglier than a monkey's arse."

"You two are about as funny as a dose of the shits," Stone said.

"Ah now, but at least you're talking," Shocker replied, the smile on his face just visible beneath the beard. "I was starting to think you'd called us here for a night of silent meditation."

"Joe Coffin. You heard of him?"

"Of course we've bloody heard of him," Shocker said. "He's all over the news right now, although depending on your point of view he's either a hero or a villain."

"He murdered my son."

"Then he's neither hero nor villain," Shanks said. "He's a dead man."

"Aye, a dead man walking," Shocker said.

"Is that what you want, Stone? You want us to take him out?"

"No," Stone replied. "You two are going to help me find him, and restrain him. Then I'm going to have a little debriefing with him, find out why he killed Isaac. Then I'm going to kill him."

"Fair enough," Shanks said.

"I need him tracking down fast, I don't want to hang around on this one."

"You might be in luck," Shocker said. "Coffin works for Mortimer Craggs, and there's a rumour going round that Craggs has lost his club to rivals. He'll be wanting to take it back, no doubt. I'll put my ear to the ground, see what else I can find out."

"Where's this club of his?" Stone said.

"Birmingham city centre, it's called Angels. You ever been there?"

"Do I look like I go clubbing?"

Shocker laughed, quietly. "It's not that kind of club, it's more like a gentleman's club. You'd feel right at home there, surrounded by all those titties on display."

Stone passed a mobile phone through the open car window to Shocker.

"That's prepaid, and it's got my number in it. Use it only to contact me, and when the job's done, dispose of it."

"Aye," Shocker said, starting up the car's engine. "We'll be in touch soon enough, but you know us, Stone. You can consider it done, already."

Stone watched as Shocker reversed his car and pulled out of the car park, back onto the road. Kept them in sight until their red tail lights had disappeared from view. He remained seated in the car, gazing into the darkness outside.

Lucy would want to be there when they had Coffin. She would want to know why he killed their son, and then she would want to see him suffer a while before he died. Stone hadn't told her yet, but he already had all the details worked out. Where they were going to take Coffin, and how they were going to kill him.

He would show her that he hadn't lost his nerve, that he still had the stomach for this. What he had planned for Coffin was so extreme, it might be that Lucy would be the one to lose her nerve, and then Stone would be back on top again, back in charge.

The thing he loved about Lucy was how tough she was, and how she thought sometimes that she was tougher than Stone.

But she wasn't, and it was time he demonstrated that to her.

Once she had seen Joe Coffin suffering a prolonged and extremely nasty death, she would know who the tougher bastard was then.

And Stone doubted she would ever question him again.

google

"What do we know about vampires?" Emma said.

"I don't know," Coffin said. "They drink blood and sleep in coffins?"

"What else?"

"Do they really sleep in coffins?"

"Who the fuck knows? Forget about the coffins for the moment, just tell me what else you know, or at least think you know, about vampires."

"All right. They drink blood, and they can live forever."

"What else?"

Coffin thought for a moment. "Sunlight hurts them, they burn up, and then they die."

"We've seen that, right? That boy, Peter?"

"Yeah."

"What else? Come on, think."

Coffin raised his glass and took a swallow of his whisky. Emma was drinking black coffee. The pub was quiet, and dark.

"Crucifixes hurt them, too, is that right?" he said. "If you hold up a cross, it scares them or hurts them, and garlic, as well. Shouldn't we be wearing necklaces of garlic bulbs?"

"What else?"

"Is this a test, or something? Are you interviewing me for the job of chief vampire killer?"

"Just shut up, and tell me what else you think you know about vampires."

"I don't know, I'm all out of ideas now, that's all I've got. How did I do? Do I get the job?"

"No, you did crap. You missed some shit out, like how a vampire can never come into your house unless you invite it in."

Coffin raised an eyebrow. "Really?"

"Yeah, really."

"So how come Angels is full of vampires? Who invited them in?"

"Well, Addison, Clevon and, shit, what did you say that girl's name was?"

"Velvina."

Emma made a face like she'd swallowed something disgusting. "Who the hell gave her that name? Don't know about you, but it sounds kind of repulsive to me."

"Her mother."

"Seriously?"

"Yeah, seriously."

"Anyway, those three, they were turned into vampires while they were inside the club, right? So they didn't need an invitation, as they were already there. Steffanie and the old man? I don't know, maybe Tom had to invite them in, or maybe just the fact that he took them there was invitation enough."

Coffin drank some more of his whisky. "Okay, so what else did I miss?"

"Vampires can turn into bats. And mist, too, they can sort of dissolve into a fog and slip through tiny gaps, and then reform into their physical shapes again."

A door opened at the rear of the pub, muffled voices, the door shutting.

"So a vampire could slip through a gap in a window, or through air vents, or anything large enough to let air through?" Coffin said.

"Yep."

"So why the hell do they need inviting in? Sounds like they can go anywhere they damn well please to me."

"I don't know, I'm just telling you the facts, okay?" Emma said. "Oh, I almost forgot, they can hypnotise you, too."

"And then they make you dance the Macarena?"

"Don't be an idiot, they make you let them drink your blood. Like, more than once, you know, over a period of days or weeks."

"You make it sound like milking a cow."

"They have to hypnotise cows to milk them?"

"Now who's being an idiot?"

"Oh."

"Anything else?"

"Not that I can think of. Except, you know, the only way to kill one is to stake it through the heart."

"That'll do it for most people, I should think, vampire or not."

"You know what I'm saying. And then you're supposed to cut off the vampire's head, stuff the mouth full of garlic, burn the body and then bury the ashes in consecrated ground. Just to make absolutely sure they're not coming back."

"Hmm, okay. Thing is, I missed out the garlic, and I didn't bury him anywhere, never mind consecrated ground. You think he might be coming back?"

"Who? Abel? No, I don't think so." Emma thought for a moment. "Holy water, vampires hate holy water, it burns them when they come into contact with it."

"Where do we get holy water from? The Vatican?"

"No, I think any water will do as long as it has been consecrated by a priest."

"Where the hell are you getting all this stuff from, Emma?"

"Um, Google, mostly. Oh, and I sort of speed read my way through Dracula."

"So, basically, everything you just told me is probably a load of horse shit."

"Yeah, probably."

"Great."

Brendan walked into the snug, followed by Gilligan.

"Cold out," Gilligan said, rubbing his hands together.

Coffin nodded an acknowledgement at Gilligan. Emma kept her eyes averted from Brendan.

"Doubt there's even any vampires out tonight," Brendan said.

Gilligan chuckled.

Brendan walked behind the bar and poured the two men a shot of dark whisky. He held the bottle up and looked at Coffin, who shook his head.

"Having trouble sleeping?" Gilligan said, accepting the glass off Brendan. "It's always the same, in the hours before a gig like this one. Get all wired up, edgy like. Ah but then, a few hours from now and it'll all be over."

"Aye, and ain't that a shame in a way," Brendan said.

"That's right, it is," Gilligan replied. "You spend ages preparing, getting your men together, and your weapons, drawing up your plans, and then before you know it you're in the heat of the battle, and in a flash it's gone." Gilligan clicked his fingers. "Just like that, and it's over."

Emma snorted, and shook her head.

"Do I amuse you, young lady?" Gilligan said.

"Yeah, you're a laugh a minute," Emma said, holding her coffee cup and staring down at it. "In fact I'm laughing so hard, my sides are aching."

"Is that right, now?" Gilligan replied, quietly. "And why is that?"

Emma lifted her head, turned to look at the two men behind the bar. "Because you're a fucking joke, that's why. You act like you're a tough guy in a Hollywood movie, all your smooth talk about the heat of the battle, you'll be bullshitting about the honour of thieves next, about loyalty and friendship and the moral code of the criminal underworld."

"And you think the newspaper business is any more honourable, do you? Live by a code of ethics, do you, always seeking the truth and exposing lies and wrongdoing?" Gilligan chuckled. "I think I know you better than you realise."

"All right, that's enough," Coffin said. "We should all get some sleep, cool off a little."

"Joe's right," Craggs said. Nobody had seen him appear in the doorway. "You should all get some rest. And lay off the booze, too. I need you sharp. A few hours from now, and we're taking Angels back."

EPISODE SEVEN

unit thirteen

Stone traced the swirling lines of Leola's tattoo with his fingertip, circling round and round and ever inwards towards her nipple. He had his head propped up on his hand, his elbow on the pillow. Leola lay on her back next to him, and they were both naked and uncovered.

The window rattled in a gust of wind, and rain spattered against the glass.

Stone looked up. "Why the hell are you staying in a shithole like this?"

"It's cheap," Leola said.

"I thought you were a millionaire businesswoman," Stone said. "You can afford the best, surely."

"No, I'm a secret agent, remember? I have to keep a low profile, avoid being noticed at all costs."

Stone draped himself over Leola, and reached down for the bed covers on the floor.

"Aren't you cold?" he said, pulling the covers over both of them. "It's freezing in here."

Leola smiled. "You weren't complaining a minute ago."

"A minute ago I was kind of preoccupied." Stone went back to studying the tattoo. "This is amazing, I've never seen anything like it before."

"It's just a tattoo."

"I know, but it's so detailed, and some of these lines, they're so fine and intricate. Whoever did this for you is an artist."

Leola ran her fingers down Stones hip and over his thigh. Even though they had only just finished having sex, she could feel him stiffening up.

"You're a greedy little boy, aren't you?" she said, taking him in her hand.

"Always have been," he murmured.

But still he kept tracing his fingers along the lines of the tattoo, sometimes brushing his fingertips over her nipple.

"Are these words, in between the lines? What do they say?"

She squeezed him, and Stone drew in a sharp gasp of breath.

"Forget about the tattoo. I want to have some fun."

The wind rattled the old sash window again. The thin curtains didn't quite meet in the middle, and the first hint of dawn was showing in the darkness.

"I thought you'd had enough fun," Stone said, kissing her breast, kissing the tattoo.

"No, I never get enough of that kind of fun," Leola replied, smiling. "Why do you think I organise sex parties for a living?"

Stone stopped running his tongue over her erect nipple, and lifted his head. "You really do that? I thought you were joking."

"I never joke about sex," she murmured, giving him another quick squeeze.

Stone sucked in his breath.

Leola climbed on top of him, pushing him onto his back. Straddling his hips, she rubbed herself slowly up and down against his erection. Stone closed his eyes, a half smile playing on his lips. He placed his hands on her hips, helping guide her motion. Leola tipped her head back, keeping up the rhythmic movement as the warmth grew between her legs, and spread up inside into her stomach.

Stone shifted position, wanting to slide inside her, but Leola moved too.

"Not yet," she whispered. "We've only just started, don't be too greedy."

Back and forth, back and forth, her movements slow and graceful, the heat growing in her middle. When she reached the point where she felt she could take no more, she pulled away. Stone let out a little grunt of disappointment, but Leola put a finger to his lips to shush him.

She slid down underneath the covers, her tongue tracing a wet line over his chest and abdomen. She took him in her mouth, her tongue playing over the end of his cock, and she could taste herself on him. This was where she had to be careful, fighting the urge to draw blood. One moment of lost control, and she would bite down, pierce his flesh and start greedily sucking his warm blood spurting into her mouth.

As she slid up and down, she could feel his cock growing even more engorged in her mouth. Stone had his hands on her head, running his fingers through her hair, tangling it up into knots. Visions of blood swam through her mind, scarlet pools of it running over cobblestones, splattered against walls and fine paintings, smeared over her face and hands. The desire was so strong, the need to feed on him almost tipping her over the edge.

Leola quickened her movements, and she heard Stone gasp. She needed to finish this before she lost control, and sank her teeth into him.

Stone arched his back and cried out, and hot fluid spurted into her mouth. She drank greedily, imagining the coppery taste of blood on her tongue, sating her desire. And still she had to keep from biting down, from letting the bloodlust overtake her, consume her totally and completely.

Stone relaxed back into the embrace of the bed, and Leola held him in her mouth a few moments longer as she regained control.

There. She had held true to her faith, to the promise she had made to herself, and to the Priest.

Stone gasped again as she pulled away.

His mobile, on the bedside table, lit up and began ringing.

Stone reached over and fumbled at the phone. It fell on the floor and Stone leant out of the bed and picked it up. He looked at the display and sighed.

"I need to take this," he said.

Leola lay down on her back as Stone sat up and swung his legs over the side of the bed, his back to her. It was obvious to her from his guarded questions and replies that he did not want her in on the conversation he was holding. But Leola could hear every word spoken by the caller. Her hearing had never been so good before she was turned by Guttman.

Leola tuned out of the discussion, and let her mind wander. She had no desire to eavesdrop, no interest in what Stone might be discussing. Today she needed to continue the task of tracking down Guttman. If he was still at the club in town, as Coffin and Emma had claimed, then that was the easy part of her plan.

Killing him would be the difficult, if not impossible, part.

Maybe she should track down Joe Coffin again. He had fought Abel twice and survived. And the second time he had killed him. It seemed to Leola that she could do with a man like that by her side when it came to a showdown with Guttman.

And what about the reporter, Emma Wylde? How had she become involved with Joe Coffin and Abel Mortenson?

Leola's attention refocused, zeroing in on the conversation Stone was having. Whoever he was talking to had just mentioned Coffin's name.

You sure you don't want us to kill him?

"No," Stone said. "Stick to the plan. You still got the address?"

Peartree Lane, Unit Thirteen.

"That's the one. I'll meet you there."

No problem.

"When is it going down?"

They're loading a van with gear now. Looks like they're about to start World War fucking Three.

"All right. Just keep an eye on the situation for now. If you see an opportunity, take it."

Oh we will, we will.

Stone ended the call, dropped the mobile on the bedside cabinet.

"I've got to go," he said, not turning around.

"Back to your wife?" Leola said.

"No, I've got business to attend to."

"Sounds serious."

Stone turned to face her. His eyes were dark, his face a blank mask.

"Yes, it is."

Leola ran a hand along his thigh, up towards his crotch, entwining her fingers through his pubic hair.

"Will I see you again?"

Stone placed a hand over Leola's, pulled it away.

"I don't know." He paused, still holding onto her hand. "Maybe."

Stone stood up and dropped Leola's hand on the bed. She looked at him, at his nakedness. He had a fine body, firm with muscle.

"Get some sleep," he said. "You've been up most of the night. I'll call you."

Leola said nothing. Stone turned his back on her and dressed quickly, picking his clothes off the floor where she had thrown them in the night as she pulled them off him. Once he was fully dressed he left without a word or a backward glance.

Joe Coffin. Why was it that he seemed so central to all of this? Leola had come to England with one aim, and that was to kill Guttman. To wipe him from the face of this earth forever with no possibility that he would ever come back.

She knew where Guttman was now. That he had been dug out of his coffin filled with blood, that he was beginning a new cycle of life. And she knew that he was growing stronger by the day, and that he had others with him.

Coffin had faced down Abel and killed him. A man capable of that? Leola needed him.

Jumping out of the lumpy bed, Leola quickly pulled on a black pair of running tights and a black top. As she tied her hair back she looked out of the window, between the gap in the curtains where they didn't quite meet. She watched Stone as he crossed the road and climbed into his car.

There was no chance of following him without transport of her own, but

Leola had a fairly good idea where he was headed.

As she watched Stone drive away, Leola noticed a second car pulling out from the side of the road and following Stone's car. She recognised it as the same one she had seen tailing Stone's cab from the hotel. And earlier than that, from the airport.

She watched until the two cars disappeared from view.

So who was following Garrett Stone?

And why?

puppydog

Leaning against the side of Brendan's dirty white van, Coffin smoked a cigarette. He kept his eyes fixed on the rear entrance to Angels as Tony Mannoia, the Noonans and Hanrahan unloaded the van. A pale, grey light was filling in the shadows as the sun rose behind its blanket of cloud.

Craggs stood next to him, surveying the exterior of the building. In its heyday, in the 1800s, what was now the Angels Gentleman's Club had been a furniture factory. The Victorian building had lain derelict during the sixties and seventies, until the former factory was renovated and opened up as a nightclub in the early eighties.

Along the rear of the building, in rows, the old, weathered windowsills were still visible. The windows themselves had long since been bricked in. The only way in through the back was a door secured with a key pad.

On the ground beside the men was a growing pile of guns, gas masks, tear gas canisters, and wooden stakes, sharpened to a wicked looking point. Coffin had insisted on the stakes. Brendan had laughed at him and said he was going soft in the head, but Craggs said if Joe wanted stakes he could have stakes.

Coffin's plan was to stake each of the vampires through the heart, once they were down. It wasn't enough to kill them, he was sure of that. But skewering Mortenson through the heart had been enough to keep him down while Coffin carved him up into pieces.

That was essentially the same plan today. Storm the club with the tear gas and the guns, bring them down long enough that Coffin could shove a stake through their chests and then drag them outside. Once Coffin was sure they were dead, each and every one of them, they were going to bundle the bodies into the back of Brendan's van. Coffin, Brendan and Danny 'The Butcher' Hanrahan were going to take them to a condemned factory Hanrahan knew of, and dispose of the bodies.

Once that was done with, Coffin could start looking for Michael again. With Steffanie and her band of vampires out of the way, Michael would be the only one left. Coffin intended to find him before he infected anyone and created more blood sucking, undead monsters. But he also needed to find Michael before anybody else did, and tried to kill him.

"Bloody hell, Tony," Craggs said, as he looked at the pile of weapons on the ground. "Where the hell did you get this lot from at such short notice?"

Mannoia smiled. "You know how it is, I can't reveal my contacts."

"No, and I respect that. But once this is over, and I'm back in my club, you come and see me. The Slaughterhouse Mob needs men like you."

Mannoia nodded, and returned to emptying the van.

"And you too," Craggs said to Coffin. "The Slaughterhouse Mob still needs you, Joe."

"What the hell's that supposed to mean?" Coffin growled.

"It means what it sounds like," Craggs said. "This business with Steffanie and Michael, it's got your head all turned around. I can see that, Joe, plain as day I can see it."

"There's nothing wrong with me," Coffin said.

"No?" Craggs said. "Then what the hell's going on with that reporter, Joe? Is she fucking you? Because whenever she's around, you act like a puppydog, wagging your tail and rolling on your back and sitting up and begging. It's getting so that it's fucking pathetic to see."

Craggs paused, but Coffin said nothing.

"I've been sticking up for you Joe, because you're family to me. You know that. But it can't go on. That reporter bitch, she's got to go, before she does something stupid and takes you down, and the rest of us with you. You can see that, right?"

Joe still said nothing. Just looked at Angels, his fists clenched by his side.

She's got to go.

Coffin knew what that meant. All this trouble with the vampires, and it had slipped by him that he was introducing Emma into a situation where she had no business being. Once this was all over, Craggs would be left with the problem of dealing with Emma, of keeping himself and the Slaughterhouse Mob safe from an expose on the front pages of the newspapers.

And there was only one way Coffin could think of guaranteeing that.

Brendan, Gilligan, Harry Frazer and Billy 'Punchy' Adams walked into the parking area.

"They're all set out front," Brendan said. "Just waiting for the word, and then they'll make such a racket, we could explode a bomb inside, and nobody'll hear it."

Craggs nodded. He had hired a team of men with jackhammers to dig up the pavement outside Angels. They had fluorescent vests, hard hats, trucks and bollards, everything they needed to give the impression that they were council employed workmen.

They had also parked a large van across the entrance to the Angels' car park, completely blocking it. There were enough men there to stop anyone from walking around the back, and discovering what was really happening this morning.

"Harry, I want you to stay out front, keep an eye on things," Craggs said.

Frazer stood up a little straighter, threw his shoulders back. "I should be in there with the rest of you, not babysitting that lot out front."

"I know," Craggs said, and put a hand on Frazer's shoulder. "But I need somebody outside, make sure the noise level stays up, make sure nobody slips around the back, sees what's going on. The last thing we need is the coppers turning up."

"Why me? Is it because of my age, is that it? Hell, Mort, I'm younger than you by a couple of decades. Maybe you should be the one doing the babysitting."

Freddie Noonan dropped the gas mask he was holding, and strutted up to Frazer. "Hey, you don't speak like that to Mr Craggs, you show him some respect."

"It's all right, Freddie," Craggs said. "Harry here is a good friend, he can speak his mind around me."

Freddie backed off. Frazer hadn't even turned to look at him, acted as though he hadn't noticed him.

"I know what you're saying Harry, but I'm going inside with the rest of them. That bitch Steffanie not only took my club, but she stole my people off me too. Addison, he was a friend of mine, and now I'm about to go in there and murder him. I'm going to see that stupid slut burn, I'm going to see her suffer for what she's done to me."

A ray of weak sunshine penetrated the cloud cover, casting its light over the assembled men before disappearing again.

"All right, then," Frazer said. "I'll do this for you, Mort. I'll do it for you."

"Thank you, Harry. You're a good man."

Craggs turned to face all of the men, who stood waiting for him to speak. He looked at them one by one, holding them in his gaze for a moment, before moving on. Coffin thought he was going to make a speech, like an officer inspiring his troops for one last assault on the enemy stronghold.

But in the end, what he said was, "All right then. Let's smoke those fuckers out of there, and take my club back."

The men murmured their agreement.

Coffin nodded at Frazer. "Go on out to the front, tell those men they can start work now. We need noise, lots of it, and continually until we tell them to stop."

Frazer nodded his agreement back at Coffin and then headed for the street.

"Grab your weapon of choice boys, and then put on your gas masks," Craggs said.

Coffin scooped up the bundle of stakes and began slotting them in between his belt and his jeans. Then he picked up a shotgun, a Remington 870, and a box of shells. He inserted four of the shells into the magazine, and pumped the slider backwards and then forwards.

The others picked up their choice of guns, mainly handguns. Coffin had asked Tony Mannoia to get him the shotgun. He preferred its directness. Its blunt power.

Picking up a gas mask, Coffin walked over to the club's rear door. He glanced back at Craggs who nodded, and then punched in the security code and pushed at the door.

Nothing.

Coffin looked at Craggs and shook his head. Billy 'Punchy' Adams climbed into the back of Brendan's van. A moment later and he jumped back out with a police issue battering ram. He strode across the car park, getting in a few practice swings with the metal tube. The others followed him.

Wearing their gas masks, and holding their guns, they looked like an alien horde intent on invading earth. Coffin slipped his own gas mask over his face and stepped out of the way as Adams readied himself to swing the battering ram at the door.

The quiet morning was suddenly ripped apart by the clamour of jackhammers breaking up paving stones at the front of the club. A moment later and the battering ram slammed into the door. It held firm. Adams pulled the battering ram back and swung again, grunting at the effort he put behind it.

This time the door crashed open, smashing against the corridor wall. He stepped back and Tony Mannoia ran into the darkened building with a tear gas grenade. He pulled the cap off, pressed the nozzle on top, and rolled the canister along the corridor. Immediately it began spraying a noxious cloud of fumes as it rolled into the club.

Coffin followed him into the darkness and the cloud of gas with the rest of the men close behind.

always causing trouble

There had been a massive problem to overcome before Coffin and the rest left to storm Angels, and Emma had been smack in the middle of it. Her mother would have sympathised, but not with her daughter. No, her loyalties would have lain fair and square with the gang of murderers, thieves and scumbags Emma had wound up hanging out with recently.

"Always causing trouble, even as a child," she would have said. "Never knew what to do with her, we didn't. Wherever there was a problem, there was Emma, right at the root of it."

Emma screwed her eyes shut.

"Get out of my head, Mother," she said.

"Hunf?" came a muffled reply.

Emma turned her head away.

That was another problem, one that she didn't want to confront right now.

That fucking Joe Coffin, she was going to kill him the next time she saw him. She had been counting on him, depending on him to stand up for her when the time came. Instead, what had happened? The big gorilla had caved in like a timid little girl.

That a confrontation was brewing, had been obvious. There was no way that Brendan in particular, or any of the others for that matter, were going to let Emma accompany them to Angels. Why would they let her do that? The criminal type tended to not appreciate reporters hanging around at the scene of a crime in progress. And even if you bought into the idea that Angels was full of vampires, and so technically already dead, within the boundaries of the law Craggs and his men were still committing murder.

So that morning, when they were all gathered and ready to swing into action with a van full of guns and tear gas grenades, Brendan had been the one to speak up first and voice his concerns.

"You know what I'm saying, Mort," he said. "She shouldn't be here, and that's the plain and simple fact of the matter."

"Didn't we clear this up last night?" Coffin growled.

"Aye, maybe we did," Brendan replied. "But now it's the morning, and we're all booted up and ready to do some killing, and I don't know about you, Joe but I don't want a reporter on the scene recording my every move for the evening edition."

"He's got a point, Joe," Craggs said.

Remarkably, Emma managed to keep her mouth shut. She had a feeling that if she started shouting and swearing and generally kicking up a stink right now, that any last vestiges of sympathy Craggs may have for her would disappear.

"I told you, she's on our side," Coffin said. "She's coming with us."

Even to Emma, that sounded pretty weak.

Craggs shook his head. "She stays here, Joe."

"Aye, and we put her down the cellar with the two coppers, and tie her up," Brendan said. "I'm not having her running out on us and blabbing as soon as we've driven around the corner."

"No," Coffin said.

"Then what the fuck else do you suggest we do with her now, Joe?" Brendan said, stepping up into Coffin's face.

The two men eyeballed each other, until Craggs spoke up.

"Joe, it's the only way. You know that."

Coffin still said nothing, continued staring down at Brendan, his lip curled back in a snarl.

"Joe, step back!" Craggs snapped.

Coffin broke eye contact with Brendan, glanced at Craggs. In that moment, Emma knew Coffin was siding with the rest of them. That she was going down in the cellar.

Coffin took her in, his arms on her shoulders, guiding her into the cellar like she was blind or elderly. His hands were remarkably gentle. He didn't take her all the way down the steps but paused less than halfway down.

"Stay here," he said, standing awkwardly a couple of steps below her so that for the first time she could remember they were eye level with each other. "Don't move from this spot. I'll be back before you know it and there will be no vampires left in the city."

"Except Michael," Emma said.

Coffin said nothing, just looked into Emma's eyes. He still had those big hands of his on the sides of her shoulders.

"Stay here," he said, finally. "Don't do anything stupid."

"Wait a minute," Emma said. "You're the one who's about to go and fight a nightclub full of vampires with the Keystone Cops, and you're telling me not to do anything stupid?"

Coffin sighed, and then smiled. It wasn't much of a smile, but it softened that battered face of his.

"You know what I'm saying," he said. "Just sit tight and wait, all right?"

"Joe, it's time we got moving," Brendan said from the cellar doorway.

"Go on, then," Emma said.

Coffin squeezed her arms briefly and then turned and climbed the cellar steps and pushed past Brendan.

Brendan was the last one she saw, standing at the top of the steps. He paused, before he shut the door on her.

"Don't you worry," he'd said, in his soft, Irish lilt. "We'll be back soon enough. Then you, me and Joe, get together shall we? We can have ourselves a little film show."

And he had shut the door, and thrown the bolts.

A film show.

Fuck.

Emma really didn't like the sound of that.

"Hunf! Errrnnnffff!"

Emma closed her eyes again. As if she didn't have enough to deal with, now she had got these two pricks annoying her with their continued grunts. Couldn't understand a word they were saying, but then she didn't need to.

It was obvious.

They wanted Emma to untie them.

"Just shut the fuck up, will you," she hissed. "I'm trying to think."

This comment was met with more grunts. One of the men kicked out in frustration, his feet bound together. Emma could just see them both, in the dirty light filtered down what looked like an old coal chute. When her eyes had first grown used to the gloom of the cellar and she had noticed the coal chute, she had wondered if she might be able to make her escape through it. On closer inspection it proved to be too narrow and high for her to fit through.

Emma had expected to find barrels of beer down here. Wasn't that what they did in pubs, when the tap ran dry? The landlord descended into the cellar and changed a barrel. But this particular cellar was small and pokey. There was an old, rotten settee, its cushions lumpy and sagging in the middle. Beside the settee stood an ancient, Victorian school desk, with a top that lifted up and an inkwell.

Other than that, the cellar was empty.

If you didn't count the two cops and the reporter, of course.

How the fuck did this happen? Of all the stupid things she had ever done, this was the stupidest of them all by a long shot. Kidnapping two members of Her Majesty's Police Force?

What the hell would Nick say when he found out?

And there was no way that Emma could see that he wasn't going to find out. At some point they had to let these two jokers go free, and then there was going to be hell to pay.

"Hnnfff!"

Except they weren't going to be set free, were they?

If Brendan had had any intention of letting them live he wouldn't have brought them back to his pub. Probably the only reason they weren't dead yet was because Brendan was too busy right now to dispose of a couple of bodies, and he didn't want their rotting corpses stinking his pub up. But as soon as this business with Angels was finished, Brendan would be the first one down here with a gun, or a knife, or whatever his favourite cop killing instrument was.

And what about Emma?

The police might hold top spot on Brendan's list of sub-species that deserved to be exterminated, but reporters were right behind at number two. Especially this particular reporter. And that crack about a film show? Emma had no idea how, but Brendan had got hold of the video of Coffin killing Terry Wu.

The one she had told Coffin she hadn't managed to find.

Once Joe found out that she had been lying to him, where would his loyalties lie then?

Emma took a deep breath, decided she had no option other than to untie the cops.

In a weird way, it kind of felt like a betrayal of Coffin. But that was just stupid. He was a murderer. Just because of all the shit they had been through together, didn't mean they were engaged to be married or anything.

"Hunff! Fernff!"

Emma held her hands up. "All right, all right! I'm coming."

She untied the younger one first. As soon as his hands were free he yanked the gag off his mouth.

"What the fucking hell took you so fucking long!" he said, his fingers fighting with the knots on the rope that bound his ankles together.

Emma tried helping him with the rope around his ankles, but he pushed her away.

"Fuck off and untie Brian, will you?"

His finger finally found purchase on the knots and the rope began to unravel. As soon as he was free the policeman scrambled for a corner of the cellar. Emma heard him unzip his fly in the darkness, and then the sound of a stream of liquid splashing against a wall.

"Ah, fuck," he sighed. "I've been holding that in all fucking night."

Emma slipped the gag off the other man. He was older, looked like he had suffered a bit more than his colleague.

"My hands," he croaked. "Untie my hands, I can't feel them anymore."

Emma helped him roll over onto his side, and worked at the knots binding his wrists together. When she had freed him he rolled onto his back again and held his hands up in front of his face. He was grimacing, the muscles in his jaw standing out as he clenched his teeth.

"Are you all right?" she said.

"Pins and needles, painful as hell," he said through gritted teeth.

"Here, let me untie your feet," Emma said.

When she bent down she wrinkled her nose, and had to bite back a noise of disgust. Brian obviously didn't have the bladder control that his younger companion did. He'd pissed himself in the night.

Emma got on with untying his feet. Decided it was best to pretend she couldn't smell a thing.

When she had freed him she scooted back on her bottom and sat on the floor, waiting for the first cop to finish pissing against the wall. Brian flexed his fingers slowly and carefully, bringing life back into them.

"Bloody hell, but I needed that," the policeman said as he zipped himself up.

"I don't know how you could hold on for so long, Jimmy," Brian said. "I tried to hold on, but I bloody pissed myself during the night."

"No shame in that," Jimmy said, heading straight for Emma. "We were tied up and locked in a cellar all bloody night."

She didn't like the look on his face.

Jimmy squatted down in front of Emma and pointed a finger right in her face. "And this bitch helped the bastards who put us down here."

"Hey, I don't know if you noticed, but I'm a prisoner too," Emma said. "You got any thoughts why that might be?"

"I dunno. Dishonour amongst thieves, and all that crap? What's the matter, did you fall out with your friends?"

"That's right," Emma said. "Because I'm the one who's been trying to figure out a way of getting you two jokers out of here."

"The fuck you say!" snarled Jimmy. "Something's gone wrong, you've had an argument or whatever, I don't know and I don't fucking care. But now they've shoved you down here with us and you're trying to pretend that you've been our best friend all along?"

"I untied you, didn't I?"

"Yeah, and you took your sweet fucking time about it, and all!"

"All right, Jimmy, calm down," Brian said. "Let's save our energy for thinking how we're going to get out of here."

"Fucking right," Jimmy said, still staring at Emma, his finger in her face.

"Did you piss on your hands, just?" Emma said. "Because that finger of yours stinks of something awful."

"You stupid bitch," Jimmy said, and grabbed a handful of Emma's hair, yanking her head back.

"Jimmy!" Brian yelled. "What the hell are you doing?"

Jimmy let go of Emma's hair immediately. He stood up, and walked away.

"Your friend's got a temper on him," Emma said.

"Which is more than a good enough reason for you to keep your mouth shut," Brian replied.

He was looking a little healthier now, stronger. He sat up straighter.

"What's going on up there?" he said.

"They've all gone," Emma replied. "We're on our own down here, apart from Patsy."

"Who the fuck is Patsy?" Jimmy said.

"Brendan's wife. Brendan's the big Irish bastard who tied you up."

"And where exactly are we?" Brian said.

"A pub, off Broad Street," Emma replied. "O'Donoghue's."

"Fucking hell!" Jimmy hissed. "I come for a pint here every now and then. I thought that bastard looked familiar, he's the fucking landlord, isn't he?"

Emma nodded.

Jimmy started prowling the cellar, looking into the darkened corners. He examined the coal chute, but obviously came to the same conclusion as Emma and quickly moved on.

"If you're looking for a secret door out of this place and into Narnia, I'm afraid you're out of luck," Emma said. "The only way out is that door at the top of the cellar, and that's bolted shut."

"Shut your mouth," Jimmy said. "When I want to hear you yapping I'll speak to you, okay?"

Emma bit her lip. Brian was right, this man had a temper and she needed to make sure she didn't provide him with the fuel to flare up. She'd be the one paying the price if he lost it.

Jimmy sat on the lumpy settee by Brian, who was massaging his feet.

"How are you doing?"

"Not so bad, life's come back into my hands and feet now," Brian said.

"Good. Let's get the fuck out of here then."

The two men stood up. Emma stood up too. "What are you going to do?"

"Take you down the police station and read you your rights," Brian said.

Jimmy ran up the stone steps to the top, and braced his hands against the damp walls. He lifted his leg, paused, and then slammed his boot into the door. It shook in the frame, but held firm. He drew his foot back and smashed his heel against the door again.

And again it held firm.

Jimmy rested for a moment.

"Bloody weak as a kitten," he said.

"You want me to come up, give you a hand?" Brian said.

Jimmy shook his head. "Nah. There isn't room for two of us up here. Just give me a minute, okay?"

"Take as long as you need."

Jimmy waited only another few seconds before raising his booted foot again, but before he had chance to deliver another smashing blow against the door a voice shouted from the other side.

"What's going on in there? Stop it, stop it now!"

Jimmy looked down the steps, into the cellar, his eyebrows raised.

"Patsy," Emma whispered. "All that noise you're making, you must have disturbed her, interrupted her TV schedule."

Jimmy pressed his cheek against the door, spoke through the tiny gap between the door and the frame.

"Patsy," he said, "this is a police officer. Open the door, please."

Silence.

"Patsy, you need to open this door and let me and my colleague out of here. I understand that you are scared, but we can help you. But you have to let us out first."

Silence.

Jimmy threw a quick glance back at his colleague. Brian gave him a quick, short nod. *Keep talking.*

"Patsy? Are you on your own out there? Is there anybody else in the pub?"

Silence.

"I think you are on your own this morning, Patsy. The others, they've left you alone, haven't they? Left you in charge. I know you're scared, and I know why you're scared, I do. But you have to let us out of here. If you let us out of this cellar we can help you. We can give you protection from your husband and the others. We can testify on your behalf, testify that you helped us. Will you do that, Patsy? Will you help us?"

Silence.

Jimmy looked back at Brian again. This time the older man held up his hand. *Wait.*

Finally, a voice spoke from the other side of the door.

"No."

"Patsy?' Jimmy said. "What did you say?"

"I said no, I'm not going to help you. Fucking pig bastards, you can rot in there for all I care."

Jimmy turned back to Brian. Emma could see the rage building in his face. In one swift movement he had braced his hands against the wall again, and smashed his foot into the door with an incoherent roar of rage.

The door shivered in its frame and shifted slightly.

"Stop that now!" Patsy screamed.

Jimmy kicked the door again, still yelling. This time he didn't stop to take a breather, he kept on kicking at the door. Looked to Emma like he had completely lost his mind.

With a splintering sound the door sprang open, swinging out hard and slamming against the wall. Jimmy disappeared through the doorway.

Emma and Brian both made for the cellar steps at the same time. They both stopped when they heard the explosion and the scream from upstairs.

Jimmy staggered back into view, clutching his stomach, a stunned expression on his face. He managed to half turn around before his legs gave way, and he tumbled down the stone steps. His head hit the floor with a sickening thud, his arms twisted awkwardly behind him.

But it was the mass of ripped flesh and blood across his stomach that scared Emma as she looked down at his still body.

"Oh bloody hell," Brian whispered. "The stupid bitch shot him."

Just at that moment Patsy began walking down the steps. Emma saw her feet first, noticed her carpet slippers, her blotchy legs, covered in varicose veins, the frayed hem of her dressing gown.

The double barrelled shotgun she was pointing at them.

Brian pushed Emma back, gave her a good shove out of the way.

"I told him to stop," she said. "I told him, I said to him, stop doing that."

"Patsy, please, put the gun down," Brian said, his voice remarkably calm and firm.

Patsy shook her head. "Brendan, he said I should shoot you if you tried anything. He said I should kill you all."

Jimmy groaned. He was still alive. But when Emma risked a glance down at him, even though every fibre of her being insisted she keep staring at Patsy and that big, fucking elephant gun she was pointing at them, she saw Jimmy was now lying in a large pool of blood.

"Patsy, put the gun down," Brian said, his voice taking on a firmer tone, like a teacher reprimanding a naughty school child.

Patsy shook her head. "I told him to stop. I told him."

"That's right, you told him to stop, and he didn't, but now he needs urgent medical attention, and if we don't get that for him he will die, and you will be on a murder charge."

"Not if I kill you, too," Patsy said, and raised the shotgun at Brian's head.

eyeballs

None of the lights in the club worked. Freddie kept flicking the switches like the lighting system might suddenly spring into life if he did it enough, but the club remained shrouded in darkness. With that and the clouds of tear gas, visibility was down to practically zero.

Coffin's hearing wasn't much better, either. Seemed all he could hear was his breath rushing in and out of his lungs. He had to shout to make himself understood to one of the others. Add to that the fact that everybody was strung out and twitchy, and they were a walking disaster waiting to happen. All it would take was one itchy trigger finger to start a shitstorm of gunfire, and Craggs needn't worry about vampires being immune to tear gas or not.

They would all be dead by their own hands.

Coffin walked slowly through the club, sliding his way along the tables, from one to another. He held his mobile out in front of him, the torch function switched on, to guide his way. Mainly it just lit up the clouds of swirling gas. In his other hand he held the shotgun, propped against his shoulder. As far as he could tell the club was deserted.

Apart from nine goons carrying guns and wearing ridiculous looking headgear.

Coffin was starting to sweat under the mask and he was already feeling claustrophobic. He had to resist the urge to rip the mask off his face and take in a deep lungful of air.

He knew how that would end.

A shadow emerged from the dark cloud in front of him, the gas mask giving whoever it was the appearance of a science fiction monster.

"Foamuchfoazelemneoafsupi," the monster said.

"What?" Coffin shouted.

"So much for the element of surprise," Brendan shouted back.

Coffin grunted. Emma had been right. This was the worst fucking plan they could have come up with. Any minute now they were going to be jumped on by a bunch of hungry vampires who, like Emma had said, weren't in the least bothered by the tear gas because they were already dead.

Coffin spun round at the touch of a hand on his shoulder. The figure in front of him held his hands up, and when Coffin peered closer he realised it was Craggs. Before they had left O'Donoghue's this morning, Coffin had tried persuading Craggs to stay behind. Said it was no place for a man of his age, that he had to look after himself, keep himself sharp for when he got his club back.

For a moment there, the old man had looked like he could have murdered Coffin. That if maybe Brendan, or one of the others, had passed him a gun right then he would have used it.

"I'm not dead yet, Joe," he said.

Coffin said nothing more about the matter.

Craggs was pointing, back in the direction of the stairs leading up to his office and the Fuck Rooms.

Coffin nodded, and turned back to Brendan and indicated where they were headed. They walked in single file along the side of the bar, and the stage where the girls danced, and out the back door. Coffin pushed past Craggs and took the stairs two at a time, the husky sound of his breath filling his ears, like a second rate Darth Vader.

Brendan had a canister of tear gas and he got ready to pull the cap off and activate it, sending it rolling along the hallway.

Coffin put a hand on his arm and shook his head. It was dark up here, but at least without the clouds of tear gas they could use their mobiles to illuminate their way.

Coffin pulled his mask off and wiped the sweat off his forehead with his arm.

"Feel like I'm fucking suffocating in this thing," he said.

Craggs and Brendan both peeled their masks off, too. Coffin swept the light from his phone across the hallway. Up here, unlike the ground floor of the club, there were windows. But they had all been covered over with layers of black bin liners, and taped up.

All the doors were shut.

"You think they left?" Brendan whispered.

Coffin shook his head.

"No. Maybe that's what they want us to think, but they're here. Steffanie wants this place for herself."

"Over my dead body," Craggs said.

"We should have brought torches," Coffin said.

"How the hell did we know they were going to throw the place into darkness by cutting the electricity?" Brendan said. "It's madness, they're just as blind as we are."

"I don't think so," Coffin replied. "I'm guessing they can probably see in the dark just as well as in the day."

"Only if you believe in all that shit you keep spouting," Brendan said. "You ask me, I think they've pissed off. They've gone, and left us to wander around and bump into each other like a bunch of blind old men."

"We need to search the place, make sure," Coffin said.

He walked over to a window and peeled the black plastic away from the glass. Pale light leaked into the hall. Coffin squinted and turned his back on the window.

"Brendan, go and get Freddie and bring him up here, search all these rooms, remember to take all the bin liners off the windows."

"Are you taking the fucking piss, Joe?" Brendan said. "I don't take my orders off you, now."

Coffin stepped up in Brendan's face. "When this is finished, you and me are going to have a little chat, sort this crap out once and for all."

Brendan smiled. "Why wait, Joe? We can dance right now, if you like."

"Have you two girls forgotten who's in charge here?" Craggs said. "When this is all done and we've got my club back you two can wave your dicks at each other all you want. But right now we need to concentrate on clearing this place of the vermin who think they can fuck with the Slaughterhouse Mob."

Coffin glanced at Craggs and stepped back. Brendan stepped forward, keeping right in Coffin's face.

"Brendan, what the hell are you doing?" Craggs said.

Before Brendan could reply, Coffin had planted his hands on the Irishman's chest and pushed him. Brendan staggered and then righted himself. Coffin tensed, waiting for Brendan to attack.

All three men turned and stared at the stairs when they heard a scream from the club.

* * *

Terry Noonan was never going to admit it, but he was practically pissing his pants. Not because of the danger they were in, this was the kind of shit he loved. A gun in his hand, with his brother, looking to fuck somebody over. Nothing could beat that feeling. Not even sex.

In fact, he had a boner the size of a donkey's right now. Always happened, every single bloody time. Freddie said he was wrong in the head, who the fuck got a hard on when they were out to give somebody a working over or on a job? Terry just told him to fuck off.

No, it was the dark that scared him. Terry never told anyone, not even Freddie, although his brother knew really. Being in dark spaces, especially enclosed dark spaces, absolutely terrified him. And despite the fact that the club was one huge, cavernous interior, Terry's primal instincts were screaming at him that he was actually stuck in a claustrophobia inducing, tiny little hole.

It was all that fucking tear gas billowing around that did it. And the hot, stupid mask on his face. He was sweating like a pig under that thing and had to keep blinking the sweat out of his eyes. The urge to rip that bloody thing off his face was almost overpowering. Several times he had caught himself raising his hand to the mask, once even tugging at it before he had stopped himself. It got so bad he had started repeating a little mantra to himself, muttering it under his breath, over and over.

Keep the fucking gas mask on, you stupid bastard.
Keep the fucking gas mask on, you stupid bastard.
Keep the fucking gas mask on, you stupid bastard.

The other fight he had on his hands was resisting the urge to turn and make a dash for the exit, get back outside in the fresh air and daylight. If he ran out on the others, that would be the end of his criminal career. Even Freddie would disown him. He'd probably have to move out of the city, find himself somewhere to live where nobody knew him.

Terry couldn't do that. He fucking needed his big brother, depended on him for everything. Without Freddie to look after him Terry didn't know what he would do. As kids it had been the same. The two of them were the scourge of their local school, the Terror Twins as some people called them even though they weren't fucking twins.

Seemed like they spent most of their school days in the headmaster's office, or in detention, or standing at the front of the class and being made an example of. It was Freddie who always got them into trouble, Freddie who came up with the stupid shit they did.

But it was Freddie who looked after his little brother, who ran screaming with fists flying whenever he saw he was in trouble. And it was his big brother that Terry still looked up to, depended upon to sort out their day to day lives; get them jobs laying tarmac, or going around somebody's place to give them a slap and a warning about a debt that was owed.

But if he ran out on them now, Terry could say goodbye to Freddie forever.

Terry shook his head, trying to dislodge more sweat running down into his eyes. Someone was shouting, but he couldn't make out a fucking word they were saying underneath the gas mask. Bloody stupid idea to come down here without thinking it through properly.

Terry stumbled over a chair in the dark and smacked his head against a wall. "Fucking hell!" he hissed.

He'd dropped his gun. Kneeling down, Terry began patting the floor. Outside, when they had been choosing their weapons, Terry had been the last one to get to choose and there had been nothing left but a couple of handguns. Terry had chosen the Glock, a semi-automatic handgun, but he wished he could have had something bigger like that fucking monster of a shotgun that Coffin had chosen.

It was always the fucking way, wasn't it? Terry was forever finding himself at the back of the queue, never got the good shit like everybody else did.

Where the hell was that fucking gun? In all this smoke and darkness he was fucking blind. He'd have to be a fucking Shaolin Monk to fight in this.

There it was.

Terry's hand closed around the grip just as his mask was ripped from his head.

He sucked in a lungful of the tear gas, and it was like breathing in fire and ice at the same moment. The gas seared through the lining of his throat, filling his chest with scorching pain. Squeezing his eyes shut was like rubbing barbed wire over his eyeballs.

Hands pulled at him, spinning him around, pushing him to the floor.

Terry screamed. The sound ripped from his throat in an explosion of agony, and he doubled up in a coughing fit so terrifyingly powerful he thought me might vomit up his lungs. The cold hands were all over him, running over his face and tearing at his clothes. Whoever it was, they were sitting on top of him. Pinning him down.

Terry tried reaching up a hand to his face, his instincts to rub at his eyes, do anything to alleviate the pain. But his attacker grabbed his wrist and with a powerful thrust, twisted his arm around. Even above the noise of the jackhammers from outside, Terry heard the bone snap in his wrist before the agony washed over him and he screamed again.

Blood pounded through his head and tears streamed down his face. His eyes and chest and mouth were all on fire. Almost senseless with the pain and fear, Terry still heard his attacker giggle.

And a tiny part of his mind regained its sharpness, its edge, just as his uninjured hand found the Glock once more. He snatched it off the floor and jammed the muzzle into the body on top of him. His attacker jerked when he pulled the trigger, but still sat on top of him. Blindly, Terry shifted the gun's position, and fired again.

This time his assailant howled, and leapt off him.

Fuck you! Terry tried screaming, but it came out as a hacking cough. He scrambled to his feet, not caring where his attacker had gone, who they were or what they were going to do next. He just had to get outside and find some air.

Holding his injured arm against his chest and coughing helplessly, Terry staggered blindly through the club. He walked into a table, his thigh smacking against it and almost fell over. Where the fuck was the exit? He had no idea in this smoke and darkness.

Someone collided with him, and Terry screamed and fired the Glock again. Through the pounding rush of blood in his ears and the noise of the jackhammers from outside, Terry thought he could hear someone shouting at him. But his head was all fucked up, his instincts screaming at him to get the hell out of the smoke and the darkness.

In his panic to get outside he hit his broken wrist against something solid, the agony swallowing his arm in a sleeve of fire. He stumbled over something, but managed to regain his balance before he fell and landed on his damaged hand.

He dropped the gun.

Fuck! Fuck! Fuck! Not again!

Terry doubled over as another particularly terrifying bout of coughing overcame him. Thought he was going to cough his guts up. He fell onto his knees and then onto his side.

And through the coughing and the crying, Terry suddenly realised he could feel hands running over him, pulling at his clothes, tugging at his trouser belt, ripping his shirt from him. He was pushed onto his back, too weak to fight off his attacker.

Another pair of hands on his face, a tongue licking the snot and the tears off his cheeks. Cold breath stinking of death and decay washing over him and the agony in his eyes ramping up more than he ever thought possible.

That wasn't just the tear gas, Terry suddenly realised.

Someone had their thumbs in his eyes, pressing and gouging, digging into his eye sockets. Terry could feel his eyeballs bulging with the pressure of being shoved to one side. With his good hand, Terry flailed at his attacker, trying to push them off. But then the red hot agony in his eyes shot off the scale, and the last thing he sensed before he blacked out was hot blood spurting from his ruptured eyeballs and over his face.

sorry

Emma had to give it to Brian, he completely kept his cool. Here was this mousy Irish woman pointing a loaded shotgun at his face while his colleague lay on the floor bleeding out from a gunshot wound, but Brian could have been looking out of his window at passing traffic for all the emotion that showed on his face.

"Patsy, if you shoot me you will be convicted of the murder of two police officers, and you will spend the rest of your days in prison," he said. "But if you put the gun down now, and allow me to call for help for my friend, then I will testify that you made the right choice in this situation, that you helped us out."

Jimmy groaned. The shotgun in Patsy's hands had a magnetic attraction for Emma, but she managed to drag her eyes off it and risked a glance at Jimmy. He was lying in a large pool of blood. His eyes were still closed, and his face was ashen white.

Emma looked back at Patsy. The woman looked absolutely terrified, and Emma could see her finger twitching over the trigger. In her present state she might actually fire the gun without intending to.

Maybe if she could distract her. Emma quickly discarded that thought. Did she really want to remind Patsy that she was here? The woman might decide to point that shotgun at her head instead.

"Patsy, please put the gun down," Brian said, his voice quiet and level, almost soothing.

Yeah, put the fucking gun down you crazy bitch! Emma wanted to scream.

Jimmy moaned again.

Patsy's eyes flicked over to him, and Brian grabbed the gun's muzzle and twisted it away. The explosion of the gunshot was deafening in the confined cellar. The Victorian school desk flipped over, the wood splintering beneath the blast.

Patsy stumbled and fell onto her knees on the damp floor.

Brian kicked her in the head.

"Stupid bitch!" he screamed.

Patsy fell over onto her side, letting out a wail of terror and pain. Emma could see a lump the size of an egg swelling on her temple, and a trickle of red ran down her cheek. Convulsive sobs racked her tiny body.

Emma stood stock still, watching Brian very carefully.

"You fucking stupid cow!" he shouted, spittle flying from his lips, his eyes bulging like they might pop out of his head. "I ought to stick this gun in your fucking mouth and let you have both fucking barrels."

Emma fought the urge to speak, to tell him to calm down. Whatever semblance of cool, calm collectedness he had needed before was gone now. He leaned over the terrified woman lying on the floor, curled up into a ball, and yelled senselessly at her whilst she wailed and cried. Did he even remember his colleague was bleeding to death just a couple of feet away?

Glancing at the steps leading up to the open cellar door, Emma's nerve endings screamed at her to make a break for it, to scramble up the steps and escape from the pub. But the logical part of her mind told her no. Any movement on her part might distract Brian, reminding him of the fact that he had a witness to his assault on Patsy. Without Emma here to say otherwise, he could claim that Patsy received the injury to her head falling over when Brian pulled the gun out of her hands.

But she couldn't just stand here, frozen to the spot, whilst Jimmy bled to death next to them. And what happened if she waited long enough that Brian calmed down and noticed her anyway? What would he do then? Was there a chance he might turn violent on her like he had on Patsy?

Jimmy moaned, sounded almost like he was trying to say something.

Brian heard, whipped around on the spot to look at his friend. His chest heaved with the effort of taking deep breaths, and his face was red and wet with sweat. Looked like he might be ready to keel over from a heart attack at any moment. Raising an arm he wiped the sweat from his face on his shirt sleeve.

Jimmy coughed blood up.

Brian knelt down next to him. "Bloody hell, Jimmy."

The older man took his friend's hand and held it.

Why wasn't he trying to find help? There would be a phone upstairs, he could call emergency services and get an ambulance out here. Why was he just kneeling there, holding Jimmy's hand?

Because he was dead already, Emma realised. She hadn't seen it happen, but she could see it now.

Brian wiped at his eyes with his free hand, whilst he continued holding onto

Jimmy. Patsy snuffled in the corner, still curled up into a ball.

What now? Emma thought. *Make a run for it, and head on over to Angels where there might possibly be another bloodbath in progress right now? Or stay here? Call the police and explain everything.*

So much blood and death over the last few days. So much violence and killing. All since Abel Mortenson had appeared. He was dead now, but the consequences of his actions were still spreading like ripples in a pond.

No, not like ripples on water, which eventually lost their power and died away. This was the opposite. It was like a virus, spreading and multiplying as it infected others. Unless they stamped it out this virus would continue to spread at a terrifying, exponential rate. And where would it end? When everyone in the country was a vampire, or dead?

And then would it spread around the world?

Which made Emma wonder where Abel had come from in the first place. How had he known to dig up the old man from the cellar? Why had there not been a vampire outbreak before this? Why now, all of a sudden?

"You," Brian said, breaking Emma out of her thoughts. "This is your fault. You and your friends."

Emma swallowed. Her throat was dry and her head was fuzzy. The blast of the shotgun still echoed around her head, along with Jimmy's scream as he staggered and fell down the cellar steps.

"You got nothing to say?" Brian said. "My friend is dead, and you've got nothing to fucking say to me?"

Emma swallowed again, tried to think of something she could say. Sorry didn't really seem appropriate in the circumstances, and she had a feeling it might tip him over the edge again.

Brian placed Jimmy's hand gently on the floor and stood up. Glancing over at Patsy he took a deep, ragged breath and let it out slowly. The woman was still crying, but softly now. Curled up in a ball, she hadn't noticed Brian staring at her.

What next?

Brian would call this in, and a huge contingent of police would appear. Emma would be taken into custody and questioned about what she knew, her part in all of this. No point in trying to hide now, or stay out of the limelight. Karl was right, she should have gone to the cops in the first place. Too late for all of that, no point in hiding what she knew anymore. She had to tell them everything, give up the video of Coffin murdering Terry Wu, all the files on the Slaughterhouse Mob.

Explain about the vampires. No one was going to believe that, she would probably get labelled as a crazy, locked up somewhere. But then the killings would start again, and when the infection had spread enough that nobody in their right mind was going outside for fear of having their throat ripped out, well, they would believe her then.

They would have no choice.

wr r u

Coffin was back in the dense cloud of tear gas, his gas mask on, and shotgun cradled in his arm. With his free hand he held his phone out at arm's length, the beam from the torch function doing little more than illuminating the swirling clouds of gas.

Over the sound of his breathing, and the racket from the jackhammers just outside, Coffin could hear nothing. Sometimes he thought he sensed movement. A disturbance in the swirling smoke, maybe. The impression of a figure darting around him, behind him.

Coffin kept swinging his arm from side to side, the beam of light like a lighthouse beacon, cutting through the fog like a special effect in a science fiction movie.

Or, considering their present circumstances, a horror film.

Coffin couldn't understand it. Craggs had stayed outside to take a breather, but that still left eight of them searching the club. It was a big space, but he should have bumped into one of the others by now. Where the hell was everyone? Had they lost their nerve and bolted?

Or were they all dead?

And who had screamed? It had been impossible to tell who it had been over the racket of the jackhammers from outside. But one of the gang was in trouble.

Coffin had the feeling that the vampires were all down here in the club, where there were no windows and no risk of exposure to daylight. How many vampires were there? Four of them. No, five counting that wizened old thing Leola had named as Guttman. Five vampires against nine men armed with guns and wooden stakes.

Movement, out of the corner of his eyes, on the periphery of his vision that the restrictive gas mask permitted him. Coffin spun round, pulling the shotgun up and pointing it at the empty space where he had sensed movement.

The wisps of gas twirled in erratic patterns in the light from his phone. As though someone had passed through that space just a moment ago.

Coffin became aware of a burning pain on his shoulder. Cradling the shotgun in the crook of his arm he placed the palm of his hand against the spot on his shoulder where it hurt. When he pulled his hand away and shone the phone's light on his palm he saw streaks of red.

They were here.

She was here.

Toying with him. When Steffanie was alive, and dancing, her sinuous movements on stage had often led to her being compared to a cat. And now that comparison seemed more apt than ever before.

Steffanie was the cat, and Coffin was the mouse.

For a big guy he suddenly felt very small.

Coffin gripped the shotgun again and switched off the torch function on his phone. He had no idea how well the vampires could see in the dark. His guess was that they could see very well. But nobody had vision good enough that they could see through clouds of smoke.

A beam of light cutting through the dark and the smoke, that was a different matter. Everyone could see that. Which meant that Coffin had been signalling his presence wherever he went with his torchlight.

Now maybe he had evened up the odds a little.

Maybe.

Coffin dropped the phone in his pocket and took a cautious step forward. His vision was completely zero now. Might as well have his eyes screwed shut.

A soft breeze, a swish of air over the flesh on his arms, and another burning sensation across his chest. Coffin jumped back, swinging the gun around, trying to make contact with whoever was there.

He paused, breathing heavily. Didn't need to explore the pain across his chest, he could already feel the warm blood seeping through his T shirt.

Coffin backed up, taking his time, resisting the urge to turn and run. His backside bumped up against something solid, a wall maybe. With his free hand he reached back and explored whatever it was.

He found a surface, wet with puddles of something, objects fixed to the surface, and something soft, like a cloth.

He was at the bar.

Coffin sniffed his fingers, flicked his tongue out and tasted his fingertips. The liquid was beer.

What the hell? Had the vampires been sitting here waiting for Coffin and

Craggs and the others, having a drink to pass the time?

Coffin edged along the bar, thinking maybe it was time get the hell out. Whoever had screamed, bringing Coffin and Brendan back into the smoke filled club, had stopped now. Although he wasn't the kind of man who liked to try and predict situations, Coffin was still pretty sure that the lack of screaming was a bad sign.

That maybe whoever had screamed was now silent because he was dead.

Maybe they were all dead and Coffin was the only one left. Maybe the Noonan brothers, Tony Mannoia, Hanrahan and Adams, Brendan and Gilligan, maybe they were all corpses now. Lying on the club floor, waiting for that spark of life to animate them, giving them that hunger for warm, fresh blood.

Coffin imagined them rising from the dead at that moment. Seeking him out, ready to sink newly sharpened teeth into his neck.

Coffin continued walking sideways, his back to the bar. When his foot bumped into something on the floor he stopped. Knelt down and reached out his hand, groping blindly in the dark.

It was a leg.

Someone lying on the floor.

Coffin's hands moved up the leg, stopped when he got to the knee. Time to switch on the torch feature on his mobile again. He'd be sending out a beacon to all the vampires who might be surrounding him at this moment, but he had to risk it. Just a brief flicker of light, find out who exactly was lying on the floor.

Coffin dug his mobile out of his pocket, activated it and flicked on the torch feature. The light hurt his eyes for a second or two, but when he could see properly he forgot all about switching it off again.

One of the Noonan brothers was lying on his back, a pool of blood leaking from his head. Coffin couldn't tell if it was Terry or Freddie because the face was obscured by the vampire straddling his chest, and sucking on his eye sockets.

Disturbed by the light, the vampire stopped feeding and lifted its head to look at Coffin. Tendrils of blood hung from its chin.

It was Addison, the Angels barman. Blood dribbled from his mouth and over his chin. His eyes had turned black, as though each eye was nothing but one big, dark pupil. His bartender's white shirt and black waistcoat were ripped and stained with dried blood.

A moment before Coffin dropped the phone and plunged them into darkness again he saw Addison snarling at him, strings of red saliva stretching out over his open maw.

Coffin lifted the shotgun and squeezed the trigger. The brief explosion of light illuminated the club for a moment, burning itself onto Coffin's retinae. Coffin heard a squeal of pain and a wet thud as Addison's body hit the floor.

Blinded by the muzzle flash, Coffin scrabbled for the phone. His hands closed over it, and he picked it up and pointed the torchlight at the body on the floor. Addison was sprawled next to his victim, a huge, gaping hole in his chest. The body was Terry Noonan. His eyes had been gouged from his head. The empty, bloody eye sockets seemed to be staring at Coffin.

Accusing him.

Coffin pulled a wooden stake from his belt. He leaned across Terry's body and shoved the stake through the ragged hole in Addison's chest.

Coffin switched off the torch and started moving again.

One down. How many more to get rid of?

Four, including Steffanie?

Coffin racked another shell into the chamber. He squatted on the floor, trying to make out any noise behind the jackhammers outside. Frazer was obviously keeping them working, but Coffin was beginning to think he could do with some quiet for a while. Velvina and Clevon were still most likely prowling through the club, invisible in the dark and the smoke. Steffanie too.

What about the old man?

Coffin wasn't so sure. He hadn't looked that strong or with it when Coffin last saw him.

What he needed to do was find one of the others, but stumbling blindly around the club wasn't working and was just going to get him killed. Like Terry.

Coffin started shuffling along the edge of the bar until he found the end, and then scooted around so that he was on the serving side. Risking switching on the torch feature on his mobile again he did a quick sweep of the area.

He was on his own. Good.

Coffin switched the light off and called up Brendan's number.

Put the phone to his ear, and then swore.

How the hell was he going to speak to Brendan when he was wearing this great big gas mask? There was no way he could make himself understood or be able to understand what Brendan was saying to him.

Coffin clicked end call and brought up the messaging feature instead.

wr r u he typed, his big thick fingers clumsily navigating the tiny screen.

He sat and waited for a reply.

His mobile buzzed in his hand. Coffin checked the display.

ovr by stge with danny n gerry bstrds r slcing n dicng us

That left Freddie, Tony and Billy unaccounted for. Coffin thought about texting them too, but then dismissed the idea as ludicrous. Despite the fact that Coffin had taken one of the vampires down they were still fighting a losing battle. Those bastards had the upper hand at the moment. Coffin wouldn't be surprised if the others were pinned down too, trapped in the dark and the smoke and being ripped apart by invisible monsters with sharp claws.

Except for Coffin. As far as he could tell he had managed to slip past whoever had been trying to carve him up a slice at a time.

It was Steffanie. You know it was.

Maybe. Maybe she had been tracking him, keeping her husband for herself. But she had to have lost him, otherwise she would be here now, slowly and methodically eviscerating him.

Coffin needed to try and equalise the odds, give himself and Brendan and the others a chance at fighting back. And the only way he could work out to do that was by flooding the club with light.

Steffanie had to have switched the power off. That was the only thing that made any sense. The circuit breaker was down in the club cellar, a huge space more like a garage than anything else. If Coffin could get down there, all he would have to do was flick the main circuit switch and the lights would come blazing back on.

Coffin's mobile buzzed again. Another text. Coffin ignored it, slipped the phone in his pocket.

Using his free hand to guide him, he made his way along the bar.

When he got to the end he paused. This was going to be tricky. Blinded in the dark and the smoke, Coffin would have to rely on his memory and sense of direction to get him down to the cellar. Down there hopefully he could take the gas mask off and switch on the torch function on his mobile. After that it would be easy to locate the electric circuit box.

Coffin gripped the edge of the bar, suddenly reluctant to leave its familiarity. It was like an anchor for him, a solid reference of location. Coffin turned in what he guessed was the right direction, let go of the bar and stepped forward. He held the shotgun gripped in both hands, ready to squeeze the trigger and fire at anything that moved. Of course vampires weren't the only things that were moving in this inky blackness, but if it turned out he shot one of his own he would just have to live with it.

He couldn't afford to pause while he worked out if he was about to blast a hole through a friend or a vampire. If he did that, he would be dead.

Coffin kept walking. Sometimes his thigh hit a table or a chair.

He reckoned he was about halfway across the club when he knocked a table so hard he heard something, most likely a glass, fall over and roll across the table and smash when it hit the floor. Coffin only just heard it over the pounding of the jackhammers from outside.

A swish of air behind him, movement sensed rather than heard or seen in the darkness. Coffin swung around, his finger squeezing the trigger and just a fraction away from pulling it right back. Edged around the table, walked backwards, broken glass crunching beneath his boots.

The problem was, in turning around he was now disorientated.

More movement in the cloud of gas. Something stalking him, staying just out of reach and moving fast. Coffin bumped into another table. Placed a hand on it to steady himself.

This was stupid. He had to switch on the torch again, get some idea of where he was. Digging the mobile out of his pocket, Coffin activated it. On the welcome screen was the text from Brendan he had ignored.

wr getin out of hre

Great, thought Coffin. The others were probably thinking the same thing, if they were still alive. As far as he knew, Coffin could be the last one left inside. Maybe Steffanie was keeping him for last and then she could take her time over him. For all he knew, she might want to turn him. That way they could go looking for Michael together and become one big, happy family again.

Coffin swept the light from his mobile in a wide arc. Trying to figure out where he was in the middle of this cloud of tear gas. A shadow moved, the cloud swirling in hypnotic patterns before a form materialised out of it.

The large, round eye holes and the bulky, alien snout peered at Coffin. Hard to tell in the darkness, but Coffin was reasonably sure that was Billy Adams under the gas mask. His arms and torso were covered in scratches, parallel lines of dark red where he had been sliced at by long fingers ending in claws.

He was breathing heavily, his chest heaving with the exertion. When he lifted his hands Coffin saw his knuckles were red raw.

Looked like 'Punchy' Adams had been living up to his name.

Coffin beckoned him closer, pointed into the fog.

This way! Follow me!

Taking Adams by the wrist, Coffin placed the man's hand on his own arm and switched off the light. Adams just had to hold onto Coffin, keep close and follow him out of the club.

Together they trudged through the darkness, bumping into tables and chairs, stumbling over objects on the floor, until Coffin found what he wanted.

that lock again

Emma watched Brian as he left his friend's body lying in a still spreading pool of scarlet blood, and stepped over to Patsy. The woman flinched as he bent over her, obviously expecting another kicking or maybe even worse. But the policeman didn't kick or hit her, didn't even speak to her. Instead he started rifling through the pockets of her dressing gown.

It only took him a moment before he found what he wanted and straightened up.

He held out another four shells for the shotgun in his open palms. They looked big enough to bring down an elephant. The cop walked back over to the shotgun where Patsy had dropped it. He picked it up and broke it open, emptied the two shells out, let them drop on the floor.

This wasn't looking good. Whatever he was doing now wasn't right. Surely he should be calling this in, getting help down here? Not messing with the evidence, covering the gun in his own fingerprints.

Emma glanced at the steps leading up to the pub. If she did it now, made a run for it, sprinted up the stone steps, she could be outside before Brian had a chance to get to the cellar door. He didn't look in good shape, all those burgers he ate at Eddie's, all that sitting around at a desk all day. Probably be out of breath by the time he even got upstairs.

Brian inserted two fresh shells in the shotgun and snapped it shut. A moment later he was looking at Emma, the shotgun held loosely in his hands.

Too late to run now.

"Shouldn't you be calling for backup, or something?" she said. At least that's what she intended to say, what she thought she had said. But she couldn't be entirely sure. The blast from the shotgun still seemed to be ringing in the confines of the cellar and Jimmy was still screaming inside her head. Her mouth was dry and her tongue seemed to be swollen to twice its normal size.

"This whole fucking mess is all your fault," Brian said. His words came out slightly slurred, as though he was having a little trouble speaking. "All your fault."

Emma shook her head. More of a jerk and a twitch than a shake, really. Nothing was working properly right now. If she had made a dash for it just a minute ago, her legs probably would have given way beneath her. Betrayed her, tripped her up and sent her flying to the floor.

Brian wiped his sleeve across his nose. When he spoke again he was on the edge of tears.

"Stupid bitch, don't you think I know who you are? We all saw you on the CCTV footage at the service station, you and Coffin and that fucking shit stain Tom Mills. You're all in this together, aren't you?"

Emma shook her head again. Worked a little better that time, but still not good. Wasn't sure she trusted herself to speak just yet though, maybe she could work up to that in another minute or two.

If she had that long.

"What happened, wasn't there enough news out there, thought you'd drum some up yourself?" He let out a heavy sigh, quickly swiped his sleeve across his eyes. "Made a big mistake though, didn't you? One big fucker of a mistake, hanging out with Coffin and those pricks in the Slaughterhouse Mob."

"It's not . . ." Emma swallowed, decided to try again. "It's not what you think."

"No, of course it isn't. You're a fucking innocent in all of this, right? Just a misunderstood little girl. That's why you were sitting in that van with Coffin and his friend, and that other woman. That's why we spent a day and a whole fucking night down here, me pissing my pants, before they decided to throw you in with us too. What happened? Did you piss them off somehow? Is that it?"

Jimmy screaming, his guts hanging out as he tumbled down the steps. Julie Carter lying on that table, Michael sat on top of her and feeding. Steffanie naked and covered in blood, a raw, hollow socket where her eye had been. Tom Mills, his head caved in like a ripe tomato. Coffin carving up Mortenson with the chainsaw, throwing his remains into a pit and setting fire to them.

All of these images flooded Emma's mind, rotating round and round like a Victorian lantern show, a phantasmagorical parade of horrors. So much blood, so much violence.

"What's the matter, cat got your tongue?" Brian said. "You reporters are usually so chatty, with all your questions and your accusations and your lies. I like it better when you're quiet. You make more fucking sense when you're not saying anything."

"I . . . I'm sorry—"

"Don't you fucking tell me you're sorry," Brian said, raising the shotgun. "Don't you fucking apologise to me, like you just spilt your coffee, or trod mud in my house. Don't you fucking dare."

Emma closed her eyes and ground her teeth. He was going to shoot her. He was going to blow a big fucking hole in her chest, or rip her head off her shoulders, and then he was going to kill Patsy and he was going to frame her for all the murders.

Hands clenched by her sides, eyes screwed shut, she waited for the shotgun blast.

It didn't come. After waiting what seemed like an eternity, Emma slowly opened her eyes. Brian still held the shotgun pointed at her, but it was shaking. He was crying, the tears rolling down his face.

Slowly, as carefully as she could, Emma edged sideways out of the line of fire. The policeman didn't notice. Or if he did, he didn't care anymore. Shuffling over to the stone steps leading to freedom, Emma kept her eyes fixed on the gun. Brian slowly lowered it, not looking at her. She risked a glance at Patsy. She was still huddled in the corner.

Emma took the steps backwards until she was high enough that she could no longer see Brian and the shotgun. At that point she turned and ran up the rest of the steps. Once in the hall she ran for the back door. That mortise key was in the lock, the one she'd had so much trouble with last night.

Emma paused at the door. What now? She couldn't just leave Patsy down there with Brian. What if he decided to take out his anger and grief on her? He might give her another kicking again, maybe this time do some serious damage. Or he might decide to blast a hole in her stomach, like she did to Jimmy.

But there was no way she was going back down into the cellar.

Emma ran for the door to the snug. There was a telephone on the wall, behind the bar. She dialled 999.

Weak sunlight filtered through a gap in the heavy curtains. Dust motes swirled in the beam of light.

"Police," she said, when the operator answered. "There's been a shooting, O'Donoghue's pub, off Broad Street."

Emma put the phone down but didn't hang up. She wasn't giving them anymore, they'd find it. Right now it was time to get the hell out. Maybe out all the way, like leave town kind of out. Leave all this mess behind and go back to live with her parents for a while. Farther out than that even, go abroad, start a new life. Somewhere there weren't any vampires or hardened criminals.

A heavy, urgent pounding on the pub's front door snapped Emma out of her thoughts.

"Hello? Is there anybody in there? Hello?"

Fuck! The police? Already?

More pounding.

"Hello? Are you all right in there?"

Muffled voices.

Not the police. Someone who'd heard the shotgun blasts, maybe? Come to investigate.

Emma ran for the back door, grateful that the pub curtains were still closed. Looked at the lock, her means of escape that had betrayed her last night. Brendan, he'd said you had to turn it in a special way, go through a special little dance was how he'd put it. And he was right, most people had something like this in their house, the kind of thing you had to explain to visitors, or if you had a house sitter, or someone come round to check on your house while you were on holiday or look after the cat.

So come on, it can't be that difficult, Emma thought. *Just give it a little jiggle and a wiggle and you'll be out of here.*

More pounding on the front door. And was that a police siren she could hear in the distance? Fuck, that was quick. And why the hell couldn't those two good Samaritans come round the back and try banging their fists on this door instead? Emma was pretty sure she could open the front door fine.

Emma grasped the key between finger and thumb, took a deep breath.

This will be fine. You know it sticks, you've just got to take it nice and easy.

The police siren was growing louder.

Emma turned the key until it stopped, halfway through its revolution, and stuck. Carefully, gently, she tried jiggling it around a little. It turned a touch more. Emma paused, took a deep breath. This was working. Just a little more and then the key would have completed enough of its revolution that the tumblers would fall into place and the door would be unlocked.

Emma jumped when she heard the shotgun blast from down in the cellar.

Oh no.

Brian had killed Patsy. What had Emma been thinking, running away without taking the shotgun off him first? Why had she left that poor woman down there in the cellar with him?

Okay, you can think about this later. First priority is to get the hell out of here before that crazy bastard comes upstairs and starts shooting at you, too.

Emma tried turning the key. It was stuck fast. Jammed so that it wouldn't move forward or back. The shock of the shotgun blast must have caused her hand to jerk, jamming the key into place.

Oh fuck, fuck, fuck, fuck, FUCK!

Taking the key in both hands, fingers wrapped clumsily around it, Emma tried forcing it unjammed.

The pounding on the front door had grown more urgent. Whoever was out there was shouting, too.

Emma's hands were slick with sweat. She wiped them on her trousers and took hold of the key again. This time, it had to work this time.

"I told him to stop."

Oh shit.

Emma didn't need to turn around to know that Patsy was standing at the top of the cellar steps. Holding the shotgun. But she turned anyway, slowly and carefully so as not to startle the pub landlady with any sudden movements.

Patsy's face and the front of her blouse were covered in a spray of blood. How close had she been when she shot Brian? Had she simply twisted the gun out of his grasp and turned it on him? Even her eyes, wide and staring, looked bloodshot.

"I told him to stop," she said. "I told him to stop."

The police car pulled up outside and killed its siren. Patsy glanced towards the front of the pub.

Emma took three quick steps, swung her arm back and knocked the shotgun from her hands. Plaster dust exploded as the gun fired and showered them in a grey powder.

Emma shoved Patsy out of the way and ran for the stairs. Taking them two at a time, she stumbled and fell face down on the carpeted steps. The carpet stank of cigarette smoke and dust.

At the top of the stairs she took the first door she came to. A tiny, cramped bedroom. There was a single bed, a wardrobe and a dresser with a portable TV on the top. From her position by the door she could just see through the window. A small crowd had gathered. One of the two policemen was doing his best to herd them back and out of the way, whilst the other one radioed in for backup.

Emma took the door on the opposite side of the hall.

Another bedroom, larger than the front one. There was a double bed, sagging in the middle, a large wardrobe with one of its doors missing, and another dresser. There was a television in here, too. Much larger than the portable, it sat on its own stand in a corner. Emma had a fleeting vision of Patsy sitting in the double bed, smoking cigarette after cigarette, watching an endless run of soaps and reality TV shows.

Emma ran to the window and looked out. Below her was the roof of the kitchen extension.

The window was the old fashioned sash type. She pushed at the bottom window, fearful that it would be stuck fast. Reluctantly it slid up and Emma swung a leg over the sill and ducked through. She was able to climb easily onto the sloping roof. She sat down and slid down the tiles until she reached the guttering. Taking a deep breath she inched forward again until her legs were hanging over the edge, and then pushed herself into space.

The drop was relatively short, but the sensation of falling seemed to last a lot longer than it should have done. Emma hit the ground and rolled over, onto her side. Before her legs had even registered the impact she was up and running.

a fleshgun

Juggling the shotgun and the mobile phone in one hand, Coffin pulled his gas mask off and dropped it on the floor. His eyes were stinging with the sweat dripping into them, and he had to rub at them with the heel of his hand. Down in the club basement the air was stale and musty, but clear of tear gas at least.

With his mobile, Coffin did a quick sweep of the cellar, checking that they were on their own. Under the motion of the light, shadows ran across the walls and over broken pieces of furniture, giving the cellar an eerie life of its own.

A quick glance at the screen confirmed Coffin's suspicions that the battery on his phone was running low. If he didn't switch on the lights soon, he would be in permanent darkness.

'Punchy' Adams hadn't got a phone with him. He stood next to Coffin, massaging his bloody hands. Coffin pulled the older man's mask off his face, and dropped it beside his own.

Adams said nothing. Just kept massaging his knuckles, his face set in a scowl. Maybe he was angry he had nobody to hit right now.

Coffin scanned the basement again, looking for the box mounted on the wall. In all his times at Angels he'd never been down here. Never had need to. But he was sure as he could be that the club's circuit breaker would be down here. The master switch for the electricity supply.

Coffin paused when he thought he saw movement in a far corner. His grip instinctively tightened on the shotgun. Had it just been the shadows cast by his mobile? Edging forward, keeping the torch trained on the corner where he thought he had seen movement, Coffin gestured for 'Punchy' Adams to stay where he was.

Shadows, that was all it had been. There was no movement now. No sound except the dull roar of the jackhammers above them and outside.

Coffin spotted the circuit breaker box, just a few feet away from the corner he had been walking towards. He had been right, the trip switch for the club's entire electricity supply was down. In one swift movement, Coffin flipped the switch up.

The cellar was flooded with light.

"Fucking hell, Coffin!" Adams shouted, flinging his arms over his eyes. "You could have warned me."

Coffin squinted against the sudden glare. He was as blind for the moment as he had been upstairs, in the dark and the smoke. He looked down at the ground, trying to ignore the instinct to close his eyes. He had to get used to the light, quickly.

The sound of movement beside him. Something falling over, clattering to the floor. Coffin spun round, bringing the shotgun up.

"Don't shoot! Fuck, don't shoot!! It's me, Frankie!"

Coffin squinted at the shape, at the movement, in front of him. "Shaddock? What the hell are you doing here?"

"Put the fucking gun down and I'll tell you," Shaddock said.

Coffin lowered the gun. His vision was returning now, and he could see the elderly Slaughterhouse Mob doctor.

He looked like he had aged another ten years since Coffin last saw him.

"Bloody psychopaths have been keeping me prisoner," he said. "That fucking wife of yours, she . . ."

Shaddock ran a shaking hand over his face. He didn't seem to know how to finish his sentence.

Coffin knew how he felt.

"Stay here," he said. "Me and Billy are going back upstairs."

"Fuck that, I'm coming with you."

Coffin placed a hand on his chest, stopped him walking off.

"No, you're not. Upstairs is filled with teargas. You wouldn't make it outside before you collapsed."

"All right, if you say so," Shaddock said.

Coffin nodded at Billy, who picked up his gas mask and slipped it back on. Stuffing his mobile in his back pocket, Coffin pulled on his own gas mask. Cradling the shotgun in his arms, he headed for the stairs with Billy.

At the bottom step he stopped, and listened. From the sounds of it, things had started hotting up.

* * *

Freddie stood over his brother's corpse, feet planted either side of him, and fired into the cloud of gas until the gun fell silent apart from the clicking of the trigger. Tears streamed down his face, and his voice was hoarse from screaming.

He disengaged the empty clip and shoved a full one in. Raising the gun again, he held it out at arm's length but didn't pull the trigger.

Freddie had stumbled into Terry's eyeless corpse just as Coffin turned on the electricity, and light flooded the club. He fell on his knees, narrowly missing the vampire's bloody corpse lying next to Terry. It had a wooden stake sticking out of its bloody chest.

Coffin had been here.

Freddie shook Terry, calling his name through the gas mask. Tears blurred his vision. Him and Terry had hardly spent a day apart their whole lives. They were closer than twins. A hot, black rage filled Freddie's chest, and he had climbed unsteadily to his feet and emptied the Glock into the gas cloud. It hadn't occurred to him that he might hit one of others, and even if it had he wouldn't have cared at that moment.

But now Freddie was calm. He blinked the tears out of his eyes and took a deep, shuddering breath.

Kill the bastards. Kill the bastards and rip their fucking hearts out.

"Come on then!" he screamed. "Come and get me. I'm fucking waiting!"

Wisps of smoke swirled and parted as a shape materialised out of the cloud. Freddie pointed the gun at the dark figure heading for him, his finger tightening on the trigger. He saw the bulky shape of the gas mask where the head was, and relaxed.

Tony Mannoia tapped Freddie on the arm and pointed over his shoulder. When Freddie turned and looked in the direction Tony was pointing he saw the gas cloud moving, forming whirling patterns which then dissolved a moment later.

"Brendan and Gerry are opening doors, get some air in and get rid of this gas so we can see what we're doing," Tony shouted through his mask.

And it was working. Already the cloud of gas was thinning out, sucked through the club by a channel of air. The sound of the jackhammers was louder, too. The doors leading out to the front of the club had been opened.

Freddie turned back to Tony, to tell him about Terry.

Tendrils of smoke billowed out and away from Tony as a dark shape dropped on top of him. Like a malignant spider it wrapped itself around him. It pulled the gas mask of Tony's head and sank its teeth into his face.

Tony screamed, a wet throaty sound that ended in a gurgle. Freddie staggered as a spray of blood splattered his mask, completely obliterating his view. Before he could fully take in what was happening he had fallen backwards. His hand holding the Glock punched into something wet and soft, with sharp jagged edges.

Freddie groaned in disgust when he realised he had fallen on top of Addison's body, and his hand had punched through the bloody mush of his chest. Pulling his hand free he tried wiping at the blood on his mask. Instead of clearing it he just managed to smear the red blood over the plastic eye pieces.

Tony was screaming again, but now it sounded like he was under water. Freddie could hear him crashing around as he fought the monster on top of him. Was that a table falling over? And a gunshot, sounded like Coffin's shotgun maybe.

As he climbed onto his knees, Freddie wiped at his mask with his sleeve. This time he managed to clear a little of the blood, and got a red smeared view of Tony thrashing wildly at the thing on top of him, its jaws still clamped around his face.

Freddie tried standing up and slipped on a puddle of blood. The dead vampire broke his fall again, with a loud squish. Freddie realised he hadn't got his gun anymore. He had to have dropped it when he fell over the first time.

On his hands and knees he started patting the floor around the two bodies. There was another gunshot, and the sound of shattering glass.

Fucking hell, where was that gun?

Despite having wiped some of the blood off his gas mask, Freddie still couldn't see that well. Like an extremely short sighted person who had lost a contact lens he kept patting at the floor and over the bodies, until his hand encountered the Glock's grip.

Oh shit.

The gun was embedded in the dead vampire's chest. Freddie had been holding onto it when he fell over. When he put out his hand to stop his fall he had to have shoved it through the wound in the vampire's chest.

Tony crashed to the floor beside Freddie. Looked like a woman on top of him, long, blond hair hiding her face. The hair was dirty and lank, looked in desperate need of a wash. And Freddie was sure he could hear her giggling.

Tony wasn't making much of sound anymore though.

Taking a deep breath, Freddie closed his hand around the Glock's grip, his fingers penetrating the oozing mass of ripped flesh and splintered ribcage.

Don't hurl, okay? Just don't hurl, not while you're wearing a fucking mask.

Freddie pulled and dragged the gun out of the vampire's chest. It made a sucking, squelching sound as it came out, like the vampire's body didn't want to give it up.

Tiny bits of ragged flesh hung from the gun's barrel. Covered in a thick layer of red gloop, the Glock looked more like an imitation gun crafted from human tissue.

Would it even fucking work now?

Freddie pointed the gun at the female vampire sucking on Tony's bloody face and pulled the trigger. The gun made a wet snapping sound.

The girl's head jerked up and swivelled to look at Freddie. Her mouth was smeared with blood and she had bits of flesh stuck in her teeth. Coffin had said they were vampires, but this one looked more like a cannibal. Or a fucking zombie.

The woman squatting over Tony's body shifted herself around and crouched lower. She looked like she was ready to pounce on Freddie, reminding him of a spider again.

He pointed the gun at her head and pulled the trigger once more. This time he didn't even get the snapping sound, and the trigger didn't release, but stayed jammed in place.

The vampire leapt for him, mouth open wide, strings of red saliva hanging from her mouth. Freddie tensed for the impact, the sensation of her jaws around his neck or his face, the teeth piercing his flesh and ripping him to pieces.

At the sound of a gunshot, the woman spun in mid-air, an arc of blood jetting from her side. She landed on top of Freddie with a wet splat.

And then she was still.

Freddie struggled out from underneath the body, having to crawl over Terry's corpse, his face only inches away from those terrible sightless eye sockets at one point.

Despite the mass of torn flesh in her side the woman started reaching out for Freddie with clawed hands. He kicked out at her, and dragged himself away. Coffin appeared out of the thinning cloud of tear gas. He had his shotgun in one hand and a wooden stake in the other. Bending low over the woman he thrust the stake through her chest. The vampire reared up, her back arched, head thrown back, and hissed at Coffin like a feral cat.

Coffin thrust the stake deeper and finally the vampire's rigid body sagged, and collapsed at his feet.

With one quick glance at Freddie, Coffin turned his back on him and disappeared into the fog.

death

Emma trudged down Broad Street, her hands stuffed in her pockets to stop them shaking. She had no idea where she was headed. Was having trouble coming up with a coherent idea.

Normal life carried on around her. Shoppers pushing by, men and women in suits talking on mobiles as they walked, teenagers loitering on steps or sitting on benches smoking roll ups. Normal, everyday activities. As though the world was a normal, safe place.

But Emma knew better now. The world she thought she knew no longer existed. It was full of blood and violence, ripped flesh and sharp teeth, guns and walking, talking corpses.

A sudden sound, a girl's high pitched, happy laughter filling the space inside Emma's head. She flinched. Only just managed to stop the scream erupting from deep inside, like a banshee set free from its prison.

In the distance she could hear the racket of workmen digging up a street, breaking apart the tarmac with their jackhammers. Something about that thought bothered her, as though it was important. But whenever she tried pinning it down, all she could see were the teeth and the ripped flesh and the blood.

Emma trudged on, thinking that maybe she should be running. But what was the point? She was far enough away now from the guns and the police.

Far enough away from the scene of the crime.

A giggle bubbled up from her chest, like gas after gulping down a fizzy drink. Emma clapped a hand over her mouth, held the laughter back. If she started she wasn't sure she could stop. And even worse, it might carry her away until she was helpless with hysterics.

That wouldn't be good. Apart from the fact that she didn't want to be noticed, and breaking up into a helpless fit of wild laughter was one sure way of being noticed, Emma was afraid that she might not finish laughing with her sanity intact.

When exactly had she lost so much control of her life? What had happened to her plans for her big, career making story? And since when had she thought hanging out with gangsters and murderers was such a good idea?

Emma jumped as two dogs started barking and growling at each other. She could see them not far ahead, their owners pulling at their leads as the dogs scrabbled furiously at the pavement, trying to get close enough that they could fight.

Emma shuddered. The dogs reminded her of Abel Mortenson and Coffin fighting each other. They had looked like wild animals, crazed with anger. Mortenson naked, his stiff cock jutting out, even in the heat of the fight. As though the fight itself was a sexual turn on.

Images swimming through her mind. Blood, teeth, flesh, guns, round and round and round. Enough to drive her insane.

Maybe she already was. Maybe she had already been tipped over the edge through the horrors that she had witnessed this last week.

Emma stopped walking, watched as the dogs were pulled apart by their owners. The two women walked off in opposite directions and both dogs calmed down. Emma shivered again. She felt weary to the bone.

I can't do this anymore, she thought. *I thought I could handle it, but I can't.*

The sound of the jackhammers registered in her mind once more. Sounded like there was lot of them.

Coffin!

That was part of the plan, to hide the noise of gunfire from within Angels. He was there now with the rest of them, fighting to reclaim the club off Steffanie and the other vampires. That stupid fucking plan of theirs to use tear gas. Why hadn't they listened to her? Why hadn't Coffin at least listened to her?

Because they were stupid.

Because they were men.

A chill wind picked up and Emma had to push hair out of her face.

What to do? Go to the club, find out what was happening?

What if they were all dead? What could she do?

What could she do even if they were alive still?

No, she couldn't go to the club. Emma needed help. It was time to get out, leave all this crap behind. People had died, and she was a part of it.

She was smack in the middle of it.

The story was over, the story was dead.

Dead, just like those two cops in O'Donoghue's. Just like Julie Carter and Michael Coffin.

Except Michael was up and about, walking and talking. And killing.

Just like Steffanie Coffin.

Emma began walking again. This time she had an idea where she was headed.

It didn't matter that no one believed her. She would tell her story and give herself up. Then it was done. The police would deal with it and she could step back, step out of the story. Become a reporter again, instead of . . . what? What was she right now?

An idiot, that's what. A complete and utter idiot for thinking she could hang around with gangsters and fight vampires. She needed help, but the question was, where to go to find that help?

Nick? No, not yet. Not while he was lying in hospital recovering from his encounter with Michael.

Who, then?

Karl.

That was where her feet were taking her, where her unconscious mind had already decided she needed to go. To the *Birmingham Herald* offices, to see Karl. Tell him that he had been right, that she should have gone to the police when he told her to.

He would listen, and he would call the police, and he would stay with her throughout.

Emma walked on, and round and round in her mind floated images of blood and teeth and ripped flesh and guns.

When she arrived at the Metropole Tower, it seemed to Emma that she surfaced from a dream. She had no memory of walking through the city centre, and for all she knew she could have been sleepwalking.

There was a small crowd gathered outside, and police cars and an ambulance. Emma pushed her way through the crowd, towards the glass doors. A policeman blocked her way.

"What's going on?" she said.

"I'm sorry but you can't go in there for the moment," the policeman said.

Looking up at the tower, at the top floor where the *Herald* offices were housed, Emma's insides felt all hollowed out.

Something's happened. Something bad.

Something dreadful.

Blood, ripped flesh, sharpened teeth, guns.

"Emma?"

The voice cut through the fog in her mind. When she turned in its direction she saw Barry. He stared at Emma like she was a stranger, and his eyes were red, the lids puffy.

"What's going on, Barry?"

Barry took her by the arm, pulled her away and back out of the small crowd. Kept walking down the street a little way, head down, not looking at Emma.

"Barry? What is it? What the hell's happening?"

Emma hauled Barry to a stop, twisted her arm out of his grip and took him by the shoulders.

Barry pulled himself free, took a step back. When he looked up, Emma could see he was crying.

"It's Karl," he said. "He's dead."

Emma held back her first response.

Don't be an idiot, Barry. Tell me what's happening.

She tried focusing on the words, the sentence that Barry had just spoken out loud. Tried to make sense of it. But she couldn't. Karl wasn't dead, it wasn't possible, had to be some kind of stupid mistake.

Had to be.

"Barry?"

Wiping tears from his cheeks, Barry looked away for a moment, back at the Metropole Tower. When he looked at Emma again his face was all screwed up, like he was struggling to keep hold of himself.

"He was shot," he said. "They found him this morning, shot in the chest. Had a cigar in his hand, burnt down to a stub, ash all over the floor."

Emma closed her eyes.

Blood, ripped flesh, sharpened teeth. Guns.

Death.

are they all dead?

The cloud of tear gas was thinning out and Coffin could see shapes, and movement. Two of the vampires were down now, so how many did that leave? Steffanie, Clevon, Guttman.

Three vampires left to exterminate.

But Terry and Tony both dead.

Gilligan appeared out of the swirling tendrils of gas. His shirt sleeves were shredded into tatters and his forearms were covered in slashes of red, but otherwise he looked uninjured. In his right hand he held a handgun.

In his left he gripped a wooden stake, his hand hanging by his side and the point facing backwards.

"Decided to take me seriously after all?" Coffin shouted, straining to make himself heard through the gas mask and over the noise of the jackhammers.

Gilligan's eyes gazed steadily at Coffin through the mask. He walked past Coffin without saying another word.

"Hey! I found one! Oh fuck! Oh sweet Jesus, no!"

Coffin ran in the direction of the shouts. Into the reception, past the cloakroom.

"Fucking hell! Fuck, fuck fuck!"

The shouting, and the sounds of a struggle, were coming from the office behind the reception desk. Coffin barrelled through the doorway, with Brendan and Gilligan close behind.

Freddie was on his back on the floor. Clevon was on top of him, snapping his jaws at Freddie's crotch. Freddie had his feet braced against Clevon's chest, but his knees were bent right back with the effort and Clevon was close to sinking his teeth into him.

Gilligan raised his gun.

Coffin slapped his arm out of the way as Gilligan pulled the trigger, and the bullet hit the wall just to the side of Freddie's head.

Coffin pulled his mask off.

"Don't be an idiot," he growled. "You'll kill Freddie."

Freddie had hold of Clevon's head now, straining to push him away. The vampire's teeth, clicking together like a demented metronome, were only inches away from Freddie's groin.

Coffin strode over to the two men, grabbed Clevon by the shoulders and hauled him upright. Using his weight against him, Coffin slammed Clevon face first into the wall. There was a crunch as his cheekbones and nose broke under the impact.

Coffin dragged Clevon back, ready to smash his face into the wall again. But this time Clevon was ready and he threw his weight behind the movement, cracking his skull against Coffin's chin. Coffin staggered under the impact, giving the former doorman a chance to whirl around and face his opponent. Droplets of blood flew from his mashed up nose, spraying over Coffin's face.

"Shoot the fucker!" Freddie shouted, scrabbling backwards out of the way on his hands and bottom.

Gilligan fired his gun and Coffin felt the heat of the bullet passing his temple before it hit Clevon in the shoulder. The vampire rocked beneath the force of bullet's impact and his shoulder erupted in a spray of blood and bone.

But he stayed on his feet.

Coffin pulled a stake out of his belt and thrust it at Clevon's chest. The vampire ducked and kicked Coffin in the knee. Coffin's leg gave way and he fell to the floor, gritting his teeth as his knee exploded in red hot pain. As he grunted in agony he dropped the stake on the floor beside him.

In his human state, Clevon had been a fanatical fitness freak. Every day he had been down the gym. He weight trained, cycled, ran, boxed and was a Seventh Dan in karate. It seemed he had lost none of his skills now that he was a vampire.

Clevon leapt at Gilligan, his foot swinging in a wide arc and kicking the gun from Gilligan's hand. With a swift chopping motion, Clevon stabbed at Gilligan's neck. The Irishman staggered, clutching at his throat and choking. He fell against Brendan and then slid to the floor, fighting for breath.

The vampire wasted no more time on Gilligan. Fighting through the red hot pain in his knee, Coffin was still trying to get back on his feet when Clevon kicked him in the head. The force of the kick snapped Coffin's head back and spun him around. He hit the floor face down.

"Coffin, stay down!" Brendan shouted, just before the room exploded with a gun shot.

Coffin rolled over just in time to see Clevon falling on top of him. His torso was a red mass of ripped flesh, but still his eyes were wide and bright with hunger and hatred and his jaws were snapping together.

The doorman landed on top of Coffin with a wet slap. Cold, foul blood splattered over Coffin's face and across the floor. Coffin reached out for the stake he had dropped a few moments earlier. His fingers crawled blindly through puddles of blood until they found what they wanted.

Coffin had expected Clevon to try and sink his teeth into his neck, but instead the vampire pushed himself down Coffin's torso.

Towards his groin.

Gripping the wooden stake firmly in his fist, Coffin rammed the point into the vampire's ear. Using all the force he could muster, he buried the stake as deep as it would go.

Clevon arched back, his mouth open wide in a silent scream. Blood gouted from his ear and his mouth. He pulled wildly at the stake, trying to yank it out. The end of the stake snapped off, and a fresh fountain of blood pumped out of the wound.

Coffin sat up and pushed the vampire over, where he lay on his back thrashing and jerking like a manic puppet. Coffin pulled another stake out of his belt and shoved it through Clevon's chest.

After a few more moments of relentless spasms, Clevon finally lay still.

"Fucking hell," Freddie whispered, sitting on the floor and his back up against the farthest wall.

On his hands and knees in the doorway, Gilligan was coughing and choking.

"Is he going to live?" Coffin said.

Brendan pulled his gas mask off and then did the same for Gilligan. He examined Gilligan closely for a moment and then stepped around him and entered the office.

"That bastard gave him a good wallop in the throat, but he'll be all right," he said.

Coffin got onto his good knee. With one hand bracing himself against the wall he pushed himself upright. Had to clench his jaw so hard to keep from crying out he thought his teeth might shatter.

"Was Clevon a fucking queer?" Brendan said.

"Not that I know of," Coffin said. "Why?"

"Because the bastard just kept going for everyone's balls. I didn't know if he was going to bite you or suck you off."

"He's not doing either now," Coffin said.

"Is that all of them?" Freddie said. "Please tell me that's all of them."

"No," Coffin said. "Steffanie and the old man. Guttman."

Freddie ran his hands over his head. "Oh fuck."

"You stay here if you want," Coffin said. "The rest of us need to—"

Silence. No sound other than Gilligan coughing and gasping.

"What happened to the jackhammers?" Coffin said. "Why the hell have they stopped?"

Billy and Danny had gathered in the office doorway, gazing in awe at the carnage before them.

"I'll go check," Danny said.

Coffin tested his weight on his injured leg. Red hot pain shot through his knee joint and already he could see his knee ballooning, straining against the fabric of his trousers. Using the wall to steady himself he limped to the doorway.

"Fuck, Joe, can you walk on that?" Brendan said.

"Yeah, I'm fine," Coffin said, and looked down at Gilligan. "Are you going to live?"

Gilligan lifted his head and looked at Coffin. His throat was a mass of angry red bruising.

"Don't worry about me," he said. His voice sounded sore and raw, but his coughing and choking had subsided and he was no longer fighting for breath.

Coffin stepped around him and past the reception desk towards the front door.

The tear gas had cleared completely out here and glancing back through the open doorway into the club, Coffin could see that it was thinning out there too.

Coffin looked outside, but kept in the shadows. Wouldn't do to be seen covered in blood.

All the workmen had laid down their tools. Some of them were sitting down and smoking.

Harry Frazer entered the club.

"What the hell's going on?" Coffin said.

Frazer shrugged. "They say they've run out of pavement to dig up. Said they won't do anymore."

Coffin scowled at Frazer. This wasn't how it was supposed to happen.

"What the hell do you want me to do?" Frazer said. "I've tried fucking kicking their arses but they won't listen to me. You want me to go out there and shoot them?"

"Leave them," Coffin said. "Come inside. You and Danny go find Billy and

Freddie. Tell them I said you need to get the bodies and dump them in Brendan's van."

"Is that it, are those bastards all dead?"

"Not quite all of them." Coffin pulled the Angels' doors shut. "Brendan, Gilligan, we're going upstairs."

Coffin limped through the club, past the upturned tables and chairs, past the bodies. Brendan and Gilligan walked either side of him.

"You need a hand there, Joe?" Gilligan said.

"No," Coffin said.

They found Craggs standing over Tony Mannoia's body. Tony was on his back in a pool of blood, his eyes wide open as though he was surprised at everything that had happened.

"A fucking crying shame," Craggs said, and looked up at Coffin. "Are they all dead?"

"Just Steffanie and the old man left," Coffin said. "They're not down here so they have to be upstairs."

"I'm coming with you. I want to see that bitch die."

They took the stairs slowly on account of Coffin's painful, swollen knee. At the top, Coffin nodded in the direction of Craggs' office. Holding the shotgun in both hands, Coffin limped over to the door with the others following him.

Brendan grasped the door handle and swung it silently open. Coffin stepped in through the doorway and swept the room in a single glance.

Empty.

The office was in darkness.

Coffin limped inside, constantly turning, looking for any sign of movement. Gilligan flicked on a light.

Craggs walked over to his desk and rifled through the papers scattered over its top.

"That fucking bitch has been going through my business," he said. "What does she think she's doing? She think she can run this club? I'll fucking kill her myself when we find her."

Brendan held up a hanger in one hand with a jacket and trousers on it and an empty hanger in the other. There were more suits draped over the sofa beside Brendan.

"I'm supposing these are yours?" Brendan said.

Craggs walked over to Brendan and took the empty hanger off him.

"Is she wearing your clothes, now?" Gilligan said.

Craggs stared at Gilligan and dropped the hanger on the floor.

"All right, so she's not in here," Coffin said. "Let's check the other rooms."

They did the same at the next room, Brendan opening the door, Coffin stepping inside with the shotgun and giving the room a quick look over.

Once they had established it was empty, Gilligan sat on the waterbed. He bounced up and down a couple of times.

"Never been on a waterbed before," he said to Brendan. "Would imagine I might get a little seasick on one of these things, especially if I was with a woman."

Coffin looked in the bathroom.

Empty.

"Let's try the next one," he said.

They gathered outside the door, Coffin gripping the shotgun. He looked back at the others, pointed.

There were bloody handprints on the door and the handle.

"The bitch is in there," Craggs whispered.

Brendan grasped the door handle and Coffin nodded. The door swung open and Coffin stepped inside, taking in the bedroom in one swift glance.

Empty.

"Check the bathroom," Coffin said.

Gilligan stared at Coffin. "Am I meant to be taking orders off you now?"

Coffin sighed. "I don't have the patience for this. Just go check the bathroom before I shoot you."

Gilligan continued staring at Coffin, maybe thinking about finding out how serious he was. In the end he shook his head, as though dismissing Coffin as a petulant child, and strode over to the closed bathroom door.

He pulled it open.

A screaming banshee leapt from through the bathroom door, a whirling mass of claws and teeth and red hair. Gilligan yelled as he stumbled, bringing up his arms to defend himself.

They fell on the floor, Gilligan and Steffanie entwined with one another so much it almost seemed as though they were one whirling mass of arms and legs.

Coffin lifted the shotgun and then lowered it again. There was no way he could shoot Steffanie without hitting Gilligan too. He flipped the gun over and held it by the stock. In two quick steps he was standing over them and he swung the gun like a baseball bat.

Steffanie's head was the ball.

The gun's shoulder stock cracked against her skull, and she flipped over and off Gilligan. Free from his attacker he scurried away on his hands and knees.

Coffin planted his foot on Steffanie's neck. She stared at him, eyes wild with hatred.

"Kill the bitch!" Craggs snarled.

Coffin didn't even think about it. He pulled his last stake out of his belt and thrust it through Steffanie's chest. She let out a high pitched scream. Coffin leaned on the stake, pushing it deeper. Hunched over her body their faces were only inches apart. He could smell the rotting stink of her breath and he had to steel himself from recoiling at the touch of her freezing flesh.

The scream died away and blood bubbled from Steffanie's open mouth. Still her eyes were wide open, staring at Coffin. She reached up, touched his cheek with her fingertips, and then her arm fell to the floor and her eyes lost whatever life-force they had possessed.

mopping up milk

They dragged the bodies outside, into the car park behind the club. Addison, Clevon, Velvina and Steffanie. The sky was heavy with dark, thick clouds but the vampires' flesh still began reddening and then popping and blistering.

Coffin, Craggs, Brendan, Freddie, Harry, Danny and Billy stood in a circle watching the grisly spectacle unfold.

"Put them in the van," Coffin said, finally. "We need to burn the bodies before they come back to life."

"They're dead, Joe," Brendan said. "They're not coming back."

"Just put them in the van," Coffin said.

"What about the other one?" Craggs said. "The one that looked like a fucking one hundred year old corpse?"

Coffin turned his back on the vampires and gazed up at the club.

"I don't know. He's in there somewhere, he's got to be."

"Me and Billy, we searched every fucking inch of that place, even the fucking loft," Harry said. "If there was anybody else still in there, we'd have found them, right Billy?"

Billy nodded, massaging his swollen knuckles.

"Too fucking right we would have."

"Looks like you got your club back, Mort," Harry Frazer said. "A pity about Terry and Tony."

"Let's get moving," Craggs said. "Freddie, help Brendan and Danny get those sacks of shit in the back of Brendan's van. The rest of you, you need to start cleaning up. My club looks like a fucking abattoir at the moment."

"What about Terry and Tony?" Freddie said.

"Put them in the back of the van as well," Craggs said. "We'll just have to dispose of their bodies the same as the others."

Freddie looked down at his feet, clenched his fists by his side. No one spoke.

"I know it's hard, Freddie," Craggs said. "Your brother was a good lad, and

I wish we could do something better for him than disposing of his remains with those pieces of shit that killed him. But we haven't got the time right now. We'll find a way of remembering him, son."

Freddie looked up. "All right, Mr Craggs."

Craggs took Coffin to one side. "What do you think? Is the club clear now? Are they all gone?"

"I'd feel better if we knew where that last vampire was. Maybe he's dead, too. Or maybe he got out before we arrived."

"But why would he do that, Joe? He couldn't have known we were coming to take the club back."

"But they did know, didn't they?" Coffin said. "That's why the lights were out, they were waiting for us, to ambush us."

"Didn't work out for them, though, did it? We fucked that bitch over good and proper, Joe."

Coffin said nothing, watched Brendan and Freddie tossing Addison's corpse into the back of his van.

"Joe? You okay?" Craggs said. "Don't feel bad about killing Steffanie, she was an evil cunt even before she turned into a vampire."

"Michael's still out there," Coffin said. "I've got to find him, catch him. Find a way of reversing whatever's happened to him."

"I'm not sure you can, Joe. You've seen what they're like. They're not people anymore. Not human."

"Hey, Joe!" Brendan shouted. "We're ready."

"You going with Brendan and Danny?" Craggs said.

"Yeah, I want to make sure they do the job properly. We don't want to have to do this again, do we?"

Craggs placed his hand on Coffin's arm and gave it a squeeze.

"You're a good man, Joe. Meet me back here after, and we'll have a drink."

Brendan slammed the doors shut on the back of his van. Danny 'The Butcher' Hanrahan had already climbed in the front.

"All right, I'll see you later," Coffin said.

He joined Brendan and climbed in the cab with Danny, who was sitting in the middle seat. In the back of the van, with the six corpses, was a large, battered toolbox containing his tools of the trade. There were also several plastic containers of kerosene.

Harry Frazer moved the van that had been blocking access to the carpark, and Brendan drove out onto the main road. Craggs' fake workmen had dug up the road and pavement outside, but laid down metal sheets and Brendan's transit van rumbled over them as he crossed the trench.

Harry reversed his van back into place.

And life outside Angels' Gentlemen's Club carried on as normal.

* * *

Danny was telling them about his career as 'The Butcher'. Neither Coffin nor Brendan were in the mood for listening, but trying to shut Danny up when he got into telling his stories was about as futile as trying to mop up a pint of spilt milk with a plastic bag.

So they sat in silence, Brendan driving and Coffin gazing out of the window.

"Me and Mort, we go back a long way," Danny was saying. "I still remember when we first met, would have been back in sixty-seven or sixty-eight, and Mort had got himself into a spot of bother. Joe, you remember Ron Wingate don't you?"

"Before my time," Coffin said.

"Yeah, of course it was, but you heard of him, right?"

"Yeah, I heard of him. My Dad used to talk about him on Saturday afternoons, whenever we were watching the wrestling."

"A wrestler was he?" Brendan said, turning the steering wheel as he took a corner.

There was a thump from the back as something shifted, and slid across the floor.

"Take it easy," Coffin said. "We don't want the doors springing open and dumping a pile of corpses on the road."

"Don't you worry about my driving," Brendan said.

"Not a wrestler, no," Danny said. "He were a wrestling promoter, and manager. But Ron never worked behind the scenes, he liked to be up front, with his boys as he called them. By the mid-sixties, Ron were more famous than his boys."

"And his son was a professional wrestler too, wasn't he?" Coffin said. He'd heard this story before, but decided it was better to let Danny talk, maybe bring them down a little after the adrenalin rush of the fight at the club. Besides, listening to Danny talk was better than arguing with Brendan.

"That's right, Johnny Thunderbolt he were called. His big moment in a fight was to climb up on top of the ropes and drop on top of his opponent, like he was doing a belly flop in a swimming pool. He was a big lad, twenty-two stone of rock solid muscle. When he landed on you, you weren't getting up again."

"Didn't he wear a vest with a lightning bolt stitched across the front of it?" Coffin said.

"A lightning bolt?" Brendan snorted. "I thought you said he was called Johnny Thunderbolt?"

"He was," Danny said. "But nobody could work out how to draw a thunderbolt."

"Still, this kind of thing pisses me off, you know? Thunder and lightning, they're two different things altogether, you know what I'm saying?"

Brendan took another corner and something shifted in the back again.

Coffin looked out of the window. Kept his mouth shut.

"Well, you get lightning in a thunder storm," Danny said.

"Yeah, and that's a lightning bolt."

"They mean the same thing," Coffin said. He was getting tired of this conversation, just wanted Danny to get on with the story.

"The fuck they do," Brendan said. "You never hear of someone being struck by thunder now, do you?"

"A thunderbolt, isn't that when lightning strikes the same time as you hear the thunder?" Hanrahan said. "Like when you're right under the centre of the storm?"

"It's still a fucking lightning bolt," Brendan said.

"Thunderbolt, lightning bolt, who gives a fuck?" Coffin said. "Let's just get on with the story."

"Johnny's career as a wrestler came to an end sometime around nineteen sixty-five. He was snorting heroin like it were popping candy by then, and it completely fucked him up. Ron tried to straighten him out, he were devastated that his own son had finished his wrestling career in such a sorry state, but it were no good."

"Aye, the drugs have ruined many a man," Brendan said.

"When it were clear Johnny was never going in the ring again, Ron approached Mort and asked him if there were a job for his lad in the Slaughterhouse Mob. Mort was happy to help out, he'd won big time on a couple of fixed fights that Ron had tipped him off about, and felt he owed him one."

Brendan snorted again. "Bloody wrestling, it's all a big fucking pantomime anyway, am I right? You remember that Jap bastard from telly in the eighties? Kendo Nagasaki? Fucker was English all along, underneath that mask."

Coffin said, "Brendan, will you shut the fuck up, and let Danny tell his story?"

Brendan twisted in his seat so he could look past Hanrahan, and glared at Coffin. A car horn blared and Brendan turned his attention back to the road, swerving around a car turning right from the opposite carriageway.

More sounds of bodies sliding around in the back, and a thump as one of them hit the van's side.

Coffin snapped his mouth shut, his teeth clicking together. He fought the urge to demand that Brendan stop driving and let Coffin take over. That would just degenerate into an argument, and then they seriously risked crashing the van. Besides, even if Coffin got his way he couldn't fit behind the steering wheel, and he hadn't tried driving a vehicle in decades.

Best just to keep quiet.

Brendan straightened the van up and continued driving, staring fixedly through the windscreen at the road ahead. They were heading out of the city now, their surroundings becoming more industrialised.

After a few moments of uncomfortable silence, Danny spoke again.

"Yeah, so Mort took Johnny on, gave him the job of muscle. He spent a few weeks learning the ropes and then he was on his own. Mort knew about Johnny's habit, but no one really knew how much he was snorting. Turned out he was in deep, and he was spending every fucking penny he earned on the monkey."

Brendan pulled onto a dual carriageway. Eased into traffic flow. His driving was calmer now, less erratic.

"Got so bad he started dipping into the protection money he was collecting, scooping out enough to top up his earnings and pay for his habit. This went on for several months until someone noticed a, what do you call it when there's a difference between what you think should be happening and what is really happening?"

The three men were silent as they thought about this.

"A disagreement?" Brendan said.

Hanrahan shook his head. "Nah, not that." He gestured, turning circles in the air with his hands. "You know, like a difference."

"A variety," Coffin said.

"Nah, you're not with me. Begins with a 'p' I'm sure, and it means when there's a difference between two things and you don't know why."

Brendan sighed. "For fuck's sake, can't we just use the word 'difference'?"

"All right, all right, so someone notices there's a difference in the figures—"

"Discrepancy," Coffin said.

Hanrahan snapped his fingers. "That's the word. There was a discrepancy in the financial figures. The thing was, nobody told Mort about it. He could be a real mean bastard in those days, and when he found out about shit like that he would go off the deep end. You remember, Joe, when he clamped Stu Jackson's head in that big fucking vice?"

"Yeah, I remember," Coffin said.

"Mort was interrogating him, and said for every lie Stu told he was going to tighten the vice a bit more. Thing was, it didn't matter what the fuck Stu said, Mort already had all the answers he needed. That was just his way of making Stu think he had a chance of getting out of there alive."

"But he didn't, did he, because whatever Stu said it was always the wrong answer, and so Mort kept tightening the vice on his head."

Hanrahan shook his head. "Bloody hell, I've never heard a man scream like that, before or since."

"At least you didn't have to clean up the mess afterwards."

"Wasn't Tom there too? I heard he's gone missing," Hanrahan said. "Anybody heard from him yet?"

"No," Coffin said. "Carry on with the story."

"So, the way I heard it, a couple of the gang decided they wanted to deal with Johnny themselves. They were worried that if they told Mort, it wouldn't look good on them. But if they dealt with Johnny themselves, maybe even got some of the money back, it would look good on them. You know, like they'd taken the initiative instead of just whining about it."

Brendan took an exit off the dual carriageway, the indicator ticking loudly.

"The one soft bastard, I forget his name now, Derek maybe, he decides to invite Johnny round to his house under the pretence of a game of poker. Then they tie him to a chair in the garage and stick his feet in a bowl of water. Derek's got this electrical cable plugged into a live socket, and he pulls Johnny's pants off and says he's going to toast his balls unless he can come up with the money that he took from the Slaughterhouse Mob."

Brendan was shaking his head now. "Fuck me, did this pair of fuckwits not have the good sense that God gave them?"

Hanrahan chuckled. "When Derek stuck the live end of that cable against Johnny's balls, he not only toasted Johnny from head to foot, but he short circuited the entire street's electricity supply."

Brendan laughed out loud and shook his head again.

"Derek's mum was pissed as all hell, she'd just sat down to watch *Armchair Theatre* when the TV blew up."

"The silly bastard was still living at home?" Brendan said.

Hanrahan snorted. "She gave him hell when she found out what had happened, and called Mort straight up. He had to come round and sweet talk Derek's mum, and promise to clear up the mess."

"And that's when Mort got you involved," Coffin said. "To help him get rid of the body."

"No, not then," Hanrahan said. "You see, Derek had toasted Johnny well good, the way I heard it he looked blacker than a jungle bunny, and his hair were all standing on end and he were smoking, like a burnt piece of toast. But he were alive still."

Brendan snorted. He looked like he was enjoying the story now.

"So Mort ordered Derek to get Johnny to the hospital as quick as possible, like. And then he decided maybe he should go and pay Ron a visit, tell him what had happened. Now Ron, by this time, he were living in a big fucking house with a gated drive, he'd done so well out of the wrestling business. But he'd let himself go, too. Like a fucking mountain range he were. Must have weighed at least thirty stone. So Mort pays him a visit and sits him down and starts explaining the situation to him, and Ron gets more and more worked up about it until he flies into a rage and attacks Mort."

Brendan turned down a cobble stoned side street, in between a row of empty houses and a disused petrol station.

"In those days, Mort used to carry a piece with him wherever he went. So he pulled his gun out and emptied it into Ron's chest. The big man fell down and died right there and then."

"Mort killed him?" Coffin said. This part of the story he didn't know. "Everyone thought he did a runner when it was found out he was fiddling his taxes."

"No, that bit were a stroke of luck on Mort's part. You see, there he was with Ron lying on his back on the living room floor, looking for all the world like a beached whale, and Ron's son is in hospital looking like a piece of burnt toast, and Mort's the one who's going to be held responsible for both of them, even though none of it was his fault. He's already regretting telling Derek to take Johnny to the hospital, thinking maybe they should have just finished him off, but with Ron dead too, it's going to start looking like Mort's wanting a piece of the wrestling action, like he's extending his empire, you know. Now this was bad news for Mort, because the last thing he wanted was a gang war, and the police investigating him for murder."

"We're here," Brendan said, parking the van.

Coffin looked out of his window. It was a perfect setting to get rid of the bodies. They were flanked by rows of abandoned, Victorian factories. Trees and bushes sprouted through empty windows and doorways, and poked out of rooves. The buildings were surrounded by high, metal fences with 'Keep Out' and 'Danger' signs on them.

Brendan killed the engine. Apart from the muted sound of traffic in the distance, silence filled the cab.

"Finish your story," Brendan said.

"Well, this is where I came in," Hanrahan said. "Mort called up his wife from Ron's house and told her to get one of the lads out to find me, and bring me over. I weren't that old back then, but I'd already got myself a bit of a reputation for disposing of unwanted mess. Mort had heard of me and decided I was just the help he needed. In his mind it was going to look less suspicious if Ron just disappeared without a trace, than if he were found dead on his back at home with his chest full of bullets. The tax dodge coming to light shortly after were plain and simple luck for Mort."

"So how did you get rid of the body?" Coffin said.

"Well, that were a challenge, I can tell you. The fat bastard was too big to carry out of the house, not without a hoist or something anyway. And we were lucky that Ron's wife had run off with a toy boy to the Med a couple of years back. It were just Ron and Johnny living there, and with Johnny in the hospital that meant we had the freedom to do what we needed to. I rolled up in a builder's van I borrowed off my mate, some rolls of heavy duty tarp and a few bone saws. We laid out the tarp in his living room and rolled him onto it, and then I spent the rest of the day sawing him into manageable pieces and wrapping them up. Construction work had started on Spaghetti Junction round about then, so we drove Ron's pieces down to the construction site that night and dropped them in one of the trenches they'd dug. A couple of days later concrete was poured as they laid foundations for the pillars that carry the motorway, and that's where Ron's remains lie to this day."

"What about Johnny fucking Thunderbolt?" Brendan said.

"He lasted a couple of weeks at the hospital, and then he did everyone a favour and died," Hanrahan said.

"Day's getting on," Coffin said. "Let's do what we came here for."

The three men climbed out of the cab and Hanrahan led them through a gap in a fence and into one of the abandoned factory buildings. The roof had long since gone, and weeds sprouted from cracks in the concrete floor amongst mounds of bricks and stone, and lengths of rotted wood.

"This place used to be a munitions factory during World War II," Hanrahan said.

"Now it's a burial site for those bastards in the back my van," Brendan said.

"We can do what you said, Joe," Hanrahan said. "We can cut them up and dump the pieces in a pile in the middle there, and then have ourselves a bonfire."

Brendan screwed his face up in disgust. "Sweet Jesus, do we really have to chop them up? Can't we just dump them here and set fire to them?"

"No," Coffin said. "We need to make sure."

Coffin lifted his face to the sky. The sun had broken free of cloud cover, and there was a patch of deep blue overhead. The sun felt warm on Coffin's face.

"Let's get on with it," he said, looking at the two men in turn.

They walked back out of the factory and over to the transit van. The rear of the van had two doors. Brendan grasped the handle on one and pulled it open.

"Fucking hell!" he said, taking a step back. "It stinks in there."

Hanrahan was standing beside Coffin. He was laughing quietly when the top of his head exploded in a shower of blood and brains, and he was propelled against the closed door. He stayed upright for a moment, eyes wide with shock, and then his body collapsed slowly, sliding down the door and leaving a trail of red and grey streaked through the dirty white.

Coffin and Brendan got down on the ground.

"What the fuck?" Brendan said.

"He's been shot!" Coffin hissed. "We're under attack!"

"Who the fuck's shooting at us?"

"I don't know. Just keep down."

"You don't have to fucking tell me," Brendan said.

Coffin crawled past Hanrahan's body and around to the other side of the transit van. Brendan joined him and they sat with their backs against the cab's grille, scanning the surrounding area for any sign of movement.

"You pissed somebody off recently?" Brendan said.

"Only vampires," Coffin said.

"You got a gun with you?"

"No. I left the shotgun back at the club. What about you?"

"No, I did the same. Fucking hell, we're sitting ducks out here."

As if to confirm what Brendan had just said, the headlamp just to the side of his head shattered, showering him with glass.

"Fuck!" Brendan hissed, and lay flat on his front. He began crawling under the van.

Coffin got down on the ground as well, but he knew there was no way he was fitting under the van. Maybe if he got inside, with the dead vampires. But then he was trapped in there, nothing to do but wait for whoever was taking pot-shots at them to turn up and shoot him at point blank range.

Coffin started crawling around the side of the van. As far as he knew they could be completely surrounded by men with rifles, but he had to do something.

He looked at Brendan under the van, his face pressed against the cobbles. His eyes were wide with fear.

Coffin stiffened as he heard the crunch of shoes against the cobbles. Someone was approaching. No, more than one.

"You can stand up now."

The voice was deep, a thick Scottish accent making the sentence almost indecipherable.

Bracing his hands against the cobbles, Coffin slowly pushed himself upright. He turned his head slowly, making sure not to surprise the men with any sudden moves.

One of the men was tall and lean, in contrast to his companion who looked like a mountain that had grown a huge, bushy beard.

They were both holding rifles, mounted with telescopic scopes.

"You under the van, you can come out now," the tall, lean one said.

Brendan dragged himself slowly out from under his van. He stood up.

"That's better," the Scottish man with the beard said.

He lifted his rifle and shot Brendan in the face.

Coffin flinched as hot blood splattered over his face. Brendan collapsed, dead before he hit the ground.

"You, you're coming with us," the tall one said.

Coffin wiped some of the blood off his face.

The tall man used his gun to indicate that Coffin should turn around and start walking.

For a moment, Coffin simply watched the two men, waiting. Weighing up his options. Didn't take him long to decide he only really had the one.

Do as they were telling him, and start walking.

The two men followed him, urging Coffin on with prods in his back whenever they felt he wasn't walking quickly enough. They arrived at a clearing, a Range Rover parked next to a chain link fence. Opening the rear door, the tall man indicated that Coffin should climb inside.

When he had folded himself into the car, Coffin expected them to close the door.

But they didn't.

The bearded man pulled a syringe from a pocket whilst his companion kept his gun trained on Coffin.

"What's that?" Coffin said.

"A little sedative," the bearded man said. "Just to keep you quiet until we drop you off."

He punched the needle through the flesh on Coffin's arm and depressed the plunger.

The tall man chuckled. "Shocker here, he wanted to shoot you with a tranquilizer dart. I said, fuck that, I'm not carrying a mountain like you to the car. Let's make him walk, and then we can tranquilize him."

Already the world was turning grey, sound growing distant.

"Don't take it personally," Shocker said. "We're just doing a job for a friend."

"Fuck you," Coffin mumbled. "When this is over, I'm going to find you, and kill you."

The last thing he heard as he drifted away was the sound of laughter.

EPISODE
EIGHT

she's a looker

Alfie Chambers poured out the last of his coffee from his flask and took a sip. Lukewarm, which he hated, but it was better than no coffee at all. Alfie screwed the cap back on the flask. Its metal casing was battered and bent and scratched from years of use. But Alfie loved that flask like an old friend.

Jobs like this, and to be honest weren't most of them like this, he spent all day sitting around in his car waiting for something to happen. He didn't smoke, and it wasn't like he could read. That would defeat the object, really. So he sat and listened to the radio, Radio Four mostly, and he drank his coffee.

That flask and his radio were his best friends. It was a lonely profession, but then Alfie didn't mind. He was a solitary sort of person anyway. Sitting in his car, watching and waiting, that was easy. Dealing with the customers was harder.

Other people were a constant mystery to Alfie. Especially married couples. Of course they were his main source of income, which sort of proved his point really. In Alfie's opinion, the world would be a hell of a better place if everyone just left each other alone to get on with their business.

Alfie had never married. When he was younger he would have liked to have found someone, but not anymore. Even back then his desire for female companionship probably had more to do with the need for sexual contact than anything else. Sex wasn't all it was cracked up to be in Alfie's opinion, and certainly didn't compensate for the difficulties and compromises involved in living with someone.

Alfie shifted in his seat slightly, and wiped at the windscreen which had fogged up a little from the steam from his coffee. He drained the rest of the cup and then screwed it onto the flask. He picked up a paper napkin from the passenger seat and wiped the flask down, mopping up any stray dribbles of coffee, before putting the flask in the glove compartment.

Beside the little pile of paper napkins was a paper bag. Alfie opened it up and looked inside. One doughnut left.

Alfie sighed. Here was another problem with sitting around all day, watching and waiting. His spreading waistline. Hard to believe how slim he had been, once. But as the years had passed the weight had crept up on him, and showed no signs of stopping. The doughnuts didn't help, of course. But along with his coffee and the radio, Alfie deserved his little pleasures in life, surely?

Alfie pulled the doughnut from the bag and bit into it. The sugar coated his lips and he licked them. Sighed with pleasure.

What he kept telling himself, was this: one day soon he was going to retire, pack it all in and move abroad maybe. France, or Italy. Somewhere by the sea. And then he was going to exercise. A morning walk every day, maybe buy himself a bicycle. He wouldn't need a car anymore, so no more sitting around for hours on end, getting heavier and heavier.

Alfie took another bite of the doughnut. Licked the sugar off his lips.

Yes, once he was active the weight would drop off him. Probably wouldn't want all this comfort food either. All that fresh air would give him a proper appetite for good, healthy food.

Alfie crammed the last of the doughnut into his mouth and chewed thoughtfully.

Sat up straighter and coughed sugar over the steering wheel and the dashboard.

There was that woman again. The one Stone had been shagging at the hotel when he got back from New York. Of course he didn't have any proof that they had been doing the dirty, but it was pretty obvious. She was hotter than a Friday night vindaloo, and why else would they have booked a hotel room together for a couple of hours?

Alfie watched as she paced up and down the road a few times, her head turned to look at Stone's car. The black, close fitting top and her running tights hardly did the job of hiding that curvaceous figure of hers. Long dormant stirrings fluttered to life in the pit of Alfie's stomach.

Then she walked out of sight again, disappearing to wherever she had come from.

Alfie finished chewing on his doughnut, swallowed and ran his tongue over his lips.

She was a looker, that was for sure. But what the hell was she doing here?

Alfie licked his finger and ran it over the steering wheel, collecting sugar granules. He stuck his finger in his mouth and sucked on it.

As much as he thought about it, Alfie couldn't work it out. Stone had shagged her at the hotel, and this morning he had shagged her in her room at the B&B.

So why was she hanging around outside, acting like she didn't want Stone to know she was there?

Did she think he was cheating on her?

Silly cow.

If he was shagging somebody else, he wouldn't have chosen this spot.

After all, an abattoir smack in the middle of an industrial estate was hardly the most romantic of places to bring a girl, now was it?

Alfie thought about phoning his client. Seeing that woman lurking around outside had put a different spin on the situation. Lucy Stone had hired Alfie because she wanted proof that her husband was shagging some other woman. And up until he had returned from the States, with that dark skinned woman in tow, Stone had proved to be as squeaky clean as they come.

But Lucy Stone was a cold one. Like one of those femme fatales in the Raymond Chandler novels he used to read as a teenager. Cool, calculating, smoking endless cigarettes. She had a way of looking at him that turned his insides into jelly. And not in a good way.

But then something very odd happened. The moment Alfie got wind that Stone was actually shagging another bird, Mrs Stone called him off the case. What the hell was that all about?

He told her all about the woman, and the hotel they had stopped off in. He told her how he could do some digging, find out who this woman was. And he told her, most importantly of all, that if they stuck it out long enough that he could get some photographs of the two of them together. Even if they weren't banging each other's bones, he should get enough incriminating shots of them that Lucy Stone could file for divorce.

But no. She was adamant. Alfie was off the case. Here's the cheque and thank you very much.

Goodbye.

It was all wrong.

And Alfie couldn't work out why.

Shouldn't have mattered, really. He'd been paid. And generously, too. He should have just let it go, moved on to another case.

But still.

Alfie decided to do a little digging into Garrett and Lucy Stone's backgrounds. Just out of interest.

Garrett Stone's history was what he had expected. Born into a tough, working class background, left home at seventeen with no qualifications, eventually joined the army, and then the SAS. From here it was difficult to track him, until he left military life behind and set up his company, a private security firm by the name of StoneColdSecurity.

Alfie thought that was a particularly shit name. Proved that Garrett Stone had absolutely no imagination. Always the same with these army types.

When Alfie looked into Lucy Stone's history, turned out she had had a similar military career to her husband's. Before she met Stone, Lucy was a member of the highly secretive Special Reconnaissance Regiment, an armed services unit so cloak and dagger they made the SAS look positively publicity hungry. The SRR was also the only UK Special Forces unit that accepted women.

It was impossible to find out anything about Lucy Stone's career in the SRR. The only interesting snippet of information that he found was that she might have been involved in the shooting of the Brazilian, Jean Charles de Menezes in London, 2005. He had been suspected of being a terrorist involved in the July 7 attacks, but turned out to be innocent.

Lucy Stone was discharged from the SRR not long after, and set up StoneColdSecurity with her then partner, Garrett Stone.

Made sense when he thought about it, that she would be the one in charge. For all Garrett Stone's toughness, she was the brains behind their business. And Alfie had a feeling that she was a tough bitch.

Tougher than her husband, even.

But what had proved most interesting to Alfie about the Stones wasn't their army history, but the killing of their eldest son, only a couple of weeks ago. Looked like Isaac Stone had gone off the rails some time ago, disgracing the Stone family name with drugs, petty crime and, probably most shameful of all for the unimaginative and uptight Garrett Stone, involvement with some weird vampire fetish group.

And then he was murdered. A shot through the back of his head at close range, along with another lad of similar age. Gang warfare, the police had said. Or a grudge killing, or a drug deal gone wrong.

Whoever had pulled the trigger was still out there, and Alfie was surprised that Lucy Stone hadn't had him looking into that, trying to find her son's murderer.

But no, she was more interested in finding out if her husband was shagging another woman. And when Alfie did find out, that was it, he was off the case.

Weird.

So Alfie had decided to continue tailing Stone.

Just for another few days, while he worked out what was going on. If he could get some decent shots of Stone and his girlfriend making the two-backed beast, he could take them to Lucy Stone and maybe get some more money out of her after all. And maybe then, when she saw how tenacious he could be, and how he could deliver the goods, maybe he would suggest that he could look into finding her son's murderer.

If he could do that, he reckoned that would be a nice little payday.

But now, after seeing Stone's girlfriend prowling around outside the abattoir, Alfie was even more confused.

He put his mobile away, decided to wait a little longer before making contact. Whatever was going on, it was all turning a bit more complicated than he had originally anticipated.

Best if he waited a little longer, found out more, maybe got himself a few shots, or even some video footage. Once he knew what was going on, then he could contact Lucy Stone.

And depending on the circumstances he might even be able to squeeze some more cash out of her, and offer to take on the case of finding Isaac's killer.

cleaning ladies

Freddie Noonan poured himself a large whisky and downed half of it in one. He grimaced at the taste and the fiery sensation as it made its way down his gullet. He slammed the glass down on the bar. Some of the whisky slopped onto his hand. Freddie sucked at his hand as he turned around to survey the mess once more.

Clean the place up, Craggs had said. That was going to be bloody easier said than done. There was blood everywhere. All over the floor, up the walls, splattered across the tables and the chairs. And then there was the shattered glass, the splintered wood and the plaster dust and bits of ceiling scattered across the floor.

And not forgetting the fucking bullet holes in the walls.

But you didn't question Mortimer Craggs when he issued an order. You just got on with it.

Freddie looked at his whisky. Picked it up and downed the rest.

Trouble was, he couldn't stop thinking about Terry.

It was all right for Craggs to be barking out orders and then saying they would do something to honour Terry's memory, but they shouldn't have taken him off in that van to dump his body God knows where with that scum that killed him.

Terry deserved better than that.

Freddie poured himself another drink, tipping the bottle carelessly and slopping more whisky over the bar.

His brother had died getting Craggs' precious fucking club back, and this was how he repaid him? It wasn't right.

"This is a woman's job, cleaning up," Harry Frazer said.

"Huh?" Freddie stirred, dragged out of his thoughts by the older man's voice.

Harry reached across Freddie and picked up the whisky bottle. He grabbed himself a glass and poured a generous serving into it.

"Fuck me, but this shit would defeat even my fucking old lady, and she scrubs the house clean twice a fucking day. This fucking place, it needs a fucking cleaning crew." Harry took a swallow of his drink. "It's going to take more than a mop and a bucket to get it all shiny and new again."

"Mr Craggs told us to clean up," Freddie said.

"Fuck that. We need professional help. All it takes is for us to miss a couple of spots and we'd be done for if the coppers came round. Did you know they've got machines now that can see the tiniest spots of blood?"

Freddie had another drink. He wasn't in the mood for listening to Harry talk but he knew better than to interrupt him. The old man could get nasty if he thought he wasn't being listened to. Especially after a drink or two.

"Yeah, these machines they've got, they shine out something called black light. Can you imagine that? What the fuck is black light supposed to be? But I'm telling you, it's true, I saw it on CSI. And they shine this black light around a room and if there's any trace of blood left after a clean-up, this black light picks it up, reflects it like it's fucking radioactive or something. Works on semen too."

Freddie thought about having another drink, but his head was buzzing and he suddenly felt very tired.

"So you see we've got to get this place cleaned up professionally. All the coppers need is a whiff of something iffy having happened here, and they'll be round poking their fucking noses in, and if we've left any trace of blood they'll find it."

Harry swallowed the rest of his whisky.

"And then we're fucked."

Freddie pushed his empty glass away, slid it across the bar. It toppled off the edge and smashed on the floor.

"Fucking hell, Freddie!" Harry said. "Haven't we got enough fucking mess to clear up without you making more?"

Freddie stood up, took a deep breath. He couldn't bear to listen to Harry talking anymore. The old man was like a wind up doll once he got started; he just would not stop talking until he finally wound down and ran out of energy.

"All right, girls, what's going on?" Gilligan stood in the doorway, gazing at the mess and then at the two men like it was all their fault.

Harry stood up. "We were just saying, how this is too much for us to clean up, and how we need a professional cleaning crew to come in."

"You know what, Harry, I think you might be right," Gilligan said. "Why don't you look through the Yellow Pages and find us a cleaning outfit, maybe get a few quotes while you're at it."

"Fuck off, Gerry," Harry said.

Gilligan laughed. Shook his head as though it was all too funny for words.

"I'll be sure and pass on your sentiments to Mr Craggs," he said.

"You don't scare me with that crap," Harry said, taking a step forward. "Me and Mort go back a long way, while you, you cocksure little bastard, you're the new boy. You should be careful, you don't want to be making enemies this early in the game."

"All right, calm down now," Gilligan said. "No one's looking to make any enemies, least of all me. We're all going to muck in with the clean-up, and when Brendan and Joe and Danny get back and start helping the work will go a lot faster, all right?"

Harry relaxed a little. "You'd better be mucking in too, you little bastard."

"I will, we all will," Gilligan said. "But right now we need to get some cleaning materials together. Mr Craggs says there's a whole load of detergent and some spare buckets and mops up in the loft."

"I'll go get them," Freddie said. It would be a relief to get away from Harry for a short while. By the time he got back down, maybe the others would be back and there would be more people for Harry to bitch and grouse at.

"Good lad," Gilligan said.

Freddie left Harry staring daggers at Gilligan. He trudged out to the back and up the stairs. Past Craggs' office and the Fuck Rooms until he found the loft hatch in the ceiling. There was a wooden pole in a broom cupboard, and Freddie used this to give the hatch a push. It clicked unlocked and Freddie lowered it open. The end of the metal steps stuck out over his head and Freddie snagged it with the hook on the end of the pole and pulled down. The ladder swung perpendicular and then slid smoothly down, extending until its feet were on the floor.

Freddie climbed the ladder until he was halfway through the loft opening. His fingers searched in the gloom along a wooden beam until they found a light switch. He flicked it on and off a couple of times, but nothing happened.

A chill, dead weight settled in his stomach. Freddie wasn't sure he would ever feel comfortable in the dark again, after today. But there was nothing to be afraid of. Freddie didn't know anymore what those things had been. Vampire, human, whatever, it didn't matter. They were dead.

Except one of them.

Didn't Joe say there was still one left?

But not here, not at Angels. Harry and Billy searched the place from top to bottom. Even up here in the loft. Harry hadn't said the lights weren't fucking working, though.

Freddie saw a torch lying next to the loft opening. It was a heavy duty one, encased in soft, black rubber. Freddie picked it up and switched it on. The powerful beam lit up the loft interior, hard edged shadows chasing each other away as he swept the light around.

The loft was empty.

Thank God for that.

Freddie climbed up the rest of the ladder until he was standing inside the loft space. The roof was pitched, but more than high enough that Freddie could walk around freely, without having to duck his head. The floor had been boarded, but the rafters were exposed, with black insulation lining the spaces between them.

Boxes of junk had been piled up around the perimeter of the loft. Freddie wandered up and down, shining the torchlight over the dusty crates and cardboard boxes. There was a stack of ancient sound equipment, a huge black amplifier, CD and tape deck, huge fuck off speakers, and even a twin deck record player.

Freddie pulled open the flaps on a cardboard box, creating a dust cloud which had him coughing and tearing up.

The box was filled with dirty magazines, looked like they must be twenty or thirty years old. Freddie pulled one out at random and leafed through it. A photoshoot of a group of girls working out at a gym. Of course they were all naked, arses thrust out at the camera, or legs spread to reveal shaved pussies. That slutty 'come and fuck me' expression on their faces.

Freddie dropped the magazine back on the pile, swallowed, swung the torchlight around the loft again.

There, over on the far side were the detergents and the mops.

Looked like there might be a problem with the roof, too. The black plastic was bulging between the rafters, like the roof slates had collapsed inwards. Craggs would have to get that fixed. Another night of rain like they'd been having recently and there might be a leak, maybe even cause some serious water damage.

Freddie walked closer, the torch beam focused on the black bulge.

Strange. The closer he got to it the less it looked like a break in the roof, but more like something attached to it.

Like something clinging to it.

As Freddie watched, transfixed, the bulbous protrusion began unfolding itself. Long, spindly arms ended in clawed hands, digging into the roof's interior. The whole thing shifted, moved like a spider suddenly aware of the vibrations running along its web, signalling the struggles of a trapped fly.

A white, skull-like face appeared from the shadows.

Grinning at him.

Freddie screamed and dropped the torch. The light flickered when the torch hit the floor, creating a manic kaleidoscope of shadows across the loft roof. The skull grinned at him, and that terrible smile grew ever wider as the thing crawled across the roof towards him like a stop motion monster in an old black and white film.

The torch gave up all together and the darkness engulfed Freddie, smothering him in its embrace. He opened his mouth to scream again, but the thing had fallen on top of him, clawed fingers raking open his face as he crumpled beneath the weight of his attacker.

Pushing frantically at the thing with its long limbs and sharp claws, Freddie cried at the agony swamping his nerve ends. Seemed like his face was being peeled off his skull.

Freddie's crying came to an end and turned to a gurgle as his mouth and throat filled with hot blood.

* * *

Gilligan didn't like the way Craggs looked, at all. Didn't like the way he kept massaging his chest, and his pasty complexion. Didn't like the way he kept pacing up and down, hardly listening to a word anyone said to him.

Craggs stopped walking by the club's front doors, and listened for a few moments. And then he started again.

"I'm thinking maybe we should get you out of here," Gilligan said. "Take you back to Brendan's."

Craggs shook his head as he paced up and down, massaging his chest. He paused by the double doors again, leaning into it, listening.

"Bloody coppers," he said. "What the hell do they want?"

He started pacing again. Up and down the carpeted hall.

Billy was standing by the cloakroom, massaging his knuckles. Looked disappointed that he hadn't been able to bust open as many noses as he had hoped he would.

Gilligan pulled a crumpled pack of cigarettes from his shirt pocket. He looked at the pack and then thought better of it, hid them away again.

Craggs stopped by the doors once more. "What the hell are they talking about out there? Haven't they got anything better to do?"

Harry Frazer walked into the reception from the rear of the club. Craggs had sent him outside around the back to see if he could listen in and find out what was going on.

"Well?" Craggs said. "What the fuck is that all about?"

"There's two coppers out there," Harry said. "And a council officer, as well. The prick from the council says there's been no roadworks planned here, and wants to know why the road's been dug up."

"Fucking hell," Craggs hissed, pacing again, shaking his head. "What are our men saying?"

"They're acting dumb. Just keep saying how they were given the job, and they're just doing what they're paid to do. That officious little prick is getting himself all worked up about something, though."

"It'll be fine," Gilligan said. "They've got no reason to connect the roadworks with the club, have they?"

"Who'd you get to dig up the road, anyway?" Billy said. "Can we trust them?"

"Of course we can fucking trust them," Harry said. "They're good lads, they'll just act dumb, and then as soon as the coast is clear they'll scarper."

"I don't like it," Craggs said. "Did they have to dig up so much of the fucking road? Looks like fucking World War Two out there."

"You told them to make noise," Harry said. "What else were they going to do besides keep at it with the jackhammers?"

Craggs said nothing.

"Let me take you back to the pub," Gilligan said. "You don't look so good."

"I'm fine," Craggs said. "Go fucking nursemaid somebody else."

Gilligan glanced uneasily at Harry.

Harry shrugged and raised his eyebrows, in a *I know, he's a stubborn old bastard* gesture.

"Where's Freddie?" Craggs said.

"He's gone up to the loft to get some more mops and detergent," Gilligan said.

"We need a fucking professional cleaning crew to clean this mess up, you ask me," Harry said.

"Well nobody asked you, so shut the fuck up," Craggs said.

"Harry, why don't you go upstairs and see what's keeping Freddie?" Gilligan said. "Soft bastard's been a fucking age."

"There you go again, giving out the orders like you're in fucking charge," Harry said. "I don't remember Mort stepping down and making you the fucking boss."

"Ah now, and I can see you're not a team player, are you Harry?" Gilligan said, a slow smile creeping across his face.

"Team player?" Harry said. "We're not on a fucking corporate adventure weekend, you know. Back in the day, you'd have no fucking teeth left by now, for a remark like that."

Craggs sat down heavily on a chair, clutching his chest.

"Will you two shut the fuck up?" he gasped.

"Mort, what's wrong?" Billy said.

"Fucking chest feels like it's on fire," Craggs said, through gritted teeth.

The three men gathered around him.

"Fucking hell, Mort, you're white as a sheet," Harry said.

"He's having a heart attack," Gilligan said. "We need to call an ambulance."

"Don't be a fucking idiot," Craggs groaned. His face was covered in a sheen of sweat. "One look in here and the cops'll be on us like a ton of bricks."

"My car, it's just outside," Gilligan said. "I'll take you to the hospital."

"No, I'll take him," Harry said.

Craggs groaned. "Fucking hell, am I going to have to die listening to you two fuckers arguing? If you're not going to take me to a hospital can't you at least shut the fuck up and let me die in peace?"

Gilligan bent down and hooked Craggs' arm over his shoulder and lifted him to his feet.

Harry stepped back out of the way, grinding his teeth.

"Stay here," Gilligan said. "Wait for the others to come back, and get this place cleaned up."

Gilligan helped Craggs walk through the club, towards the rear entrance.

Harry and Billy watched them go.

Finally, Harry stirred, and said, "I'm going up to the loft, see what's keeping Freddie."

i was
a hero once

Someone had removed Emma's brain and stuffed the empty skull with wet cotton wool. At least that's how her head felt right now. Soft and mushy, and with an inability to form a coherent thought. At times she seemed to be hovering over her own body, watching from a dispassionate distance, observing herself going through the motions.

A police woman had talked to Emma outside the Metropole Tower for ten minutes, asking her about Karl, about his relationships, his working hours, any death threats he might have received at the paper, any stories he had been working on. Emma had answered all her questions truthfully.

She just left out a few details.

Barry had bought them both a coffee while they waited to find out when they could leave. Emma felt lost in all the hustle and bustle, lost in the crowds of morbid sightseers, the police, the scene of crime officers, and reporters.

Emma had sat with Barry on a bench and Barry put his arm around her shoulders. For once she wasn't ready with a quick put down. Emma clutched the coffee in both hands, ignoring the pain as the heat seeped into her palms.

After a few moments, Barry had taken his arm from around Emma's shoulders and put his hands over his face.

"I can't believe it," he said, his voice muffled. "It just feels like a nightmare, and I'm going to wake up any moment."

"Yeah," Emma said. She knew how he felt. Hadn't that been her life for the last week?

"I mean, who could have done this? It's not like Karl had any enemies."

"No," Emma said.

Barry took his hands from his face and looked at Emma. His eyes were damp with tears.

"Do you know of any stories he was working on?"

"No," Emma said.

Barry wiped at his eyes with the heel of his hand.

"I bet it's got something to do with Joe Coffin," he said.

Emma kept quiet, couldn't think of anything to say.

"Have you seen him, recently? Been in touch with him?"

"Who?"

"Joe Coffin."

"No.

"It's got to be him," Barry said. "It's got to be."

Emma stood up, threw her coffee into a waste bin. She hadn't touched it at all.

"Barry, I've got to go," she said. "I'll catch up with you later."

Barry stood up too. "What do you mean, you've got to go? Where? Where have you got to go that's more important than this?"

"I've just got to, all right?" Emma said, trying to keep cool, keep her temper under control. "Fuck all is happening here, the cops don't need me, they don't need you either."

"But that police woman, she said to stay here until they told us we were free to go."

"Yeah well, she knows where I live. I'll see you later."

Emma left Barry standing there, his mouth open, watching her as she walked away.

And now here she was, God knows how much later, outside Angels wondering what the hell had gone on in there. The road had been dug up out the front of the club, and the trench extended down the street, and round the corner. No sign of any workmen now. No sign of any activity at all.

Emma crossed the road at a point where the trench ended, and walked back along the pavement until she was standing outside the club. She tried pushing at the doors, but they remained firmly in place. She walked along the front of the club until she got to the entrance to the carpark. There was a van blocking the way, but Emma was able to easily walk around it.

The back door, the one she had walked through only a couple of nights back, was open. Emma stood and watched it. Waited to see if anyone might come out.

Going back in there wasn't an option. No way. Not after her last experience. She would be a complete idiot to even think about walking through that open doorway. What if Steffanie was still in there? And the old man, Guttman?

But what if Joe was in there?

Wasn't that why she had walked all the way over here?

This last week it had seemed like there were three men in her life. All competing for her attention, demanding different things from her. But now one of them was dead, and the other was in hospital.

That left Joe Coffin.

Maybe Joe was dead, too. Maybe they were all dead, Craggs, Gilligan, Brendan and the others. All of them lying in pools of blood, their throats ripped open. And maybe one or two of them were already starting to wake up. Eyes fluttering open, a growing thirst for blood consuming them.

But what if Joe was in there? Alive.

Emma needed to talk to him. Tell him about the cops, about Karl.

The blood and the guns and the teeth.

No, that wasn't right.

Emma rubbed at her face, tried clearing her head.

Joe already knew about the blood and the guns and the teeth. He was a part of it all. Always had been.

No, that's wrong too. The vampires, Joe was never a part of the vampires.

Why was it so difficult to think?

Teeth snapping shut, arterial blood spraying, screaming and crying, body parts tumbling from black plastic bags, Steffanie and her empty eye socket, Tom Mills' head bashed in like a ripe tomato.

Emma balled up her hand into a fist and punched herself in the forehead.

Get a grip! You're losing it!

She punched herself again. It helped a little, the pain clearing her head slightly.

What was happening to her? Was she losing her mind?

Abel, naked, slashes of blood smeared across his chest.

Emma stuffed her fist into her mouth and bit down hard on her knuckles.

Julie crying as Michael squatted over her, baring his teeth.

A shadow appeared in the doorway of Angels. A man's figure, standing just inside, out of the light.

Emma held her breath, waiting to see if he would step outside or if he would stay where he was. Wondering if he was a man or a vampire.

The figure stepped outside, put a cigarette in his mouth, struck a match against the wall and lit up.

Emma breathed again.

She recognised him, one of the men that Craggs had gathered together to reclaim Angels. If he was there, smoking, loitering outside, that must mean they had got the club back. Emma realised she hadn't seen Brendan's van anywhere.

That settled it. Brendan had to have taken the vampires somewhere to dispose of them. That had been the plan.

Emma pulled herself together. Joe was here. He was alive, and he was here.

As she walked towards the club's rear entrance the man looked up and saw her, and his eyes widened.

"You're that reporter, aren't you?" he said. "What the hell are you doing here?"

"Where's Joe?" Emma said. "Is he inside?"

"No. He's gone with Brendan and Danny."

"You're Billy Adams, aren't you?"

"Yeah. Let's get you inside."

Billy pulled the door shut behind him, and Emma shivered as she walked down the corridor. The last time she had been here she had run straight into Guttman.

"Where is everyone? It's so quiet."

Billy pulled her up short before they walked into the club. "I wouldn't go in there, it's like a bloody slaughterhouse." Billy looked at her. "Let's go upstairs, we can use Mr Craggs' office."

Emma let Billy guide her upstairs and into Craggs' office. She sat down on the leather sofa, and noticed Billy looking uncomfortably at the floor. When she followed his gaze she saw a large, dried bloodstain on the carpet.

She started laughing.

"What's so funny?"

Emma couldn't answer. The laughter had taken hold of her, was swallowing her up in a wild, uncontrollable grip. She tried to take a breath, but she couldn't.

I'm going to die here. Not at the hands of a vampire, but I'm going to suffocate because I'm laughing so hard I can't draw breath!

Billy slapped her across the face. Emma's head snapped back and silenced her laughter like a television that had suddenly been switched off. She jumped to her feet, a snarl growing in the back of her throat, her hands balling up into fists.

Billy grabbed her by the shoulders and pushed her back into the sofa.

"Snap out of it, young lady," he said. "You're hysterical."

The world came back into focus. Lifting a trembling hand, Emma touched her cheek. Her flesh still stung where Billy had slapped her.

"That's better," he said. "Now, I think we could both do with a drink."

Emma watched him as he shuffled around the office looking for alcohol. She took a deep, juddering breath and exhaled slowly. That slap, it had been an old fashioned, male cure for hysterics. But she had to admit, it had worked.

For the moment.

The madness, the hysteria, was lurking just out of reach on the edges of her consciousness. She had to be careful, keep it at bay.

"Bloody hell, there has to be a bottle of something in here somewhere," Billy said.

"What about the globe atlas?" Emma said.

Billy looked at the huge globe standing on legs on the floor. He placed a hand on it, over Canada, and pushed. Nothing happened, the world staying firmly in its position. Billy ran his hands around its perimeter and found a catch. The top half of the world lifted up on a hinge, revealing bottles and glasses.

He lifted a bottle of whisky out of the stand, held it up and examined it.

"Looks expensive," he said.

He lifted two glasses out of the globe's interior and placed them on a small table. With practiced ease he uncorked the bottle and poured a generous portion of whisky into each glass.

"Here, drink that," he said, holding the glass out.

Emma took it and held it under her nose, had a sniff, wrinkled her nose.

"People seriously drink this poison?" she said.

Billy threw his drink back in one and smacked his lips appreciatively.

"Drink up," he said.

Emma took a tentative sip, swallowed, coughed.

She put the glass down.

"No more. I'm fine now, really."

Billy poured himself another drink. "Last time I saw you, young lady, you were being locked up in the cellar back at Brendan's. How the hell did you get out?"

"Patsy," Emma said. "She went crazy, opened up the cellar door and walked down the steps with a bloody great shotgun in her hands. Those two cops, they're dead. She killed them."

Billy shook his head. "That timid little mouse? A shotgun? I don't believe you."

"Fine," Emma said. "To be honest I don't give a flying ratfuck what you think. It's quiet in here, where is everybody?"

Billy downed his second whisky. Put the empty glass on the table. Looked at Emma for a while as though he was sizing her up.

"You used to be a boxer, didn't you?" she said, eventually.

Seemingly unaware of what he was doing, Billy stood a little straighter, pushed his shoulders back.

"A long time ago now, yes," he said.

"I remember seeing you on the front pages of all the papers," Emma said. "I was only young, maybe six or seven, and I was in a shop with my mother, and we were in the queue, and I remember seeing that photograph on the front page of every single newspaper in the shop."

Billy nodded, picked up his empty glass and rolled it around and around in his fingers.

"You were standing in the ring, standing over your opponent who was lying on his back. And the referee, he had his arms around you, like he was trying to pull you away, and there were a couple of other men there too, hands around your arms, holding you back."

Billy nodded, gazing at his glass, kept rolling it around.

"And I remember the photographs in newspapers were still printed in black and white then, except there was this one newspaper that was colour. And in that paper, in the photograph on the front page, I remember seeing a streak of red on one of your boxing gloves."

"You've got a good memory," Billy said softly.

"Not really," Emma said. "But that's always stuck in my mind for some reason."

"That's the fight that got me banned from boxing forever. Served time as well."

"He died, didn't he?"

Billy nodded. "Brain haemorrhage."

"But that wasn't your fault, was it?"

"I had a habit of losing control. If I got angry, or when I was in the ring in a fight, I got so that the red mist came down, and I wasn't myself anymore. That's what happened that night. I can't even remember it myself now. All I remember is the fight beginning, and then sort of coming out of a trance, and seeing Ray McDonnell lying on the canvas, his face all busted up, blood leaking out of one ear. They told me afterwards that I wouldn't stop hitting him, long after I should have stopped. Long after everyone else could see he was in trouble. Even when he was down they said I was hitting him, like he was a punching bag lying on the floor."

Emma couldn't think of anything to say.

"I was a hero once. I was the lad from the rough part of town, from no-hope parents, who was going to be big. I was going to make everybody proud. I'd always wanted to be on the front page of the papers. But not like that."

Billy poured himself another shot of whisky.

"Not like that," he said, and tossed the whisky down in one.

"Where is everybody, Billy?" Emma said.

"Joe, Brendan and Danny, they've gone to get rid of the bodies. Terry and Tony, they're both dead."

"What about the others? Where's Craggs?"

"Mr Craggs took ill, and Gerry took him to the hospital."

"Ill? What do you mean, ill?"

"I don't know. It were like maybe he were having a heart attack. That's what Gerry said, anyway."

"What about Freddie? Is he dead, too?"

Billy shook his head. "No. Him and Harry are up in the loft, looking for mops and cleaning fluid."

Emma looked at the dark stain on the carpet. "It's going to take more than a mop and bucket to get that up."

"That's what Harry keeps saying." Billy looked at the bottle, obviously considering another drink.

Emma tilted her head back, gazed at the ceiling.

"Seems awfully quiet up there considering there's two men wandering around looking for mops and buckets."

Billy stood up. Was it Emma's imagination, or did he suddenly look a little unsteady?

"Stupid bastards have been up there forever," he said.

Emma watched Billy as he walked over to the door, and stepped out onto the landing. Suddenly possessed by a fear of being left on her own, she stood up and followed him.

Towards the end of the landing there was a ladder extending from an open loft hatch.

"Oi! Freddie! Harry! You found those fucking mops yet?"

Silence.

Billy placed his hand on a rung, ready to climb the ladder. He paused, took his hand off the ladder and looked at it.

The palm of his hand was smeared with red.

"What the hell?"

Harry Frazer dropped from the loft hatch, his limbs getting tangled in the ladder as he fell.

"Fucking hell!" Billy shouted, scrambling to get out of the way.

But he was too late, and Harry's body crashed on top of him. Billy hit the floor face down, Harry on top of him.

Sightless eyes stared up at Emma, the gaping wound slashed across his throat like a red, grinning mouth.

put him out
of his misery

Darkness.

Pain.

Lights, dancing and flashing.

Movement.

Eyes all gummed up.

Pain in his back and neck.

Streams of light, dancing before his eyes in the darkness.

The movement. Swaying, swinging gently.

Head pounding fit to bust open.

The smell.

Blood.

Raw meat. Like in a butcher's.

Coffin had to struggle to open his eyes. Wanted to wipe the stickiness out of them, but his wrists were bound behind his back.

More movement, more swaying. Where was he? On a boat, at sea?

Light streamed in, hurting his eyes. Squinting, he turned his head, trying to ease the kinks out of his neck. Why did his back hurt so much? And his stomach and chest, too? Something digging into him, a pressure on his torso, holding him up.

Every movement he made increased the swaying sensation. As his vision slowly returned, Coffin could see that he was spinning slowly. First one way, then the other. Not much, but enough to turn his stomach over. The inside of his mouth was sticky, and his tongue thick with a foul tasting coating, but at least he hadn't been gagged.

Coffin worked his jaw up and down, ran his tongue over his teeth. What he needed right now was a drink.

Didn't look like he was going to get one.

As his vision settled down to normal, Coffin took in his surroundings.

Rows of hooks hanging from the high ceiling on runners. Chains and pullies, rusted with age. Sheets of stamped aluminium had been fixed to the walls of what appeared to be channels leading to drains, the concrete floor stained dark brown. Walls at roughly waist height, designed to herd cattle to a place where they were gated in. A trap for their heads to be fastened in.

The hooks hanging from the ceiling, they were meat hooks.

Coffin was in an abattoir.

He had been bound tightly, with his arms behind his back. And he had been hung from one of those meat hooks. Just like a huge side of beef, waiting to be quartered and carved up.

Directly underneath his swaying feet was a large, rectangular opening on a raised ledge. The sides of the ledge were caked with brown lumps and dried stains. Inside the rectangular opening were what looked like a series of cogs and gears. They were also caked with an unidentifiable muck.

The whole thing reminded Coffin of the teeth of a huge dinosaur, waiting to swallow him up and chew him into digestible pieces.

He flexed his upper arms and his shoulders and then his lower arms, testing the strength of the rope. There was no give at all. Whoever had tied him up knew what they were doing. There was no way he was making a Houdini like escape from these bonds.

He wondered briefly about shouting, but decided there was no point. If there had been any danger of Coffin making his presence known through shouting then his captors would have gagged him.

Which left him thinking about the two men who had murdered Brendan and Danny, and sedated him. Brought him here, and hoisted him in the air on the end of a meat hook.

Coffin had to work hard to concentrate. The sedative those two bastards had injected him with had left him with a nasty headache, and his thought processes were slow and sluggish.

But he thought about his two kidnappers all the same.

Were they working on their own? Coffin hadn't recognised them. They had given off an air of military efficiency, but they hadn't looked like soldiers. Maybe they were working for somebody else. Somebody who had a grudge against Coffin?

That didn't make much sense either. Coffin had made plenty of enemies over the years, but he couldn't think of one who would go to these elaborate lengths. Or kill Brendan and Danny as casually as those two bastards did.

What about the Seven Ghosts? Terry Wu had said the Triads would exact their revenge for his murder, and Coffin had laughed in his face. But neither of those two men looked as though they had even a hint of Chinese in their ancestry. And Coffin got the feeling that if there really was a secret organisation named the Seven Ghosts, that they wouldn't be hiring out their dirty work to a bearded Scottish man and his lanky friend.

Having thought through all the ideas and suspicions he had available and come to no conclusion, Coffin decided his best option was to simply bide his time. Whoever had left him here would obviously be returning at some point to finish off whatever it was they had started. All Coffin had to do was wait.

And it wasn't exactly like he could do anything else.

He didn't have to wait long. Coffin heard a door open and slam shut. The noise echoed around the vast interior.

Coffin's shoulders and back felt like they were on fire. But his head was clearing of the dulling effects of the sedative, and his headache was easing off, too.

A man walked into view. Someone Coffin had never seen before. That answered one question, then. The two men who had taken Coffin had been working for this man. That was why he hadn't recognised them. The problem was, he didn't recognise this man either.

He stopped walking at about six feet in front of Coffin, and he had to crane his head to look up at him.

The two men regarded each other silently for a while.

"Over the last couple of days, I've thought of many different things I could say to you at this moment," the man said, eventually. "That's the way it happens in the films, isn't it? There has to be a speech or a philosophical discussion of some sort, before the killing happens."

Coffin grunted. He wasn't in the mood for philosophical discussions.

"The problem is, I'm not a particularly imaginative man, Joe Coffin. I've been racking my brains for something to say for the last couple of days, ever since I started the job of tracking you down. In the end I thought maybe it would be better just to kill you, and spare us both the embarrassment of me attempting a philosophical discussion on death and revenge."

Coffin shifted his shoulders slightly, trying to alleviate some of the pain.

"Revenge," the man said. "There is a saying about revenge, isn't there? How does it go, now?"

"Revenge is a dish best served cold," Coffin said.

The man snapped his fingers. "That's the one. A fine, Shakespearian line. Or maybe ancient Japanese or Chinese. Such a powerful sentence, full of cold, hard meaning. You see, you obviously have more imagination than I have. If only I had thought of that."

Coffin grinned.

"What's so funny?" the man said.

"Your fine, Shakespearian line is from *Star Trek: The Wrath Of Khan*." Coffin said. "Khan delivers it to Kirk."

"Really? That's a disappointment. Still, I wouldn't know. I don't go to the movies, I don't read books, it's all a waste of time as far as—"

"You talk a lot, don't you?" Coffin said.

The man paused, thought this over.

"Well, no, not usually. This is an unusual state of affairs for me. Perhaps we should just get down to business, forget about all that other rubbish. My name is Garrett Stone. I am Isaac Stone's father."

"Congratulations," Coffin said. "Now that we've cleared that up, perhaps you could get me down from here and then I can cave your skull in with my bare hands."

"His name means nothing to you, does it?"

"Never heard of either of you. Should I have?"

"Maybe not. But whether you knew him by his name or not, you murdered my son."

Coffin thought about this. He'd killed a lot of people in his time, starting with his father when he was a teenager. But he couldn't ever remember killing anyone with the name of Isaac.

"You sure you've got the right person?"

"He was also known as Jet."

"Nope. Still not ringing any bells. You got the wrong guy. So, like I said, how about untying me and we settle this the old fashioned way?"

"By caving my skull in?"

"It could go that way, yeah. Or I could rip your spleen out first."

Stone put his hands on his hips, cocked his head to one side like he was examining a zoological specimen in a glass case. He was wearing a shirt, open at the collar, and trousers. Coffin had the impression of a businessman come straight from the office, removing his tie enroute in an attempt to look a little more casual.

But Coffin could see the muscle rippling beneath his shirt. Whatever he did for a living, Stone wasn't just an office drone. He was fit and strong and powerful.

"Why'd you do it, Coffin? Why did you kill him?"

"If I knew who you were talking about, maybe I could tell you," Coffin said. "Right now, I haven't got a fucking clue."

"Two weeks ago, a shitty block of flats in a shitty suburb of Birmingham. You'd just got out of jail, the same day in fact. You and another man forced your way into my son's apartment and shot him point blank in the back of his head."

Now Coffin knew who Stone was talking about. Instead of opening his mouth right away, Coffin decided to keep quiet for a little while, act like he was thinking on it.

"Yeah, I remember him," he said, eventually. "Scrawny little fuck was supposed to have killed my wife and son."

Coffin saw Stone visibly stiffen. Saw his throat move as he swallowed.

"Supposed to have?"

"Yeah. I was inside when they were murdered. The man I was with? He met me on my release, told me he'd found out who killed my wife and boy. Brought a gun with him to the prison. Can you believe that? Took me straight to your son's flat, and I shot him and his friend. They were both strung out on drugs, hardly knew what was going on. Thing is, this man, he purposefully provided me with false information, because he was involved."

"What's his name?" Stone said.

"Tom Mills. He's already dead. I killed him."

"Is that supposed to make me feel better?"

Coffin smiled. "It worked for me."

"Do you feel any remorse or guilt, that you killed my son when he was innocent of your family's murder?"

Coffin thought about this for a while. Thought about lying, but decided it wouldn't make much difference. Stone had obviously decided to kill him whatever he said.

"No. Your boy was killing himself anyway, with all that crap he was injecting. I just put him out of his misery a little sooner than he expected."

"That's what I thought," Stone said.

"Now what? Is this the part where you kill me?"

"No. Not yet. We're waiting for my wife. As soon as she arrives, we'll start having some fun."

"Great. How sweet."

"That machine underneath you?"

Coffin looked down, at the gunked up cogs and wheels with teeth.

"It's a meat grinder. Churns out minced meat. I would have liked to have ground you up completely, and then I could have spent the next few months feeding you to my dogs. I have a feeling the motor will overheat and pack in before you're fully turned into minced meat, though. Doesn't matter. You'll be dead by then."

Coffin kept his mouth shut.

He'd run out of things to say.

billy back
in the ring

"We need to get out of here," Emma said.

Billy finished pushing Harry's body off him and stood up.

Looked up at the open loft and shouted, "Freddie?"

"We need to go," Emma said, tugging at Billy's sleeve.

Billy glanced at her, massaging his knuckles. Looked up at the darkness in the loft hatch.

"We killed them all," he said. "And then we searched this fucking place from top to bottom, even the loft." He took a deep breath, and bellowed, "Freddie!"

"All of them, you sure you killed all of them?"

Emma was backing up a little now. An unconscious movement, but once she realised what she was doing, she thought, *Yeah, good idea, get the fuck out of here now.*

"Yeah, all of them, except. . ." Billy's brow furrowed, ". . . the old man. Joe said something about an old man."

Emma's stomach tightened up into a tiny knot. "What old man? What did he say?"

"He said we never found the old man. Said he should be here somewhere, we should've found him."

Footsteps behind Emma, the hiss of an indrawn breath. The hairs on the back of Emma's neck stood up, her flesh tingling as she anticipated sharp fangs sinking into her throat and ripping a gaping wound wide open.

Spinning around, Emma held her arms up to ward off the vampire's attack.

And immediately relaxed.

"What the fuck's going on?" Frankie Shaddock said.

"Frankie?" Billy said. "Where the fuck did you come from?"

"I've been down in the fucking cellar this whole fucking time, practically shitting my fucking pants and waiting for one of you fucking fuckers to come down and tell me the fucking coast was clear."

"No one told me you were down there," Billy said, hands extended in an apology. "When did you arrive?"

"You stupid bastard, aren't you listening to a fucking thing I'm telling you?" Shaddock wiped a shaky hand across his lips. "They've been keeping me prisoner down there. Joe found me a while back, told me to stay put until it was safe to come out."

"The vampires have been keeping you prisoner?" Emma said.

Shaddock looked at her, turned back to Billy.

"Who the fuck is she?" he said.

"She's a reporter," Billy said.

"Are you fucking serious?" Frankie said.

He bent over at the waist, put his hands on his knees.

"You all right?" Billy said.

"No, I think I'm going to throw up. All this excitement, it's playing fucking havoc with my IBS. I haven't had a shit in two fucking days straight."

Billy looked back up at the black hole in the ceiling.

"Freddie's up there," he said.

"Freddie's dead, Billy," Emma said. "And so are we unless we get out of here."

Frankie straightened up again. "You telling me one of those blood sucking bastards is still here?"

"Freddie!" Billy shouted.

Both Emma and Shaddock flinched at the sound of Billy's voice.

"Yeah, the old man, they never found him," Emma said.

"You know, we could have done with you earlier," Billy said, looking at Shaddock. "Mr Craggs, he had a heart attack."

"Mort? Is he dead?"

"No, Gerry took him to the hospital."

"Gerry? Who the fucking hell is Gerry?" Shaddock passed a hand over his forehead. "Wait, don't bother. I don't give a fucking shit who Gerry is."

"You know, I think it's time we got out of here," Emma said. "If that creepy old vampire is still here we need to leave before he comes looking for his mid afternoon snack."

"We need to find Freddie," Billy said.

Shaddock glanced up at the loft. "Be my guest, but there's no fucking way I'm hanging around here any longer. Let's get out of here."

No one moved. Billy continued looking up at the loft hatch, massaging his knuckles.

"What are you thinking?" Shaddock said to Emma.

"I'm thinking it's awfully quiet up there," Emma said.

"Which makes sense if Freddie's dead," Shaddock said. "Did anybody else go up there?"

"No," Billy said. "Just Freddie, and then Harry."

"So there's nobody up there," Shaddock said. "There's your answer, that's why it's so quiet."

Emma held Shaddock in her gaze.

"Oh shit," Shaddock said. "You're thinking of that creepy old corpse. If he isn't up there, then where the fuck is he?"

"Could be anywhere in the club," Emma said. "Waiting for us."

"Billy, you're coming with us," Shaddock said. "We need to stick together."

"Anyone got anything we can use as a weapon?" Emma said.

Billy held his hands up, curled them into fists. "I've got these."

"Fucking great," Shaddock said.

They all turned and faced the hall. Still no one moved.

"We don't have to go through the club itself," Shaddock said. "If we go out of the back door he might miss us altogether."

Emma decided to take the lead. It didn't look like either Billy or Shaddock were keen on going first.

Leave it to a woman, as always, she thought.

Placing a hand against a wall to steady herself, Emma began edging down the hallway. Shaddock followed her with Billy in the rear.

If the old man, Guttman, had been in the loft, when had he come down? Had it been while Emma and Billy were in Craggs' office? Had he even known they were here?

Shaddock groaned and Emma turned back to look at him. He was doubled over and clutching his stomach.

"Oh fucking hell," he said, looking up at Emma, panic on his face. "I think I'm going to shit myself."

"Can't you just hold it in until we get outside?" Emma hissed.

Shaddock lunged for the door to Craggs' office, shoving past Emma.

"I don't fucking believe this," Emma said.

Billy massaged his knuckles, and looked up and down the hall.

"Mr Craggs has got his own private bathroom in there," he said. "We should wait for him."

"No way," Emma said. "If you want to hang around and risk getting a love bite from a corpse while your friend takes a shit, be my guest. I'm getting out of here."

Not waiting for an answer, Emma began walking slowly towards the stairs. Her legs were weak, hardly seemed able to support her, and she could feel a faint tremor in her knees. Once more images of blood and guns and sharp teeth snapping at her threatened to overwhelm her tired mind. If she could just get out and find Joe, find somewhere safe to hole up and rest, she would feel much better.

Her eyes registered the black shape clinging to the ceiling, but it took her mind a second or two to catch up. To fully comprehend what she was seeing.

Guttman, in his black suit, stained with dried blood. His long limbs stretched out, fingers splayed against the surface of the ceiling. His head rotated and his dark eyes locked onto her. Red lips peeled back to reveal long teeth. Blood had run down his chin and dried out, and it cracked and flaked as his facial muscles moved.

Was it Emma's terrified imagination, or did he look younger than when she last saw him? His hair was darker, streaked with grey now rather than fully grey. His pasty flesh still clung to his skull like parchment, and his eyes were large and bulbous in their deep sockets. But he looked stronger.

With a whispering susurration the thing on the ceiling began crawling towards her. And he was fast, slithering from the ceiling and along the wall as he drew closer.

Emma backed up.

"Billy!" she said.

She bumped into him and heard his sharp intake of breath as he saw Guttman crawling towards them.

"Fucking hell!"

He grabbed her by the arm and pulled her into Craggs' office. Guttman increased his speed, crawling along the wall towards the door.

Billy pushed the door shut, slamming it in its frame.

But it didn't quite shut.

Guttman had shoved his arm through the gap between the door and the doorframe. He had made no sound as Billy smashed the door against his arm. Long, crabbed fingers clawed at the space just in front of Billy and Emma. The nails were ragged and crusted with dirt and dried blood.

Billy put his back against the door, his feet digging into the carpet as he strained to keep the ancient vampire from throwing the door wide open. As strong as he was, the ex-boxer looked like he was struggling.

"Is there another way out of here?" Emma said.

"Don't think so," Billy grunted.

"Why the fuck aren't there any windows in this place?" Emma said, looking wildly from side to side.

A bare foot inched its way through the door, followed by a leg. Emma watched, fascinated. Even Guttman's toenails looked like claws. Had he taken his shoes off so that he could crawl along the ceiling and the walls?

"Don't just stand there," Billy gasped. "Help me out, will you?"

Emma snapped back into the present, out of a dreamlike state where she had felt more like an observer than a participant in the action. She ran over to Craggs' desk, thinking maybe he had a gun in one of the drawers.

One by one she pulled them open, rifling frantically through the contents. Nothing.

Except, a small knife, maybe a fancy letter opener.

It might do.

Emma picked up the knife and ran across the office. Grabbing Guttman's wrist she twisted his arm back against the wall and shoved the knife through his palm, and into the wall.

Guttman howled.

Billy kept up the pressure on the door, and held Guttman's wrist in place.

"Get something to hammer the knife in deeper," Billy said. "Maybe we can pin him into place."

Emma ran back to the desk and found a glass paperweight. Picking it up she ran back over to the door and began hammering the knife deeper into the plaster, until the handle suddenly snapped off.

Billy stepped back and Guttman staggered into the room. The door slammed against the wall. Before he could regain his balance, Billy had punched him in the face. The vampire's head snapped back, and Billy punched him again. Dark blood had begun streaming from Guttman's nose and over his mouth and chin.

Billy danced back out of the way of Guttman's outstretched claw.

He's smiling, Emma realised. It was as though the years as an embittered ex-boxer had suddenly fallen from Billy, and he was back in the ring again. He leapt from foot to foot and took another swing at Guttman, this time connecting with his chin. The click as his teeth snapped together was hideously loud.

Guttman lunged at Billy again, but the knife pinning his hand to the wall held him back. With a cheeky grin that made the boxer turned enforcer look almost handsome, Billy looked at Emma and gave her a wink.

In a spray of blood, Guttman ripped his hand from the knife pinning it to the wall and flew at Billy. Emma screamed Billy's name as the vampire slammed into him, propelling him across the room. They hit the bathroom door, to a muffled cry from Shaddock inside.

Guttman held Billy's head in both hands. His long fingers seemed to have grown even longer, like creeping vines or tree roots, as they covered Billy's face and scalp. The ex-boxer was gripping Guttman's wrists, trying to pull his arms apart and peel those hideous hands from his head.

Blood started leaking from between Guttman's fingers, running down the backs of his hands and dripping off them. Billy's feet started kicking out in a jerky, spasmodic rhythm, and Emma realised Guttman was actually holding him off the floor by his head.

Billy was making unintelligible grunting sounds, and his struggle to free himself was growing weaker. Finally his arms dropped by his sides and his feet stopped kicking. Guttman let go of Billy's head and he slid to the floor, leaving behind a long, dark trail of blood and hair on the bathroom door.

Emma couldn't move. Her mind was screaming *RUN! RUN!* but it was as though her body had given up. That it was refusing to take orders anymore from her head, and that her legs and arms were now simply nothing more than useless appendages.

Back hunched, clawed hands dripping red gore, the vampire slowly drew closer. His suit, stiff with dried blood and dirt, rustled with each movement he made. In his skeletal face his teeth were so long it didn't seem possible they could fit into his mouth.

Emma backed up a step and her leg hit an obstacle. Falling backwards she sank into a large, leather sofa. Guttman approached her slowly, his head cocked to one side as he regarded her. He raised his hands, his long fingers ending with their broken, dirty fingernails were crooked like the branches of a gnarly tree. The knife Emma had used to pin him to the wall was still protruding from his hand.

When he was up close and hunched over her, his foul breath washing over her and making her gag, the vampire leaned in even closer. There was no escape now. As much as she tried to sink into the sofa, willing it to swallow her up, there was nowhere to go.

Guttman's mouth was only inches from Emma's, his head still cocked at that odd angle. She twisted her head away, coughing and gagging at the stench emanating from his mouth and his body. A long tongue flicked out, and Emma screwed her eyes shut at its sandpapery touch as Guttman licked her cheek.

That filthy, crusted suit rustled and creaked with every movement the vampire made. Flakes of dried blood fell into Emma's lap. Up close, she could see the lines in his face were still caked with dark crusts of blood, and in his hair.

Emma flinched at the touch of Guttman's fingers on her cheek. A delicate touch, as though he was afraid of hurting her. Clenching every muscle in attempt to keep from shuddering violently, Emma held her breath as the vampire's fingers traced a delicate line down her neck. Down over her collarbone and her breasts, and down to her belly.

Where his hand rested.

A single sob racked her body. Guttman gazed at her. Head twisted away and into the sofa back, Emma could just see the vampire's ancient face. He seemed genuinely curious about her. Leaning in even closer until his cold, cracked lips were touching her neck, the vampire sniffed Emma's flesh.

He sniffed again and again, examining every inch of her. With his hand still on her stomach the vampire snuffled at her jawline, and her hair, and her neck again. He sniffed at her breasts, his tongue flicking out to lick his lips. And then he moved further down her body, and sniffed at her belly, and then the crotch of her jeans.

Emma screwed her hands up into fists and bit down on her tongue.

And waited for the agony to end.

grow a
pair of wings

The Nikon D4 was probably the most expensive bit of kit he had ever bought. Which seemed a waste when he thought of what he mainly used it for.

To be honest he hadn't needed to spend all that money on a flash camera like this. He could have saved himself a grand at least by going for a cheaper camera, one that would have done the job just as well. But Alfie Chambers liked cameras. He was a frustrated photographer at heart and had promised himself that when he retired he would take his passion for photography seriously. There would be plenty of photo opportunities and beautiful panoramas to record wherever he settled down, he was sure.

Right now though, this expensive bit of kit had a much more practical purpose. Mainly taking photographs of errant husbands.

Preferably caught in the act.

Not that that was an easy one to pull off.

There had been that silly bastard who'd tried shagging his girlfriend on Fistral Beach in Newquay. It had been the middle of summer a couple of years back, and the damn place had been stuffed to the gills with blond haired surfer boys and their girlfriends. This middle aged loser, Reg he was called, owned a photocopying shop in Milton Keynes and thought he was God's gift to women, had been cheating on his wife for a good while.

Alfie, employed by the suspicious wife, had tailed the man down to Newquay, where his girlfriend was entered into a surfing competition. According to the movies and the glossy magazines, all surfers, boys and girls, looked like supermodels. Tanned, toned bodies, perfect teeth, blond hair, chiselled good looks and overflowing with sex appeal.

Not Reg's girlfriend. Despite obviously being a talented surfer, her body still managed to look vaguely dumpy, her white skin never seemed to tan no matter how long she spent baring it to the elements, and her face looked like something he'd once trodden in after an accident in a pizza shop.

Which explained why she was hanging around with Mr Charisma himself, Reg.

Alfie had begun to despair of ever snapping a photo of the two of them getting it on, which is what the wife particularly wanted for some reason.

And then came that night with the BBQ on the beach, and the sex session doggy style in the sand dunes, Reg with his trousers round his ankles grinding away at the girl's doughy arse and her yipping like Shih Tzu being spanked.

Alfie was pretty damn pleased with himself for the pictures he got that night. Bloody camera had outdone itself, especially in the low light. A bit too well, really. Alfie wasn't sure he would ever be able to forget the sight of Reg's hairy arse thrusting away like a piston on a steam engine going at full speed.

Alfie didn't really hold out much hope of catching Stone in flagrante in an abattoir, but he'd had no chance at the hotel and the B&B. Maybe he would get lucky, and catch Stone giving that Creole woman a good banging on the office desk, or maybe even on a butcher's block, if that was the kind of thing they had in these places.

But then the job had suddenly grown interesting, and the camera had come into its own. A Range Rover had pulled up, parked in front of the abattoir beside Stone's car. Two men had got out, and then hauled a third out of the back. Alfie couldn't tell if he was dead or simply unconscious, but he had chuckled as he watched the two men trying to manhandle him inside. He was a huge slab of muscle, and Alfie had snapped off a few photographs in between laughing.

Then he had sat and waited some more. Alfie's interest had been piqued by this latest development, and he was keen to find out more. But not while there were three of them inside. More chance of being spotted if he went snooping around now.

Eventually the two men came back outside and climbed into the Range Rover.

As soon as they had driven away, Alfie climbed out of the car, cradling the D4 and its massive 70 - 800mm lens. Bloody thing was so heavy, Alfie could have done with a trolley to wheel it around on.

He stood by the car and looked at the slaughterhouse.

Just what the hell was Stone up to in there?

The rational part of his mind told Alfie to get the hell out and take his photographic evidence to the police. They would be very interested in seeing what he had to show them. But Alfie was intrigued by what he had seen, and this was about the most exciting his job had been since . . . well, since ever, really.

Alfie approached the abattoir slowly, ready for the door to swing open at any moment and for Stone to come striding out. Alfie had had a story all ready about going out bird spotting and getting lost. Pretty lame, but he couldn't think of a better one.

Even if he hadn't get the money shot, and Stone realised who he was, and that he was working for his wife, or at least had been, Alfie had enough photographic evidence of his extra marital misdemeanours to go to a divorce lawyer with.

But now the situation had changed dramatically. Alfie realised that if Stone caught him snooping around with his camera his first thought wasn't going to be that he'd been caught banging that woman. No, Stone was up to something here with much higher stakes than that, and how far would he go to protect himself from discovery?

Still, in for a penny, in for a pound, as Alfie's dad used to say.

The abattoir had a wide roller entrance, big enough to drive a lorry through. It was closed at the moment. There was also a person sized door leading into what looked like a small reception area, with a desk and little else.

Alfie decided to check around the rear of the abattoir before going inside. He hefted the camera in his hands, the weight awkward and unbalancing him. To be on the safe side he had hung the strap around his neck, but the lens was so bloody heavy that if he dropped it, the whole thing would just pull him over anyway.

The abattoir was huge, and it took Alfie a little while to walk all the way around it. Apart from two fire escape doors, both firmly shut, there were no other entrances or exits.

And there was no sight of that woman, either. Had she given up and left? Or had Stone let her in through one of the doors at the back?

When the two goons with the Range Rover had left, they had let the door swing shut behind them. But the latch hadn't caught. Alfie pushed at the door and it opened. On the floor he could see scuff marks where they had given up trying to carry the big man and had dragged him inside instead.

The faint smell of blood and raw meat hung in the air, even out here in the tiny office. Metal shelves lined the back wall of the office, stacked high with folders. A coating of dust covered the desk, with its ancient IBM computer, an electronic typewriter and an old fashioned telephone. Sheets of paper were scattered across the floor, looked like invoices and inventories.

The place was obviously abandoned, and had been for a good long time. What had happened that production had to be ceased and the building left like this? Maybe the meat had been contaminated through shoddy hygiene protocols, and the company had been shut down and prosecuted.

Alfie imagined that when this place had been in full operation it would get pretty noisy. But today the building was silent. Apart from quiet, muffled voices, somewhere deeper in the abattoir. Alfie followed the sound, walking through the office and pushing slowly at another door.

The voices grew louder.

Alfie walked around a channel in the floor, crusted with a brown stain which he guessed was dried blood. There was an opening ahead, but his view of the next room was obscured by long, wide strips of opaque plastic. Pushing one of them aside he peered through the gap.

The big man he had seen being dragged inside was hanging from a meat hook. Stone was standing in front of him, and they were talking.

Alfie swallowed, suddenly nervous.

Whatever the hell was going on here he didn't like it one bit. Maybe he was in a little too deep now. Whatever Stone was up to, it wasn't good. And Alfie had done his research, had a pretty good idea what this man was capable of. If Alfie were to be discovered in here, with his D4, he wasn't sure what Stone would do.

But it wouldn't be pretty.

Best to get out now before he was noticed.

Alfie slipped between the plastic strips and ducked down behind a row of sinks bolted to a low wall. What possessed him to ignore his instinct to run, he couldn't say. Perhaps it was the excitement, after a lifetime of mindless jobs revolving around unfaithful partners. The lure of danger, the risk, the intrigue.

Hugging the D4 closer to him, Alfie strained to hear what the two men were saying.

* * *

Coffin watched Stone pacing up and down. He kept checking his watch, and then his mobile. Neither of them had spoken since Stone had explained his intentions to Coffin.

Didn't seem much point in talking. Stone had obviously made up his mind about killing Coffin in the most gruesome way possible. All they were waiting for was the arrival of Stone's wife. Once he had his audience, that was it. Maybe there would be another reprieve of a few moments while Stone made some idiotic speech about revenge, but then he would flick the switch and Coffin would begin the descent into the open maw of the meat grinder.

And Coffin couldn't think of a single thing he could do to stop him.

Maybe Stone's wife, when she arrived, would be horrified at what she found. Maybe she would talk her husband into letting him down, taking him to the police instead.

Maybe Coffin could gnaw his way free of his bonds and then grow a pair of wings and fly away to freedom.

Coffin was used to taking action. If he saw a problem, he attacked it head on. Never much had the patience for sitting down and discussing things. Something needed to be done, you just went ahead and got it done, in his opinion. That was what was wrong with the world today, too much talking going on. Not enough action.

But right now, all Coffin had left was his voice. Tied up like a chicken ready to go in the oven, he was utterly helpless. Which left him no option but to attempt to talk his way out this mess.

If Emma was here he knew what she would say to that.

Oh, shit. You're fucked.

Coffin knew he couldn't appeal to Stone's better nature. Beside the fact that he wasn't sure he had one, Coffin wouldn't know where to start. He couldn't remember the last time he had tried appealing to anyone's better nature. And he sure has hell didn't have it in him to start begging for his life.

Maybe that would change when the meat grinder started up, and Coffin's feet were only inches away from the whirring blades.

Or maybe he could talk to Stone about his son. Talk about why he had ended up living in a filthy squat in Birmingham, injecting himself with shit and filing his teeth down to points so he could pretend to be a vampire. His girlfriend, she had pointy teeth, too. She must have been the one to identify Coffin. Should have killed her, too.

Tom Mills was still fucking Coffin's life up, even though he was dead. If he hadn't lied to Coffin about who had murdered Steffanie and Michael, he wouldn't be here right now. And Stone's son would still be alive.

What would that mean to Stone, though? It didn't seem much like the two of them had been close before Coffin had put that bullet in the back of his boy's head. With all the resources that Stone evidently had, why was he letting his son live that shitty life?

Coffin looked at Stone, still pacing up and down.

"You ever thought to yourself that maybe I did your boy a favour?" Coffin said.

Stone stopped walking. Turned around.

"What did you say?"

"Your son, he was a fuck up, right? You ever try straightening him out?"

Stone walked closer.

Stared up at Coffin.

"What are you trying to do, Coffin? Rile me, goad me into doing something stupid?"

"Nope. Just trying to make conversation. It's getting a little boring up here."

Stone grinned. "You've got balls, I'll give you that."

He turned his back on Coffin, began walking away again.

"But I was thinking," Coffin said. "Seems to me that if I hadn't shot your son, if he was still living in that crappy flat, boning that skanky girlfriend of his and rotting his brain with whatever fucking crap he was stuffing up his nose or in his veins, I was thinking, would you even have remembered you still had a son?"

Stone stopped walking again. Didn't turn around this time, just kept his back to Coffin.

"I seriously doubt you would. Poor bastard was an embarrassment to you, right? What are you, ex-army, something like that?"

Stone turned around. "You're observant."

"It's the way you walk, the way you hold yourself. I'm betting you were SAS, or SBS maybe."

"And your point is?"

"My fucking point is this, that if your boy was such an embarrassment to you, I would have thought you'd have been glad to see the back of him. No more chances of him turning up on your doorstep, begging for a handout so he could score some crack. You should be thanking me for putting that bullet in his brain, instead of all this stupid shit."

Coffin's words hung in the silence between them. If Stone was getting riled by Coffin's words, he was doing a good job of hiding it. He stared impassively at Coffin. Didn't matter what Coffin said, he was the one trussed up like a Christmas turkey and hanging from a meat hook, whilst Stone had the freedom to do whatever the hell he wanted.

"This whole sorry mess started with the murder of your family," Stone said. "You wanted revenge, and you took my son's life in exchange for your son. But you got it wrong. I'm doing the same as you, only I made sure to get my facts right."

"What about this vampire cult he was a part of? You find anything out about them?"

Stone checked his watch. "Lucy should be here any minute now. Then the fun will start."

"You didn't answer my question."

"No, I didn't bother looking into their sordid little club. Why would I? I found out who murdered Isaac, I didn't need to know the details of his pathetic little life, now did I?"

Coffin tried shifting slightly, to alleviate the pain in his back and shoulders. His hands had gone numb and even if Stone were to let him free right now Coffin doubted he would be able to do anything other than lie on the floor in agony. The pins and needles in his arms as his circulation started up again was going to be extremely uncomfortable.

But nothing compared to being turned into minced meat.

"So, he meant fuck all to you," Coffin said. "How long had he been a junkie, Stone? How long had he been shagging Little Miss Vampirella and filing his teeth into cute little points? You must have been so proud of him. Did you brag about him, Stone? Those two goons who killed my friends and drugged me, did they know what a fine, upstanding young man your son had turned into?"

Stone said nothing. But Coffin could see a nerve twitching in his jaw.

"You got any more children?" Coffin said. "You looking forward to seeing them take the same path?"

"My family are my own concern, Coffin," Stone said.

"Is your wife bringing the family with her? She should bring a blanket and a hamper of food, you could all have yourselves a picnic while you watch me being ground down into mince. Maybe make burgers out of me afterward."

Stone's mobile vibrated into life. He held it to his ear, listened, spoke a few words.

Slipped the phone into his pocket.

"She's here. She'll want to talk to you."

Coffin rolled his eyes. "Great. I can only hope that she's not as tedious as you."

Stone turned his back on Coffin and walked away.

Coffin thought through his options.

Nothing had changed.

Looked like today was the day he died.

Fuck that, he thought.

meat grinder

Leola watched as Lucy Stone drove into the parking area, and stopped the car behind her husband's. Lying flat out on the roof of a neighbouring warehouse, Leola's sharp eyes had a perfect view of Garrett Stone's wife. She was beautiful, but cold. Even from this distance, Leola had the impression of a woman who demanded to be the one in control.

She couldn't imagine the two of them having loving sex. It would be more like a battlefield, a war to see who could dominate, be the one in control. No wonder Stone preferred being on top. It had nothing to do with the view, or any other stupid shit he might say. It had everything to do with feeling emasculated underneath a woman, of not being in charge.

Leola kept down low as Lucy Stone locked her car and then made her way into the abattoir. Dressed in a smart business suit, she looked out of place here, an alien body in a hostile environment. But Leola had no doubt in her mind that she could take care of herself.

As Lucy Stone disappeared through the door, Leola noticed her hand slipping around behind her back, feeling for something, checking it was secure.

Was she carrying a gun?

A wave of giddiness washed over Leola and she put her head down, cheek against the hard, dusty flat roof. To Leola's heightened senses, the rich, coppery smell of blood was strong, even though the abattoir had been abandoned for many years. The desire to seek out fresh, living flesh and sink her teeth into an artery was overwhelming. Leola bit down on her lip, drawing a bead of blood. Her tongue flicked out and licked it away.

How quickly her teeth had grown sharp again. The Priest had told her that her cure was an article of faith, and she had promised to hold dear to that faith, to keep that promise. But what was faith in the face of a body that revolted against her? A desire for blood, threatening to swallow up all of her self-control and leaving her at the mercy of her vampiric impulses?

Leola was back in the Louisiana mansion, amongst the bodies of the guests, the air thick with the smell of their blood. With Merek Guttman and his travelling tribe of blood sucking night creatures. All of them drowsy after a feast.

But the baby was crying. The sound cutting through the fog of inebriation, slicing open her mind, dragging her to full wakefulness.

The slaughterhouse office door slammed shut behind Lucy Stone, snapping Leola back into the present. She lifted her head and looked at the abattoir, letting the memories fade. Returning to the present.

Joe Coffin was inside that abattoir. She had seen him being dragged inside. Why had he been brought here? What did Stone want with him? Was he going to kill him?

And why did Leola care so much what happened to Coffin?

Because he killed Abel.

Was that it?

If Coffin could fight and kill Abel he had to be strong.

And Leola needed an ally to take on Guttman.

She couldn't do it by herself.

Leola watched the abattoir, as though expecting it to give her the solutions she needed. But even her finely tuned senses couldn't detect what was happening in there.

You've got to go in.

Leola closed her eyes.

Your new life is an article of faith. You have been reborn in Christ, you are of God the Father, and you are filled with the Holy Ghost.

Leola opened her eyes again.

But watch out that the serpent does not fill you with his lies, and entice you back into a life of sin and bloodlust.

She pulled herself up and began climbing down the side of the warehouse.

* * *

Coffin held Lucy Stone's gaze in his. As well as his back and shoulders being in agony, now his neck was hurting too. It was the way he was hanging from the meat hook, he had to keep lifting his head to talk to Stone. When he got down from here he was going to inflict some serious damage on these two.

Might even shove *them* through the meat grinder.

Stone's wife was an attractive woman. Obviously kept herself in shape, took care of herself. Coffin admired that in a person. But she looked colder than a winter's day in Alaska. Her face, handsome as it was, seemed set on the verge of a permanent scowl. As though the world had disappointed her, when she had expected so much more from it.

Coffin had wondered if Lucy Stone, the moment she saw the gruesome fate her husband had lined up for him, might say this was too much. Might try and persuade Stone to let Coffin down, that they couldn't feed a man through a meat grinder.

But no. If anything, Mrs Stone appeared to be a supremely cold hearted, manipulative bitch. What was it she had said when she walked into the abattoir and saw Coffin trussed up like a Christmas turkey, and dangling over a meat grinder?

Oh, Garrett. How imaginative!

Her voice dripping with sarcasm.

Lucy Stone might well flick the switch herself. Of course she would stand back, far enough that she didn't get any of his blood on her expensive suit. But she wouldn't take her eyes off Coffin once. Not until the motor on the meat grinder had burnt out from the effort of chewing up his bones.

Not until she was sure he was dead.

"Well," Coffin said, breaking the silence, "I suppose I should just come right out and say it."

"Say what?" Lucy Stone said.

"I'm sorry I killed your son. He obviously meant a lot to you, and you were very proud of him. There, does that make you feel better? Can we be friends now?"

"Is he for real?" she said.

She didn't look at Stone when she said this. Just kept her eyes fixed on Coffin.

"You want me to switch the meat grinder on now?" Stone said.

"Oh please, let's get this over with," Coffin said. "I am so fucking bored with you and your shit."

Lucy Stone glanced at her husband, and then back at Coffin. Like she couldn't take her eyes off him for more than a second at a time.

"You certainly outdid yourself this time, Garrett." Again she kept her gaze centred on Coffin while she talked to her husband. "You could have just put a bullet through his head, like he did to Isaac. Or maybe, if you'd wanted to make a big scene out of it, you could have shot his kneecaps off, and then his balls, and then put a bullet through his head. But this?" Finally she turned and looked at her husband. "Don't you think this is all a little . . . over the top?"

She turned her attention back to Coffin.

"What do you think, Mr Coffin?"

"I vote for getting me down from here and you putting a bullet through my skull."

"It will probably come to that anyway," Lucy Stone said. "This old thing will most likely give out before it's finished chewing up your legs, and by that point you will be begging me to shoot you. Of course we could just leave you to bleed out, you would soon be dead. And even if you survived, you'd only be half the man you are now. I wonder how that would feel for you, being only half Joe Coffin."

Coffin rotated his head, cricked his neck. Seemed like his entire upper half was on fire, and below the waist he was going steadily numb.

He lifted his head again, looked over at Stone standing behind his wife.

"Do you let her talk to you like this all the time?"

Stone kept his mouth shut.

"Yeah, I bet you do. You've been acting like a tough guy in front of me all this time, but really you're nothing more than a snivelling, pussy whipped, skullfucking, piece of shit. You like to think that you're the big man, a cock on legs, but you're not. You're her bitch, aren't you? I'm surprised she doesn't lead you around on a chain, and make you beg for your dinner."

"Be quiet now," Stone said.

"Fuck that, I'm only just getting started. What happened to your balls, Stone? Did they shrivel up and drop off? Or maybe your wife's got them in a jar by the side of her bed? I bet you can't even get it up, can you? What does she do for her jollies every night? Strap you face down to the bed with your arse sticking in the air and buttfuck you with a wine bottle?"

Stone glanced at his wife.

"What, you want to hide behind her skirts, Stone? Does she fight all your battles for you? If you were a real fucking man you'd let me down and we could settle this properly. But you don't have the balls to do that, because she cut them off, and ate them for breakfast."

"I'm bored with this," Lucy Stone said. "Just flip the switch and lower him down. I want to see him scream."

"Yeah, do as you're told, bitch," Coffin snarled.

Stone clenched his hands into tight little fists. Looked to Coffin like he was torn between doing what his wife had commanded him to, or rebel. The trouble was, this had been his idea all along. He needed to lower Coffin into the meat grinder.

Coffin saw the change in Stone's eyes before he made a move. Saw him make that decision.

"Fuck you, Coffin," he said.

In one swift move he stepped over to the meat grinder and flipped a switch. A deep, electrical hum stuttered into life beneath Coffin's dangling feet. Stone flipped another switch, and the hum was drowned out by a ratcheting, metallic whining. Like massive tumblers in an old lock being constantly rotated.

Coffin looked down.

Metal parts rotating, crunching together, ready to churn him up and grind him into bloody pieces.

Stone grabbed a chain hanging down to the floor and began pulling at it. Coffin glanced up, saw it was attached to a series of pulleys.

At that moment he began the slow descent towards the meat grinder's churning metal teeth.

it's complicated

Alfie sat down and took a deep breath. He couldn't believe what he was seeing. Crouching behind the row of sinks, hidden from view, he had watched Stone and Coffin talking. Then, just as he had been thinking about risking taking a couple of shots on the D4, he had heard the outside door open. Alfie had ducked back behind the sinks sharpish as he saw Lucy Stone making her way through the abattoir towards her husband and Coffin.

What the hell was she doing here? Had she known about this all along? Was this why she had told him to stop following her husband?

Bloody hell, Alfie, but you're in a bloody mess here, aren't you?

Alfie raised a shaking hand and wiped sweat off his forehead. Odd that he was sweating, it was bloody cold in here.

Alfie hefted the D4 and its enormous lens. The camera was difficult to hold in his sweat slick palms, and he had to grip it as tight as he could to keep from dropping it. Calming his breathing, Alfie tried attuning his hearing to the Stones and Coffin. They were talking again. He couldn't quite make out what they were saying, but Coffin suddenly seemed angry. Not surprising considering his current situation, but up until now he had been calm and collected.

Just what the hell was going on? Was this some kind of revenge thing the Stones were involved in? Had they found Isaac's murderer, and this was their twisted form of payback? No wonder Lucy Stone had taken Alfie off the job of tailing her husband. The last thing she would have wanted was for him to see this.

Because what were they going to do? Murder him?

Of course they're going to murder him. What did you think they were going to do? Ask him to apologise and then let him go? Tell him not to do anything like that again?

Alfie changed his grip on the D4, struggling to keep hold of it. Bloody thing seemed heavier than ever.

What the hell was he going to do?

Call the police you idiot!

As Alfie fumbled for his mobile he heard the rumble of machinery starting up. He dropped his phone into a drainage channel and it fell down the wide hole where blood and bodily fluids from animal carcasses drained away.

Oh shit!

There was nothing he could do now. Whatever the hell they were doing over there, and Alfie was thinking he might have an idea but it was too horrific to contemplate, he needed to get the hell out. Get somewhere he could find someone with a phone and then call the police.

It would be too late to save that poor bastard hanging from the meat hook, but at least the police might catch Mr and Mrs Stone before they got the hell out of here.

Alfie braced himself, ready to run for the exit in a low crouch.

But then he thought of his camera, and that great big lens he had been lugging around.

Thought maybe he should get himself a photograph before he left. He could show it to the police, use it as evidence. He switched the camera on, set the zoom to 400mm. Got up on his knees, straightened up until he could see Coffin hanging from the chain.

Garrett Stone was pulling on a chain, lowering him down. Lucy Stone was watching, her hands on her hips. Alfie raised the camera to eye level, and framed the three of them in viewfinder. The lens was too bloody heavy though, and the image was shaking around so much he could hardly keep the three of them in the same shot. Bloody picture was going to be blurred as hell too, with all that camera shake.

The low wall he was hiding behind, with the metal sinks bolted to it, that would make a good place to rest the lens on, stabilise the picture.

Eye glued to the viewfinder, Alfie leant forward to carefully rest the end of the lens on the wall.

But he misjudged the distance. The heavy lens fell forward, the momentum carrying Alfie behind it. The clang of the camera hitting the metal sink reverberated around the empty abattoir.

When Alfie looked up he saw Garrett Stone and Lucy Stone were both staring at him.

* * *

Coffin had to bend his knees and lift his feet up under his backside to avoid the spinning metal teeth of the meat grinder. The one mistake Stone had made when he bound Coffin up was not tying his ankles together. If he timed it just right, and his numb legs didn't give way underneath him, he could straddle the open maw of the meat grinder and plant his feet on the ledge either side.

After that he wasn't sure what he was going to do.

Stone was going to have to climb up onto the ledge to attempt to push him back out over the meat grinder again, and Coffin could only hope that he might be able to fight him off.

Of course that left Lucy Stone, and Coffin had no doubt that she was carrying a gun somewhere on her person. But he could only think of one thing at a time, and right now that was working on how to prevent his feet from being shredded into tiny little scraps of bone and flesh.

The clang of something heavy being dropped in a steel basin echoed around the abattoir. Coffin's descent towards the mincing machine was halted as Stone stopped pulling on the chain and looked towards the disturbance.

Coffin didn't bother checking out who or what had made the noise. This was his chance. He kicked his feet back and then underneath and out in front to try and propel his body into a swing. He was close enough to the ledge that he could have planted his feet on there from where he was, but then his arse would still have been hanging over the meat grinders spinning teeth and he wouldn't have had the leverage to stand up straight.

Coffin managed to create a tiny bit of movement, but not enough. He immediately kicked back and out again, and then again. Garrett and Lucy Stone both had their backs to him, and they were running over to the source of the disturbance.

One last kick and the chain swung Coffin over the ledge enough that he was able to plant his feet on the side and lean forward, to keep from falling backwards.

Coffin snapped his teeth together as his numb legs erupted into red hot flames of pins and needles. The machinery rumbled on behind him, only inches away. One slip or stumble and he would fall back into the grinding, spinning teeth, and then he would be dog food.

Hunched over, Coffin tried inching his way forward, but the meat hook stopped him. He couldn't move forward and he could move backward.

Stone glanced back, and his eyes widened as he spotted Coffin. With a shout of dismay and anger he started running back.

Fuck! One good shove and I'm in the grinder! Coffin thought. *Stand up at least before that bastard gets to you.*

Coffin stood up straight, his legs protesting at the sudden movement. With the sudden slack on the chain the meat hook slipped from beneath Coffin's bonds and fell, to dangle over the meat grinder.

Stone leapt up onto the ledge beside Coffin. Before he could make another move, Coffin head butted him, smashing his forehead into Stone's nose.

He fell off the ledge and onto the abattoir floor.

Coffin followed him, using the other man as a cushion to soften his landing. Stone expelled a bellow of air when Coffin landed on top of him, blood spraying from his busted nose in a red mist. The noise of the machinery was overwhelming down here, beside the meat grinder.

When Stone tried to push him off, Coffin head-butted him again. Even over the noise of the meat grinder, Coffin heard Stone's nose snap. Rolling off him, Coffin lay on his back, panting. The pins and needles in his legs were starting to wear off, and he thought he could risk standing up. But his back and shoulders were red hot with pain, and he needed to get his hands free before Stone's wife returned.

Coffin struggled into a sitting position.

There was no sign of Lucy Stone. Whatever the disturbance had been had taken her away, and she probably had no idea Coffin was free. He swivelled himself around onto his knees and then stood up.

Registered movement on the periphery of his vision at the moment he realised Stone had gone. The swish of air over Coffin's head as he ducked, Stone narrowly missing piercing Coffin's head with a barbed meat hook in his hand. Looked like a giant fishing hook.

Coffin kicked out, smashing his foot into Garrett Stone's thigh, sending him howling to the floor. The movement overbalanced Coffin, and he stumbled and then fell on his back into a drain, dark with crusted blood. With his hands tied behind his back he couldn't break his fall, and the impact jarred his spine, sending spikes of pain up his back and neck and into his skull.

Stone dragged himself to his feet first, and limped over to Coffin. In his right hand he held the meat hook, and his face was split wide with a crazed grin, his teeth white against the mask of blood from his broken nose.

"You killed my son, Coffin," he shouted. "You don't deserve to live."

Coffin kicked out at Stone again, but he was ready and stepped out of the way. Before Coffin had chance to move, Stone had kicked him in the thigh, deadening all sensation in his leg. Then he lifted his foot and smashed his boot down hard on Coffin's knee, the same knee that Clevon had kicked earlier that day.

His deadened thigh exploded with pain, along with rest of his leg. Stone walked alongside Coffin's prostrate form until he reached his head and then kicked him in the temple. A wave of darkness washed over Coffin along with searing bolts of pain and a high pitched humming that was even louder than the rumble of the meat grinder. When his sight returned and the pain receded enough to allow him conscious thought, Coffin saw that Stone was squatting over him.

He held a meat hook in each hand now.

"You know what I'm going to do?" he shouted. "I'm going to stick these through your eyeballs, and then hoist you up by your eye sockets. And then I'm going to lower you into the meat grinder, inch by fucking inch. I'm going to take my time enjoying this one."

Stone walked around behind Coffin. Coffin's head was still spinning from the kick, his vision greying in and out. Like a vision from hell, Stone's face filled Coffin's view, a grinning red mask of hate and insanity. He leaned in close.

"Fuck you, Coffin," he said. "Your days of shooting defenceless kids in the back of the head are over now."

Coffin spat in his eyes. Stone jerked back instinctively and Coffin rolled over. On his front he got his knees under his chest, ready to push himself upright. Still holding onto the two meat hooks, Stone kicked him again. This time the kick went wild, glanced off Coffin's hip without any real power. But it was enough to push him over again and onto his back.

Before Stone could make another move, Coffin smashed his boots into Stone's ankles and then scooped his feet out from beneath him. Throwing the meat hooks up into the air with a cry of surprise, Stone flipped over and smacked his head against the concrete drainage channel.

He was out cold.

Coffin rolled over onto his side, panting heavily.

Got to free my arms before that bitch comes back, he thought. *There must be something around here I can use.*

Rolling onto his front he pushed himself up onto his knees. He had to wait a moment then, let the dizziness subside. His sight was clearer now, at least, but his head still throbbed like a bastard, pounding in time to the powerful rhythm of the meat grinder.

Coffin stood up. Legs a little shaky, but okay.

On the floor, Stone groaned, and his eyelids fluttered open.

Coffin kicked him in the head.

"Stay down you fucker," Coffin muttered.

He walked away from Stone, past rows of S shaped meat hooks hanging from a rail, and away from the meat grinder.

No sign of Lucy Stone. Whatever had caused that noise, it had spooked them enough that Mrs Stone was out of action for the moment dealing with it. Maybe someone had been spying on them. One of Craggs' men?

But although Danny hadn't kept it a secret where they were going to dispose of the bodies, neither had he been that specific. Coffin couldn't see how anybody would know where he was. Not unless somebody had been following them.

Right now that didn't matter. What he had to do was concentrate on freeing himself and then getting the hell out of here.

Maybe deal with Stone first, though.

Coffin found a section of wall with a sheet of stamped metal bolted to it. Part of the metal had been ripped away along its side, leaving a jagged edge. Coffin was able to back up to it and start sawing at the rope around his wrists. It took him a few minutes until the rope finally snapped and began unravelling.

With his arms free, Coffin massaged life back into his muscles.

Couldn't waste too much time, though. Get out of this place before the killer bitch returned. If she caught him here still, the odds were stacked against him. She had a gun, and he didn't have that much fight left in him anyway.

Coffin returned to Stone. He was still out cold. Couldn't leave him alive, the bastard would just come after him again.

"Turn around."

Coffin closed his eyes.

Oh shit.

"I said turn around."

Coffin opened his eyes and slowly turned around. Lucy Stone was holding a gun on him, a handgun of some sort, Coffin wasn't really sure. Looked to be on the small side, but he had a feeling Stone's wife was a crack shot.

"Put your hands on your head, and then get down on your knees," she said.

"Aren't you going to shoot me?" he said.

"Just fucking do it!"

Coffin did as he was told.

"Where's Garrett?" Lucy Stone said.

Coffin looked over at Stone lying on his back, still out cold. Realised Lucy Stone couldn't see him from where she was standing.

"He's taking a nap," he said, and tilted his head to indicate where Stone was lying.

She moved closer, looked at her husband. Coffin couldn't read her expression that well, but he was sure there was no compassion in there. Maybe disgust, or a weary disappointment.

"Is he dead?"

"Do you care?" Coffin said.

"You're right, it doesn't matter," she said.

"You're a cold bitch, aren't you?"

"Did Garrett ask you why you killed Isaac?"

"Yeah, he did," Coffin said. "I told him—"

"I don't give a shit what you told him. I don't care why you killed Isaac. He was an embarrassment, a total fuck up."

"You don't mince your words, do you?"

"He was weak, just like his father."

Coffin shifted position slightly, trying to ease out a kink in his back.

"Don't move!"

"Easy," Coffin said. "I'm not going to jump you or anything, I'm just trying to get a little more comfortable. It's not easy kneeling with my hands on my head after spending the last hour hanging from a meat hook."

"Lie down."

Coffin sighed. "Really?"

"Yes, really. Lie down, face down and put your hands on your head again."

"What if I said no?"

Lucy Stone shot him.

Coffin doubled over as the bullet hit him in the gut. A red bloom of blood blossomed on his T-shirt and began spreading. Clutching at his stomach, blood oozing between his fingers, Coffin pitched slowly forward, his cheek scraping against the concrete floor.

Waves of pain radiated from the pit of his stomach and up through his chest and down into his groin. Already there was a growing pool of blood on the floor, the coppery smell swamping his senses. Through the pain he was vaguely aware of Lucy Stone walking past him, around and behind him. What was she going to do? Shoot him again? In the back of the head, the way he murdered Isaac?

Coffin screamed as a red hot knife sliced into his back. The blade punctured deeper, probing, scraping against bone. He tried to crawl away, but something held him back. The knife was caught in his back, it had a hooked blade, and the hook was caught beneath his shoulder blade.

A wave of nausea rolled over him as the pressure on his shoulder blade increased, and Coffin was slowly pulled upwards. It wasn't a knife at all, the thing in his back was a meat hook.

And it was hoisting him into the air.

Coffin let go of his stomach and grabbed at the chain behind him, and over his head. Tried to release the intolerable pressure on his back by lifting himself up, but his hands were too slippy with blood.

Back on his knees now, his shoulder blade was being pulled so tight it felt like it was about to pop out of his back. Now Coffin's knees lifted off the floor, and although he hadn't thought it possible the pain in his back notched up to an even frighteningly higher level.

Up he went a little more, in agonising, incremental jerks. Each one another scrape of metal against bone, another sickening bout of pain. Coffin tried to stand, to ease the pressure beneath his shoulder blade, but his feet slipped in the dark pool of blood on the ground.

His blood.

As his feet scrabbled for purchase on the blood slick floor, Coffin slowly rotated on the hook until he could see Lucy Stone. A sheen of sweat on her face, she was pulling on a chain, hoisting him higher. The chain was on a pulley system, and attached to a mechanism beneath a rail in the ceiling. The rail ran over the meat grinder, its metal teeth still churning and rumbling.

Coffin groaned through clenched teeth as he was hoisted higher and higher. The blood on his hands was drying out, becoming stickier, but still he couldn't get any purchase on the chain to relieve the pain of the hook piercing his back.

Lucy Stone stopped pulling on the chain, stepped back to take a good look at him. Her breath came in short, sharp gasps. She wiped a hand across her forehead.

"Good, you're still conscious. I thought you might have passed out by now."

Coffin groaned again. His sight greyed out, went to black and then returned to grey again. Despite the agony he was acutely aware of the blood running down his legs and splattering on the floor.

Lucy Stone approached Coffin. Planting her hands in his back, she gave him a good shove. The chain juddered along the rail, moving Coffin towards the meat grinder. She gave him another shove, grunting as she put all her strength into it.

The meat hook travelled closer to the meat grinder. Coffin's boots bumped into the ledge. She hadn't hoisted him quite high enough, and Coffin was able to plant his feet on the lip of the meat grinder, and take the pressure off the point of the hook scraping against the inside of his shoulder blade.

Blood ran down his legs from the bullet wound in his stomach, forming pools on the meat grinder's concrete lip. Everything greyed out again, and for a moment Coffin thought he might faint. But then the world came back into focus, and he gripped the chain above his head tighter.

And started to lift himself up.

"No! No!" Lucy Stone shouted.

Coffin roared, a primal, guttural scream as he focused all his strength and willpower into his arms, lifting his bodyweight up until the pointed end of the meat hook slid from his flesh.

"No!" Lucy Stone screamed again as she scrambled up onto the ledge beside Coffin.

Her shoes slipped in Coffin's blood, her arms cartwheeled for a moment that seemed to last forever, and then she fell.

Coffin clenched his jaw, willing himself to stay upright. If he fainted now, he would fall into the churning teeth beside him.

Lucy Stone was hanging onto the chain dangling over the meat grinder, her feet still on the ledge, her body at a forty-five degree angle. She stared at Coffin, eyes wide, lips peeled back in a snarl.

Coffin looked back at her. She was stuck. All he had to do was reach out a hand and pull her to safety.

He kicked her feet out from beneath her.

Her scream was cut short as she fell into the meat grinder's churning teeth. Her body flipped over, wide eyes beseeching Coffin for help before the skin was torn from its skull. She tried to lift an arm but her torso was flipped over again by the rotating teeth, and her arm disappeared in a fountain of scarlet blood.

Coffin watched until her body had disappeared completely, consumed by the machine's revolving metal teeth.

And it was as though she had never existed.

A bullet whizzed past his temple, smacked into the wall.

Slowly, carefully, Coffin shifted his weak, sluggish body around until he saw Stone. He had Lucy's gun. And he was pointing it directly at Coffin's head.

"You don't look too good," he said.

"I feel just great," Coffin replied, but his voice was sluggish, and he had to speak slowly to get the words right.

"I'm going to kill you now," Stone said.

"Yeah, I know," Coffin replied.

A dark shadow fell from the ceiling. A monstrosity of arms and legs, enveloping Stone in its embrace. The shadow landed on top of him, throwing him to the floor. The gun skittered across the concrete.

Coffin put all his diminishing willpower into focusing on what was happening.

"Leola?" Stone cried.

Coffin recognised her now. She was straddling Stone on the ground, pinning his wrists in place, her hips on his. She hovered her face over his a moment.

And then she sank her teeth into his neck.

* * *

"You're a vampire," Coffin said.

He was sitting propped up against a wall. More blood was gathering beneath him, spreading outwards.

"Yes," Leola replied.

"Are you going to drink my blood?"

"No." Leola looked back at Stone's corpse, his throat ripped open. "I've already had my fill."

Coffin licked his lips, tried to concentrate on what he needed to say.

"But we saw you, in daylight."

"I know. It's complicated."

Sirens, in the distance, growing louder.

Coffin lifted an arm. Felt like he had a dumbbell in his hand. He pointed at Stone.

"Is he coming back?"

"Maybe."

"Do me a favour." Coffin licked his lips again. Swallowed. "Get rid of him."

Leola nodded.

She lifted Stone's corpse like he was a feather, and carried him over to the meat grinder. She threw him inside, and watched as the teeth chewed him up.

When he had gone, she turned the machine off.

The sirens were much closer.

"I should go now," she said.

Coffin nodded, and closed his eyes.

When he opened them again, she was gone.

emma

Barry popped open a can of lager and drank straight from it. He was going to get filthy drunk tonight, completely and utterly shit-faced. Maybe go out later, down to the Blockade, see if he could chat up that barmaid some more.

What the hell was her name? Beverly? Beatrice? Belinda?

Fuck knew.

Barry finished the can and threw it in the kitchen sink. He pulled another one out of the pack he had bought on the way back to his flat earlier, and popped the tab on that one.

No, he was going to stay in tonight. Get so fucking drunk he wouldn't be able to remember his own name.

Maybe that way he could forget about Karl for a while.

Wasn't going to work, though.

Barry put the fresh can to his mouth and tipped his head back. Drank the lager down in one. Had to put his free hand on the kitchen counter to steady himself. When he had finished he dropped that one in the sink with its companion, and opened up another.

He looked at the can for a while, the lager frothing out of the opening in its top.

And then he realised he was crying.

A spoken word, a name, filtered through into his brain. The television was on in the living room, the sound of it drifting through the open door into the kitchen. The speaker was a news reporter, and he was saying something important.

Barry walked into the living room, stood in front of the TV, can of lager in his hand dripping onto the carpet.

Something about a crazed woman found wandering the city centre, clutching at a bloody wound in her neck. She was rambling, incoherent. A photograph appeared on the screen.

Barry dropped the can. Lager fizzed from its opening, spreading across the carpet.

"Emma," Barry whispered.

* * *

As the afternoon wore on the cloud cover increased once more and then the rain started falling. The white transit van sat alone, abandoned. The rain pattered against its roof, and mingled with the pools of blood on the ground, leaking from the two bodies lying next to it.

Brendan lay on his back, staring sightless at the sky, the raindrops falling on his eyes, running over his face. Danny 'The Butcher' Hanrahan lay in a crumpled heap, blood and bone and brains splattered over the ground next to him.

The rear doors of the van were open, just as they had been left by Shocker and Shank.

And all was still, and silent.

But if there had been anybody around later that afternoon, they would have seen some movement. The van rocking slightly, as something inside stirred.

And then they would have seen a hand reach out from inside the van, and slam the doors shut.

JOE COFFIN

SEASON THREE

sneak preview
joe coffin season three

the seven ghosts

Coffin was back on the Fatboy. It was good. He headed into the city, used the time on the bike to forget about the dreams, forget about Leola and Michael. He headed down to Edwards Number Nine. The evening was closing in, and lights flickered on in the pubs and the clubs.

Coffin had slept most of the day, and now here he was wide awake and ready to stay up all night. Seemed like he was turning into a vampire himself. Now he was free again he felt vulnerable. Had to stay alert, and that meant not sleeping. Not at night. Not anymore.

Coffin parked the bike and had a good look around. A car drove past him. Bland colours, bland design, Coffin wasn't even sure what make it was. He watched it take a corner at the end of the road and disappear from view.

Edwards was quiet, but later on it would be full of kids. That was how it had always been. Craggs had always said that Angels was for the sophisticated man, which made Coffin chuckle. But Edwards was for the kids, the grungy rock kids.

Stut met him at the door.

"Hey J-J-Joe, it's good t-to see you."

Coffin shook his hand, glanced around. "How's things here?"

"You know, s-s-s-same as ever."

Stut's black hair was piled up on his head in a rockabilly quiff. He wore a black leather jacket over white T-shirt and jeans. In amongst all the indie rock and Emo kids he looked about as comfortable as a vegetarian at a hog roast.

"How's the leg?" Coffin said.

Stut had accidentally shot himself in the thigh at Angels when he first encountered Guttman.

"It's g-g-g-good, I don't even l-limp anymore."

"Mort put you in charge of this place?"

"N-no, Gilligan did," Stut said. "The place was c-c-c-closed while I was in h-h-hospital. With Rob dead, they had n-n-n-no one to run it."

"And so as soon as you were out, Gilligan put you in charge. You talk to Mort about it?"

"N-no. Is there a p-p-p-problem, Joe?"

Coffin clapped him on the back. "Of course not, just catching up on what's been going on while I've been away."

"You w-w-want a drink, Joe? On the house."

"Sure."

They found Coffin a bottle of Old Crow and Stut poured him a generous slug. Coffin stood at the bar. Watched the place filling up with kids. Long hair, ripped clothes, studs, tattoos. Coffin fit in about as much as Stut did.

A few of the kids recognised him and stayed out of his way. Some of the others didn't, but stayed out of his way anyway. The music got ramped up, indie rock mainly. A fight broke out, nothing more than a spat, really. Coffin stayed out of the way, let the bouncers deal with it. Saw a long haired lad weaving his way through the crowd, high as a kite.

Coffin decided it was time to check outside.

It was full dark out, street lights on, pavements busy with clubbers. A car parked further down the road, on the opposite side. Bland colour, bland design. Easy to miss.

Coffin walked away from it, round the corner. There, that was it. Exactly what he had been waiting for.

A Chinese man, young, chubby, talking with one of the indie rock kids. Performing a transaction in a shadowed doorway. Coffin caught a glimpse of a tinfoil package exchanging hands. No money.

Coffin pulled the kid away by the scruff of his jacket, yanked him around so they were face to face.

"Get the hell out of here," he said. He pulled the packet off the kid, squeezed it in his fist and dropped it on the ground. "Go home, back to mummy."

The kid turned and ran.

Coffin grabbed the Chinese man before he could get away. Slammed him up against the door.

"What's your name?" he said.

"L-Lester." Eyes wide, chubby lips trembling.

"All right then, Luh-Lester, this is how it is," Coffin said. "You don't get to hand this shit out around here anymore. You want to sell it? Fine. The Slaughter-house Mob gets thirty percent."

"No way!" Lester said. "That's too much, man."

"Of course it isn't," Coffin said. "You're giving the shit away at the moment, so what's thirty percent?"

"Mr Xian will never agree to that."

"Jimmy Xian will agree to whatever I tell him to agree to." Coffin shoved Lester harder against the door. "You got more supplies?"

Lester shook his head.

Coffin let go of him. "Empty your pockets."

Lester shook his head again.

Coffin smacked him around the side of the head and Lester crumpled to the ground. Coffin picked him up.

"I said empty your pockets."

Lester shook his head again. His lips were trembling.

Coffin smacked him in the face and Lester crumpled again. Coffin picked him up. Lester's lips were bleeding.

"We can do this all night if you like," Coffin said.

Lester emptied his pockets. Dropped silver tin foil packets all over the ground.

Coffin stepped back. "Get the fuck out of here. Go tell Jimmy I'm coming to see him. Maybe tonight, maybe not."

Lester eyeballed Coffin, tried putting on a tough attitude. "You should watch out, be careful. You don't want to mess with the Seven Ghosts."

Coffin stepped in close, smacked Lester across the side of the head. Coffin caught Lester before he hit the ground again.

"Say that to me again," he growled.

Lester wiped blood off his lip with the back of his hand. Shook his head. Coffin punched him in the face. Just a gentle tap. Lester hit the ground hard. Coffin grabbed him by his jacket collars and hauled him to his feet. Blood ran from Lester's nose and down his chin. His left eye was blossoming into a bruise.

"Say that to me again or I will hit you so hard you won't wake up for a week," Coffin said.

"You don't want to mess with the Seven Ghosts," Lester mumbled.

"And just who the fuck are the Seven Ghosts?" Coffin said.

"A Triad faction," Lester said.

"Are you one of them?"

Lester nodded, kept his gaze averted from Coffin.

"And what about the club, Angels?" Coffin said. "Is that who's in there now?"

Lester nodded again. Wiped his sleeve across his bloodied chin.

"You really don't want to mess with them," he said. "There are some bad motherfuckers in that club now."

"Yeah, I know."

Coffin let go of Lester and his legs gave way. He slid down the door and to the ground.

Coffin walked back out onto the main road. The bland car with its bland colours and bland design was still parked up where Coffin had seen it last.

He walked on over, casual like.

Tapped on the window.

The man inside cranked the window down.

"Can I help you?"

Coffin grabbed him by the back of the head and smacked his face against the steering wheel. The car horn let out a short, sharp honk.

"What the fuck?"

The man looked up at Coffin, eyes wide and tearing up. The VW logo was imprinted on his forehead.

Coffin smashed his head against the steering wheel again. This time he heard the crunch of bone underneath the car horn. Pulled the man back upright again. His nose was bent sideways. Blood poured from it, dripped on his shirt.

Coffin knelt down next to the car, got on the same eye level as the driver.

"Why are you following me? Did someone put you up to it?"

The man in the car said nothing. Touched his nose and winced.

"Fucking hell, you broke my nose."

"Who's paying you to follow me?" Coffin said.

"Fuck you."

Coffin smashed his head against the steering wheel again. The car horn honked again.

"Who's paying you to follow me?"

The man licked blood and snot off his lips. Gasped at the pain.

"Fuck you," he said.

Coffin smacked his face against the steering wheel. Once, twice, three times. The car horn honked every time.

His eyes rolled back in his head, and Coffin thought he was going to black out. He recovered.

"Are you enjoying this?" Coffin said. "We can keep going if you like."

"Archer," the man said, his voice thick with phlegm and blood.

"Detective Nick Archer?"

The man nodded. Coffin let go of his head.

"Go tell Archer to find himself another lackey," Coffin said. "You're quitting."

The man nodded again.

Coffin returned to his bike, got back on it. As he drove past the car he saw the man inspecting his broken nose in the rear mirror.

Coffin headed on over to Angels. Parked the Fatboy where he could see the front entrance, but he was out of the way. There was a crowd milling around outside. Didn't look like the usual sort of crowd. Lots of flesh showing. Black

an american werewolf
in london

Looking at the wall of DVDs, row after row of horror movies collected over years and years, he realised he was spoilt for choice. And not in a good way.

Darren Dilnott ran his fingers along the spines of the DVD cases, reading the familiar titles.

Basket Case, The House by the Cemetery, Suspiria, Anthropophogus, The New York Ripper, Freaks.

He had been a horror fan ever since he first crept downstairs late one night as a child, and watched *Terror Express* on the TV, the sound turned down so low he could barely hear it. His parents, strict Methodists, would have been horrified if they had known what he was doing.

So he sat there in the dark, his parents asleep upstairs, and almost cried with fear as he watched Peter Cushing, an actor he grew to love and already knew from *Star Wars*, hunting down a monster on the Siberian Express. Tame even then, the film still scared the young Darren enough that he was hooked on films, and horror films in particular, from that moment on.

Now he was a grown up, and held a collection of DVD and Blu-ray films so huge that most of them were in trunks in the loft. And some of them were so bad he doubted he would ever watch them again.

But here, lining one whole wall of the living room, were his favourites and his newer, unwatched purchases. Film posters in frames decorated the other walls, and there was a fifty inch HD screen mounted at the one end of the living room, with surround sound cabled in discreetly behind the plaster board.

It was a movie lover's paradise.

And with Julia gone, he had it all to himself now.

Darren pulled a DVD case off the shelf and looked at its garish cover. *Zombi!* Julia had hated his obsession with horror movies. She was more of a romcom girl, chick flicks. Saturday night, they'd decide to sit in with a bottle of wine and some snacks, and watch a film together. More often than not, by the time they'd finished arguing about what they wanted to watch, they had eaten the snacks and drunk the wine, and the evening was half over.

And when they did agree on something it was always a disaster. Either she got her way, and Darren had to sit through an awful, saccharine story featuring that sack of irritating non-talent that was Jennifer Aniston, or he got his way and Julia sat next to him emanating waves of disapproval and disgust as they watched one of his all-time favourites.

Seriously, what had he been thinking when he asked her to move in with him? Maybe it had been the sex. He had to admit, she was pretty good at that.

But now she was gone, and Darren was on his own again. It was a relief, if he was honest with himself. No amount of fantastic sex could compensate for her constant whining, and her demands, and especially her insistence that they start thinking about having a child.

What the hell did he want a kid for? Bloody snotty, whingeing, annoying shits. And he knew what would happen next. As soon as they had a child in the house, Julie would have demanded that Darren get rid of all his DVDs. That it wasn't a suitable environment for a child.

So yeah, it was a bloody good job she was gone.

Now he had all the time and the freedom to watch what he wanted.

But he was spoilt for choice. Couldn't make his mind up. Felt like if he had a smaller collection, if he had less of a choice, it would be easier for him to make a decision. He was even thinking about venturing into the loft and opening up the trunks, having a sift through his collection up there.

Bloody stupid idea.

How ironic. His first Saturday night of freedom in years, when he could watch exactly what he wanted when he wanted without Julia sitting next to him with a face on her like she was sucking a lemon, and he couldn't make up his mind.

Darren ran his hand up and down the shelves of DVDs and abruptly chose one at random.

An American Werewolf in London.

His all-time favourite film.

He had already seen it hundreds of times before, but he never grew tired of it, never grew bored.

He pulled the disc from the case and slipped it into the player. Switched on the flat screen TV, mounted on the wall. Settled down on the sofa, stretching his arms out across the back. The fridge was stocked with beer, and he had enough snacks to keep him going in the event of a national food shortage.

Darren closed his eyes and dropped his head against the sofa back at the soft knocking on his front door.

Really?

Maybe it was Julia come back, full of apologies, wanting to make another go of it. Or maybe she'd forgotten something.

Either way, he was going to tell her where to go. This was his place, and it was up to him who he let in.

"All right, bloody hell, I'm coming," he said, when he heard the knocking again.

He dragged himself down the hall to the front door. The door was a big, old heavy one, in keeping with the rest of the Victorian built house, and had one small stained glass window.

Darren swung open the door, a sarcastic comment ready to be unleashed. But he never said a word.

The odd couple standing on the front doorstep were inside the house before Darren realised what was happening. The man shut the door behind him. He was tall and rake thin, wearing a stained suit that was too short for him in the arms and legs.

His companion was a short, fat woman with dark greasy hair tied back in a ponytail. She was wearing a black leather jacket and black leather trousers. She placed an index finger to her lips.

It took Darren a moment to realise that there was something very odd about that hand, very strange. And then he realised. The hand was plastic, a mannequin's hand, the fingers stiff and unmoving, the whole thing yellowed with age and shiny.

"What the bloody hell do you think you're doing?" Darren said, ignoring the request for silence.

The woman's arm shot out, her plastic hand smashing into Darren's face. His head snapped sideways, his teeth cutting into his lip. Darren yelped and stumbled sideways, his hand over his mouth.

"What the hell?"

Before he could say any more the woman had hooked a foot around behind his legs and he crashed to the floor, banging his head on the cold Minton tiles.

"Mr Corpse, would you be so good as to check out the rest of the house to make sure we are on our own here?" the woman said. "It would be most distressing to be interrupted in our work."

Corpse peered at Darren lying on the floor and smiled, revealing his chipped, rotted teeth. "But Mrs Stump, I wants to be interrovestigating with the manthing."

"You can play later, right now we need to check the house is empty."

Corpse turned and looked at Stump with, Darren realised with a growing sense of horror, something approaching love.

"Go on, my love," Stump said, caressing him on the cheek. "I promise, you can play soon."

When Corpse had gone Stump squatted beside Darren and gently patted his face with her plastic hand.

"Now, now, don't worry, Mr Corpse can be quite gentle when he needs to be," she said. There was a crash from upstairs as something toppled over. Both Stump and Darren looked up at the ceiling. "Oh dear, he can be quite clumsy sometimes too."

"Just take what you want and get out of here," Darren said.

Stump looked back at Darren. "Oh don't worry, that is exactly what we're going to do."

She caressed Darren's cheek, running the plastic fingers up and down the side of his face. The plastic stank, a foul, bitter, unwashed smell. Stump took a deep, slightly jagged breath and sighed.

"It's a shame, really," she said. "Mr Corpse has all the fun, but then I did make a promise to look after him, the poor dear. But I do think I should allow myself a little playtime occasionally. I'm sure Mr Corpse wouldn't mind."

The tendon's in Darren's neck felt like they were about to snap as he tilted his head away from Stump's hand. The stink was overpowering, settling in his stomach in a sour, bubbling soup. He was trying to breathe in short little gasps, and his lungs were aching with the effort.

Corpse came back.

"This homeciliary is fulled up with nothingness, Mrs Stump," he said.

"Very good." Stump stood up, and Darren sucked in a lungful of air now that filthy hand had been removed from under his nose. "Let's go get the things from the van, shall we? The sooner we can get the job done, the sooner we can have some fun with our friend here."

"Ooh, smashioning!" Corpse cried, clapping his hands together like an excited toddler.

The odd couple walked towards the front door. Darren couldn't believe it. Were they just going to leave him on his own whilst they went outside and got whatever it was they needed? This was his chance to get out of the house, and away from these two freaks. Most likely it was going to be his only chance.

Darren placed his hand flat on the cold tiles and pulled himself quietly along the floor. He kept his eyes fixed on the odd couple all the time. If he could just get to the back door without them noticing him he could run outside and climb over the garden fence. Go find help.

Because if he stayed here he had no doubt these two freaks were going to kill him.

Stump and Corpse had reached the front door when Darren's shoulder bumped the leg of a table. He looked up just in time to see the vase on the table tottering over the edge. It shattered on the tiles, the sound like a gunshot in the confines of the hallway.

Both Stump and Corpse turned at the sound.

"Oh dear, Mr Corpse, how disappointing," Stump said. "I had hoped we weren't going to have any trouble."

Corpse grinned. "Shall we yankers inside outs his wormygutserings, Mrs Stump?"

Darren climbed shakily to his feet, the shards of porcelain crunching beneath his feet.

"You two are a pair of freaking psychopaths," he said.

Darren grabbed a standing lamp and levelled it at the odd couple, still standing by the front door. He felt faintly ridiculous, a knight jousting with a lamp complete with shade and tassels. Like he was in a Monty Python sketch. But he was desperate enough to not care.

Darren backed up until he was against the kitchen door. On his right was the cellar. All he had to do was get through the kitchen, into the utility room and then outside, in the back garden. It wasn't far. The only real impediment was the locked back door, but he always left the key in the lock. When he made his move he just had to be fast.

Because those two freaks would be behind him then.

Stump and Corpse stared at him, neither of them making a move. Corpse in particular seemed bored with the situation, and stuck his finger up his nose, began rooting around. Darren became fascinated with that finger, so far up his nose that it was pulling his top lip up.

It was obvious they were prepared to stand there all night if needs be, and wait for Darren to make the first move.

"Oh fucking hell," he muttered.

Darren dropped the lamp and spun round, grabbing for the kitchen door handle. Scuffling movement behind him, a grunt. Darren's palm was slick with sweat, and his hand slipped off the handle. Another grunt from behind and then a searing pain across his back.

A wetness spread down his back and over his hips. His legs were giving way and as he slid to the floor he twisted around to face his attackers. A blur of motion, and what looked like a long, vicious blade swiped across his field of view. More hot, scorching pain across his face and his vision turned red.

Darren began falling. Reaching out blind, his hand encountered empty space where he had thought the wall would be. He realised he was at the top of the cellar steps.

And then he was falling.

He tumbled down the cellar steps, hitting his head, his shoulders, twisting his back, until he landed at the bottom on the gritty dirt floor with a neck twisting thump. Hot pain shot through his spine and into his skull. He lay in the dark, unable to move.

The light from upstairs shifted and changed. Shadows danced across the bare brick cellar walls. Stump and Corpse descended the brick steps carrying torches. Corpse also had a pick axe and a spade.

Ignoring Darren, Mrs Stump unfolded a tiny camping stool and sat on it.

Corpse gripped the pick axe in both hands and lifted it over his head. He sank the pointed end into the ground with a grunt.

By the time Darren finally slipped into unconsciousness, Corpse had dug a hole deep enough that it reached his knees.

By the time his spade hit the wooden lid of the coffin buried in the ground, Darren was long dead.

acknowledgements

First of all I want to thank all of you who read and enjoyed Joe Coffin Season One. It seems a lot of you think it would be great to have Joe Coffin on your side, especially if Stump and Corpse were around!

Whilst I am handing out rosettes I must give a big shout out to the community of independent authors, publishers, reviewers and bloggers out there in the digisphere. You people are awesome, generous and hugely supportive, and I'm proud to be a part of that community.

And I really do need to give a special mention to my beta readers, Carrie Rowlands and Duncan Ralston. It's great to know I have two trusted readers waiting to ~~rip my work to shreds~~ give me constructive feedback.

Well, as the saying goes, *That's all folks!*

At least for now, anyway.

Because Joe Coffin will be back.

other books by ken preston

Joe Coffin Season One

Joe Coffin Season Two

Joe Coffin Season Three

Joe Coffin Season Four

Population:*DEAD!*
and Other Stories of Horror and Suspense

Young Adult

Planet of the Dinosaurs Book One: Project Wormhole

Planet of the Dinosaurs Book Two: The Journey North

Caxton Tempest at the End of the World

The Devil and Edward Teach

Romance

Twenty Seconds to Free Fall

Christmas in Paris

Lethal Injection

Hollywood Adventure

The Ocean's Slave

join my
mailing list

If you enjoyed this special edition of Joe Coffin you might want to sign up to my **VIP** readers' list.

First up, I will give you my collection of short stories **POPULATION:*DEAD!* AND OTHER TALES OF HORROR AND SUSPENSE**, featuring **HOW TO EAT A CAR** and **MRS DE RUNTZEN'S JEWELS**, both of which have been adapted for radio by Tall Tales and **THE MAN WHO MURDERED HIMSELF, DRIVE FAST SHE SAID** and the title tale **POPULATION:*DEAD!*** a horror/western mashup, plus more.

WANT EVEN MORE?

YOU GOT THAT TOO!

Every week I send out an email with ***giveaways and prizes***, including books by other authors who I think you will like too, plus updates on my work and ***member only*** books for sale which are not available anywhere else, including Amazon!

Sign up here:

www.kenpreston.co.uk

Printed in Great Britain
by Amazon

57929419R00227